Art historian David Webster left his childhood home of Saugerties, New York ten years ago and hasn't looked back. Intelligent, successful, and proud of his sexuality, David has built a comfortable, if lonely, life in Chicago. But when he learns his father has suffered a debilitating stroke, he decides to leave his prestigious museum job and move home to care for his dad. Until now David has never questioned his devotion to academic and professional success. Suddenly he's forced to confront and reevaluate his desires, chief among them, his former best friend Nick.

Nick Patras has spent his entire life trying to be the perfect Greek son. From devoting himself to football, to forgoing an athletic scholarship to work at his family's diner, to denying his sexuality and getting married to his high school sweetheart, Nick got used to putting his family's dreams ahead of his own. The facade shattered, however, when Nick divorced his wife and left the family business to follow his dream of starting an organic farm. Finally content with the life he's built for himself, Nick is still haunted by the mistake that ended his friendship with David a decade earlier.

When David and Nick reunite their old feelings are undeniable, but can David trust Nick with his heart a second time around? As David embarks on a new career as an artist, he must decide whether or not Nick fits into this composition.

LOVE ON THE HUDSON

KD Fisher

A NineStar Press Publication

Published by NineStar Press
P.O. Box 91792,
Albuquerque, New Mexico, 87199 USA.
www.ninestarpress.com

Love on the Hudson

Printed in the USA
First Edition
September, 2019

Print ISBN: 978-1-951057-57-2

Also available in eBook, ISBN: 978-1-951057-53-4

Warning: This book contains sexually explicit content, which may only be suitable for mature readers, depictions of homophobia, parental illness, parental estrangement, and recounted sexual assault.

To my family—found and blood

Chapter One

David

March

I step onto the salt-white sidewalk and into a stream of traffic noise. Rush hour commuters pour their anger into their car horns, laying on them for what feels like minutes at a time. The familiar scents of bus exhaust, cigarette smoke, and the caramel-sweet fragrance of roasted nuts from the stand on the corner overpower the rich steam rising from the to-go cup of coffee in my hands. It's cold. I know March in Chicago is always cold, really still winter, but the bite of the wind makes me edgy. I find myself constantly checking the weather forecast the moment I wake up, hoping I can stow away my heavy, unattractive coat for the season.

I rush toward the museum, knowing I'll be early for my meeting but hurrying nonetheless. As I walk, I mentally go over the presentation I'd practiced endlessly the night before. We can work with Chicago Public Schools to widen the reach of the museum and diversify visitorship. I've already talked to the assistant superintendent, and she loved the idea, saying the partnership would help supplement the arts programs that got cut a few years ago when the state couldn't agree on a budget. I'm lost in thought, half hoping I'm not practicing my talking points aloud, when I realize I'm already standing at the bottom of the lion-flanked steps of the museum. It bothers me that I do this—zone out and navigate the streets on autopilot. I chastise myself for taking the aesthetics of the city for granted. On any given day I pass the spaceship-like hulking form of the Thompson Center without batting an eye. I breeze by major public artworks by Picasso and Miró. I whisk past Burnham and Sullivan buildings with my eyes trained on the ground.

When I first moved to Chicago for undergrad, I was fascinated by the city. Everything was vibrant and engaging, unlike Saugerties, the small town where I'd grown up. Every chance I had I hopped on the bus, pretentious leather sketchbook in hand, and went north from my school's South Side campus to the center of the city. I took silly architecture boat tours filled with tourists who largely tuned out the information pouring from the scratchy PA system as the boat chugged through the dingy river. Spending hours on Google Maps, I planned walking tours of Oak Park for myself, enjoying the lull of the suburban streets as I basked in the gorgeous lines and thoughtful details of the Frank Lloyd Wright houses.

Again I'm lost in thought because I'm now enveloped in the quiet of my office, coffee still in hand, coat and scarf still on, but seated behind my desk. Shaking my head, I set my coffee down and busy myself with the tasks of a Monday morning. Check my voicemail, start my computer, glance at the Post-it-covered Stendig calendar tacked to my wall. As I'm about to reread my notes for the thousandth time since I woke up, my desk phone rings and the small light for the main museum reception line blinks red.

I pick it up on the second ring, running my fingers through my hair as I speak. "This is David Webster." I always lower my voice when fielding an unexpected call. Although I tell myself it's to sound professional, I'm a bit self-conscious about the soft, lilting cadence of my words.

A timid female voice responds. "Uh, hi, Mr. Webster? I have a call for you from a, uh, hospital. The nurse said she tried your cell but..." The woman's voice trails off, growing somewhat hoarse.

"Oh, sure. Okay. You can go ahead and put her through." The tremble in my voice does not surprise me. My heart races and my fingers shake as I reach for my bag to retrieve my cell phone.

"Mr. Webster?" My name is tinged with the upstate New York accent of my youth.

"Speaking," I squeak out. "What's going on?" I know it's something with my dad. Or fuck, could it be Anna? There's a sickening swooping sensation in my stomach. Did something happen to Nick? Unbidden, his intense gray gaze appears in my mind's eye. I shake my head to clear the thought. No one would call me about him.

"You're listed as next of kin for Dr. Richard Webster. You are his son, correct?"

"Yeah. Yes. Is he okay?" I hold down the button on the side to start up my phone. I always keep it off between the hours of midnight and seven to preserve my sanity and mitigate my technology addiction. It had been my New Year's resolution. Clearly this is not a good choice when your elderly father who lives alone hundreds of miles away is hospitalized.

"Yes, sir. Your father's condition is stable. We were unable to reach you on your primary contact number. He suffered an ischemic stroke. We have him on tPA and he's resting in the ICU. We'll keep him for a few nights for monitoring and scans. Then we can start talking about rehab. A…" She pauses and I hear a few mouse clicks over the phone. "James Webster is with him now."

Jimmy must have called me. Quickly I unlock my phone to see a barrage of texts and missed calls from my uncle's number, as well as three voicemails from an 845 area code, very likely the hospital's number. I scan through Jimmy's increasingly panicked then calm texts without responding to the nurse.

"Mr. Webster?" she asks, a note of irritation creeping into her voice.

I tear my eyes away from my phone screen. My hands clench white and my arms are suddenly insanely heavy. My torso is hollow. "Yes. Sorry. I'm in Chicago. Like, I live in Chicago so I need to fly up. But he's okay, right?"

Line two rings on my desk phone—startling me—and I know it means the superintendent has arrived. My head spins and I lean forward, scrunching into myself and trying to resist the urge to collapse even though I'm sitting. A few moments later I have wrapped up my conversation with the nurse and managed to write down the relevant information on the back of a deli receipt on my desk. I'm about to return one of Jimmy's dozen calls when Marc blusters into my office, eyes wild.

"Uh, David?" his voice is shrill, and it's one of the first times I have ever seen him look so irritated.

"I know. She's here, right?"

"Yes!" he hisses, running his slender fingers through his perfectly messy dark hair. I notice he's even wearing a tie today. A nice touch for the meeting, I think, and I smile to myself.

"My dad had a stroke," I say softly. Repeating the information I was told makes my stomach twist sharply and a wave of nausea rolls over me.

The irritation drains from Marc's face and he quickly crosses over to my desk. "Shit. David, when? Why didn't you call me?" His groomed eyebrows are raised, earnest.

"I just got the call here... You know, my phone was off."

Marc groans. "You and your stupid phone thing. I knew it was going to be a problem someday." He claps a hand over his mouth. "And I'm nagging you right after you found out your dad's sick." He paces my small office, from the wall plastered with my calendar and some framed landscapes to the window overlooking Millennium Park. "Okay. Okay. Okay. Here's what we'll do. I'll take care of the meeting. Call, well normally I would say call me...but Vic can handle booking you a flight to New York. You should be able to take leave for this." He runs his fingers over his lips, leaning back against the window. I know his mind is vibrating at its highest frequency. "Lane and Nisa and I can handle everything for a few days or whatever you need. Go, David."

FIVE HOURS LATER I find myself behind the wheel of a white rental sedan barreling up I-87 in the direction of Saugerties, a perfectly nice town I'd hoped never to see again. The sky is the same mottled gray as it was back in Chicago, the snow along the highway the same dirt-tinged pewter. The passing cars are spattered with white salt stains. I drive in silence, every radio station bothering me with shrill commercials or horrendous blends of the 80s, 90s, and today.

My mind falls into a chaotic tailspin. I want to call Marc and see how the meeting went. I want to call Jimmy again and see if there is any update on my dad's condition. The doctors are worried his vision was compromised but needed to run another test. I want to call Anna to hear her soothing voice and ask the one question that absolutely shouldn't be on my mind right now. Has she seen Nick recently? Again, his gray eyes and those dark lashes flit across my mind and I grip the wheel harder. I need to focus. Plus I won't even see him. He moved across town when he got married. He doesn't live in the house across the street anymore.

Our old house, however, looks entirely unchanged. Same bluestone exterior, same red front door, same neat garden beds outlined with smooth white rocks. I look away from the winter-brown tangle of plants, my jaw tight. Jimmy's truck, dotted with environmental and leftie bumper stickers, rests out front. Although they were born ten years apart, my uncle and father are incredibly close. It was Jimmy I could thank for my dad's health and safety over the past few years since his first stroke. As if on cue, I hear the groan of the wooden garage door around the back of the house. Jimmy strolls down the brick garden path clutching mismatched coffee mugs. I grin, knowing my coffee will be made exactly right, with almond milk and way too much honey, a combination almost everyone I know finds utterly disgusting. Jimmy wears his standard uniform of olive green hiking pants, a zip-up fleece, a disarmingly bushy beard, and a gleaming bald head.

"I bet you're exhausted, kiddo." He hands me the chipped public radio mug he knows used to be my favorite, full almost to the brim.

I take a grateful sip before responding honestly. "I am. I had a big meeting this morning, so I barely slept at all."

Jimmy nods seriously, taking a long sip of his own coffee. "Your dad's okay. Thankfully I was over when it happened. We were playing cards on the patio. Anyway, they said at the hospital he's gonna pull through." Jimmy trails off, staring down at his hiking boots. "But son, I don't know if he can be on his own anymore." His gray eyebrows crash together and his grip around his mug tightens. He heaves a weary sigh, and it occurs to me he looks much older than he did when I last saw him. "Let's go in. Get freshened up. We're due over at the hospital in an hour and a half for some appointment or other. I think they want to go over what to, you know, expect."

I follow Jimmy into the house. It's surreal. Grief has kept me away since my mom's death almost ten years ago, but there is evidence of her everywhere. The green plaid couch, still draped with the colorful knit throw blanket she made feverishly after finding out she was sick. The living room walls, adorned with framed posters of Met exhibitions she and my dad took the train into the city to see. I avert my eyes from her paintings, still proudly displayed in a large cluster above the fireplace. Even with my gaze rooted to the oak floor I can picture the fast brushwork and heavy application of pastel paint forming delicate flowers and vibrant leaves.

The kitchen smells the same too, a mix of turmeric and coffee and lavender that always clung to her clothes and hair. I always thought our house smelled like her rather than the other way around. Part of me hoped I would never have to set foot in this house again. I'd tricked myself into believing I could turn my shoulder on the gaping reality of her absence. I could call my dad on the phone and perform mental gymnastics to delude myself into thinking she was alive, out working in the garden or seeing a patient. That she hadn't chosen to let herself die. The ghost of a sob bubbles up in my throat and I hurry up the stairs, swallowing hard.

After depositing my duffel bag in my childhood bedroom, the walls plastered with high school painting projects and Death Cab for Cutie posters, I dart to the bathroom to freshen up. A sharp twinge of nostalgia momentarily incapacitates me as I step into the stone-tiled shower. I quickly scrub down with the all-in-one peppermint soap, the only bath product my dad seems to own.

Standing in front of the mirror where I'd obsessively combed my hair into questionable styles as a teenager is strange. Sure, I'm the same person I was when I looked into this mirror ten years ago, but I am profoundly altered. My narrow eyes, serious, too-straight eyebrows, and rumpled auburn hair are unchanged, but my face is tired. A few fine lines have appeared on my forehead from constantly raising my eyebrows or knitting them together. I'm taller now too, thanks to a final growth spurt around my twenty-first birthday. I'm not as tall as my dad, though. And not nearly as tall as Nick. And fuck. I'm thinking of him again. I've been in New York for all of an hour and he's taken up far too much space in my mind already. Grumbling to myself, I pull on fitted dark jeans and a thin black sweater. I packed in such a hurry, I'm thankful I have a single presentable outfit to put on.

As I brush my teeth, I reach for my phone, hoping again for an update from Marc or a voicemail from the hospital with some new information. No luck. There is however, a frantic text from Anna.

Anna: *You're here! Jimmy told me about your dad and that sucks. But you're here! I'm glad he's okay. I went by the hospital this morning but they wouldn't let me see him. I guess I kinda thought the whole visiting hours thing was just on TV?? Then again I never go to hospitals so... Yeah. When you're all settled TEXT ME. Btw your uncle couldn't get ahold of you because of your dumb phone rule. Stop doing that. And make sure you eat something because coffee doesn't count as food. Or maybe it does. But not in my book.*

I laugh to myself softly. My best friend always texts like this, in lengthy stream-of-consciousness bursts. I quickly tap out a reply.

David: *Heading over to the hospital in a few. Haven't seen my dad yet. Honestly I'm really freaked out. I guess I won't believe he's okay until I see him. I'll swing by the library after?*

Immediately a little bubble pops up on the screen indicating Anna is typing. She sends a smiling sunglasses emoji, three hearts, and a thumbs-up.

THE HOSPITAL ROOM is painted a shade of beige that I know was likely selected to be soothing, but ends up looking grimy. A tangle of cords and monitors surrounds my father's bed. The fluorescent light keeps flickering, making me feel like my eye is twitching even though it isn't. My dad looks awful. This is his third stroke and the worst yet. I didn't come home for the other two because they were so minor that Jimmy and my dad and Anna convinced me I could stay in Chicago and focus on work. Plus my dad knows my thoughts about coming home. But this stroke was bad, largely robbing him of his ability to speak and move and really do anything at all for the time being. His tall, lean frame, so much like my own, looks small and crumpled in the hospital bed. The pervasive tang of antiseptic cleaner and the occasional glance at the IV lines in my father's arms fill my stomach with a watery queasiness. I can tell he's trying hard to stay awake while I'm in the room but I wish he would sleep. He radiates pain and exhaustion. His bloodshot green eyes remind me too much of the weeks after my mom died.

While she was sick, I made all kinds of dramatic pronouncements to myself that I wouldn't set foot a hospital again until I was dying. And, honestly, right now I kind of wish I'd kept that promise because I'm shivering even though the room is pleasantly warm.

I'm watching this all at a remove. I keep trying to blink myself present. It doesn't work. My dad's face is almost as gray as his hair. I hold his hand in mine. The skin is dry and looks cracked in places. Absently I wonder if the nurses will put lotion on him. Do they bathe him? Will I have to do that? Will he be embarrassed? He tries to say something, and his normally measured voice has been replaced with slurred sounds, like someone has stuffed his mouth with cotton. My vision blurs and I wish I could sit down but I don't want to let go of his hand.

The doctor, a woman with shiny black hair who I would guess is around my age, in her late twenties or early thirties, bustles into the room. She explains to me that my father will need months of rehabilitation to return to normal. She keeps using the word normal and I wonder if she couldn't find a better term. I'm sure they taught her a more clinically appropriate word in medical school, right? What does normal mean for my dad? Certainly he won't be going on the Appalachian Trail through-hike he's been planning with Jimmy. He probably wouldn't be embarking on the trip to Ireland he had planned either. Nor would he be putting up his customary jars of salsa and pesto from the tomatoes and herbs in his garden. No. Normal might mean living at home again, but not on his own and not on his own terms. Normal means walking and bathing himself. Normal means not having another stroke and dying alone in his home while his son is off in a city far away.

"Mr. Webster?" the doctor asks, a sculpted eyebrow raised, clearly aware I'm not listening to anything she's saying. She seems impatient with me.

I nod slowly, racking my brain for context clues. Physical therapy...occupational therapy...insurance...

Surmising my lack of focus, she repeats herself. "So, Mr. Webster." She pauses and looks into my eyes. Something shifts in her expression. "David. You know what has to happen. Someone has to be with your dad to help him around the clock. He's not stable enough to be at home by himself. He will need a great deal of help with simple physical tasks. Of course we're able to recommend in-home care or nursing facilities, although both options are likely going to be quite costly on your father's insurance plan." When she looks at me again her face is sympathetic. She reaches to give my arm a soft squeeze. I'm contemplating her perfectly buffed fingernails but then my vision wobbles. Tears slide down my cheeks too fast to wipe away.

Before my mind even has the chance to catch up to my mouth, I'm saying the words. "No. I'll stay with him. Tell me what I need to do."

And that's it. I call Marc as I leave the hospital and beg him, not that he needs to be begged, to go over to my place in Andersonville and pack up my clothes and toiletries and ship them to my dad's house. I guess I'll have to break my lease, but I push all but the most pressing practicalities into a folder in my mind and lock it up in a drawer labeled *Do Not Think About or You Will Have a Panic Attack.*

Not once as I talk to Marc do I even wonder about work. After a while he mentions the meeting, saying it went incredibly well, but already my job is a relic from a distant past. Something I'm reading about with mild interest but no longer invested in.

I can practically feel Marc's panic vibrating through the phone. "Are you, like, quitting, David?" Marc has largely banished the word *like* from his vocabulary so its appearance clues me in that he's truly concerned.

I weigh his question in my mind, considering my life in Chicago since I took the job at the museum. There's my apartment, a roomy two-bedroom walkup in my wonderful neighborhood. The gorgeous back balcony with its twinkly lights and potted ferns and the vintage mosaic table Christopher and I found at a shop down on Clark Street. The exposed brick walls dotted with paintings made by friends. Then there's my work, waking up each day to take the L to a job I genuinely care about. After years of school, laboring over my master's thesis and making myself sick over my dissertation, years of academic anxiety and competition, now I go to work every morning invigorated, knowing what I do matters. But there's also the reality that most of my friends from my doctoral program moved to New York or scattered to far-flung universities to teach. Aside from Marc, I barely have anyone I can talk to or count on in Chicago.

On the surface my life looks exactly like I wanted it to when I got on the Greyhound bus to study at the University of Chicago when I was eighteen. I have a great apartment, a fantastic job with benefits and a comfortable salary, and I can go out to bars and meet interesting queer men whenever I want. Not that I take advantage of that perk very often anymore. Deep down, though, my life feels totally hollow.

My stomach clenches. I'm lonely. Even when I was with Christopher I would sometimes wake up early in the morning sipping a cup of the expensive coffee he always bought and think, *Is this really my life?* It was like I'd spent years sewing an elaborate costume and occasionally I would give it a tug only to realize it didn't fit quite right. As a kid I always felt so passionate and connected, ready to take things on. Seeing the autumn light cast long shadows in my mom's garden and being filled with sudden energy. Wanting to find the perfect combination of oil paints to recreate that light. Lying in the grass with Nick—*Shit. Don't go there.*

Just like at the hospital I find my mouth moving ten steps ahead of my brain. "Yes," I finally answer Marc's question, "I guess I am."

Chapter Two

David

March

The library looks the same. The American classical façade, all red brick and white columns, was such a comfort to me as a kid. I loved walking the half mile from our house to sit in the quiet stacks and flip through the small collection of art books or put on the colossal black headphones to listen to The Smiths for hours on end.

Anna suggested we grab dinner together at a restaurant that had opened since I'd moved away. As I wait for my best friend, I wrap my wool coat tight against the sharp edge of the wind blowing in off the Hudson. The air is wet and heavy with cold. Forcing my attention to the gray clouds as they tumble across the night sky, I curse myself for scanning the streets for any member of the Patras family. Their diner is around the corner from here and I keep worrying one of Nick's sisters or his brother or one of his million cousins might walk by and recognize me. Hopefully not his dad though. That's a face I could do without seeing ever again. I know I'm being paranoid, but it's not without good reason. That family defines tight-knit and I remember with a twinge how much power Mr. Patras's anger could wield.

My reverie is interrupted, however, as Anna tumbles out of the library entrance, gaze fixed tightly to mine. Her red hair is longer, tied back in an elaborate fishtail braid. She's wearing a truly enormous purple knit scarf wrapped around her neck and a giant smile.

Her familiar smell of grapefruit and coffee and paper envelops me as her arms twine around my neck. "Jesus Christ, I've missed you." She leans back and grins at me, even bigger now, her warm brown eyes shining.

Something releases in me seeing her again. Sure she was in Chicago for the New Year, but this is different. We're back on familiar ground together.

"Missed you too," I mumble as she squeezes me into another viselike hug. We walk in a calm silence and I realize that the town doesn't look quite the same. Numerous funky little restaurants, cafes, and shops have opened along Main Street, replacing the vacant and boarded-up storefronts of my high school and college years. Anna gestures toward a once-abandoned mill by the river and tells me a luxury hotel has opened and that they have a decent bar.

"If you need a drink at the end of the night we can swing by." She winks and grabs my hand, pulling me into a cute restaurant, the front window adorned with vintage half aprons in lieu of curtains. As we push in through the front door I'm surprised by how full the place is, the bar packed and most of the tables occupied. There are young couples who look distinctly like city transplants, bearded guys in high-end workwear and willowy women in skinny jeans and suede ankle boots. Older couples and families huddle together too, sharing artfully arranged plates of assorted cheeses and meats and sipping wine and cocktails. And I see people I immediately recognize as queer. Men sitting close together and talking animatedly, a woman stroking another woman's face in an absent, fond gesture. I realize with a jolt of happiness just how much the town has changed.

I turn to Anna and she's smiling at me. "See, this place isn't so bad. As I've been saying for like eight years."

The cute young host leads us to a two-top in the back of the restaurant. His eyes meet mine as he hands me my menu and a bit of heat creeps into my cheeks.

"You've still got it!" Anna giggles, shrugging off her pea coat and unraveling her gargantuan scarf.

We've been saying this to each other since college, always ribbing the other when someone seems to check one of us out. I laugh but then a gentle quiet settles between us as we both peruse the menu.

"You going back to the hospital tonight?" Anna's voice is soft. "I can come with you if you want."

I shake my head. "No. Visiting hours ended at eight. Plus my dad was super out of it. He knew I was there, but he's on a lot of medication and he's still in the ICU. I'll go back in the morning. I have a meeting with some other doctor. The one overseeing his recovery, I think?" I huff out a long breath and my shoulders finally relax a bit.

The warm chatter, the delicious smells of browned butter and garlic, the soft light emanating from the antique fixtures overhead all make my eyelids heavy. We place our orders, Anna getting the vegan option, me the roasted chicken with spring vegetables. Each of us takes a grateful sip of white wine. As we wait for the salad we opted to share, I tell Anna about the four hours I spent at the hospital, about all I know so far regarding my dad's condition, and finally about my decision to leave my job and move back to care for my dad full time. At this, Anna's mouth falls open.

"David, are you serious?" Her thin eyebrows rise. Masking her feelings has never been Anna's strong suit. Concern and excitement war in her expression as she waits for my reply.

I nod. I still don't know how I feel about my choice. The rational part of me is aware that leaving a job I was incredibly lucky to get at one of the best museums in the world after spending roughly twelve years in school is a huge mistake. But something about the decision just feels right. My father is my only family left. He needs me.

"I'm sure the museum would let you take a leave of absence, right?" Anna asks, looking a bit confused. "Jimmy and I are both here. If you want to take a few months to help your dad recover..." She trails off when her eyes meet mine, then her expression softens. "Well, not to be selfish, but I'm pretty fucking excited you'll be back here. I've missed your whiny ass."

I watch as a new expression crosses her delicate, elfin features—the mischievous, *I have gossip* face she used to make in high school so often when we sat on my parents' couch drinking herbal tea.

"What?" I chuckle. I'm grateful for a change in topic. My mind is exhausted from churning over fears about my father and the career suicide I'm about to commit. I'm ready to shut my anxiety off for a bit and listen to Anna's tales from the library and town gossip, like her hilariously disturbing story of the elderly pharmacist and his wife having loud, vigorous sex in the library's local history room.

"You're going to hate me for bringing him up. He who shall not be named." She pauses, but the lifted eyebrow and smirk remain fixed on her pale face.

I groan. "Anna. No. Come on. Not after all the shit today." It's our agreement that she doesn't fill me in on anything to do with Nick or the Patras family. I can't deal with details of his wedded bliss or—

"He got divorced," she blurts out, a bit too loud. A few people at the tables next to us glance over, looking alternately amused or irritated.

My neck is hot, and my muscles clench tight, like I went for a long run and forgot to stretch or drink any water after. I shouldn't care. This information should not matter. Nick is straight. He insisted on this fact. What happened between us over and over was a mistake. He insisted on that. But he had also insisted he loved Christi and now they're divorced?

My voice is a croak when I finally speak. "When?" I take a big gulp of wine, hoping it will hydrate my utterly parched throat. It doesn't.

Anna looks abashed. "Like...two years ago."

"And you didn't tell me?" I can't tell if I'm angry or impressed. Anna kind of sucks at keeping secrets or withholding information. After I pleaded with her to stop giving me a blow-by-blow description of every time she ran into Nick around town or at the library it still took her a while to remember not to mention him. She thought, rightly so, that I was being dramatic.

"Well, you asked me never to bring him up again. And it always made you seem upset to hear about him. So yeah, when I found out I didn't think it would matter. Honestly I hoped you were over it anyway. But since you're back...and single, I thought maybe I should tell you."

The mischievous expression is still on her face and my exasperation grows. Honestly Nick is the last thing I want to deal with right now. Of course even though I've barely heard from him in ten years he can still find a way to fuck up an already horrendous day.

"Okay, but get this..." Anna's voice is positively tinkling with delight and I'm about to ask her why she insists on torturing me, when she continues. "He's a farmer."

Then we're both laughing and I'm not sure why. But the idea seems too absurd. High school heartthrob, hulking star of our varsity football and basketball teams, destroyer of my adolescent psyche. Girls in our class actually called him "The Greek God." Now he's a divorced farmer? Tears well at the corners of my eyes as I laugh at the image of Nick's hulking frame in denim overalls, a straw hat covering his thick, dark hair. Okay, that's weirdly kind of hot. *Fuck.*

The waiter delivers our food and Anna and I are both grinning like idiots still as he walks away. "I see him almost every weekend at the farmers' market," Anna states matter-of-factly, taking a small bite of mushroom pasta. "He actually grows the nicest eggplants I've ever seen. Even if he is a dick. Hah!" She laughs at her own lame joke. "But yeah, anyway, he and some friends started this whole organic farm somewhere outside Woodstock, I guess."

I haven't even touched my food. It smells amazing, the chicken skin is perfectly bronzed and crisp and the accompanying new potatoes and English peas look delicious. But my stomach is so full of butterflies I don't think I could fit any food in.

"Do you know why he got divorced? Christi couldn't get into the whole farm lifestyle or something?" I'm trying to keep my tone light, but my voice is doing its whole nervous shrill thing and I know Anna sees right through it.

"I have no clue why. He's only been doing the farm for the last year or so, so that can't be it. The rumor was that he had an affair with a woman in the city and Christi left him but I don't think that's true." Anna holds my gaze for a long moment and I can tell she's trying to decide how much she can push this topic.

I sigh. "Go ahead. Give me your theory." I already know what she's going to say.

She beams. "Okay. So."

Clearly she has been bursting to tell me this and I feel momentarily guilty for getting so angry with her over bringing Nick up in the past. I was being kind of a baby about something that happened a decade ago.

She drops her voice to a dramatic whisper. "I think he's gay. Like, my guess is he couldn't live a lie anymore." I scoff but Anna continues. She never bought that he was straight to begin with. "Look at the facts, David. I mean, fact number one—you guys hooked up like, what, ten times? And he was always kissing you and stuff."

"Eight," I quickly interject. But wish I hadn't because Anna looks smug and it makes me sound like a weirdo.

"Exactly. You should call him! I mean, you're single...he's single."

I interrupt. "Anna, no. I'm here for my dad, not to torture myself with Nick. Plus, he is not gay." My voice gets hoarse again. "You know what he said to me. You know why I can't see him." My wine glass is empty and I contemplate ordering another, or a whole bottle, for that matter, but I have to drive and I know drinking will do nothing to help this mess. "Can we drop it? I want absolutely nothing to do with Nick."

Chapter Three

Nick

April

The farm is quiet and still as I swallow the last of my coffee and wash out the mug at the sink. The sun won't rise for about two hours. Jenna and Hector aren't set to arrive until around seven. But I like working alone in the dark with only the chatter of the early morning birds and the soft sound of the breeze rushing through the mostly bare trees. Mentally I run through my morning to-do list: finish packing up the pea shoots, wash and bag the spinach, divide the red potatoes into one-pound bags, and get the cash box ready. Jenna and Hector can take care of the rest before we head into town at eight. I glance over at Archie, who's still snoring loudly on the sofa, nestled in his favorite wool blanket. His too-big front paws twitch in his sleep.

As it does almost every market morning, my chest constricts and my heart starts to race. The thought was on my mind first thing today. The word that seems to float to the surface at random moments, causing me to squeeze my eyes shut or bite the inside of my cheek. *Gay.* I remember the first time I let myself think it. Waking up in the middle of the night from a dream that I'd been kissing a boy. Not even a boy I liked very much. Not the boy who I couldn't stop looking at in class. Not the boy who sometimes held my hand absentmindedly when we crossed the street. Not the boy who played with my hair while we watched TV. No, the star of my dream had been Paul Robins, a loudmouthed kid with crazy black hair who teased the girls in our homeroom nonstop. My pajama pants had been damp and sticky and at first I'd thought I'd wet the bed. The shame of that had been enough. But sneaking into the bathroom I'd realized that I had ejaculated in my sleep, while my brother Jason snored in the bunk under me.

I'd always been hyperaware of the boys around me in a way I just wasn't with girls. If my fingers brushed another guy's when he handed me papers in class. If I looked too long at my teammates during basketball practice. The thought materialized, making my cheeks burn and my breath go shallow. Then David came out in eighth grade and what I felt had a name in our house. A different name. A name harshly uttered by my father and laughed about by Jason and his friends.

I make myself take a few deep breaths, but they come in shaky and thin. The more I try the weaker my breathing gets. I sink down onto the couch. Okay. I can calm down. I take stock of the room around me, running my eyes over the low pine bookcases I finished building a few weeks ago. They're crammed with gardening books and dozens of sci-fi paperbacks with creased spines. I need to organize them. Trying to distract myself by mentally alphabetizing the titles does nothing to calm me. I tell myself I'm okay but I'm starting to get lightheaded and I scoot toward Archie and push my fingers into the shaggy gray and brown fur on his back. The big dog groans in his sleep and his eyes creak open.

"Sorry, buddy," I say softly, genuinely feeling bad for waking him. But being near him always makes my shoulders drop and my heart rate slow. I can't keep letting this happen. Fear is running my life like it always has. Recognizing the root of my anxiety doesn't make it go away. It's better now that I live out here. Not as many questions and way less lying. I can stop the panic attacks before they start for the most part. But still, I shouldn't be having them at all. The thought of seeing my father and brother should not make me physically sick. But it does.

Once I throw myself into work, things are better. My mind shuts off the way it does when I run or lift weights, the way it used to when I was on the football field. I hum quietly as I work in the barn, adding new things to the ongoing to-do list as I notice them. Archie, who followed me outside, snuffles to sleep on a towel I keep folded by the door as a makeshift bed for him. Since the day I'd adopted him he'd loved anything soft and fuzzy. Initially I'd tried to keep him out of my bed and off the couch but it was pointless. Anytime I left him alone in the house I'd find my quilt covered in dog hair anyway, so it was better to vacuum regularly and resign myself to the fact that the only one I'd be sharing my bed with was a seventy-five-pound ball of fur.

I'm getting the cash box and produce labels ready when I realize the sun has risen without me noticing. A pang of sadness that I didn't go outside to watch the pink and gold creep into the deep blue of the morning sky twists in my chest. Stepping out onto the gravel driveway I turn into the sharp face of the wind, smelling earth and water and green. I'm grateful that I have this space to call my own. At least I made the decision to live my life somewhat honestly. Even if it means I only have Archie for company.

But the unmistakable creak of the rickety metal gate at the end of the driveway reminds me that I'm not entirely right about that. I grin as Hector's banged-up sedan crawls up the gravel and thuds to a halt next to my Jeep. Jenna is in the passenger seat, her bleached natural curls pulled back with a tie-dyed bandana. Except for David , Jenna is the best person I've ever known. Jenna is beautiful, with tawny brown skin, amber eyes that always seem to gleam with humor, and truly impressive abs. She is also incredibly sharp and endlessly kind, engineering creative solutions to challenges around the farm and pushing Hector and I to do more to give back to the community.

"Morning!" Hector calls with far more energy than I can ever imagine feeling as his lanky frame unfolds from the driver's side.

"Morning, guys." I return their smiles and gesture toward the house. "Coffee and muffins in the kitchen if you want some. Last week Will promised us a breakfast pizza, so I didn't make too much. But if you want—"

Jenna cuts me off, shaking her head fondly. "Nick, calm down with the mother hen routine, will you? Your muffins are perfect." Her wink makes the comment seem playful and dirty.

"Did you do the spinach yet?" Hector asks and I follow him and Jenna back into the kitchen, deciding on another cup of coffee.

"Yup." I nod. "Pea shoots and spinach are in the greenhouse and I pulled the potatoes from the cellar. You want to do the herbs, lettuces, and leeks? Jenna and I can start loading up the truck then come help you finish up."

Although Jenna is only five feet tall, she's easily as strong as I am due to her lifelong yoga practice and recent stint as a CrossFit instructor. Hector, conversely, is a brilliant soil scientist and knows more about organic pest control than anyone I've ever met, but he isn't exactly brawny.

After a quick break for a second lemon poppy seed muffin and a third cup of coffee, Jenna and I get to work loading up my ancient Jeep. Since this is the farm's first fully functional year, the yields are still small and our offerings are still somewhat limited. My mind drifts to the projects we have planned for next year: getting the overgrown orchard productive again, establishing breeding flocks of chickens and turkeys, and experimenting with different legume cover crops. I'm mentally flipping through the seed catalog when Hector's voice pulls me from my thoughts.

"Okay dude, I'm all set. It's almost eight. Should we head out soon?" I nod and Archie and I hop into the Jeep.

The market is already hectic with other vendors by the time we arrive. Now that the sun is fully up, the sky is a crystalline cloudless blue. It's nice to have some decent weather in the spring to break up the endless days of low, gray skies and wet, cold winds. As Hector, Jenna and I hurry to unload the vegetables and arrange them attractively on our table, Will from Wandering Monk Pizza sidles over, bearing three small pizza boxes and smiling. My cheeks heat. And I'm embarrassed to feel my cock twitch in my jeans. *Shit*. Will is cute. Small and pretty and sweet. And I know he's gay. His blond hair is tousled, and his blue eyes meet mine as he hands me the still-hot breakfast pizzas.

"Thanks, man," I say, doing that stupid thing I've always done involuntarily around attractive guys, dropping my voice low and finding it impossible to make eye contact. David always used to tease me about being shy, but I didn't know how to act around men. And shit, was I trying to give myself a heart attack this morning? Thinking about David is not something I need to be doing.

Thankfully Jenna comes to my rescue, asking Will about sourdough starters between giant bites of pizza. I can kind of zone out and finish prepping the stand. The pizza is delicious as always, with thinly sliced spring onions and asparagus scattered around a large sunny-side-up duck egg in the middle. I try to eat slowly and appreciate Will's handiwork but I'm starving and I know people will start trickling into the market soon, so I end up eating almost as quickly as Jenna.

"Dude, he's cute. You should ask him out. He's always coming over and talking to you," Jenna whispers as Will walks away.

I become fixated on making sure the price sign for the scallions is straight. Jenna is one of exactly five people in the world who knows my secret. Well, plus the guys from the apps but I push that thought from my mind too.

"He's just being nice," I mumble, still not meeting her amber eyes.

She scoffs. "Uh huh. Sure. That's why he only gives *us* the free pizza and he can't take his eyes off you. Okay. You know you're hot, right? I don't go for guys at all and sometimes I still wish I could jump your bones." She pinches my arm and chuckles.

"Stop harassing me," I tease and I see Hector stifle a laugh out of the corner of my eye.

"He does seem into you," Hector offers quietly. Even though they're speaking softly and there's no one close enough to hear our conversation, a fist of panic clutches at my chest.

"I do not want to talk about this." I don't mean for my voice to sound so clipped and angry. But it does. Hector holds up his hands and raises his eyebrows in a *don't look at me* gesture. Jenna softens, casting me an apologetic look and patting my hand gently before wandering off to grab a coffee before we get too busy.

The market is four hours of uninterrupted motion. Little kids and dogs dart all over the place, creating a pleasantly chaotic atmosphere. I answer questions, make change, and do my best to keep the table looking neat and attractive. With the warmer weather, more and more people start coming upstate from the city. Already I spot a few, young couples in their twenties and thirties taking dozens of pictures and paying with inconveniently large bills.

There's always a twinge of jealousy when I see guys together, holding hands or huddling close to debate the merits of one bundle of herbs over another. I want that. That easy intimacy in public. That affection and companionship. And as if conjured up by me thinking gay thoughts my dad and brother appear in front of the table. Jason looks exhausted with bags under his eyes and a grayish pallor to his olive complexion. I'm sure he was out until early this morning pounding shots and snorting coke at a bunch of his buddies' houses.

"Ugh, I don't know how you do this early morning shit, bro," Jason says, scrubbing a hand over his stubble and taking a long sip from a giant canned energy drink.

My dad, who doubtless was up as early as I was, shoots Jason a scolding but slightly amused look. Jason is five years younger than me. He was constantly messing up throughout our youth and his adulthood: getting busted for selling pot, showing up at school drunk, missing countless shifts at the diner. And the icing on the cake, getting his girlfriend Lexi pregnant at the age of seventeen. They got married in a hurry and Lexi moved into our parents' already overcrowded house. Jason still half-heartedly works at the diner, too busy cheating on his wife and ignoring his son to try to make anything of himself. I have no doubt in my mind my dad sees Jason as the better son. Jason is a ladies' man. He gave my parents a Greek grandson. And he isn't a divorced loner who sells "overpriced" vegetables and abandoned the family business.

"Spinach looks good," my dad grunts in his combination Greek-upstate accent.

"Take some if you want." I gesture to the bags and grin, taking his praise too seriously.

"All of this won't be enough to make a single pan of spanakopita, Nick." He shakes his head like I've suggested something truly idiotic.

"Maybe mom would like some though?" I push, knowing I'll regret it. "It's super fresh. She could make a nice salad."

My dad barks out a laugh. "A salad?"

I know for him salad means one thing. Chunks of iceberg lettuce, dried oregano, a few canned black olives, rings of red onion and a single pickled pepper. We used to get into arguments like this all the time when I was still cooking at the diner.

Jason looks up from his phone. "Hey, I saw Christi the other night at Red's. She's looking real good, bro. I don't know why you let a girl that hot get away. I mean damn, I wish Lexi kept it that tight." Again Jason gets an amused look and an elbow to the ribs from our dad. My brother re-glues his eyes back to his phone screen, no doubt DMing underage Instagram models or posting on one of the lifting forums he frequents.

I mumble something that sounds vaguely like, "Oh cool" and quickly turn to help Evelyn, a frizzy-haired, bright-eyed hippie lady who buys half our herb stock every week. Today she's loaded up her canvas tote with bunch after bunch of parsley, cilantro, and chervil. Once Evelyn has paid and sweetly offered to let me keep the quarter owed her in change, my father turns back to me, his bushy gray eyebrows furrowed.

"Your mother wants you at church for once. Come before supper. Last Sunday Katie Kostopoulos was asking about you." He gives me a meaningful look and I clench my fist under the table in an effort not to immediately tear my eyes away and stare at the ground. He knows I stopped going to their church regularly when I turned eighteen, but he continues to nag me about coming back as often as humanly possible.

"Dad, you know I'm not looking to date." My voice is a low, coarse sound. I'm grateful that Hector and Jenna are used to helping our other customers every week when my dad and Jason come by to pester me.

My father waves a wrinkled, dismissive hand. "You're already thirty-one, Nick! You need to start a family." He looks proudly over at Jason. "But you'll come over for dinner, yes? Your mother is making her chicken. You can even bring some of the spinach if you want."

I almost want to laugh at his attempted goodwill. He's being nicer than normal. Still, the idea of spending the entire afternoon in my parents' house makes my stomach turn as it always does. Sunday supper is sacred for my family, my mother in particular. It's the only time they all take off from the diner, handing things over to my uncle for the day.

Every single Sunday is the same. Yiayia makes snarky comments about me being divorced while working on her puzzle. My younger sister Doria ignores me, sulking on the couch, texting her friends, and occasionally glancing up to roll her eyes at our mother. My older sister Cassie hovers, asking me a million questions and shooting me knowing glances. Usually, the only high point is sitting in the backyard with Cassie while she sneaks a cigarette and gives me advice.

I almost cave and say yes to church, knowing it will make my mom inordinately happy, when my dad speaks again. "Your mother invited Katie to eat with us. You two can get to know each other. Think about it, Nick."

He and Jason exchange a few more words with me then turn to leave, not stopping by any other stands. They always come on their way to the diner, taking over for my mother who runs the early morning shifts. They never buy anything or talk to anyone but me. Hell, I don't think my dad knows who Jenna or Hector are by name. I don't even have time to wallow in my family shit though because the one other customer I dread seeing bounces up to our table.

"Hey, Nick!" Anna's infectious grin almost makes me smile back, despite my slightly sour mood and the fact that seeing her always makes me a little dizzy and freaked out. David's best friend. The connection to the man whose face is the last thing on my mind before I fall asleep, or first thing I think of when I'm in the shower stroking myself.

Okay Nick, focus. I need to stop being so weird. But since Anna started coming by the market I couldn't help thinking about David. And she makes it even worse by giving me occasional updates about his life: informing me that he got his dream job at some important museum, telling me she was in Chicago visiting him, mentioning he broke up with his boyfriend at Christmas.

"Good morning, Anna." My voice is even and professional. "What can I get you today? We have some nice leeks left—"

"David's back in town." Anna interrupts me, a grin spreading wide on her angular, pale face.

I try not to react, but my mouth falls open. No words come out. A wave of fizzy heat rolls from the top of my head down to my aching feet.

"His dad had a stroke a few weeks ago." The smile disappears as she shares this information. "Well, another one, but this one was bad. He was in the hospital for a little over three weeks. He's home now and David's living with him. Taking care of him. He moved back." Anna selects some vegetables as she drops this bombshell on me. "And I'll take the leeks."

She seems to be deriving some kind of sick pleasure in the fact that she's stunned me into silence. Jenna hands Anna the last two bunches of the pale green stalks and handles the transaction, shooting me a concerned look. A stab of sadness for David's dad, one of the kindest men I've ever met, mixes with a whole bunch of anxiety about potentially seeing David again. And then there it is. The lightness in my chest and a swoop in my belly. I'm excited. Really fucking excited. I want to see him. I want to hop into my Jeep and drive over to his house and pull him into my arms and never let him go.

"Nick?" Jenna's voice is soft and tentative.

My brain searches for the words to ask if David would be okay with me stopping by to see him. I wish I could at least work up the courage to finally ask for his new cell number. He changed it when he moved back to Chicago. Instead I mumble, "Well, give Dr. Webster my best."

Great. I'm sure when Anna inevitably goes over this conversation with David he'll be nothing but enthusiastic to reconcile with me.

I scrub my hand over my face. I'm fucking stupid sometimes.

Chapter Four

Nick

April

I savor the familiar wood-smoke dark of my house. I'm exhausted. The kind of bone-deep exhaustion that comes from exerting both mind and body to their limits. Normally I love feeling this way because it's one of the only times I can actually relax. But today was too much. Seeing my dad and brother always sets me on edge. But knowing David is back for the first time since he left for good ten years ago has unmoored me. I'm desperate to see him and wholly terrified at the same time.

As I step into the hot stream of the shower I let my mind wander to David as it has probably thousands of times over the last decade. His sculpted, high cheekbones and long, straight nose. His perpetually messy auburn hair and intense green eyes. His lanky frame stretched out under me in the back of my Jeep.

Giving up any pretense of not fantasizing about him, I reach for my cock, now pulsing up toward my stomach. I stroke myself gently at first, keeping my fist loose at the base of my shaft, avoiding the sensitive head as I remember that night. The last night I saw David.

We were sitting in my Jeep, parked out at the farm, then nothing but my uncle's abandoned land where we would go to talk or smoke weed or swim in the frigid creek. It was one of those shatteringly cold nights, where every star glints clear and every breath is bracing and vital. The air smelled like snow. Although the heat was turned up to its highest setting David was still shaking, teeth chattering, sitting hunched in the passenger seat.

I had no idea what to say, so I let the silence stretch out between us, not exactly uncomfortable. Guilt consumed me; I had no words to comfort my best friend. He had put his favorite CD into the stereo and we stayed there, car running, the same album, *Dummy* by Portishead, playing over and over. To this day hearing the opening chords of "Mysterons," the first track, never fails to get me hard. I'm embarrassed to even think of how many times I put that CD on while I tried to make love to Christi. She just thought I liked nineties electronica.

David finally cut the silence, making a comment about not wanting to go back to school. I gave him some bullshit line about how hard he'd worked to get into Columbia. That he only had a year left in his master's program anyway. I put my hand on his shoulder, gripping his thin frame through his fancy wool overcoat. That's when he started sobbing. At first it was too dark in the car for me to tell, but then I heard his shaky breaths and soft whimpers. Tears slid down his nose, leaving dots of moisture on his black dress pants. I lifted my hand to his face, cupping his cheek gently. Recalling tracing the line of his jaw and running the pads of my trembling fingers over his swollen lips, my dick surges and I start working myself harder, biting back a moan.

I'd hated myself in that moment because as my best friend sobbed next to me, my cock had gotten so incredibly hard it strained against my already uncomfortable khakis. I knew I should comfort him some other way. I knew only a few weeks earlier I'd told David unequivocally we couldn't keep fooling around. But damn if I didn't lean across the center console and pull his shuddering body into my arms. I pressed gentle kisses into his soft hair, which always smelled like peppermint and lavender. Nonsense words of comfort, probably too quiet for him to even hear, escaped my mouth in a steady stream.

The justification that me holding him like this was only to calm him down quickly flew out the window when he shifted slightly in my grip and his gaze locked with mine. The memory of the lust in his green eyes, pupils blown and long eyelashes fluttering, makes my knees buckle and I palm my balls, grabbing them and pulling lightly.

"Fuck," I murmur and I tip my head back, letting the hot water rush onto my neck.

He'd kissed me then and my whole body buzzed hot. It had been the first time he'd ever initiated a kiss. I was always the one to kiss him, pulling him to me roughly or pushing him up against a wall when I couldn't take it anymore. But David's kiss felt so different. So honest and open and giving. At first his lips brushed mine tentatively, like he assumed I'd push him away.

"Sorry," he'd murmured, pulling back and covering his pretty mouth with his hand. But I was too turned on to even think about stopping and a low growl rumbled from my throat. I pulled him against me and pressed my lips firmly to his. At first his mouth stayed closed and I could almost feel his brain working in overdrive. Then his lips parted, so soft and supple against my own. His mouth tasted sweet like the super sugary coffee he'd been drinking and like something else, a fresh flavor I always associated with him, like newly fallen rain. David started mewling softly as I slid my tongue against his plump bottom lip. The kiss became fierce then; we were making out in earnest, the way we had in his dorm at Columbia. I couldn't think about anything but his smooth skin under my hands. I'd yanked at his overcoat and suit jacket, my movements jerky because of the awkward distance between us in the front seat.

In all the years I've replayed this night in my mind I can never remember which one of us suggested we move to the back seat. But we did, quickly getting out of the car and going around to the back. I know I'm the one who laid the seats down and threw the worn cotton blanket over them, hoping if we did have sex that it would make David more comfortable. I'd undressed hurriedly, turning to pull the door shut behind me once I'd stripped off my shirt. The air outside was freezing. The heater was too weak to get the back of the car very warm, and I remember David grinning, the bright, playful smile that made him look so boyish and so fucking cute and asking me to help him warm up. Then I said it.

"I want to be inside you. Is—is that okay?" I'd wanted to sound firm and confident, to reassure him that I wanted this too, but my voice was hoarse, barely a croak. David blushed in the soft overhead light of the back seat. Damn, he was adorable. He nodded enthusiastically, his grin widening and his eyes bright.

"Um, yeah. I'd love that." And I knew that was true. The last time we'd been together he'd asked me to fuck him over and over. He'd even been all mock-sullen about it when I'd said I didn't think it was a good idea. "Are you sure though?" A slight tremor had edged into his voice.

I hated myself for making him doubt me. For being so hot and cold and unfair to him for so long. As I stroke myself in the shower this memory gives me momentary pause, my hand stilling on my throbbing erection.

"I'm sure," I'd said and we both silently finished undressing, eyes locked together. He was so beautiful, slim with features that were somehow incredibly delicate and profoundly masculine. Serious eyebrows and a full, luscious mouth. "I haven't been able to stop thinking about you since last time," I admitted, embarrassed by the truth. He'd been on my mind every waking moment, and honestly a lot of nights when I slept. I was a twenty-one-year-old man who was still having wet dreams about his best friend.

Then we were down to our boxers and David was shivering again so I pulled him close, lying down on the scratchy blanket with him on top of me. His normally silky skin was pebbled with goose bumps and I smiled, running my hands up and down his back. David shifted against my body, scooting up so our erections lined up perfectly, the friction amazing even through the thin cotton of our underwear. The head of my cock had slipped out through the fly of my boxers and I'd been wildly desperate to feel skin on skin. I couldn't get him close enough.

"Oh god," I'd moaned and David smiled against my neck, kissing and nipping softly as he continued to grind and rub against me.

The thought alone of the pressure of his cock against my own, almost makes me come. I let go of my dick, momentarily running my fingers over my chest and circling my nipple with my fingers before giving it a rough pinch.

David had flashed an impish grin and slowly pulled my dick fully out of my boxers and bent gracefully to close his hot mouth around my twitching hardness. I moaned his name along with what I'm sure was total nonsense as he sucked me deep, his hand fisted at the base of my erection. The slick warmth of his mouth was almost too much to bear as his tongue danced in a sultry circle around the tip of my cock. Slowly but surely he dropped his mouth lower and lower around me until his lips met the top of his clenched fingers and I'd had to stop him. I knew I couldn't take much more of him sucking me that deep or I would come. And I knew where I wanted to come.

I must have indicated my desperation to be inside him somehow because he'd reached into his pants, lying crumpled on the car floor, and fished out his wallet to extract a lubricated condom. Gently, he placed it on the seat between us and leaned over to press a chaste kiss to my lips. I wrenched him toward me and tugged down his boxers and my own in a few rough motions. Flipping him onto his hands and knees, I bent over him. My skin thrummed with nerves and the pure joy of being with David. I felt so alive when I was with him like this. Most of the time I was pretending to be this straight jock, a good Greek son, the man's man my dad needed me to be. With David I didn't have to pretend.

I'd wanted so desperately to capture that feeling, to etch every detail into my memory. The clean wash of moonlight. His lean, lithe body under my bigger frame. My cock pressing and pulsing into the cleft of his perfect, shapely ass. Our combined panting fogging up the frosty windows of the car. I pressed my lips to his still chilly skin and dragged my face down his pale, lightly freckled back.

Knowing I hadn't shaved in a few days, I figured my stubble might scrape his skin a little, but if it bothered him he didn't say so. David groaned and reached for his own cock, giving it a few slow tugs. Taking his escalating, raspy breathing and soft cries of "oh god" and "yes" as an indication he liked what I was doing, I kept going, kissing down the small of his back and slowly dipping my tongue into his crack.

We'd never done any ass stuff, sticking firmly to kissing, jerking each other off, and the one other time he'd blown my mind by taking me down his throat. I'd been unsure in theory but as I licked down to the tight pink bud, I realized there was absolutely nothing to worry about in reality. He smelled musky and masculine and like his peppermint soap and so good. I never wanted to stop. When I pushed the flat of my tongue against his hole, I felt David tense and a brittle whine escaped his lips. He swallowed audibly and shifted a little.

"Nick." His normally melodious voice was thick and raw. "You don't have to—"

I cut him off by circling my tongue around his entrance again and moaning into him. My own dick was achingly hard at that point but I didn't want to feel anything until I slid into his ass. I knew I couldn't slam right into him so I put my finger in my mouth, slicking it up with spit, and gently slid it into David's channel. Holy shit. He'd been hot and tight and perfect. This was nothing like putting my fingers awkwardly inside girls. The sensation of his slick muscle clenching almost made me come.

"Oh my god. Nick, that feels so good. Please. Oh god." David's voice was so needy. Remembering the sound of him keening underneath me, I start to pump my cock harder now, my knees buckling as hot sparks of pleasure lick at my balls. Still stroking my shaft with my right hand I slide my left index finger into my ass, curling it toward my prostate. Again I have to bite back a growl of pleasure.

I slid two more fingers slowly in and out of him, fucking him and exploring and making sure he would be ready. When I'd asked him if he was, he'd laughed and begged me to please fuck him already. So I did. Well, after he had to get up and help me put on the condom, that is. My overeager fingers were shaky and kept slipping around on the lubricant. I hadn't told David, but it was my first time putting one on. It was, in fact, my first time having sex. The fooling around he and I had done was the closest I'd come to any sex at all. With girls I had always tried to make excuses and be a "gentleman" to avoid anything other than hands and making out.

David got back on his hands and knees, head dropped down, whole body tense as he waited for me to line up and press into him. I was so afraid of hurting him as I pushed the tip of my cock into his tight hole. And fuck, it was tight. I'd been worried I couldn't do it, couldn't get inside.

"It's okay," he whispered and pressed his perfect ass back toward me.

With one shaking hand I gripped his hips while I guided my cock with the other, pressing a little harder into his entrance. I gasped at the electric shock of pleasure that almost blinded me as I slid in through the tight ring of muscle and into his heat. And I'd almost lost control because then I was buried in him and he was crying out under me. At first I'd panicked, thinking I'd hurt him, and I started to pull out. But then David spoke.

"Don't you dare," he said, and even though I couldn't see his face I could tell he was smiling. "You feel amazing. I've wanted you inside me for so long."

I started rocking my hips again, slower this time, gripping his muscular, pert ass with both hands. Loving the sensation of his flesh against mine as I pumped into him. I'd already been pathetically close to coming, but I held off, needing David to come first. I needed to hear him let go, to feel him clench around me as he found his pleasure.

I'd tried to focus on pretty much anything else, looking closely at the ugly orange and teal stripes of the blanket bunching under us and noticing that the CD had started over again as I drove steadily into David. Then I found it, that spot I'd located with my fingers, and I surged against it hard. David gasped and whimpered under me and I did it again, this time reaching to wrap my fingers around his cock. All it took was a few pumps, and he fell apart.

"Nick. I'm going to... Ah. Fuck. Nick." His hot channel was like a vise around my throbbing erection and I felt his warm release spilling into my hand and down onto the blanket.

"I've got you, baby," I said, pushing deeper into him, right on the edge myself. My balls tightened, and I felt my ass clench as I pulled him flush up against me. It was like nothing else mattered but our bodies, me squeezing him tight as my orgasm took over.

"Nick, I... Please," he'd whined and shook as I'd started to spill into the condom.

And then I'm coming, jacking my own cock rough and hard, white-hot energy racking my body and blurring my vision. I'm spilling all over my hand, my knees buckling as I have to brace myself against the wall. Waves of pleasure slowly give way to sadness as I come back to myself. The water has gone cool and the familiar shock of loss hits me like a slap to the face. What I'd done right after collapsing on top of him. The words that had ended our friendship for good.

I know what I need to do.

Chapter Five

David

April

The air smells like rain as I step onto the front porch, fingers wrapped tightly around the hot mug of coffee, my copy of *Kafka on the Shore* tucked under my arm. Once again the sky is a depressing shade of white-gray and the diffuse morning light renders the brown grass and tangled dead plants in the garden especially dingy. I'm utterly exhausted. Dad had a rough night, falling out of bed and getting angry with me when I tried to help him to the bathroom. He'd wet himself and the shame and rage in his face had made me feel almost sick to my stomach.

I'd always been close with my parents, having the kind of open and honest relationship that precluded us from ever acting self-conscious around each other. But this was so different. Because I felt embarrassed too, seeing him like that. As I'd helped him to the bathroom and into fresh pajamas, he'd started mumbling. It was still difficult for me to understand anything he said since half of his face sagged from the stroke. Then I'd realized. He was saying he wished he'd died. His words hit me like a punch in the middle of my chest. Like her. He's doing the same thing my mother had done when she'd chosen to ignore her doctor's treatment plan. Was he going to stop trying too? Anger surged in me, hot and vicious, but I'd said nothing, just tucked my dad back into fresh sheets and returned to my room to lie awake for hours.

I try to read but I can't focus, my vision blurring as I scan the same paragraph over and over. After last night I'd yearned for the comfort of a favorite book, hoping to lose myself in the familiar story and relax the tension thrumming under my skin. But I'm cold and jittery and especially irritated because my eyes keep flicking up to the Patrases' driveway. Nick's Jeep is parked out front. Well I assume it's still his. It's the same forest green '97 Grand Cherokee he'd driven throughout high school and the whole time I was away at college. The same Jeep we'd fucked in before he decided to show me what a complete asshole he was. Ugh. Nope. Not thinking about that.

Clearly unable to use reading as a distraction, I pull my phone out of my pocket and check my Instagram page. I have a few new followers and a tiny flame of excitement flares in my chest. Maybe nothing will come of this but the joy of sharing my art even in this small way brings a smile to my lips.

"Hey."

A low, rumbling voice and footsteps startle me so much I fumble my phone and it clatters against the stone porch. Thank god I sprung for the protective case. Before I even look up I know it's him. Years of sleepovers and phone calls and teasing each other has seared the low cadence of his words into my mind. I don't want to look up. My face is stupidly hot and my heart is hammering so hard I have to imagine he can hear it.

"Hi," I say, still looking at my phone on the ground. Why am I acting like this? I've rehearsed seeing him again an embarrassing number of times, and it never was supposed to involve me dropping things or being stunned into silence. In my fantasies I'm always cool, impassive, not giving him the time of day.

Grudgingly I raise my eyes and he's still perfect. Perfect because I know the sleepy smile he makes first thing in the morning. Perfect because I know how tight his big body scrunches up during scary movies. Perfect because I know his flaws but I don't care. But honestly though, why does Nick have to look like that? He is almost comically tall, standing a good half foot taller than me. And his broad frame has gotten broader since I saw him last, like he's started to seriously work out. He is massive. His dark brown hair, once a shaggy tangle, is cut shorter and parted on the side. It's still long enough, I note, that the messy waves make me want to run my fingers through it. Nick's stupid handsome square jaw is tight and his dumb gorgeous thick brows are pulled together. He looks nervous.

"Um. How are you?" He seems to be frozen at the bottom step of the porch, hands stuffed into the pockets of faded gray jeans that probably were at one time black. Nice to see he still dresses like a dad in an L.L. Bean catalog. He's probably owned this entire outfit since last time I saw him: a light blue T-shirt that I pretend not to notice is deliciously tight across his built chest, and a green and blue flannel with the buttons undone.

"Tired," I reply honestly. My face gets hot again. It's still weirdly easy to talk to him even though I am so uncomfortable I wish a bolt of lightning would zap out of the overcast sky and kill me on the spot.

Easing myself back down into the Adirondack chair, I gesture vaguely for him to sit in the one next to me. He grins sheepishly and bounds up the porch steps. He seems pretty nervous. As soon as he sits his knee starts bouncing and I have to look away because even through the denim I can see the powerful muscles of his thighs clenching. We sit for a long, tense moment in silence. Then we both start speaking at once.

"So what's up?" I start to say.

He laughs a little as if to acknowledge the awkwardness. But I don't want to laugh with him. As happy as I am to see him—well okay, maybe not happy, but something in me eased the moment he sat down next to me—I'm still angry at him. I mean, he basically tortured me from the time I was sixteen until—well, until I got that damn wedding invitation with that damn note in his damn handwriting saying he was in love with Christi and he hoped I could make it to their damn wedding.

"I'm really sorry to hear about your dad. But he's doing better, yeah?"

"Thanks." My voice is cold and sounds kind of sarcastic. "So did you need something?" I'm being bitchy.

A touch of pink floods Nick's olive skin and my heart softens. His abashed expression has always done that to me. His emotions are so clear on his face. He opens his mouth then scrubs a hand over the back of his neck. "My mom wanted me to give you guys her best." He pauses as if he regretted saying that. "Uh, yeah. My parents still do the whole Sunday supper thing. They're trying to set me up with some girl from their church." His eyes dart toward mine and I can see pain in his face.

Nope. David Webster, you are not going to feel sorry for him.

"Right." Something like a sneer flashes over my face and I focus my energy on softening my expression. "I was sorry to hear about your divorce." Again it comes out snarky and insincere. I mean, he has to know I'm not too broken up over his divorce.

He shrugs like he isn't all that upset over it either. I guess it was more than two years ago. It's possible he's moved on to this new church girl. "Anyway," Nick continues, "I don't want to be over there. And Anna told me you'd moved back? So I thought I'd come see how you're doing."

He looks like he wants to say something else, so I wait, but he just grips his knees and stares down at his brown work boots. Wait, when did Anna see him? She never told me she talked to him. Traitor. I almost want to text her on the spot to pump her for information but I refrain.

"Yeah. I'm back for a while. I broke my lease, quit my job and everything. It's so weird being back here. The town has changed a lot. And I'm pretty bored because other than taking my dad to physical therapy and his doctors and stuff, I haven't been doing much." I'm rambling but I can't make myself stop. "Like for so long my whole life has been all about school and work, and I finally was getting settled in at basically my dream job and now I'm living at home and unemployed. I kinda feel like the whole doctorate thing was a waste of time. But my dad needs me." I try not to think about last night and my dad's apparent lack of desire to live. I have to figure this out. I have to help him get better.

I can hear the softness of sympathy in Nick's voice. His gray eyes are locked on mine. "That sucks. I'm so sorry to hear he's sick. Anna told me how much you loved your job. That must have been a tough decision."

My stomach is weirdly hollow and my throat tightens. I have to change the subject. "So what's your mom making for dinner?" Nick's mother is a phenomenal cook. When we were kids I loved going over to their house to eat fresh baklava and dolmas and her amazing homemade pita.

Nick's whole body relaxes, and he leans back into the chair. He's too broad for it and I find myself smirking. "She's making roasted chicken. The one she does with lemon, you know? And potatoes and, probably a million other things. I'd invite you over but…" He pauses and he looks even more nervous than he did when he initially sat down. His full lips pull into a tight line. "My dad hasn't changed much."

Nick's dad is a bigot. He's super religious and big-time into the brand of political conservatism that pushes hardcore anti-gay rhetoric. When he found out I was gay, he told Nick in no uncertain terms I was no longer welcome in their home and that I shouldn't come by their family's diner anymore either. This marked the end of years of Nick and I stopping by his parents' restaurant after school to eat fries and guzzle soda and do our homework at the counter. Not only did I get cut off from pretty much their entire family but I also was cut off from my only source of being able to eat any meat or junk food. It was back to seaweed salad and carob cubes as after-school snacks from then on out. I groan. I can still remember how good Mrs. Patras's roasted chicken is, all crisp and tangy and studded with rosemary and garlic.

"But hey," Nick grins. His smile is the warm wash of genuine sweetness that drew me to him as a kid. "If you want, I can make it for you. I finally convinced her to give me the recipe and I've gotten pretty good at making it." I can tell he's trying to act confident but his knee is bouncing again. "Maybe you could come over one night this week for dinner?"

My whole body feels like it's filled with helium at his words. I can't help but return his grin and I stare down at my Bensimon sneakers. "Sure," I say quietly.

Nick startles me by springing up from his chair. For a second I think he might pull me into a hug as he closes the distance between us. His gaze is hot on my skin. But then I realize he's handing me his phone. "Here." His smile is huge, his heavy eyebrows raised. "Put your number in. I don't have your new one."

I quickly add myself as a contact in his phone, noticing his wallpaper is a picture of him arm in arm with a tall Latino guy with big ears and a bigger smile, and a small, pretty black woman with honey-colored natural curls. I wonder who they are. He sends me a quick text so I have his number. It's a smiley face, but he's typed it out :-) rather than using the emojis. Goofball. I'm about to make some excuse to go inside so I can call Anna and panic at her about this whole situation when Nick speaks again.

"Thanks, David. I really, um." He swallows loudly and I can't look away from his Adam's apple bobbing in his stubbled throat. "I need to say some stuff to you, okay?" He pauses again as if speaking is starting to cause him real physical pain. His breath, I notice, has gotten uneven and shallow. Does he still have panic attacks? He drags his fingers through his hair and starts to make his way down the porch steps. "So text me and let me know what day works." Then he's jogging across the street and disappears into his family's garage.

I hustle back inside, already unlocking my phone. My head spins and thoughts fly around so quickly I can't possibly grab onto one. Nick is somehow more gorgeous than he was in his twenties. Now he looks less like an Abercrombie model bro and way more like if Superman ditched the cape and got really into hiking. I force myself to focus. Does he want to apologize? Maybe he wants to try to be friends again? Or maybe he just feels guilty and needs to absolve himself. Or maybe Anna is right and he wants to—no. I can't go there.

I'm in the middle of drafting an airtight contract in my head that I cannot under any circumstances allow myself to sleep with him when I hear grumbling and bumping from upstairs. My father is up, and it sounds like he's fallen again. I take the stairs two at a time, my pulse racing, all frivolous thoughts sweeping out of my head like raindrops on a windshield. Relief washes over me cool and soft when I enter my dad's dim bedroom. He's okay, just awake and slightly tangled in his sheets.

"Hey, Dad." I smile at him and give his shoulder a gentle squeeze. "Do you want some breakfast?" He can't eat solid foods quite yet because his facial muscles are weak so I've been making him lots of smoothies and soups. Mostly I've been eating the same liquid diet and I notice my jeans hang loose around my hips.

His gray hair is matted and his skin looks almost chalky. I forget sometimes, or at least I used to before this stroke, that my father is going to be seventy-one next year. My parents were in their forties when they finally had me, both of them academics who spent their twenties and thirties amassing degrees and flying around the country to give conference papers and conduct research.

He nods and the two of us make our way slowly to the kitchen, me holding him up. He doesn't have any doctors' appointments today and I've checked out a bunch of books and DVDs for him from the library. But he hasn't seemed interested in anything over the last few weeks. I'm so used to the version of my father who breathes NPR and reads political science journal articles for fun, I hardly recognize this man.

"Want to watch something?" I ask softly once I have him settled on the couch with the kale, banana, and tofu smoothie I made him when I woke up this morning. "I got a few documentaries you might like. One of them was produced by Dr. DePalma. He was in your department, right?" My dad shakes his head and stares into space. The steady ticking of the ornately carved German clock on the wall is the only sound in the room.

"David." My dad's voice, still slurred and thick, but getting better every week thanks to his fantastic occupational therapist, startles me.

"Yeah, Dad?"

"Who was here?" The words come out slowly, a labor.

I feel a flush creep into my face. "Um, Nick, actually. He wanted to see how you're doing. Said his mom sends her best." Absently I'm surprised she didn't send any food over. But Nick's dad probably forbade it. He hates my father almost as much as he hates me. My father's liberal op-eds in the local paper hadn't exactly been George Patras's cup of tea.

Even though he struggles to control the muscles around his mouth, I can see a flicker of amusement on my father's face. It's nice to see. "You talked to him?" he inquires slowly.

I only laugh and shrug in response.

"Nick's a good kid, David. Always liked you two together."

I blush hotly but say nothing. While I never told my dad exactly what happened between Nick and me—that would be too much information—I imagine he'd pieced some of it together. I would get irritable any time my dad or uncle mentioned my former best friend. But he never pressed for details.

After my dad finishes his breakfast, I keep myself busy cleaning the kitchen, doing laundry, and deep cleaning the bathrooms. I glance at the clock, intensely grateful that it is finally late enough in the morning that I can call Anna. She spends her weekend mornings running and I know she never brings her phone.

Thankfully she answers on the first ring. "What's up, buttercup?" she chirps and I can hear the crumpled sounds of wind blowing into the receiver.

"Where are you?" I ask in response.

"Sitting on my porch having some coffee. Want to come over?"

"Been there, done that," I tease. "And guess who showed up?"

"No. Way." She gasps. "Yay! It worked!"

Damn, she's perceptive. But I love how we're always on the same wavelength, like she can read my thoughts. It's always been this way with her. "Anna! Why didn't you tell me you talked to him? You're so shady!" My voice is teasing but I'm a little angry at her. I know she means well, but sometimes I wish Anna would leave well enough alone.

"Well...I may have seen him at the market yesterday. And I may have told him you were back. But man, he acts fast. I thought I'd have a chance to warn you. Oops. But tell me everything."

I quickly fill her in on Nick's visit this morning. "What do I do? Like, why does he want to see me?" I nervously pace around my bedroom, compulsively picking up random objects and putting them back down.

"Stop pacing," she scolds. "I can tell you're pacing."

I sink down onto my neatly made bed, running my fingers over the blue linen duvet, but I get fidgety and stand up to look out the window. Great. I can see Nick and his sister Cassie sitting on the porch swing, a big brown and gray dog snoozing next to Nick's feet. I turn around to keep pacing.

"You should see him, I think." Anna's voice is gentle. "I mean, you guys were friends for so long." Her voice shifts from soft to playful. "And let's be honest. You're still pretty hung up on him. Like, you get so damn touchy about him and you used to always compare sex with Christopher and even Julian to the infamous Nick hookups."

My cheeks flame. "I did not."

Anna scoffs. "Okay. Whatever you have to tell yourself, bud. But worst-case scenario he gives you an awkward apology, and it's kind of weird. Best-case scenario, I'm right, he's queer and you guys fall in love and have a beautiful gay wedding and adopt a bunch of kids and animals."

I press my palm to my forehead. Hearing that hypothetical makes my eyes lose focus and my neck go hot. "No," I grind out. "Worst-case scenario he, like, messes with my head all over again. What if he still thinks being gay is wrong or whatever the fuck? Or what if he still doesn't know what he wants? Or what if he wants to be friends again?" I pause and stare at the boxes of books I still haven't unpacked from my apartment. "Because I don't know if I can be his friend." I open my mouth to spin out more horrible possibilities but Anna interjects.

"David, stop." Anna sighs. "I know he hurt you. What Nick did wasn't fair. We both know that. But I also think you need to give him a chance. I mean, not everyone gets to be as comfortable with their orientation and coming out as you did. Not everyone has a family like yours."

Anna always gets frustrated with me over this point. I think she's committed to this idea that Nick is just closeted partially because her parents stopped speaking to her when she finally worked up the courage to come out to them in her early twenties. Unlike me, she understands why someone might deny something so basic about who they are.

My shoulders sag. "Sorry," I murmur. "I know you're right. I should see him. Even if it is only to talk this out. And who knows, maybe we *can* be friends."

"I'm still convinced he's got it bad for you." Her tone is cheeky again. "I mean he's making you dinner. It sounds kind of date-like, no?"

I sigh.

"What night are you going? Want me to come over and hang out with your dad for a while?"

I love Anna. Since the day we met in studio art freshman year of high school, she's always shown herself to be one of the most compassionate and thoughtful people I've ever known. Sure, she can be a nosey pain in the ass sometimes, but I know her heart is in the right place. I want to reach through the phone and hug her.

"Anna, have I told you how much I love you lately?" I ask. I almost feel like I could cry.

"Not often enough, honey," she jokes. "But I love you too. I want you to be happy."

We end the call a few minutes later after Anna asks me a few practical questions about helping my dad and tells me to let her know what night I want to go over to Nick's.

"Oh," she gibes before hanging up, "and let me know if I should pack an overnight bag."

I'm tempted to text Nick immediately and tell him I'm free Tuesday night, but I force myself to wait. His Jeep is still parked outside his parents' place. And not that I'm looking, but around noon I see a VW Bug pull up. A curvy woman with glossy brown curls walks up to the front door clutching a cellophane-wrapped bouquet of flowers. Church girl. A zing of jealousy rages through me but I tamp it down. Nick didn't seem that excited to see her, did he? And so what if he is? Disgusted with myself I go around to the backyard with my painting supplies.

Once I settle into working, the world slows and softens. I lose myself in the task of putting paint to paper. I don't even think about Nick. Well, not very much. I'm working on a watercolor of two men flirting at a bar, the colors all pastel and the brushwork light. I'm kind of liking it. The sexual tension between the men is palpable and I'm pleased that the image I had in my head translated onto the page.

I want these paintings to look gay. I want my work to celebrate queerness and the beauty of the male form. So much of art has historically focused on idealized female beauty but I want to express masculine attractiveness in a real and vulnerable way, to highlight the potential warmth of male interaction. I'm trying to capture what drew me to love art in the first place. Flipping through the big Caravaggio coffee table book in my mom's office, getting uncomfortably turned on by *Boy with a Basket of Fruit* and realizing for the first time how simultaneously pretty and powerful masculinity could be. And I hope my work expresses that. I take a quick picture of my painting and text it to Marc, since a date he told me about was the inspiration for the piece.

> Marc: *I don't hear from you for a week then you text me a random painting? I love it though! Hot guy in it too ;)*

> David: *Sorry. I know I've been a shitty friend. I don't even have an excuse either since I basically don't do anything up here. I was thinking of uploading it to the page? Is that cool with you?*

> Marc: *Hell yes! Tag me in it! I saw you already have like 50 new followers. This is such a good idea. I've always liked your work.*

> David: *Thanks. I hope everything's good at the museum.*

I almost type that I missed it, but that's not exactly true. What had felt like my dream job had been weirdly easy to leave behind. I probably just have whiplash from the extreme left turn my life had taken. I was always bad at sorting out my own emotions, opting instead to go along with things until I was freaking out but couldn't understand why.

My phone buzzes and Marc replies saying he'll call me this week. I do miss Marc, his all-black outfits and snarky commentary. I wonder what he'd make of the whole Nick situation. He's pretty adamantly opposed to dating guys in the closet so he probably wouldn't think too highly of it. And why am I thinking about Marc's opinion of Nick? I need to pull it together.

By nine at night I'm exhausted since I'd barely slept the night before. My dad seems better. He ate more for dinner than usual and even agreed to let me read an article to him from the local paper, intent on expressing outrage at the columnist's views on redrawing local voting districts, which was much more like the old him.

I collapse onto my freshly laundered sheets and pick up my phone to set the alarm. I have a text from Nick.

> Nick: *Hey David. I hope it's okay that I'm texting you. I just wanted to say it was really good to see you today. I missed you. I hope you'll come over.*

My heart does a little backflip. After years of hooking up with hipster art academics who ironically used flip phones and scoffed at texting, and then living with Christopher who almost never expressed his feelings, it's strange to get such an honest and vulnerable text. I type out and delete a few replies before sending off my response.

> David: *Sure. It's okay. It was weird to see you honestly. It's been so long. But yeah, I'd like to come over. Is Tuesday okay?*

My hands shake and I quickly darken the screen of my phone. In order to avoid the horrible waiting game, I scamper off to the bathroom to wash my face and brush my teeth. But I should have known Nick's response would be immediate. When I get back to my bed, I see two texts.

> Nick: *Yeah it was weird, I guess. I was nervous if you couldn't tell.*

> Nick: *Tuesday is great. I got some tips from my mom today too, so the chicken should be good. :-)*

David: *Well you've officially gotten my hopes up, so it better be.*

This all feels too flirty so I send a second text, then immediately regret it. I'm not sure why I insist on torturing myself.

David: *How was hanging out with church girl?*

The little gray bubble hovers on the screen to show he's typing, then disappears only to reappear again for what seems like an eternity. My head spins. What is he doing, typing a Russian-novel-length description of their time together? When my phone buzzes again it almost flies out of my hands in my haste to unlock the screen.

Nick: *Fine. She's a nice person.*

I want to throw my phone out the window hard enough that it finds Nick and hits him on his perfect head.

Chapter Six

David

April

Tuesday dawns bright and clear with a warm edge to the breeze. I'm in a terrible mood. Not only am I seriously second-guessing agreeing to go over to Nick's for dinner, but my dad's regular physical therapist is out sick. The man filling in for her is pushy and impatient with my father. He's a macho bro with the kind of cut, sculpted body that shows he spends a huge amount of his free time at the gym. He's about a head shorter than me and I can tell he does not accept his stature with grace. At the end of the session when I walk into the harshly lit physical therapy gym to ask how the rehabilitation is going, the guy shrugs and says my dad needs to try harder if we want to see results. While my dad doesn't react at all, anger rises up my spine like water boiling over.

"Excuse me?" I ask, hoping my voice sounds civil.

The physical therapist—Tim, his badge reads—puts up his hands. "Sorry, princess." He smirks at me and I'm half embarrassed, half enraged and then more angry with myself for feeling any shame at all. "Tellin' it like I see it. If your father wants to walk again for more than a few steps at a time, he's going to have to do the exercises at home too. If you're too busy to take his rehab seriously, he should be at a facility."

I wonder what I could have possibly done to offend this man so much. Is it that he can tell I'm gay? Did he think my father was being lazy? I want to punch him or, I don't even know, yell at him. Something. Anything. Instead I take a deep breath and calmly thank him for his input. My father's face is equally impassive.

On the way out my dad stops by the nurse's station and quietly requests that Tim not be his physical therapist again. She looks abashed and apologizes, saying that's just Tim's manner. That he likes to tell it like it is. My anger is back in a flash. I hate that men are allowed to get away with being assholes under the guise of being straight shooters or tough guys. But I say nothing and my father and I air our grievances to each other in the car.

By the time we get home and finish lunch it's already late afternoon. I quickly text Nick to ask what time I should come over. He doesn't reply and I wonder if he's having second thoughts. Trying not to be a nervous wreck I poke around in my closet, wondering what I should wear. I have everything neatly hung up and arranged by color in the gigantic walk-in closet in my childhood bedroom. This closet is certainly one perk of being an unemployed art historian back in my dad's house. I may be flushing six years of painstaking doctoral research at the University of Chicago down the toilet, but at least now I have a closet that fits all my clothes. After some deliberation, I settle on a pair of dark purple pants I bought a few months earlier on major sale at Barney's, a fitted white T-shirt, my favorite black leather motorcycle jacket, and black Chelsea boots. I quickly snap a selfie in the full-length mirror on the back of the door and text it to Anna.

David: *Thoughts? Too much?*

Anna: *No such thing, love. You look hot. What time do you want me over tonight to hang out with Papa Richard?*

David: *I'm not sure. I still haven't heard from Nick. I'm kind of panicking to be honest. Does he not want me to come over?*

Anna: *David he's a farmer. He probably doesn't keep his phone on him while he's out, like, hoeing the fields or whatever.*

David: *Haha hoeing. You're probably right. When I hear from him I'll let you know.*

I try to keep my mind occupied by making sure everything is ready for my dad's dinner and writing out a detailed description of his exercises and medications for Anna. Finally, Nick texts me asking if seven thirty is okay. I quickly respond, unlike him, and then let Anna know what time I'll be heading over. Then I realize I have no idea where this farm of his is or how long it's going to take me to drive there, so I text him again and ask for his address. His message pops up on my screen and my mouth actually falls open. He lives *there*? Nick fucking lives and started a farm on the piece of property where we had sex. The place where we used to go to smoke and talk for hours and later to fool around. The place where he said the words that ended our friendship for a decade.

I google the address to be sure. It's there plain as day. The first result is the website for Laurel Creek Farm. Even though I'm freaking out and confused as hell, curiosity gets the better of me and I tap the link. The website is well designed, a white background with a simple font and nice photos of the farm and the produce they grow. I learn that they use biodynamic practices and will be offering a farm share this summer. Feeling like a kind of a creep I tap the "About" tab. There is a picture of Nick, looking insanely hot in a fitted, slightly sweaty gray T-shirt and a plain navy baseball cap. His colossal form is flanked by the two people I'd noticed on his phone background. There is also a paragraph of information about the farming practices.

Laurel Creek Farm was co-founded by Nick Patras, Jenna Watson, and Hector Flores. After more than a decade working as a cook at his family's diner, Nick became interested in sustainable agriculture and began growing small quantities of produce as a hobby on the property that now houses the farm. The land, a former horse ranch owned and operated by Nick's uncle, Gus Patras, sat abandoned for over twenty years. When Uncle Gus passed he willed the land to his nephew.

Jenna Watson and Hector Flores joined the team shortly after the farm's humble beginnings. Jenna brings years of experience in organic farming from her time spent working in Sonoma, California for a variety of wineries, farms, and restaurants. Hector graduated from Cornell College of Agricultural Sciences with a degree in Plant Sciences. Prior to co-founding Laurel Creek Farm, Hector served as the Farm Director at The Red Barn Center for Agriculture in Tarrytown, NY. The 50-acre property is home to apple and plum orchards as well as our heirloom vegetable and herb gardens. Next spring we will be introducing breeding flocks of Rhode Island Red chickens and Narragansett turkeys.

Laurel Creek Farm is not currently certified organic but we strongly believe in a healthy, holistic approach to farming and we do not use any artificial chemicals, pesticides, or fertilizers. Our goal is to provide healthy, nutritious food to all members of our local community. Laurel Creek Farm is committed to equal food access. To ensure the whole community has access to healthy food, we donate produce to the Catskill Food Bank and will offer a sliding payment scale for our upcoming CSA. Please feel free to come visit us and say hello!

Jesus Christ. I don't know what to be more surprised by: the fact I am going to be seeing Nick in the exact place our twenty-year friendship and any potential for a relationship imploded, or by how professional and legitimate this whole farm operation seems. Not that I should be surprised. Nick has always been single-minded about projects and goals. When he set his mind to making the varsity football lineup our freshman year, he trained and practiced almost obsessively. A shiver rushes up my spine as I remember what it was like to be on the receiving end of that focused determination.

I close the internet browser on my phone and groan. Now dread sits cold and heavy in the pit of my stomach. I genuinely do not know what to do. Can I handle this? I was already nervous to go over there, but this setting might put me over the edge. And why would he want to live there, in a place where he did things he regretted so much? I don't know if I can deal with something else going to shit in my life right now. I've already abandoned my career and detonated the life I spent years building in Chicago. And my breakup with Christopher still feels a little raw, inevitable though it was. My heart may be unable to bear the burden of more hurt.

After an embarrassing amount of deliberating, including changing out of my date outfit then putting it back on, drafting then deleting an angry text to Nick, contemplating not showing up at all, and finally driving the ten minutes to the fancy wine boutique and buying a bottle of Chablis in case I need to drown my sorrows, I decide to go. I'm a grown-ass man with a doctorate and a healthy relationship with my sexuality. I can handle one night with my hulking hunk of a former best friend. At least I think I can.

My dad looks happy to see Anna as she blusters through the door around six thirty and greets him with a big hug. She'd always loved my parents and continued to check in on my dad, taking him out for breakfast a few times a month after I'd moved to Chicago. They both had an unhealthy love of tofu and were total news nerds, rapidly exchanging opinions on world affairs and name-dropping UN Assembly members like it was totally common knowledge. She looks nice in her customary high-waisted jeans and thin black turtleneck. Her hair, which is almost always pulled back into intricate styles she finds on Pinterest, is down tonight, the copper-colored waves brushing the middle of her back.

"Get a haircut, hippie," I tease and she flips me off.

"So Richard, did David tell you where he's going tonight?" she asks innocently but eyes me slyly.

"He must have a date," my dad says slowly and gestures to my clothes.

Before Anna can run with that, I pipe up. "No! It's not a date." My voice has the shrill edge it gets when I'm nervous or lying. But I'm not lying. This is so not a date. "I'm going over to Nick's farm to check it out. He invited me when he stopped by the other morning."

I can tell my dad is not convinced and Anna looks smug. "At night?" he asks and his bushy eyebrows rise. haltingly.

"Nick is making him dinner," Anna says primly, sounding like that annoying kid in class who reminds the teacher they didn't collect the homework. Thankfully my dad says nothing but I can see a small smile on his face.

As I dash out the door, gripping the bottle of wine like it's a life raft, and somehow running late even though I've been ready for hours, Anna follows me out onto the porch. The evening air is chilly and I'm glad I have my jacket on.

"Have fun, okay? Try to relax. I know you're probably freaking out, but remember he was your best friend. Well, second best. Obviously I'm number one. But hear him out."

I nod. Part of me wishes I could hit fast-forward on the night and be back here already, sitting on the couch with Anna and eating the weird coconut milk ice cream she loves so much, laughing about how I'd been agonizing over nothing.

"Oh, and by the way. I did bring my toothbrush and pajamas. So feel free to have *a lot* of fun." She tries and fails to wink and I hit my forehead with my palm before waving dramatically at her and pulling the car door open.

Kate Bush's voice carries me along the tree-lined roads toward Nick's place. I review the things I want to say to Nick in between humming along with "King of the Mountain." I'll tell him he hurt me but I won't be all dramatic about it. I will absolutely, under no circumstances kiss or hug him. I won't even shake his hand, I decide. Although why we might shake hands is beyond me.

As I pull up to the long gravel driveway, now marked with a little wooden sign reading *Welcome to Laurel Creek Farm!* I realize I drove here on total autopilot. I hate myself for remembering how to get here so well. Nothing about the driveway has changed. It's still long, bumpy, and dusty, flanked on either side with dense foliage. But with a shock I realize the driveway is the only thing that has remained unchanged.

Even in the fading light, I can see that the rusted-out trucks, falling-down fence posts, and overgrown tangles of weeds and grass around the old farmhouse have been replaced with a patchwork of neatly ordered vegetable beds dotted with what look like miniature plastic greenhouses. Where there was once a small, collapsing building filled with rusty tools and paint cans there's an actual greenhouse, its glass walls reflecting the light shining from the house. And holy shit, the house. The pile of rubble masquerading as a structure that had stood ten years ago has been transformed into something that looks like the platonic ideal of a farmhouse. In place of the caved-in, peeling shingle roof is a green standing seam metal one. The once-crumbling brick chimney now juts toward the inky sky, a wisp of smoke dissipating in the breeze. There's a wide porch, and a curved bluestone pathway. Neat flowerbeds surround the house in a riot of colorful spring blooms. The wooden siding has been repainted too, the peeling green paint now a crisp, clean white. Every window on the first floor glows with soft yellow light. I approach as if a magnet pulls me in.

As I step onto the dark wooden slats of the porch, a dog barks inside, followed by the low rumble of Nick's voice. I can't suppress a smile when I also catch the bubblegum country stylings of the Dixie Chicks escaping through the open windows. Although I'd resolved to be angry at Nick, not to allow anything to topple the wall of indignation I'd constructed around myself, I chuckle and shake my head fondly. I've read too much Judith Butler to be thinking this way, but Nick's taste in music is hilariously girly. Growing up he always put on a front, playing the same metal and rap that all the other guys on his teams blasted from their trucks. But anytime I went through Nick's iPod it was all Dolly Parton, Linda Ronstadt, JLo, and Beyoncé. When I teased him about it, he would get all flustered and claim it was because of his sisters. It had been something I loved about him.

And that was the thing about Nick. Anytime I tried to stay angry with him, he always did such adorably sincere and unexpected things that it was impossible to hold on to any malice. He's so damn sweet. Like the night of my seventeenth birthday when he promised he would come with Anna and me to see *The Rocky Horror Picture Show* in Albany. At the last minute he'd bailed, opting instead to get trashed in a random field with his football buddies. I'd dashed at my tears the whole drive back. Anna had gripped the wheel hard as she navigated the winding dark roads, telling me not to bother with that jock asshole. But the next morning Nick showed up at my house, looking exhausted with dark bags under his eyes, unsteady on his feet. He'd stayed up all night to make me a chocolate raspberry cake, knowing it was my favorite.

Or there was the night he'd kissed me for the first time a few weeks later, when we were stoned out of our minds lying in my parents' backyard beneath a canopy of pinprick lights. Nick loved smoking weed and stargazing for hours, most of the time saying nothing at all. It was the only time he ever seemed genuinely relaxed. But that night, out of nowhere he'd rolled over onto me, almost crushing me under his bulk before he slid his arms under my body and pulled me close. I had freaked out a little as he crushed his lips to mine, worrying he was more out of it than I'd thought. But then Nick sighed in what seemed like relief as my lips parted against his. He pulled back gently and nuzzled his nose against mine and whispered my name, telling me I was beautiful. After that night Nick was everywhere: in the rising notes of the jazz standards my mom played while painting, between the lines of every novel I read, in the smell of freshly cut grass.

I realize too late that I'm standing at the door, staring blankly at the wreath of lavender adorning it, when Nick pulls it open and dazzles me with his enthusiastic grin. His gray eyes are bright and crinkle at the corners with his smile. He's wearing a navy blue henley that hugs his large biceps. The sleeves are pushed up, showcasing his thick, powerful forearms. I dart my eyes down. His enormous feet are bare and for some reason I can't stop looking at them. I get this overwhelming feeling, like I'd missed seeing his bare feet. *Nope. Absolutely not.*

I am not letting myself get all sentimental about this. I am keeping this quick and painless. Eat some dinner, listen to whatever he has to say, then go home. I'm still standing on the porch, gaping at him, when the big brown and gray dog I saw the other day pads over, bushy tail wagging. The dog has one blue eye and one brown eye and sits right in front of me, serenely waiting for me to pet it.

"Hi, buddy." I can't suppress my smile. The dog is so gentle and sweet, pushing its cold nose against my face as I squat down to stroke its wiry fur.

"That's Archie," Nick says and I glance up at him, realizing I am now at eye level with the man's denim-clad crotch.

"He's cute," I reply and quickly rise. I have to tip my head up to meet his gaze. Damn, he's tall.

"I adopted him when I moved out here. Christi never wanted a dog because she had two cats, but he keeps me company. He's kind of the farm mascot." Nick chuckles and pushes his fingers through his hair in the same nervous gesture he's done since he was a little kid. "Oh," he says like it just occurred to him, "come on in."

He steps back and I toe off my boots, lining them up on the small jute rug next to the door alongside a few pairs of Nick's huge work boots and mud-caked sneakers. He's turned the music off. When I finally look around the house I have to work to keep my face neutral, hiding my surprise. We never went inside the old farmhouse much because it always seemed structurally unsound, but once again I can barely believe this is the same place. The whole first floor is open, with butter yellow walls and wide-plank pine floors that softly reflect the warm overhead light. All the light fixtures look antique and vaguely industrial. There's a small woodstove in one corner of the living room with a neat pile of logs stacked next to it. And there are plants everywhere: big potted palm trees, cacti, and lined up along the wide stone kitchen windowsill there is a collection of herbs in white ceramic pots. The place looks more like a spread out of *Martha Stewart Living* than the bachelor pad I was expecting.

"Wow. Nick, this place is gorgeous," I murmur as I follow him and Archie across the living space and into the kitchen.

He looks a little shy then and bends down to pat the dog's head. "Thanks. It took a while to do all the work but I like how it turned out."

Now I really can't reign in my surprise. "You did this?"

He nods. "I mean, Jenna and Hector, they co-own the farm, helped me. So did Cassie's husband, he did some of the plumbing. But yeah, I did pretty much everything else." He gestures to the gingham curtains, looking proud. "I even made those. The only thing I didn't want to touch was the electrical, so I hired someone to do that. Didn't want the place to burn down." He laughs.

"That's amazing." I look around again and my eye catches on the painting hanging over the low pine bookcases in the living room. No way. He kept it? He even framed it in a simple wooden frame. It's a painting of the creek we used to swim at. The creek that I can hear rushing faintly through the open windows. Nick had always said it was his favorite place in the world, so I'd painted it for him. It was done in oil, all cool shades of green and blue and brown, in the hyperrealistic style I'd been into while working on my AP studio art portfolio.

Nick follows my gaze to the painting and I can tell he's nervous. "Yeah, I kept it. It's a nice painting." His hands are shoved deep into the pockets of his jeans.

Trying to hide that I'm out of breath, I crouch down to look at his collection of books. I want to hug him. I want to close the few feet of space between us and wrap my arms around his solid frame and forget all the stupid anger I've carried for years. Instead I shrug and mutter something about him needing to get out more and see better art. I regret my snarky comment the minute it comes out of my mouth. Desperate to change the subject, I thrust the bottle of wine at him. He thanks me graciously and pours me a glass before stowing the bottle in the vintage-looking white refrigerator.

"Dinner's almost ready," he murmurs as he turns back to a cutting board and begins slicing a tiny bulb of fennel into paper-thin slices.

I perch uneasily on one of the metal stools pulled up to the butcher block island. Nick's movements reflect his time in a professional kitchen, all focused and spare. Everything is chopped perfectly and arranged in small glass bowls.

After a few moments of awkward silence Nick glances up at me and smiles a sweet, tentative smile. "Thanks for coming over, David. I get that you probably weren't psyched to see me."

The back of my neck gets hot and tingly. How am I supposed to respond to that? I try to return his smile and take a small sip of wine. "What made you move out here?" I ask.

Nick takes a moment to respond. The timer on the oven goes off and he bends over to pull out a perfect-looking, delicious-smelling chicken. In an effort not to stare at his ass, I focus on the food he's preparing. Small golden potatoes and wedges of lemon are arranged in the roasting pan around the chicken. Nick quickly sprinkles everything with chopped rosemary before transferring the chicken to a platter and tenting it with foil. "It's kind of a long story," he says, not meeting my eye and taking a few gulps from a can of beer.

"Okay," I respond simply and I welcome the little bloom of irritation. Anger is easier than whatever the hell else I'm feeling.

He says nothing as he carves the chicken perfectly and arranges it on stoneware plates along with a spinach and fennel salad, roasted potatoes, and some kind of green sauce. I follow him silently to the long wooden table set with a cluster of candles and a pitcher full of daffodils. Damn. He really put the effort in. I don't think in three years of dating, Christopher ever treated me to a meal like this. And I certainly never did for him either. Mostly we grabbed sushi at the place down the street or ate takeout on the couch while watching Netflix.

Is this a date? Is Nick gay? I mean, I don't want to be too rigid about gender performance but do most jockey-straight guys prepare elaborate candlelit meals for their friends?

I sit down across from Nick and start eating. The food, not surprisingly, is delicious. The flavors are perfectly balanced and everything tastes incredibly fresh. "This is even better than your mom's," I mumble with my mouth full.

Nick has already eaten almost half the food on his plate. He's always been a fast eater with a huge appetite. He beams at me. "I won't tell her you said that, but thanks." Without another word though he goes back to eating, his eyes cast down. I almost want to ask him to get on with it. I'm about to break the silence with lame small talk when Nick puts his fork and knife down with a bit of a clatter and blurts out, "I'm gay."

Chapter Seven

David

April

Gently, I place my fork down on my half-empty plate and force myself to look at Nick. His square jaw, peppered with dark stubble, is set tight and his full lips press together. Honestly, he looks like he might either cry or be sick. Whole body radiating tension, his eyes bore into mine.

"Okay," I say mildly because I have no idea what else to say. My world has tipped on its axis but at the same time I'm not exactly surprised. I mean, we did have sex— amazing, mind-numbing sex. But he'd also shut down so quickly after. He'd been so adamant about it being a mistake. I decide to wait for him to go on.

His cheeks are flushed and when he finally does speak his voice is raw. "I mean, that's kind of why I moved out here, I guess. Once I knew for sure. At first, for a while I thought, you know, maybe I was, like, bisexual, and that I could choose not to be with guys. Turn that part off or whatever."

The words are tumbling out of him in a rush, but he's still got his eyes locked on mine, as if he promised himself he would look at me while he said this. This was probably not a good time for me to interject that bisexuality doesn't exactly work that way, then.

"So I got back with Christi. I'd had fun dating her in high school and I thought if I focused on women I could be straight. But it didn't work. Obviously. I was fucking miserable. I mean, Christi's a great woman. She was an awesome wife and my folks loved her. But being with her felt wrong. And it was hard for me to...you know, to have sex with her. I was drinking a lot."

Now his cheeks flame. "I started having a lot of panic attacks. I never cheated on her or anything but I knew what I was doing to her was cruel. Unfair, you know? She started talking about having a family and I couldn't do it. And I think she kind of knew something was wrong. At first she thought I was having an affair since I never wanted to have sex. And I felt super guilty so I would, like, buy her big gifts sometimes and go out of my way to be perfect in every other way."

He shakes his head and pauses for a long time. I'm glued to his every word and my body feels almost floaty. I realize I'm hunched toward him and I force myself to relax back into my chair.

"She found out. I forgot to clear my browser history, and she saw I'd been watching gay porn. And of course it all made sense to her. I couldn't really deny it, so I told her the truth. Made her promise not to tell anyone. I felt—I feel horrible about what I did to her. She basically understood, though, and even offered to stay married to me and both see other people. But she deserves better than that. And I knew I couldn't keep lying all the time."

Another long pause and sip of beer.

"I was still working at the diner but I couldn't go back to living at home. You know how my dad is. I told Christi she could keep everything. We were living in a condo down the street from the diner. I was coming here a lot to think anyway, so I started camping out and planting vegetables and stuff. It was the only thing that kept me sane. And then my Uncle Gus told me I could have the land right before he died. He willed it to me and everything—even left me some money. But naturally my parents, my dad especially, lost it when I told them about the divorce. He told me not to come back to work. That he didn't want to see me. And of course *now* he acts like I abandoned him, like I chose to leave..." Nick laughs bitterly.

"Anyway, I started kind of living off the grid out here for a while. It's easier for me. Living out here, I mean. The idea of starting a farm had occurred to me, but I didn't really know how to do it until I met Jenna and Hector."

Nick smiles fondly when he mentions his friends.

"I knew Jenna from the diner. I had overheard her saying something about working on an organic farm, so I decided I'd run her food out myself. You know, so I could ask her more about it. She'd started coming in every morning. She would tell me everything she knew about growing and stuff. Pushed me to start educating myself about sustainable practices too. I went to this New York organic farming convention. Hector was there and we just kind of hit it off because he's insanely easy to talk to. I think you'd like him a lot. So yeah, when I mentioned that I wanted to get into farming and had the land, he said he would invest and move to the area since he has family here and... Yeah. I guess that's it." Nick trails off and shrugs, as if he's run out of steam to keep talking.

My mind vibrates with questions and I squeeze my eyes shut so I can try to make sense of all this. Finally I glance at Nick. He's back to looking like he's going to be sick. He bounces his leg under the table across from me. Archie comes to sit next to him and I swear the dog looks worried.

"So you're not out?" It's not what I'd meant to say and my words sound harsher than I wanted. Nick just told me all about reinventing his life and I'm nit-picking. *Really nice, David.*

Nick's eyebrows pull together. "Not exactly," he responds slowly. "I mean, Christi knows, obviously. And Jenna and Hector both know. And Cassie figured it out."

At this my face must register surprise. I'd always liked Nick's older sister, but the idea that he was out to any member of his family was surprising.

"She was fine with it," he says quickly. "She's been great. And she knows better than to tell my parents. I mean, getting divorced was already a huge failure in their eyes. Shit, if they found out I'm gay they'd never speak to me again."

This has always baffled me about Nick's relationship with his family. Why did he care? He had always been desperate to be the perfect son. While his brother Jason had permission to fuck up nonstop, Nick forced himself awkwardly into the impossible mold his father created for him. Whether it was turning down the unbelievable football scholarship at Syracuse to work at the diner, or apparently denying a huge part of his identity, he did everything he could to make his father happy.

But his dad was a jerk, always complaining about Nick. Nothing was ever good enough. When Nick led our school's football team to a state victory, his father hadn't even shown up to the final game, claiming he was too busy at work. When Nick had started cooking at the diner after high school he'd been amazing at it, mastering the recipes and enthusiastically coming up with specials. Whenever we Skyped while I was away at undergrad in Chicago, Nick would excitedly tell me about ideas he had for new menu items. His dad always shut him down.

I hear Nick's intake of breath and I know he's about to bring it up. "David, I'm so sorry. About how unfair I was to you too. I mean, I was so fucked up and I know I jerked you around..."

I had promised myself I wasn't going to be dramatic, or cry, or show him how much he'd hurt me, but as I push back from the table violently, my eyes filling with burning tears, I'm furious with myself because I know I'm about to break all of those promises. "So you expect me to forgive you?" Although I feel nothing but sadness, my voice sounds venomous. "You want me to feel bad for you, so I won't be angry that you fucked me right after my mom's fucking funeral and then you basically told me I disgust you?"

Nick looks at me like I slapped him. "That's not what I said, David..." His hands are up, and he's coming around the table toward me.

I turn away, striding over to the kitchen to pour myself another glass of wine. Shit, I better not drink too much. I put the cork back in the bottle, shove it into the refrigerator, and close the door with too much force. "Right. Nick. What was it?" I repeat his words back to him and sag against the fridge. "'I can't be like you. I'm not messed up. I like girls.' That was it, right? When I tried to touch you, you literally shoved me away. Remember that? When I called you the next day, you didn't even answer."

A few tears inch down my cheeks and my face burns with the shame of it all. "Do you not get it, Nick? Having sex with you was the culmination of so much for me. I'd wanted it for so long but I didn't even want to let myself fantasize about it. Then it happened, and it was so fucking perfect. Like I'd been thinking you were going to want to be with me for real. That everything was going to fall into place. That the guy I'd been in... That my best friend..."

I pause and step back from the conversational precipice I'd nearly stumbled over. "But then the second you pulled out of me, you shut down. I know it wasn't easy for you, but you were so...I don't know, mad at me. And then you stopped talking to me. Right after my mom's fucking funeral." My voice is shaking and brittle.

His big arms come around me and even though I want to jerk away from him, I collapse into Nick's embrace. I nuzzle into his warm chest to hide the thoughts I know are etched on my face: *touch me, put your mouth on me, want me.*

I inhale his smell, still familiar after all these years. The warm musk I associate with him is intoxicating, and I press my face into his neck to breathe it in. Growing up, Nick had always smelled like soap and fabric softener. All his T-shirts carried the slight chemical tinge of bleach. But the scent of artificial clean is gone. Now Nick smells distinctly earthy and herbal like sage, and pine, and fresh air.

"Baby, I'm so sorry." I can feel his words as much as I hear them, pressed against his body like this.

Desperate as I am to balk at the term of endearment, as much as I want to keep railing at Nick over how much he hurt me, my body is a traitor and his words only make me melt against him.

"I know that saying sorry won't ever make up for it, but what I said to you, pushing you away... I made a mistake. I was terrified. You were always there for me. And you put up with my bullshit when you didn't have to. I know I was a coward. Making love with you that night..." He trails off and his arms tighten around me. My cock starts to fill at the memory of him inside me. "It was so good. I still think about it. I think about you."

I press my forehead into his muscled shoulder and force myself to breathe. My arms hang limply at my sides as his big hands slide down my back, pulling my hips toward his. After a long moment, I shift away from him and lamely gesture toward his couch. Nick settles down, leaning back and spreading his large body out wide. I scoot to the far end opposite him and tuck my legs under me. Immediately my body cries out for his heat and heady scent.

"Can you give me another chance?" The naked hope in Nick's face sends a jolt of warmth right through my heart. "I know I don't deserve it but I want to at least be your friend again. And if you'd be willing, I want to be with you for real." He pauses and rubs his hands up and down his thighs, clearly trying to gather his thoughts.

"Do you hate me too much to try again? Because when I found out you were back, I needed to see you. I missed you so much." His shoulders sag like he expects me to say no. He has always been so passive, so willing to accept any criticism or anger directed at him. My mom once described Nick as a docile, overgrown puppy. The label is pretty apt.

I want to reach out and touch him but I hold myself back. "I never hated you. You hurt me. You rejected me and made me feel like an idiot. Like I was this delusional, pathetic person. You fucked with my emotions for like all of my late adolescence."

Shit. I need to reel this in. I've already broken two-thirds of the rules I set for myself. I've kind of hugged Nick and I've also cried so I certainly cannot let myself devolve into histrionics. Whenever I'm upset I have a tendency to ramble and spiral. Words I don't mean tumble out of me as I lash out blindly. I used to do it with Christopher all the time. He was always so stoic and dispassionate with me, which would work me up into a fever pitch of trying to say the most hurtful thing possible in order to get any reaction at all. Slowly I breathe in and out before continuing. "Look, Nick, I can't be your secret person again." And I do mean this.

When we were little kids, our friendship was uncomplicated joy. I could cross the street to his house to spend the afternoon watching cartoons and eating junk food or we could hang out in my backyard digging in the dirt and adding to our rock collections. We would talk for hours and fall asleep whispering into the walkie-talkie set I'd gotten for my birthday.

But when we started middle school something changed. Nick ignored me at school. I was his home friend. He might nod to me in the hallway or chat with me for a few minutes before class, but at school we existed in decidedly separate worlds. He hung out with his basketball and football teammates and I found my own small tribe. He was the popular, likable jock, and I was a queer skinny kid. Sometimes his friends would even hassle me in the halls—nothing terrible, muttered comments and chuckles—and Nick would half-heartedly tell them to shut up. But basically he did nothing.

He would grind with girls at school dances and make out with them under the bleachers after football games. I would pretend not to notice. And despite the I-hate-sports-and-everything-mainstream rep I tried to uphold, I always went to his games, excited to see him succeeding at something he cared so much about. And he would pretend not to notice.

On the weekends or in the blue hours of evening, though, things were the same between us. We'd sit on his parents' porch swing talking or hole up in my room for hours listening to music, imagining what our lives would look like in the magical realm of someday. Even when he started dating Christi junior year, we still drove out to the farm and spent long afternoons and evenings together. Then he changed everything, adding another layer to the whole messy dynamic. He started kissing me, pulling me to him in frantic bursts of desire, and giving me everything I'd always secretly wanted.

With effort, I refocus on the present and try to smash down the ever-expanding balloon of hope that's filling in my chest. This is thirty-one-year-old Nick. The man who just told me that he is gay and that he wants me. But this is also the man who can't be out because he's terrified of his family. "Okay"—I'm happy to hear that my voice has softened—"I don't want to force you to come out or anything like that. But I love being gay. It's important to me. It doesn't embarrass me. I can't be a secret. I can't do that again."

Nick has dropped his head, pressing his face into his clenched fists. The thin cotton of his shirt stretches over his back and shoulder muscles as they ripple with tension. "I understand." His voice is thick and muffled. Then he looks up, his eyes glassy, but I can tell he's trying to look calm. "You always were out of my league. But it was worth a shot, right?" He barks out a laugh, but it sounds almost strangled.

Wait—does he think I'm turning him down? Is that what I'm doing? I try to take stock of what I want. Experimentally I shake my head, hoping some epiphany will get knocked loose with the movement. No luck. Nick's eyes slide over my body. His gaze is as solid and sure as his arms around me. The air between us is thick now and I realize I still haven't said anything. I don't want to torture the poor guy.

Before I can talk myself out of it, I slide my body over on the couch so I'm sitting right next to Nick, our thighs touching. I turn toward him enough that I can look at his face. His pupils are dilated but I can still see the stormy slate of his eyes, the irises ringed with a fine line of dark blue, almost navy. His eyes are so striking against his olive skin and dark hair and my mind wanders to how I could mix colors to capture that complex gray and the almost luminous bronze. Nick's lips part and he looks confused. Those beautiful, storm gray eyes dart to my mouth and his breath hitches. I lean forward, closing the distance between us, and press my mouth to his.

Immediately Nick's strong hands are on me, gripping my waist like I'm magnetic. He groans into my mouth, a powerful sigh of relief. I love the way he tastes, a little like the beer he was drinking and the dinner we just ate, but also spicy and warm and achingly familiar. Wanting to taste more of him I trace his bottom lip with the tip of my tongue and I'm rewarded with a moan from Nick as he opens to me and slides his tongue against mine.

"Jesus, David," Nick murmurs against my mouth.

I pull back and trace his square, stubbled jawline, shivering at the rough sensation under my fingertips. I'm already embarrassingly hard, because honestly, I've been keyed up all evening. It's like all my energy is pulsing in my cock. Suddenly Nick grins, tightens his grip on my waist, and hauls me up onto his lap as if I weigh nothing at all. Now that I'm straddling him, his erection drags against mine, and I momentarily forget how to take in oxygen. His arms are around me again, pulling me flush against his bulk. Even through the layers of fabric, his heat and the friction are almost too much. I bend down to kiss him, cupping his face with both hands. Why does kissing him turn me on so much? I never got that into kissing Christopher, but then again we didn't have the world's greatest chemistry.

"David, I want you so bad," Nick whispers. All I can do is nod.

My whole body feels almost weightless. The desire is overwhelming. My throat is dry, like waking in the middle of the night desperate for a drink of water. He rocks his hips up into me again, gruffly simulating sex, and I cry out, already dangerously close. I pull back again, forcing myself to breathe and slow this all down. Without thinking I press two fingers to my pulse point in my neck. My heart is racing.

If we're going to do this, we have to take it slow. Nick looks dazed, his dark eyelashes fluttering closed. I'm about to speak, to tell him to take it easy, when he presses his lips to the point in my neck where my fingers just were. Then he's kissing all over my jaw and throat, rubbing my skin a little raw, making my eyes squeeze shut with the sheer pleasure of the sensation.

"You're gorgeous," he says softly, punctuating each word with a kiss to my neck.

Somehow I've shed my jacket—did I take it off after dinner? I can't dwell on the thought for too long, though, because Nick slides his palms up my bare back under my T-shirt. Of course his hands are rough and callused. If he keeps touching me like that, keeps rutting his erection against mine, I will actually come in my pants, something I have managed to avoid my entire life.

"Nick, stop." I pull my mouth from his and our lips part with a soft smack that makes me want to laugh.

He looks bereft. "You don't want to?"

I glance down to where our hips are joined, at the evidence of my arousal. A small wet dot is visible through the somewhat thin fabric of my pants. Nick follows my gaze and his body relaxes under me. That sweet, shy smile plays at his lips.

"I think it's pretty obvious that we both want to." I draw a shaky breath. "But we have to, like—" I wave my hand vaguely. "—talk and take things slow and stuff." Very articulate. It's pretty much impossible for me to focus with his hands still on the bare skin of my lower back, gently rubbing up and down. I try to shift away but that only results in Nick's hardness pushing up closer against my erection. He lets his head fall back against the couch with what sounds an awful lot like a growl.

"You're right," he mutters, as if it is causing him actual physical pain to admit it.

"If you want to do this," I start and Nick quickly interjects, his eyes wide and nostrils flaring. Ugh, that nostril flare. Nick's nose is slightly too big and wide for his face and it somehow makes him even more attractive.

"I do." He looks desperate. "I want you. I know myself now. I'm sure. This won't be like before. I know that I acted like, well 'an asshole' doesn't even cover it, but I care about you. I never stopped caring about you." Nick's words sound rehearsed, like he'd practiced this apology speech a few times.

His admission forces another breath of air into that hope balloon lodged in my chest. I remember him doing this when we were younger, planning out and practicing his words when he had something important to say. He tended to get tongue-tied when he was nervous.

His hands move from my waist and now he's playing with my hair, running his fingers through it absently and occasionally grazing his nails over my scalp. All this contact is making it hard to focus. Pressing a quick, chaste kiss to his lips, I slide off his lap and reclaim my seat next to him on the couch. Still touching, but much easier to form coherent thoughts.

"We haven't seen each other in a long time," I say even though we are obviously both quite aware of this fact. "A lot has changed in my life, and clearly in yours too. We're not the same people as when we were twenty-one. I basically blew my whole life up moving back here, and I know that navigating your sexuality isn't easy."

I pause because this is a lie. I don't actually know this. I have no idea what Nick is going through. For me, coming out was as simple as saying the words. Being open about who I am has always been as natural as breathing. I never had to second-guess it. But when your parents are left-wing academics with tons of queer friends, I suppose that makes being gay a whole lot easier.

"I know it isn't easy for you anyway. I get it. But you can't assume that because we felt something a decade ago, it's still going to work."

When I glance over at Nick, I know I've said the wrong thing because his handsome face has gone serious, his mouth tight again.

"Hey," I whisper and cup his cheek, turning his face to look at me. "I'm not saying it can't work. Just that we have to get to know each other again. Okay? I didn't even know you got divorced until a few weeks ago. I didn't know you were figuring out your sexuality. And I definitely didn't know about this whole *farm* thing." My attempt at humor is rewarded with a low chuckle from Nick. "You don't know about the job I left or my total failure of a three-year relationship."

Nick's eyes flick down to the floor and the corner of his mouth quirks up.

For a moment I'm confused by his reaction. Then I realize he knows more about my life than I know about his. "Anna?" I ask, unable to stop my eyes from rolling. She is such a busybody.

He chuckles and gives a small, resigned shrug. "Yup. I never used to see her much, sometimes at the library but, I mean, she would never come into the diner since my dad refused to add a single vegan option to the menu." Nick's voice goes bitter, but he continues. "Anyway, she was one of our first regular customers at the market and I used to get nervous seeing her, since she was your friend and, well, she kind of hated me."

I don't bother protesting because throughout high school and college Anna had not made any effort to hide her disdain for Nick.

"But one day she was buying some stuff—tomatoes. I remember it was the first crop of green zebras, and she casually mentioned that you had gotten this big job at a museum in Chicago. She sounded so proud of you. So yeah, she told me things sometimes, random stuff about you. Like that you were living with this guy, Christopher, and she wasn't so sure about him. Then after she visited you last time, she told me that you guys had broken up. I, uh, was pretty fucking jealous of that guy." Nick's jaw tenses. "But you're right. I do want to get to know you again." His voice is so gentle.

We sit next to each other on the couch, legs pressing together. The silence quickly becomes charged and slightly awkward. As much as I'd like to ask him dozens of questions and unpack every single thing from our past, either that or climb back up on his lap and resume our make-out session, I also don't want to come across like the neurotic stress ball or total hypocrite that I am. Nervous rambling is right on the tip of my tongue when Nick does the damn cutest thing. He does the classic yawn-stretch and puts his arm around me, pulling me close to him.

"Very smooth," I snort. But I'm delighted because he's warm, and I hadn't realized how much I missed his arms around me.

"Hey, this is all pretty new for me," he retorts, giving my shoulder a playful squeeze.

The comment sets my mind spiraling though. Am I the only man he's ever been with? I want to ask him, but I also know that grilling him about his sexual history, especially at this tenuous moment, would be invasive and inappropriate. "Do you want to maybe watch a movie or something?" I suggest lamely. But then I realize Nick doesn't have a TV. The walls are mostly dedicated to windows or bookshelves.

His arm around me tightens. "My TV's in my room."

Of course. "That's okay." I'm trying to play it cool but half of me hopes he takes it to mean I don't want to go there. Because I'm not sure if I can be in bed with Nick and expect myself to make rational decisions.

But he hauls me to my feet and I follow him up the stairs to his bedroom. It seems the entire second floor is also an open plan, consisting of his large bedroom and three other doors, one of which I can see leads out onto a balcony and the other two I can only assume lead to a bathroom and a closet. If I thought the rest of the house was gorgeous, this bedroom is truly remarkable. The ceiling is vaulted and high, paneled in whitewashed wooden planks. A second woodstove with a similar neat pile of logs next to it stands unlit. A modern pine bedframe houses an enormous mattress draped with a colorful quilt. And as if it's an afterthought, balanced on the dresser, there is a somewhat dated flat-screen TV.

Like it's nothing, Nick flops onto the bed and reaches for the remote resting atop a neat pile of books on the pine nightstand that matches the bed frame. Clearly this is his side of the bed because the other night table is bare aside from a folding metal desk lamp.

"Anything you wanna watch?" Nick asks, sprawling his long limbs out on top of the weirdly garish quilt.

I shrug and gingerly perch on the bed, again scooting far away from him like a total prude.

"Do you like *Blue Planet*?" he asks, clicking through his Netflix.

I try not to creep on what he's recently watched but I can't help myself. Nature documentaries, that well-produced show about famous chefs, and *Gilmore Girls*. I choke back a laugh. Nick follows my eyes and shoves my shoulder.

"Shut up. Not everyone can have your fancy taste in movies. *Gilmore Girls* is awesome."

I shake my head and relax back into the pillows. "I'll take your word for it."

Nick shuts off the lamp next to him, plunging the room into the diffuse, cool light of the TV, and puts on an episode of *Blue Planet* about the Arctic seas. Watching the polar bears and ice floes makes me start to shiver. Then I realize it's cold up here since the temperature has probably dropped outside and the fire isn't lit.

"You cold?" Nick asks, his eyes still fixed on the penguins waddling around on screen.

"No, I'm fine," I say, but my body language definitely gives me away. I'm all scrunched up and my arms are crossed tight against my chest. Naturally, Nick takes this as an invitation to slide over toward me and hoist me up on top of him again. I'm sure neither of us can see the TV now, but I also do not care. His heat immediately relaxes me and I whimper with pleasure as he grips my ass.

"Is this okay?" he asks, his lips ghosting over mine.

How is it possible for a man to look like he does and to smell so damn good? I grin against his lips and nod.

"You make me crazy," he whispers and then his mouth is engulfing mine and my whole body is pulsing.

We're moving together at a delirious, delicious slow tempo. My head spins. His strong hands are still kneading my ass, almost overwhelming me with pleasure. I trace my fingers up under his shirt, loving the flex of muscle and tickle of hair. His heart hammers in his built chest and I'm rewarded with a feral growl when I experimentally tweak his taut nipple. The same desperation-like thirst builds again and I start to drag a hand down his body, dipping into the front of his jeans.

"David." Nick's breathing is uneven as he pulls back. He looks almost nervous. Our legs are twined together and we are both rock-hard, pressing against each other. "We should stop."

I lift my hand to gently cup his face and nod. He's right. I'm the one who said we should take things slow, and there I was with my fingers inside the waistband of his boxers. I extract myself from him and start to move away but he stops me.

"Stay here?" It's less of a command and more of an invitation but he keeps one arm wrapped around me, my face resting on his chest.

Surrounded by the tranquil sounds of the ocean and images of sea life, Nick falls asleep within minutes. Nick's breathing slows under me and his grip around me relaxes. For a long moment I consider giving in to the warm comfort of Nick's bed and his body. After all, Anna did bring her overnight stuff. My dad is fine with her. But I need time to think and it's almost impossible for me to be rational when I'm surrounded by Nick's herbal, earthy scent.

Quietly I slip out of bed and flip off the TV, pulling the other side of the quilt over Nick's large frame. He looks so boyish as he sleeps, his full lips parted and curved up, his long dark lashes fluttered closed. I press a soft kiss to his forehead, but he doesn't stir. He's really out.

As I pad down the stairs I'm greeted by the gigantic dog, Archie, who is sitting next to the front door, his mismatched eyes regarding me expectantly.

"Do you need to go out?" I ask, glancing around for a leash. As if the dog understood what I said he paws at the door. I open it a crack, throwing out a silent prayer that he doesn't bolt into the dark and I won't have to wake Nick up and explain that I lost his dog. But he does just that. When I step out into the hazy black of the night, I don't see any sign of Archie. I whisper-scream his name a few times into the darkness, my heart now somewhere right at the top of my throat. But the dog comes trotting right back and lopes up the porch stairs, tossing an *Are you coming?* look back at me. Laughing to myself I follow him inside and quickly do my best to clean up the dishes and scrawl a note for Nick on the magnetic whiteboard mounted to the side of his fridge. I'm not sure what to say, so I keep it simple and light.

> *Nick,*
>
> *Thanks for a great evening. The food was delicious and so were you ;) I took Archie out around 11. Call me tomorrow?*
>
> *David*

I know the line about him being delicious is cheesy as hell, but I also bet he'll love it.

When I finally get home, my dad is in bed and Anna is asleep on the couch, her fingers tangled in a knitting project. When I gently shake her awake, her eyes narrow for a moment then zero right in on my face. Her voice is soft and I lean down to hear what she says.

"You have beard burn."

Chapter Eight

Nick

April

The sun pries my eyes open and I'm immediately in the kind of panicked state I still associate with oversleeping for school, only half aware of the world around me and failing to slow my racing heart. I should be waking to pale gray silence, not dappled sunlight and birdsong. Several things occur to me at once: I am still wearing my clothes from last night, I have a painfully hard morning erection, and David is not in my bed. Struggling to dislodge myself from the quilt cocoon I've wrapped myself in, I also discern two familiar soft voices downstairs and the scent of coffee and something warm and cinnamon. Oatmeal?

Quickly I pad to the bathroom to wash up and change into work clothes. As I'm tugging on jeans, Archie prances into my room and guilt weighs heavy on my chest. Poor guy didn't go out last night. I always take him out before bed, but last night I conked out. And shit, thinking of last night does very little to deflate my hard-on. The feeling of David on my lap, rocking his hips, the soft brush of his lips on mine, the intoxicating fresh smell of him. *Okay, focus.* I take a few deep breaths and walk down the stairs.

As I round the corner into the kitchen, I see Jenna and Hector both perched on the metal barstools, sipping coffee and tucking into steaming bowls of oatmeal.

"Hey, guys." I hope my voice sounds at least somewhat normal as I pour myself a large cup of black coffee. With a small jolt I realize the kitchen is spotless and I feel bad that Hector probably cleaned up the dishes from dinner. Jenna wouldn't clean up after me. She would sooner blast an air horn in my ear to wake me before she cleaned up my messes. Hector, though, is one of the most considerate human beings I have ever met.

"You're up late." Jenna's voice is singsong, loaded with innuendo. When I glance at her, her amber eyes glint with devious joy.

She's right. The digital clock on the oven reads 7:22, about three hours later than I normally get up. Usually by this time I've worked out, made a big breakfast, played with Archie, and gotten started on answering e-mails or working in the greenhouse.

"Yeah," I grumble. Unsure of how to explain myself, I go with the truth. "Someone came over last night for dinner." Conversations are always easier when I have something to do with my hands so I pick a few brown leaves off the sage plant in the windowsill.

"He left you a note." Hector's voice is placid as he gestures toward the small whiteboard on my fridge.

My face is red-hot as I read over David's note. But my legs also get the relaxed jelly feeling I associate with a long run. My mouth stretches into a wide smile.

"Oh shit, Hector. He's blushing," Jenna coos without malice. "So *delicious*, huh? What the fuck happened?"

Hector laughs, shaking his head at both of us.

I start running my fingers through my hair. The back of my neck is tight and itchy.

"Leave him alone," Hector chides. "It's none of our business."

Jenna pouts and her eyes don't leave mine.

"We talked," I say as I push up onto the counter and start shoveling food into my mouth. If my mouth is full I can't be interrogated, right?

"And." She rolls her hand in a *keep going* gesture. Hector shoots her a death glare and eyes me sympathetically.

"And, we might have kissed." My voice is quiet, and I am in that moment very focused on making sure the maple syrup I added to my oatmeal is well incorporated.

"De-lic-ious!" Jenna shouts into her cupped hands. Archie slinks into the living room to settle on the couch.

"Screw you." I laugh and turn toward Hector. "Hey man, thanks for cleaning up the dishes. You really didn't have to do that."

A wide grin illuminates his face. "Dude, that wasn't me." I glance at Jenna skeptically but she snorts.

When we finally get outside to begin transplanting the herbs and hardier peppers we started in the greenhouse, the sun is already warm and I immediately strip off the flannel I threw on over my T-shirt. Normally I don't keep my phone on me while we're working, but the thought that David might text me has me tucking it into the back pocket of my jeans.

As I pull weeds and lay a mixture of recycled newspaper and hay over the lettuce beds my mind drifts yet again to David. I'm giddy, buzzing with almost uncontainable excitement that he agreed to try again with me. In all the scenarios I'd played out in my head I didn't think he would end up in my arms, on my lap, grinding against me. Okay, I need to cool it because I do not need to be going about my entire day agonizingly hard.

I can't stop thinking about him, can't stop my mind from picturing David moving through his day. Wondering what he would think if he could somehow see me moving through mine. As I work, I imagine David waking up in his old bedroom, the sage green walls covered in his amazing art and less amazing emo band posters. His hair would probably be even more mussed than usual, the auburn waves on top soft and rumpled. I picture him making coffee, squeezing in a gross amount of honey and pouring in milk. Would he be checking his phone, seeing if I called him, or was he busy with his dad first thing? Quickly I extract my phone from my pocket and check the time. It's only nine and I know David never was an early riser. Although maybe that has changed. I should probably wait until at least noon to call him though.

At exactly noon I call David. Jenna and Hector have gone inside to eat some lunch. My footsteps sound weirdly loud as I pace the porch. The phone rings, once, twice—shit, he's not going to answer. He's probably busy.

"Hey." David sounds out of breath and heat travels down my body. I picture him on the other end of the phone, his lips parted as he breathes heavily. It sounds like he's outside, birds chirping in the background.

"Hi," I say and my throat feels thick. *Pull it together, Patras. It's just a phone call. Okay, a phone call with the most beautiful man you've ever seen who is giving you a second chance you totally do not deserve.* But still, just a phone call right?

"Sleep well?" His voice is teasing and I'm embarrassed.

"Yeah. Sorry for passing out like that. I get up early so I'm not usually up late." I pause and sink into one of the wooden deck chairs I built. Idly I notice it's a little wobbly.

"Hey, did you clean up the dishes? Because you didn't have to do that."

David laughs, a light, contagious sound. He always blinks a lot and covers his mouth when he finds something funny. Again I can't stop myself from visualizing it. "I didn't want you to wake up alone and with a mess to clean up. Well, not that kind of mess anyway." He drops his voice. Is he flirting? I think of the painful erection I woke up with and my cock twitches slightly.

"Yeah, I have kind of a bad case of blue balls this morning." The words are out of my mouth before I can stop them. Jesus Christ. I want to punch myself in the face.

That light laugh again. "Okay, I definitely jerked off when I got home last night," David deadpans.

And if I can't help visualizing his laugh or him going through the motions of his morning, I absolutely cannot stop my mind from conjuring the image of David stroking himself, the soft sounds he makes, the way his eyes clamp tight as he comes. Great. Now I'm fully hard. Again.

I clear my throat and quickly get up from the chair. Sitting is not very comfortable at the moment. "So are you free at all this week?"

"Well, I'll have to check my social calendar..." he teases. "But yeah, my dad has an important check-in with his doctor this afternoon so probably not tonight. Does Thursday or Friday work for you?"

I almost want to jump up and down the way Cassie used to when she and her friends would talk on the phone with boys in middle school. But I pull it together and do my weird low voice. "Uh, yeah. Thursday is better. I get up super early on Saturdays for the farmers' market and I'd rather not disappoint you by going to bed so early."

"Not unless I can go with you, no." David's tone is teasing. Was he always so flirty? I kind of love his confidence.

I clear my throat again and throw my head back with a dramatic groan. "You're going to make me miss lunch."

"What?" David's confusion registers in his voice.

"I can't go inside and eat with Jenna and Hector with this fucking erection."

David's laugh is distinctly triumphant. "Okay, I'll stop. Do you want to go out to eat on Thursday? Anna took me to this awesome restaurant a few weeks ago. Diana's Kitchen, I think?"

My smile slides off my face and the lightness in my chest is swiftly replaced by hot guilt. I can't take him out. If someone sees us together, eating dinner, that would look too weird, right? Plus I basically can't keep my hands off him for more than about five seconds. And Diana's Kitchen isn't far from the diner. "Um..." I hedge, and David, perceptive as ever, immediately knows what I'm doing.

"Right. No dinners out in town. And you probably don't want to come over to my dad's either, living across from your parents and all that."

"Yeah." I feel like an asshole. "You want to come over again? We're going to harvest the artichokes tomorrow, so I can do a pasta?" This artichoke pasta better be pretty fucking delicious. Should I tell him I'm sorry? That I would love nothing more than to take him on an actual date.

David's voice is flat. "Sure. That sounds great. Around seven?"

We confirm and quickly end the conversation after that. And seeing as self-hatred and guilt have eclipsed my arousal, I have no problem dragging myself inside for lunch.

BEADS OF SWEAT slide down the back of my neck as I drive to the Saturday market, the branches of the newly green trees stretching out to cast flickering shadows over the road. The weather has taken a turn from breezy and cool to worryingly hot for spring. I really should take the Jeep in to get the AC fixed.

The drive, sweltering as it is, gives me an idea. While Saugerties, where my sprawling extended family and my parents' even bigger, nosier church community loom large, wouldn't be the ideal spot for a date with David, that doesn't mean I couldn't take him out a few towns over. As the Jeep crawls through the traffic in town, I notice a ton of quaint restaurants and file their names away to ask Jenna about. She seems to know every chef in the county, so I'm sure she'll be able to give me some recommendations.

Last Thursday's dinner with David was nice, if not a bit awkward at first. When he loped up to my door wearing very slim-fitting blue pants and an expensive-looking cream-colored sweater it was hard to keep myself from pushing him up against the door and dropping to my knees. He was just so damn cute.

Growing up he'd always been pretty into fashion, reading those thick glossy magazines that Cassie said were for rich people with weird taste. But David must have learned a lot from them because he puts clothes together in a creative way that reflects who he really is. Like he could express some indefinable David-ness when he got dressed every day. Personally, I basically only care about comfort. Most of my T-shirts, if they don't come in a three-pack, are ancient relics from high school sports or less ancient leftovers from races I'd run when I'd been obsessed with training for a triathlon. But David, with his sculpted cheekbones and full lips and slightly delicate features, looks like an actual model. He makes simple things like sweaters and button-down shirts look somehow interesting and cool.

Because I'd still been consumed with guilt over the whole 'not taking him on a real date' thing, I tried hard to make dinner at my place seem at least somewhat special. Once Jenna and Hector left for the day I quickly cleaned the house, vacuuming thoroughly and mopping the floors since Archie sheds constantly and coats everything in his fur. I set the table with the blue and green striped runner I made, an assortment of tapered beeswax candles from the market, and a few sprigs of forsythia arranged in a weird ceramic jug Uncle Gus had left behind in the house. It looked good. Not wanting to get caught again listening to the Dixie Chicks, I shuffled through my music library until I found something David might like. Did he still listen to The Cranberries? I knew my little sister Doria was pretty into them, so maybe David liked their music too?

Thankfully the pasta had turned out great. I made fresh tagliatelle and tossed the noodles with the most delicate artichokes we harvested, even though they definitely should have gone to the market. But that didn't matter. David loved it, even saying he could tell I made an effort and that he understood about dinner out.

This time we kept it together long enough to do the dishes and clean up the kitchen before retreating to the couch to make out for what felt like hours. When I pulled him on top of me, this time lying down so every inch of our bodies pressed together, I had been worried I would lose it. I wanted, needed to go further. I wanted to pull his sweater over his head and lick every inch of his creamy, freckled skin. I wanted to wrap my lips around his shaft and taste his release. And I really, really wanted to be inside him. But I needed to figure out how to broach...what? There were things I wasn't ready to tell him. How could I possibly bring up what happened last year? Whenever I thought of that night in the city, my head buzzed so loud and my heart hammered so unevenly it was difficult to even put the words together.

By the time Saturday morning's market rolled around I had jerked off quickly and unsatisfyingly in the shower a grand total of three times and pushed my body to the absolute limit lifting weights every morning. I was exhausted and horny and far too eager to see David again. We hadn't made any firm plans to get together, and aside from some lighthearted texting, we hadn't spoken much.

So when David breezes into the market dressed in yet another pair of his adorably sexy slim-fitting pants, this time olive green, a navy and maroon sweater, and a pair of gray high-top sneakers, I can't hide the grin that breaks across my face. Jenna must notice me staring at him because she follows my gaze and gives me an approving nod. "Is *that* David?" she asks, watching as he scans the vendor tents and the crowd. "He's so..." She shakes her curls. "Pretty. Seriously, is he like an actor or something?"

"No," I reply, still looking at David. Thank god for Hector and his ability to focus on actual tasks like helping customers. "He used to work at a museum in Chicago. Something with education? I think it was a pretty fancy job. He's insanely smart. He moved up here to help his dad." I can't keep the pride out of my voice. Whatever—David is awesome and everyone should know that.

Even though I feel a like a creep, it's nice to watch David from afar. He moves gracefully through the crowd and the morning sun catches in the reddish golden strands of his perfectly messy hair. A few women and men cast lingering glances in his direction and I realize my grip on my coffee cup has tightened considerably. The cup crumples and searing hot coffee sloshes onto my wrist and the sleeve of my shirt.

Glancing back up from my stupid jealousy spill, I realize David is talking to Will from the pizza truck. And—are they flirting? David is gesticulating wildly like he always does and Will is laughing, standing awfully close to him. Instead of jealousy though, now I only feel sadness.

That's what David deserves. A man who can flirt with him, touch him, be with him in public without looking over his shoulder and trying to cover his tracks. A moment later Anna walks up behind David and gestures in the direction of our stand. Ripping my gaze away I start to actually help customers, trying to focus all my attention on bagging vegetables and making correct change.

When Anna and David start in our direction Anna is beaming and David is shooting her a death glare. The pink flush on David's cheeks undoes me and my shoulders drop. Knowing he's nervous too makes me feel so much better.

"Hey." He's breathless.

"Hey." I know I'm smiling like a total fool at him. But the fact that he's here to see me makes my stomach do a somersault.

"Hi!" Anna says loudly and David and I both laugh. "So I joined your CSA. I'm confused though. Do we pick up here at the market or at Bluebird Café on Sunday?"

I'm grateful for the distraction. Although most of the time I've known Anna she's seemed to hate me, she's also always struck me as keenly observant and sensitive to others when she wants to be. If she hadn't said anything, David and I might have stared at each other like awkward morons for hours.

I explain to her that she can choose the option that is most convenient for her and ask if she thinks we should send a follow-up e-mail to clear up any confusion. David is eyeing the piles of produce in the fixed way he looks at things sometimes. It's almost like all his senses except his vision shut off and he's taking things in with this clear, focused intensity. Of course the moment I can actually talk to him is the time a huge line forms, and Jenna, Hector and I hurry to answer questions, weigh produce, and handle transactions. Finally the line dies down and I'm unreasonably happy to see that Anna and David are still standing off to the side of the tent.

"So you're David?" Hector asks and stretches out his hand. He never seems uncomfortable around new people. He's just friendly.

"Yeah. Yes. Hi." David shakes his hand. He's blinking a lot. Is he nervous?

Hector introduces himself warmly and then Jenna shakes David's hand too. But she's way more subdued than usual. It's possible she doesn't like him? But no, I realize her gaze keeps darting to Anna. Interesting. We're all chatting about stupid stuff like the weather and how many people from the city are starting to stay in town since the new hotel opened, when I spot my dad and

Jason. Thankfully everyone in our family is tall, so I see them coming from a ways off.

I'd been so preoccupied with thoughts of David all week that the dread of seeing my family didn't even get to me much this morning. Something in my body language must change though, because Anna and David exchange an unreadable look before glancing over their shoulders. When David sees my dad a dark look crosses his face. He never liked my dad at all. Not that I can blame him. My dad treated David's family coldly even before he found out David was gay and banned him from our house.

When my dad and Jason stop by our stand, I can tell my father is not happy to see David. Not happy at all. His bushy eyebrows pull together and his weathered face is coldly impassive. He doesn't acknowledge David though, just glares at me as if I conjured my gay friend into existence. I don't even let myself look at David. Shit—my breathing is coming in shallow again, like something's stuck in the bottom of my throat that refuses to let any air into my chest. Tiny black dots buzz at the edges of my vision.

"Hey, Mr. Patras. Hey, Jason." David's voice is so warm and friendly you would think the three of them got together every week to drink beer and shoot the shit. Jason grunts hello but my dad keeps looking at me. "Um, well anyway, Nick, it was nice to see you."

David hurries away, not even looking at me while Anna quickly buys a few vegetables before rushing after him. I want to put my fist through the table but the warm, strong weight of hand on my shoulder grounds me. Jenna shoots me a soft smile, then starts restocking a depleted pile of Swiss chard.

Jason snorts out a laugh and lets his wrist go limp as he pushes one hip out to the side. "Bye, Nick." His voice is exaggerated and girlish and he bats his eyelashes. "Bro, I can't believe you used to hang out with that guy. He seriously walks around like that? That fucking sweater." He shakes his head as if David's sweater deeply offended his sensibilities. But I know it's not the clothes.

I'm used to hearing my brother and dad, and even sometimes Cassie's husband talk that way. Sure it always makes me mad, always makes me clench my fist and change the subject. But now I actually want to punch Jason. I want to tell him David is a far better man than he could ever hope to be.

"Nick." My dad's voice is sharp, the same rebuking tone he used to tell me my ideas at the restaurant were foolish or that my grades weren't high enough. "I don't want you hanging around with that kind of man." Now his eyes, so much like my own but so much colder, bore into me. "The last thing you need is for people to get the wrong idea and think you're...messed up too."

An all-too-familiar toxic mix of rage and shame detonates in my chest. I'm shaking and hot and now I can't breathe well. But then I look at the two of them. Jason is once again hungover, slouching and sullen in his tight black T-shirt and elaborate designer jeans. Jason, who has probably spent less time with his own son than I have. Jason, who gets to mess up and goof off and get away with every last thing. And then there's my dad. I know I resemble him. We're both tall and broad. We're both athletic. My father boxed and played baseball. We share the same wide nose and heavy brows. But the similarities end there.

I want to build a responsible business that gives back to our community, not fight the town board over any and all progressive policies. My father is cruel. Belittling my mother's cooking anytime she tries something new. Always telling Cassie she needs to quit her job and have babies if she wants to keep her husband happy. Complaining that Doria should grow out her hair to look more feminine. In that moment I'm desperate to come out. The words are ready in my mind but they falter in my dry throat. I shouldn't do it out of spite. Instead I shrug and turn away to help a waiting customer.

Thankfully the rest of the market goes smoothly and quickly. We sell out of everything. Jenna even chats with Asha, a sweet and hilarious Somali woman who runs a private catering business and is hoping to open her own restaurant next year, about supplying her with produce. So, aside from my family being awful, overall it's a good day. Neither Jenna nor Hector says anything about the interaction with my dad and brother until we're loading up the cars.

"Your dad is a fucking asshole." Hector's words startle me. Not only because I have never once heard the man swear but also because his normally relaxed voice has gone hard and sharp. "Sorry if that offends you, but man."

His outrage sets Jenna off and she wheels on me. She looks angry, but I know it's misdirected rage. "I don't get why you let him talk to you like that. Why you have anything to do with those jerks. When my dad freaked out, I told him he could deal with it or not see me again. So he dealt with it."

I know Jenna means well. She cares about me and wants me to be happy. But she also doesn't know what the hell she's talking about. Jenna's dad, a minister at a fairly prominent African-American Baptist church in South Carolina, is a thoughtful, well-educated man. When Jenna came out, he talked it through with his daughter and reached out to members of their church for support. He read books about being a queer Christian and now works to help gay youth in their church community.

But my father is small-minded. He wouldn't research or talk. In fact, I've wondered from time to time if he wouldn't be violent if I told him the truth. Would he blame my mother like he did for anything else that went wrong in his life? Although I'm not sure why, I can't walk away from them. I'm already so distant. I miss things when I avoid family parties or bow out of events at the church. The tightness returns to my chest and I can tell Jenna knows she pushed too much.

"Sorry, Nick," she mutters. "I think you deserve better than them. And I want you to know we've got your back." There's a long pause then her expression shifts from thoughtful to cheerful. "So David's gorgeous."

I grin, again feeling weirdly proud of him.

Jenna's cheeks darken. There's something else. When she speaks her voice is overly breezy. "So what do you know about his friend? Anna, right? The redhead who always buys a ton of kale. She's cute."

Aha. "You mean do I know if she likes women?" I cut right to the chase, not wanting to torture Jenna the way she always insists on torturing me. "I think you're in luck. I remember in high school she and David helped start the gay alliance at our school. And she had a girlfriend for a while, I think? I don't know that much about her because she hated my guts. Rightfully so because I used to be a dick."

"You still are," Jenna jokes. But I hope it's not the truth.

Chapter Nine

Nick

May

It's odd walking back to the creek with David, navigating the narrow, rocky footpath leading from the house to the rushing water. As I follow his slim frame, I'm struck by how many times the two of us made this walk in the past. I used to be so nervous then. I would always suggest hiking to go for a swim and we would usually end up in our underwear and laughing, me trying hard and failing not to start something with him. That same thrum of arousal is here now, thankfully without the weird anxiety and guilt. Or at least not as much of it.

I force my body to relax, surrounded by the chirping of birds and the rush of the breeze through the new growth in the woods. It's still unseasonably warm and David is dressed in a pair of white shorts and a loose blue button-down. Totally impractical for hiking but he looks adorable. Trying to avoid staring at his ass, I shove my hands in my pockets. And close my fingers around the two condoms I'd tucked into my pocket, just in case. Okay, the thought of using them isn't going to help get rid of my desire. The soft trickle of water rises as we approach the creek and David turns to face me, his eyebrows raised and a wide smile on his lips.

"You know this water is going to be freezing, right? No way am I getting in." He pauses on the trail and leans toward me. "I'm happy to watch you swim though." His lips quirk into a flirtatious grin and I can't stop looking at that full, beautiful mouth.

Unable to resist, I drop the bag of blankets and snacks and close the distance between us to stroke my fingers into his soft hair, tugging on it as I tip his head back. David's eyes drift shut, and his mouth falls open. As I stoop to brush my lips over his, his breath catches in his throat and he returns the kiss, pushing up toward me and grabbing the fabric of my T-shirt. His tongue slides against mine, warm and a little minty. I smile at the thought that he and I probably both aggressively brushed our teeth before going out for this walk. Usually David is clean-shaven but today a slight edge of stubble scrapes my skin. I'm desperate for him. My skin is buzzing and tight and I'm frantically trying to press every inch of our bodies together. Because David is a good five or six inches shorter than me, I bend my knees so I can press our clothed hips together, aligning my cock with his.

"Oh god," he sighs and his body arches, pressing even closer to me.

But he jerks away. And for a moment I worry I've done something wrong, pushed too hard, gone too fast. Then I see he's hurrying toward the clearing at the water's edge, fumbling with the buttons of his shirt as he walks. No way he's undressing to swim. Following his lead, I pull my shirt over my head. And, okay, David is taking his shorts off, so I do too. Before I know it we're both in only our underwear, our erections straining the thin fabric.

"Come here," I say softly and I pull him into my arms. Desire burns in my throat. The feeling of his hardness against mine, the warm glide of his freckled, smooth chest against my own, knowing how quickly I've turned him on—it all makes my dick surge. He moans softly as our lips meet again and I breathe in slowly through my nose, loving his fresh smell.

He breaks away for a second, looking down at our erections rubbing together. "This is so weird." His voice is shaky, and he's out of breath. "I feel like I'm nineteen again, coming out here and jerking each other off."

I can't quite read his tone. Is it too weird for him? Is he still pissed at me? "We can stop," I say softly and relax my arms around him. Gently I run my fingertips up and down his spine. He sighs and presses up on me, rolling his hips in a way that tells me he probably does not want to stop.

"God no. I want... I want to keep going. It feels like déjà vu is all." David kisses me again, cupping the back of my head and pulling me down to him. He buries his face in my neck, nipping at the sensitive skin of my throat before dragging the tip of his tongue up to my chin.

Fuck. I yank him toward me by the waist, hopefully not too roughly, and grab his ass, the perfect muscular globes supple under my hands. I need his bare skin against me so I shove his briefs down. David shivers and licks his lips.

"Okay?" I ask, barely able to get the word out I'm breathing so hard. It's like I've just run a mile at a full sprint. His head is tipped back, but he nods and groans something that sounds like *yes*. David's skin is unbelievably soft as I knead his tight ass and pull him up toward me. His teeth sink into my shoulder now, not too hard but enough that I groan with the shock of pleasure the bite sends through me.

"Off," David huffs out and tugs weakly on my boxers. I quickly shed the plaid cotton. Immediately David's fingers close around my cock and I buck up into his grip. But I need his bare erection against mine, need that silky hardness on my skin. I reach down between us, shifting so the sensitive heads of our erections glide against each other. We sigh in unison at the contact. I wrap my hand around both of our cocks, and David must understand what I'm going for because he moves his hand to grip my ass and whispers, "Oh fuck, Nick. That feels amazing."

It does. The slide of my hand over our erections and the hot friction is perfect. Already I'm thinking about coming, wanting to pump hard and fast until we're both collapsing into each other. David is fucking into my hand, whining and panting. His erection leaks precome and the occasional warm slickness only makes me move my hand faster over us. My knees ache from bending to even out our height, but I could be standing on broken glass for all I care. I need to be inside him. Slowly I trace the fingers of my free hand up and down over his crack and he whimpers. Again, I ask if it's okay, and he nods frantically. Still stroking our cocks together I press my finger to his lips, hoping he'll understand what I want. And fuck. He definitely understands. His hot mouth closes around my finger and the sensation rockets directly to my cock. When I slide from his mouth and stroke the slickness over his hole he moans, a strangled, beautiful sound.

"Please." David's voice, normally so even and calm, is wild and high now, like everything is pulled tight.

Then I slide my finger into him and I have to bite my cheek and slow my strokes to keep myself from tipping over the edge. The velvet heat around me is intoxicating. He clenches as I start sliding my hand faster. Every inch of David is warm and needy and pliant against me.

A delicious ache starts in the pit of my stomach and sends sparks of white-hot pleasure down to my balls. The want is overwhelming. I want to come, to watch David come. I want to feel him shoot onto my stomach and to hear him cry out as an orgasm racks his lean body. But at the same time I never want this to end. I want to stay in the state of suspended, all-encompassing pleasure forever.

"Nick," David cries out. His eyes squeeze shut and his lips part. "I'm—I'm going to come," he whines.

"Come, baby." I need him to fall apart so I can too, need to see him let go. I crook my finger inside him to massage his prostate.

David's cock jerks, spilling jets of hot release onto both of us as he groans incomprehensibly. My release is no longer a choice. It's inevitable. My body shakes and my legs buckle as that thick, needy feeling breaks and I am nothing but searing relief. Everything seems to be spinning around the axis of my body and David's as my orgasm takes over.

"Fuck," I growl and pull back as the evidence of my release hits my own fist and the ground between our feet. My legs are unsteady and my heart is still racing, but the guilt burns my cheeks. Not guilt over what David and I have just done. Guilt over the painful truth I'm hiding. I need to tell him, to put the brakes on this whole thing until—

"That was amazing." David's voice, still shaky, interrupts my spiraling thoughts. He is grinning almost maniacally as he swabs at the come on his legs and stomach with his underwear. "I mean, holy shit, Nick. Thank you." His smile softens, and he presses a sweet kiss to the corner of my mouth. Something in my chest goes funny and my eyes burn. I shrug and wander away to the creek, plunging myself into the deepest section of the rushing water before I can think twice. The water is breathtakingly, achingly cold. So cold it seems impossible that it isn't frozen. I splash some on my face, the back of my neck. *Okay. There. Now I can focus.*

"Are you out of your mind?" Shock registers on David's face when he turns and sees me in the water.

"I guess so." I laugh before stepping out of the rushing creek. My skin is covered in goose bumps and I'm shivering hard.

David looks horrified and his hands are moving a mile a minute as he talks. "Your skin is blue, you idiot." He thrusts one of the blankets I brought at me and gratefully I wrap myself up in it.

I smile at him, shaking my head. "I'm fine. Needed to cool down." I manage to get the words out through chattering teeth and open the blanket up. He comes toward me and I wrap both of us up, awkwardly pulling him down with me as I sit. "But now I think I need your body heat," I tease and spread my legs so he can settle between them. His warmth is everything I need. David is quiet for a long moment and I give him a squeeze with my thighs, hoping he's not regretting what we did. "What's up?" I ask.

He turns to face me. A soft flush colors his pale cheeks. "Um. This blanket. Is this the one you had in your truck when we had sex?" His eyes flick down to the orange and teal fabric.

It is. I hadn't even thought about it when I packed up the tote bag this morning. I laugh. "Yup. Sorry if that's weird."

David's body relaxes against mine. I'm finally starting to get warm again.

"Hey, can I ask you something?" David asks. His voice sounds genuinely casual, and he's still leaning against me, so I try not to let dread sink into the pit of my stomach at his words.

"Sure," I reply, hoping my voice sounds neutral.

"I'm not asking out of jealousy or anything weird like that. I'm just curious. But you don't have to tell me if you don't want to—"

I cut him off, chuckling, but also nervous now. "What? You can ask."

He moves his hands down to my thighs and starts stroking and playing with the dark hair. It feels good.

"Am I the only guy you've been with?" David doesn't sound tense or weird about it. But shit.

This is certainly the opening. I have to tell him. I wish I was dressed and facing him to do it. He must take my long silence for irritation because he sits up away from me and repeats that I don't have to tell him if I'm not comfortable.

"Uh, no it's fine." I stand up quickly, letting the blanket fall around me. "Let me get dressed, okay?"

If David thinks my desire to be dressed for this conversation is weird, he doesn't show it. He simply pulls on his shorts and shrugs into his button-down before laying out the blanket, sitting down on it, and patting the spot next to him.

I take a long, shaky breath. I'll start with Matt. "A few months after we, uh..."

"Fucked?" David supplies.

"Had sex," I say with emphasis. To me that had been a lot more than fucking. "But yeah. A few months later, after all that..."

I break off for a moment, remembering my desperation to get David back into my life. The nights I spent staring at the phone, debating calling him. The e-mails I wrote but couldn't bring myself to send. The fear and self-loathing that kept me from doing right by my best friend. The shaky nausea in my stomach when I was sure I'd lost him forever.

"I met someone online. I was pretty active in this gardening message board and there was this guy, Matt. A farmer in Idaho. We were both trying to grow these Trinidadian scotch bonnet peppers. I had it in my head then that I was going to make homemade hot sauce for the diner. Anyway, we hit it off. Started texting. He let it slip that he was gay. So he ended up being the first person I came out to. It was easy since he was basically a stranger. But yeah, so we kind of started, um, sexting, I guess. Exchanging pictures and stuff. We talked and video chatted sometimes. It was nice. But I mean he was halfway across the country. It went on for like a year but then it kinda fizzled out. I think it bummed both of us out to have that kind of relationship. He was a great guy though. After, I was fucking lonely and confused so I tried dating women for a while. That's when I got back with Christi."

I tell David about how trapped I felt in my marriage. Then about how confused and lost I felt right after Christi and I divorced. About how I had no idea how to be gay or what to look for in a relationship. Eventually, though, the solution to the question of exploring my sexuality came in the unlikeliest of places. My father. One afternoon when I was over at my parents' house helping my dad clean the gutters and do some yard work, he mentioned scornfully that my cousin Ben had moved to New York from Boston a few weeks earlier to take a fellowship at Columbia.

"Oh yeah, I remember Ben. He was super hot. He came to that big family reunion you guys had at the lake, right? That was the last Patras family party I think I ever attended," David interjects, grinning up at me. He's arranged our bodies so his head is in my lap. I run my fingers through his hair, appreciating having something to do with my hands while I talk.

I laugh. "Yeah. That Ben." My fingers freeze in his hair. "Wait—Ben was like eighteen and we were, what, thirteen? What the fuck, man? I didn't know you had a thing for older guys," I grumble teasingly.

"I don't." David winks. "Just for tall, dark, and handsome men. What can I say?"

"Anyway," I say pointedly. And David settles back down, all serious again. "My dad was pissed because my Aunt Helene had called him to let him know that Ben moved to the city. They hadn't talked in years because she called my dad a bigot—"

David interjects with a "Go Helene!"

"Right? My aunt didn't take any shit from the family about Ben being openly gay. So she cut ties with a lot of us. Which sucked because they were my favorite relatives by far."

I go on, explaining to David how I got Ben's number from my aunt and I called him to ask if I could visit him in the city. It had been so awkward meeting him in some ultra-hip coffee shop in Brooklyn after not seeing him for years. Thankfully my cousin had always been pretty even-keeled, so he was gracious and put up with my boring small talk. After a few minutes of talking about the weather and my train ride down I blurted out that I got divorced because I was gay. He'd gotten this big smile on his face and clapped me on the back and told me he was proud of me.

But of course Ben, being all intellectual and comfortable in his own skin, had shaken off the question when I asked him about how to "be gay." He explained that there was no monolithic queer culture and that I shouldn't get so hung up on fitting in. Finally, after I asked him dozens of questions, he suggested I make an online dating profile (of course he knew nothing about online dating himself) and gave me the names of a few gay bars (that his friends had been to, but he, himself, had not visited).

So I downloaded a few dating apps on my phone and after meeting up with Ben I decided to stay overnight in the city. When I logged on I was immediately intimidated by the acronyms and labels I knew nothing about. Gayness was its own complicated world, and I was completely clueless about how to navigate it. My profile was simple and kind of bland: a few pictures and a little information about myself. I was embarrassingly frank about being new to the whole gay thing. I received messages from guys looking to show me the ropes, quickly followed by dick pics or highly detailed, graphic descriptions of what they wanted to do with me.

I'd been so overwhelmed I was ready to throw in the towel when I'd gotten the message from Shawn, a cute guy who suggested we meet for a drink near where he worked in Queens. So I said yes and proceeded to sweat right through my shirt on the seemingly endless subway ride. Thankfully Shawn was nice enough and even cuter than he'd looked in the pictures, with close-cropped light brown hair and big brown eyes. He was a high school gym teacher, and we slipped into an easy, if not slightly dull, conversation about football.

The exchange took an odd turn when he harshly mentioned he was glad he'd found a guy who wasn't "so femme" and complained that the app we'd met on was overwhelmed with "queens." While I understood that femme meant men who embraced more feminine traits, I was confused by the rage in his voice. So what if that was how people wanted to express themselves? But I'd stayed silent and taken a long sip of beer, ignoring his mini-rant.

That night after getting a few more beers we went back to his place and had sex. He said he was a strict top and, I'd seen enough porn to know that this meant he would be the one to fuck me. That wasn't exactly what I'd wanted, but I also didn't know, so I went with it. It meant, I learned, that he would fuck me hard and fast and stop when he came, letting me finish myself off. I couldn't get into his aggressive style, but I liked the feeling of his body against mine and I'd enjoyed getting to know him, so I chalked up my lack of enjoyment to nerves and told him I'd call him.

Over the next couple of months we sexted almost daily and got together a few more times, me coming down to the city to grab a beer with him before going back to his place for sex that left me feeling excited but somehow more confused. He never kissed me. And that bothered me because I love kissing, and I'd been eager to experiment with kissing other guys. I'd thought of asking Ben about how rigid the whole top and bottom thing was but even if he hadn't been my cousin, it would have been way too weird. He was one of those people that seemed somehow indifferent to sex and relationships, more interested in astrophysics than sexual chemistry.

Then one weekend when I took the train into the city, arriving at the sports bar Shawn had given me the name of, he never showed up. I texted him. Nothing. So I sat at the bar for a while, sipping my beer, thinking he was stuck on the train or busy at work. But he still didn't show. I started to feel kind of bad for myself. I didn't know why he would blow me off like that. I had tried pretty hard to be open-minded, and I knew he was attracted to me. It didn't make sense. Maybe the connection wasn't there for him. Honestly, it wasn't for me either. Or maybe I was messing something up about this whole being gay thing.

I must have been pretty down though because after a while I realized I was drunk. The whole time I'd been waiting I hadn't eaten anything, but I'd managed to put away a good number of beers. So I was tipsy enough to look up a gay club on my phone and take a cab over. I wasn't dressed for it, since Shawn seemed to prefer when I dressed in athletic clothes. And of course the place I found online was pretty fancy, with a long line out the door and tons of men dressed in stylish outfits, smoking and laughing and texting at lightning speed. Somehow the bouncer let me in, and for a while it was fun.

I realize David is sitting up now, looking at me intently. My hands are balled into fists. The tightness in my chest is back, worse than it has been for a while.

"Anyway," I continue. My voice is gravel rough. I swallow hard in an effort to smooth it out. "I got totally wasted. I mean, I was pretty far gone when I got there but a few guys bought me drinks, and I was real nervous because the whole thing was so new. So yeah, I got way too drunk." My face flushes hot as the memories come back to me. The fun rush from dancing and the flattering high of attention. The crush of bodies moving in time to thumping music. The flashing colored lights and mix of so many colognes with the bite of liquor and the slight edge of cigarette smoke in the air.

David puts his hand on my arm, squeezing gently and meeting my gaze. There is no anger or judgment in his eyes, so I keep talking, my mouth thick and sluggish as I try to speed through this part.

"I don't know. The last thing I remember from the club was talking to this guy at the bar. I don't even remember what he looked like. I'd had a ton of shots. I was, you know, slurring and stuff. Falling-down drunk, which is fucking embarrassing. I know I said I needed to head out but he asked me to dance so we did. And I kind of remember dancing? But then."

I pause and drag my hand over my face, momentarily pressing my fingers hard into my eyes so my vision goes black and greenish patterns swirl behind my eyelids. Shit, I can barely breathe all the sudden and a loud sound, like water, rushes in my ears. I'm dizzy. "I woke up the next morning in a hotel. The guy was gone. I basically didn't remember anything. I sort of pieced together him waking me up in the cab and bringing me up to the room. But yeah. I was, uh, sore when I woke up. And I could tell he didn't use a condom."

My body remembers the shame and I shiver, my muscles tensing involuntarily. I don't tell David about the blurred fragments that slammed into my consciousness without warning in the days that followed. The dizzy, sick feeling as I sat on the floor of the unfamiliar hotel shower, searing water stinging my numbed skin. How do I put into words my sense that this whole thing was better left balled up tight and buried deep enough that I didn't have to think about it anymore?

David traces patterns on my arm, his fingers cool and gentle against my burning skin. "Nick. I'm so sorry."

Wait, why is he sorry? Confusion blooms on my face. "No. I'm sorry. I fucked up. I got trashed and now I don't know if I'm, I don't know, sick or anything like that because I'm too freaked out to go get tested. I mean, when I first found out you were back I made a damn appointment with my doctor but what was I supposed to say? He's the same old dude my dad sees. He goes to their church. Was I supposed to tell him I got wasted and had sex with some random dude and I woke up knowing he hadn't used a condom? That I waited almost a year to get tested? You deserve more than some fuckup who can't even take you on a date and can't even be bothered to have responsible sex." My voice breaks and I hate the wetness on my face.

Like always when I have one of these panic attacks, I'm simultaneously acutely and very distantly aware of what's happening. My heart races. My body shakes. My face is wet. My chest hurts. I can't breathe.

Shit. I really can't breathe. Everything feels detached, almost like I'm watching myself on TV. Then there it is, that cool touch, the soft brush of fingers on my face, grounding me.

Chapter Ten

David

May

Nick had always suffered panic attacks. He was an anxious kid, losing sleep over quizzes, crying hard when he thought he upset his siblings, revisiting disagreements with his dad or coaches ad nauseam. And when we'd started making out and hooking up, sometimes afterward he would turn in on himself, not speaking, jaw and fists clenched tight, breath shallow and ragged. Of course I always felt horribly guilty, but Nick insisted it wasn't my fault.

Usually the attacks followed a similar trajectory: something would upset him, I would watch his eyes lose focus, and he would go silent and still, almost like he went somewhere else for a while. The first time I saw him get upset like that, when we were about ten, I'd been so scared I'd told my mom about it. She quietly suggested growing up with a dad like Nick's probably caused him to disassociate from himself as a coping mechanism. That night I had looked up the word disassociate in the dictionary and learned it meant the same thing as detach, which made sense. Nick did seem to separate from himself, disappearing to a place where I couldn't find him.

And I thought as soon as Nick started talking about what happened he would do just that. The words would die on his lips, his eyes would go blank and he would sit there, silent as stone. I would rub his arms while I waited for him to come back. But he'd kept talking, and for the first time ever I saw tears slide down his cheeks. Sorrow swept through me then, like a wind rushing through a tunnel. But that wind cleared something in my head and I turned off the tenuous new maybe-boyfriend mode and let my LGBTQ+ youth advocate training kick in.

"Nick." I'm glad my voice is strong and clear as I cup his cheek. He's stopped crying now. He's breathing hard, his head dropped between his knees. His skin, which had been so cold before from the water, is feverish.

I give him time to breathe, running my fingers through his hair. Fleetingly, I worry that my touch might be bothering him—I know when I get upset I hate being touched. But when I draw my hand away he looks up sharply, his body relaxing when I tangle my fingers back into his short, dark hair. Slowly Nick's breathing evens out and he sits up, face flushed but otherwise calm. He opens his mouth, and I'm sure he's about to apologize for getting upset so I cut him off.

"That was not your fault." I'm aware that the words can sound hollow, but one of the first things I learned working at the youth center in Chicago was that many victims of sexual assault need these words. That they can be a tiny, soothing balm for a terrible hurt. "What that guy did to you—that was not okay. It sounds like you were visibly drunk and couldn't consent to sex. People should know better than to try anything with someone who is clearly unable to participate willingly." My words are emphatic and somewhat rote. I remember giving a similar speech to teens at the center.

Nick glances over at me, his face now calmer but etched with incredulity. "I mean, but I probably let it happen. Maybe you don't get it..." He seems like he's working hard to convince me. "I was fucked up. And it wasn't like I got, you know, drugged or anything like that. I just drank a ton."

I stop for a long moment to consider this. How can I help him understand the reality of what he told me without making him further relive the encounter, or negating his telling of the experience? "Okay, think of it this way," I begin, my voice thankfully still soothing. "If I came over to your house for dinner and I was hammered drunk, passing out or whatever, would you want to sleep with me? Like, I'm still me and you know normally I'd be into it but I'm out of my mind drunk. Would you do it?"

Nick shakes his head quickly. "No."

"And why not?" I ask softly.

"Because it wouldn't be right. It would be taking advantage." And as he says the words, I see his shoulders drop. "Okay," he hedges. "I guess I get what you're saying. But still I should have gotten tested or whatever right away. I should have told you. I mean, I don't want to put you at risk."

I smile at him, gently teasing. "Babe, I think we're pretty safe with frottage."

Finally Nick gives a small laugh and the tension seems to be draining from his handsome face. But then his gaze drops to the ground and when he speaks his voice is almost imperceptibly low. "I know I should have told you about this right away. But I didn't know how to bring it up. And I didn't know where things were going and even if you would want to see me."

I know this is his anxiety talking. This is such vintage Nick—earnest panicking, raised eyebrows, words rushing out, big body all tense—that even though what he's saying is heartbreaking, I can't help but smile sadly.

"And I'm going to go get tested. I promise. I know it's fucked up that I didn't. I'll show you the results and everything." He breaks off and looks at me, his gaze so intense it's hot on my skin. "But what if I'm sick. Like I'm..."

"Positive?" I supply gently. "Then we deal with it. I can go on PrEP. And I know your dad probably wants you to believe that every single gay man is a walking petri dish of STIs, but that's total bullshit. Okay, yeah, clearly the guy who did that to you isn't a stellar human being, but that doesn't mean he gave you a bunch of diseases too." I draw in a deep breath, trying to calm the anger filling my body with heat.

"We can go get tested together, okay? Hell, we can drive over to Planned Parenthood in Albany tomorrow if you want. And I won't speculate about what the results will be, because there's no way for us to know. But we'll deal with it no matter what. It will be fine." I take his hand in mine and squeeze it tight. Unbidden, the thought that I no longer have health insurance since leaving my job at the museum springs to mind, but I tamp it down. I can cross that bridge if and when I get to it. Thank god for the Marketplace.

"Planned Parenthood? Isn't it..." Nick's voice is hesitant, not quite skeptical.

I hastily interrupt. "If you say the words 'abortion clinic' I will kill you for real."

"Easy there..." Nick laughs. "I was going to say a *women's* clinic. I took Doria there last year so she could get a prescription for birth control. She used to get insane cramps and stuff."

Another of the icicles in my heart melts. Even when he was the almighty quarterback, Nick had always doted on his sisters. Especially Doria who is quiet and small and never seemed to fit in their big family of tall, gregarious athletes.

"It's a health clinic. They offer services for men too. For everyone. And they have great resources for the LGBT community. I mean there are even support groups and counseling services if you want to talk to someone about what happened or get help with coming out." I totally know I'm pushing. And as I expect, Nick tenses up and looks at me out of the corner of his eye.

"I'm fine. I wasn't trying to make a big deal about that." His voice has dropped into the intense growl he sometimes uses.

I shrug and lean over to plant a quick kiss on his lips. "I want you to know you can talk to me about this. Anything. Always." I give him a long look before kissing him again, this time on the tip of his nose. "So you're okay though?"

Nick doesn't answer. Instead he pushes me down onto my back and kisses me senseless.

NICK FUSSES WITH the radio endlessly as we drive along the heavily wooded roads up to Albany. Apparently Nick still likes to avoid highways when he drives. And apparently the CD player in his Jeep died a few years earlier, leaving us with his radio that only seems to pick up two stations, bad pop country and bad Top 40. Of course he settles on the bad country.

"Holy shit," I mutter as Nick sings along with a truly saccharine song, his hands relaxed on the steering wheel. He knows all the words to this crap. And I have to pretend I don't find it kind of adorable.

"Hm?" He glances over at me quickly but then returns his eyes to the empty road. He's a careful, patient driver.

"This is *awful*. Your taste in music is the actual worst." I beam at him.

"Shut up," he scoffs. "This song is great! Listen to the lyrics." He turns the dial on the stereo and sings along even louder.

I'm thrilled he isn't nervous. Or at least that he isn't visibly tense and taciturn as we drive toward the state capital. Because, honestly, I feel a little anxious myself. During my college years of casual sex I had always been religious about testing, going in for an STD screening a few times a year and always insisting on condoms. My parents had been big into sex-positive health education and had drilled the "no glove, no love" slogan into my head like an embarrassing mantra. Nevertheless, I haven't been tested since Christopher and I split up, since I found out he was not entirely faithful.

Nick glances over at me again. "What's up? You got all tense. Are you worried about the appointment? Because it's okay if you're having second thoughts. I mean I get it if..."

"No," I sigh heavily, pressing my face into my hands. "No matter what, I'm with you." I turn to him to emphasize this point. "It's just. Okay. I think you know I dated this guy Christopher. For like three years. We lived together. But after about a year of living together we almost never had sex. And part of it was definitely my fault. I had my job at the museum so I was exhausted all the time. But we also, like, had zero chemistry. I realized we made better roommates and friends than boyfriends, but god forbid I say that to him. And when I finally did, he told me he had gotten back with his ex, some blond finance guy. Then he shared the lovely news that they were having threesomes and stuff. When Christopher and I did have sex, we'd stopped using condoms. We'd agreed to be monogamous. So, yeah. I get it. I haven't been tested since we broke up."

Nick's grip on the steering wheel has tightened considerably. "I would never do that, you know," he growls, eyes still trained on the road. "And I only want to be with you. You're everything I want."

Heat rushes to my face. He sounds possessive, and damn if that doesn't turn me on a little. Or a lot. "I want to be monogamous too," I say softly. The fantasy Anna had teased me about—me and Nick living on his farm with kids and pets—pops into my mind and my heart starts hammering in my chest. I could set up a small studio. I could make a go of working as an artist from up here. The farm gets amazing light. And it's not that far into the city.

And what in the actual fuck am I thinking? Jesus. Way to get ahead of myself. Here I am planning out a whole future with Nick when I don't even know what we are to each other. Not to mention the fact that I'm not even sure when I'll be able to move out of my dad's place.

I've skirted around the topic of Nick coming out, unwilling to be the one who pushes him into a decision that could sever his ties with his family. I know his father. I know his fear. But I also know I'm itching to pop the bubble we've surrounded ourselves in. I want a partner:

holidays together, shared meals, meshed schedules, pointless arguments over dumb TV shows. A full, imperfect life. And I want that life with Nick.

WE'RE BOTH BUOYANT as we sit down at a Thai place Nick dragged me to after we left Planned Parenthood. I tried not to be thrilled that he grabbed my hand as we followed the directions on his phone to the strip mall housing the restaurant. The clinic had rapid result testing for HIV in addition to the standard STI screening results. All negative for both of us. I tried to ignore the wave of calm and desire that immediately ran through me when I found out.

"I was worried I wouldn't have an appetite," Nick says between large bites of his Panang beef curry. "Jenna told me that this place is good. I'm glad we can enjoy it."

The relief and joy are so plain on his face that for a moment I am enthralled by his beauty. The sun glows behind him through the dusty plate-glass window of the crowded restaurant. His hair is a bit rumpled from him running his fingers through it again and again as we sat in the clinic's quiet waiting room. Those thick eyebrows have relaxed, his face soft and open. A strange emotion builds inside me. The swell consumes me for a moment, but I don't want to stop to examine it. Instead I grab my phone off the table and snap a picture of him. I think I'll remember everything for later but I want to be sure.

"Did you take a picture of me?" Nick laughs. He doesn't seem offended, only confused. I flush.

"Yeah. Is it okay if I paint you? You look beautiful in this light. And, I don't know, you seem so relaxed." I'm not being very articulate.

But Nick nods enthusiastically. "Yeah! That would be cool! I've been dying to ask you about your art. You're so talented."

And there's that weird emotion again, a heady mix of pleasure and anticipation and comfort. The way I felt the first time Nick kissed me. The way I felt when he showed up with a potted plant at my Columbia dorm then pinned me to my bed and rubbed us together until we were both sweaty and falling apart. The way I felt when he put his arms around me when I went to his house for dinner. Had any other man made me feel this way?

"Thanks," I reply, unable to look at him now. I push my bowl of half-eaten soup toward Nick and he hesitates for a moment before diving in. "It's been nice having so much time to paint, to be honest. A couple days ago my Instagram hit over five hundred followers which is kind of crazy because I straight up suck at social media." As much as I love painting, I hate talking about it. I chew on my lower lip, worried like I sound like one of Christopher's pretentious friends, forever droning on and on about their influences and the social impact of their work.

"For real?" Nick's eyebrows shoot up. "That's amazing. Our farm account has like ten followers. Can I see?"

I unlock my phone and open the app before handing it to him. He stares at the screen for a few silent moments, swiping through the images slowly. A few of the pieces I posted recently lean more toward the erotic. I wonder what he'll make of the piece I posted this morning, an extreme close-up of a strong hand grasping two erections, rendered in indigo ink. It's more abstract than most of my stuff but I'm pretty pleased with it. I painted it in a hurry the night after Nick and I hiked out to the creek.

Nick's eyes are wide as they meet mine. "This is amazing, David." His voice is soft. "I mean I knew you were good at painting, but...wow. These..." He pauses for a long time and stares down at my phone. "These make me happy I'm gay."

I reel at his words. Not only because Nick is saying out loud in public that he is gay. Not only because his praise sounds so sincere, it's almost reverent. Not only because his statement encapsulates exactly what I want people to experience when they see my work. Everything I want is becoming real. I'm on a date with Nick. We trust each other after years of misunderstandings. And I'm making art again. Even though today has been wonderful, Nick so at ease for our first lunch out together, I'm suddenly desperate to get home. I'm desperate to paint and to have Nick inside me. And I kind of want that forever.

Not for the first time I wonder if Nick can read minds because he reaches across the table and covers my hand with his. Every part of him is so big and warm. "Saturday night I want to take you to dinner. In Kingston? I'm still not ready to come out to my parents so I should be careful I guess. But I want to be with you. For real. And after dinner I want to have sex." His voice is low and my ass clenches at his words. His honesty is disarming. And thrilling.

I'm so used to dating being a game, making slight tweaks to myself for other men. Taking stock of what a guy wanted and putting together the perfect outfit, making sure I emphasized the right aspects of my personality and hid the wrong ones. With Christopher everything kind of flowed along in neutral. We met at a mutual friend's party, fucked a few times, fell into dating, fell into living together, fell apart. But with Nick this time around everything is so bright and clear. He's direct about what he wants and how he feels. And I love it. I love him.

I do an internal double-take at my own thought. It's been a month. There's no way... I shove the notion to the back of my mind, filing it away for later examination.

Nick looks tentative now. "Would you like that?" His hand is still on mine. I wonder if he'll still take my hand in his when we're closer to home. If he'll ever hold my hand when his family might see.

I nod, head bobbing hard. "Yes, please." I try to lighten the mood with a flirty grin but Nick's face is still heated and serious. "And I do think you should be out to your family. I want that because I want you to feel okay being honest with them. But I also get why you're not comfortable with that yet. I know how your dad is."

Our conversation is interrupted by the waitress coming to clear our plates. She glances down at our clasped hands but says nothing. Part of me expects Nick to jerk his hand away but a more of me starts to fall for him when he doesn't.

WHEN I CALL Anna to give her the highlights reel from my adventure in Albany, her excitement over my solidifying relationship with Nick and the news of our upcoming date quickly shifts to disappointment.

"Crap. I can't hang with your dad Saturday night. I have to go to an ALA conference in Saratoga this weekend." I can hear frantic jazz in the background along with the clatter of dishes and I know she's sitting in her favorite spot at the Bluebird Café guzzling a chai before the library opens. I wish I was there with her, chatting face-to-face instead of standing in a litter-strewn hospital parking lot sweating through my shirt. The occasional breeze is nice but also blows the trash into a grotesque tornado of fast food wrappers and plastic bags. Who throws all this stuff here?

"That's okay. I'll call Jimmy later. Daisy's doing a lot better so they've been coming by more. I think it's good for my dad too. Jimmy hovers less than me." My cousin Daisy in on the autism spectrum and struggles with self-injury and communication. A few days after my father's stroke Daisy hit her head hard and had to spend two nights in the hospital. Jimmy worried it was the change in routine since he'd been accompanying me to so many appointments and helping out around my dad's house. He'd shared this with me apologetically, but the guilt I felt over it was agonizing. I relied too heavily on him to help me sort out the mess of calls and forms and emotions that swirled in the wake of my moving back. But lately Daisy has started to enjoy coming by my dad's house again, working in the garden with Jimmy while my dad sits on a deck chair reading. So that has been a welcome relief on all fronts.

"I'll bet he does. You need to learn to chill. But yeah, I'm sorry I can't help out. Your dad seems a lot better though, especially his walking."

"Yeah, we're at OT right now. He always pitches a fit about coming but it helps a ton. Anyway, you excited about the conference?" I ask sarcastically. Anna hates networking and public speaking with a level of repulsion I reserve for icebreaker games and being serenaded on my birthday.

"Ugh. Not. At. All. I don't know why they always send me to this. Joseph knows that I can't mingle for shit."

"Right. But you're the hip, young face of the library. You can do Twitter. You're relevant. You have tattoos." I laugh, repeating back the funnier choice lines her older, well-meaning boss has thrown at her.

Anna falls quiet for a long moment, and if it weren't for the background noise, I would think the call had dropped. When she does finally speak, her voice is studiedly casual. "Do you go out to the farm much during the day?"

The question is odd and I rack my brain for why she might be asking. "Um, not really. Only the one day Nick and I went hiking." I had provided Anna with a PG-13 recap of that afternoon, leaving out the specifics of the story Nick told me. "Why?"

Again her voice is weird, light and purposefully even. "Oh, I was wondering if you know the other people who own it. Hector and, the woman, I forget her name."

I snort hard into the phone. "Jenna? Are you asking what I know about Jenna? Because unfortunately the answer is almost nothing. Nick seems to love her to death. He takes her word as gospel too, the way he went on about her restaurant recommendations. Want me to do some recon tomorrow night? Try to feel out if she's queer?"

"No," she says quickly, then sighs. "Yes? If it comes up. She's cute, right?"

"Very." I grin. "I'll bring it up tomorrow, okay?"

Once Anna and I hang up I quickly text Jimmy to see if he and Daisy want to come over tomorrow night. His reply is immediate and teasing, asking me if I have a hot date. God, I hope it will be hot. The memory of Nick fucking me in his Jeep all those years ago has fueled far too many emotionally confusing jerk-off sessions. So yes, the thought of what will come after the date has me adjusting myself slightly and glancing around, hoping I don't look like a total creep lurking in this parking lot. Blushing, I text back that I'm getting dinner with a friend. I don't know how comfortable Nick is with random people in my life aside from Anna knowing about our relationship. And that sucks. Because I'm pretty much constantly overjoyed to be with Nick. It's like I won the lottery but I have to keep it a secret so random relatives don't start calling and hitting me up for cash.

I remind myself that I can't pressure Nick to come out. I understand his reluctance. That horrible thought, the one I had time and time again after my mom died, bubbles up. Why couldn't it have been Nick's dad instead? Why did my empathetic, soft-spoken mom have to die, but Nick's spiteful, small-minded dad continues to plug away, making Nick feel diminished and anxious? I know what I'm thinking is beyond fucked up. But I can't stop the feeling from slithering through my mind. I lean back against the bricks of the hospital. They're still cool from the morning air. For an instant I look directly into the sun. Then I squeeze my eyes shut tight and watch the repeating circles of light dancing in the dark.

Chapter Eleven

David

May

The sky is mottled pink and orange when I pull up the driveway to Nick's house Saturday night. The air at Nick's farm always smells good, like warm grass and freshly turned soil with an edge that's slightly floral and sweet. Was it lavender or roses? Neither are in bloom this early, at least that I can see. Nick is in the large, neatly maintained front yard throwing a Frisbee to Archie. He looks happy. He also looks painfully handsome and my heart flips because he has clearly dressed up to go out to eat with me. I can count on one hand the number of times I have seen Nick in a shirt with a collar that wasn't flannel. But this one, a crisp light blue button-down, is neatly tucked into a pair of navy pants. And okay, yes he's still wearing boots but these aren't his usual leather hiking boots with mismatched laces. Archie bounds over to me and waggles crazily as I reach down to stroke his coarse fur.

"You look great," I say to Nick. He laughs and shakes his head.

"I'm glad I still have this shirt. Bought it for Cassie's wedding. Lucky it fits." I remember Nick's crazy final growth spurt around his nineteenth birthday. He'd suffered growing pains in his legs like a third grader, climbing from his already tall six foot two to his ridiculously tall six foot five. He bends and brushes a soft kiss over my lips and I am momentarily tempted to forget the whole dinner thing and drag him inside to his bedroom. His outdoorsy, herbal smell surrounds me as I deepen the kiss. He groans into my mouth. "Dinner. Then this."

The restaurant Nick directs me to is romantic, a small place with brick walls and a large mirrored bar. Although it's cool out we decide to sit on the back patio. The sun has set fully, and the sky is now a deep indigo. For a moment the whole thing feels slightly off and I'm reminded of how strange this date is. I know this man so well, but in actuality I know the outdated model. I barely know Nick the gay organic farmer. After the waitress brings our drinks, a dark beer for Nick and a glass of red wine for me, a not quite tense silence settles down between us again. It's almost like an awkward online date.

"So how's your dad?" Nick asks, looking down at his hands. He's fiddling with his fork.

"Better," I say honestly. I fill him in on the details of my dad's progress with occupational and physical therapy, the fact that he's better able to speak now, and how my uncle and cousin have been spending more time at the house like they used to before my dad was hospitalized.

"It's weird though," I say absently, not thinking before I speak. "This is my life now. Like I never thought I'd be back here. And now that I'm back it kind of feels like, I don't know, like I hit pause on my life or something. I was so excited when I landed my job at the museum. My whole dissertation was about community building through art so it was like a tailor-made position for me. Honestly, I was good at it too. So it's bizarre now that I don't do anything except cart my dad around to appointments and make these stupid paintings and post them on Instagram. Like, why the hell did I spend six years busting my ass to get my doctorate? It was all a fucking waste of time." I realize I'm ranting and that I sound bitter. I stop myself. This is not casual, light date conversation.

Nick looks apprehensive, but it's clear he is trying not to. He takes a deep breath before saying anything. "Okay. Number one, your paintings are not stupid. You know that. I mean, it's awesome that you got your PhD. It made sense since you're so smart and with your parents being professors and stuff. But when you went away to Chicago for college, the first time I wondered why you didn't keep making art instead of studying art history. Anyway, I mean that I think it's awesome that you're painting again. I guess I don't know if you still did paint and stuff while you lived in Chicago..."

He pauses and takes another deep breath. It's like I can see him trying to organize his thoughts. "So yeah, my second point was supposed to be that you didn't waste your time with your degree. But maybe I covered that? So number three is that I understand how shitty it must feel to be back here after your life in Chicago. But you're taking care of your dad. And you're doing a great job of it. He's lucky to have you." Nick sips his beer and smiles tentatively at me. God, he's sweet. But I can tell he has something else he wants to say.

"Is there a point number four?" I ask, grinning at him.

He hesitates. "Do you think you're going to move back? To Chicago, I mean. I know it's hard to know one way or the other right now. But if your dad gets better... Are you happy here?"

Honestly, despite all my self-pitying and worrying I was a failure for leaving the museum, I haven't stopped to consider whether or not I'm happy living here again. Seeing my dad and making sure he's healthy brings me a sense of relief I didn't know I was missing. Being able to stop by the library and gossip with Anna whenever I want comforts me. Having the time to paint for hours on end makes me excited to wake up every morning in a way I haven't felt in years.

And being with Nick... Being with him makes me feel whole. I open my mouth to try to articulate all this, when the waitress swoops over and delivers a highly detailed litany about the specials. It is abundantly clear that Nick is not listening, which is surprising to me because the man is obsessed with food. I nod along and order one of the specials while Nick orders a random bunch of things from the menu, a flatbread and steak and a side of roasted vegetables. When she finally leaves, Nick's eyes are locked on me.

"No, I'm not unhappy here. It's complicated, but I'm definitely not *unhappy*. I don't think I would move back to Chicago."

Nick's body must have been tense as he anticipated my answer because I watch his shoulders fall and I can practically hear his sigh of relief even though the patio is crowded and noisy. I decide not to share with him that I do miss living in a city, even if our town has changed enough that I don't exactly hate living there.

"I used to think about your life in Chicago a lot," Nick admits. "I knew what your life looked like when you were at Columbia. I saw your dorm and stuff." He smirks. The two times he came to visit me, we barely left that tiny dorm. "But I've never even been to Chicago. I would get kind of, jealous, I guess? Not of you being with other guys and stuff. I mean, sometimes I'd think of that too and it made me feel like a real fuckup. I messed things up between us so bad. But, yeah, I'd picture you living in this cool apartment. One of those big places...all brick and open." He pauses like he's searching for the word.

I want to laugh at how distant that image is from my life in Chicago while I frantically taught intro-level art history classes and wrote my dissertation. First, I lived in a cramped apartment in Pilsen I shared with two other PhD students from the University of Chicago, then in the relatively nice but certainly not glamorous apartment in Andersonville. "A loft?" I supply, shaking my head at Nick and failing to contain my grin. "No, I never lived in a loft. Christopher moved into one when we broke up though, oddly enough. His ex that he got back with, Greg, had a gorgeous place in the West Loop."

Nick furrows his brows. "Yeah, well I always pictured you living in a loft. And going to fancy parties and having this big group of cool friends and stuff." He shrugs, seemingly embarrassed to admit this to me and it kind of breaks my heart.

I thought of Nick a lot during those intervening years but it was always with a mix of anger, shame, and yes, a lot of the time lust. But he had built me up into this cool gay sitcom star in his mind. I'm about to interrupt to thoroughly disabuse him of this notion when he continues.

"I just—I worry that this won't be enough for you. That I won't be enough." His eyes are downcast, beer glass drained empty.

Sliding my hand across the table to his, I squeeze his fingers tight. "That's not true. My life was nothing like that. I was busy and stressed and exhausted. When I was in grad school, I spent pretty much all my time either holed up in the library or teaching. That, or crumpled in some corner of a coffee shop trying to consume enough caffeine to stay awake. Any free time I had I worked at a youth center, which was awesome, sure, but not exactly fancy. When I got my job at the museum I was so desperate to prove that I belonged there I worked crazy long hours. I barely hung out with anyone other than my friend Marc, and that was because he worked with me and didn't let me get away with blowing him off all the time."

I clasp Nick's fingers tighter so he lifts his gaze to mine. "I missed you too. I thought about you too. When I pictured your life it hurt so much because I thought you were happily married to Christi. I figured you had a house and kids and the whole life you wanted with her. I didn't know. But being with you now, knowing that you want me..."

I draw in a steady breath, not sure how much I should reveal. Do I tell Nick that I had been in love with him basically all throughout high school and college? Do I tell him that this is pretty much the only relationship I've been in that matters? I go with a toned-down version of that truth.

"Nick, when we were younger, I, like, idolized you. I mean, you were this fantasy guy. The fucking quarterback. And all of the sudden you wanted me exactly how I wanted you. Now it's like I'm getting that again, but you mean it this time. I know it hasn't been easy for you to figure out your sexuality. But I feel lucky to be with you."

I keep my voice soft so I don't embarrass Nick, talking in public about him being gay. And if I let my voice lift above a murmur, I know it will break. Somehow I didn't quite manage to say what I wanted though and Nick still looks uncertain.

I smile at him flirtatiously, desperate to lighten the mood, and I drop my voice to a whisper. "And I can't wait for you to fuck me."

Nick shakes his head and laughs but I can tell I successfully distracted him from being all guilty and hard on himself. The rest of the meal is pleasant, fun even. Nick tells me about some plans for the farm and I admit to him that I stalked his website before I went over to his house. I also ask him, trying and failing to be casual, about Jenna. He grins when I ask, revealing he suspects Jenna is into Anna too. So of course I immediately send Anna a quick text confirming that yes, Jenna is into women and that there is a chance she is into her. Nick floats the idea of a double date, something "fun" like kayaking. I agree enthusiastically even though kayaking sounds like absolute torture.

As usual Nick eats an insane quantity of food: all his steak and sides and almost half of my salad. Which is more than fine with me because as dinner goes on I'm too turned on to even want to eat. Nick all clean-shaven, his hair neatly combed, is sexy as hell. Not that stubbly, flannel-wearing Nick is any less sexy. Watching his large hands as he eats makes me think of his hands on my body, tracing down my back, palming my ass, sliding his fingers inside me.

"David?" Nick looks amused and I must have been spaced out because I realize both he and our waitress are waiting for me to say something.

"Uh sorry, what?" My ears are hot.

"Can I get you anything else? Dessert? Coffee? Another glass of wine?"

"Oh, no thanks," I mumble. Nick shrugs and asks for the check.

"Are you okay?" he asks. I love the little wrinkles he gets on his forehead when his eyebrows draw together like that.

I nod quickly, embarrassed that I was too busy thinking about sex to be present during the date Nick planned. "Hey, thanks for tonight. I hope it doesn't make you anxious, though, being out with me."

He shrugs, glancing around the patio. "Not really. No one here we know." I wonder what he would have done had he recognized someone here. I try not to let the speculation turn my stomach.

The bill arrives and Nick brushes off my insistence that I pay for at least half. I grumble that I'll pay for our next meal and he beams at me. He bought the Thai food the other day too. Absently, I wonder about his finances. I mean I still have some savings from when I was actually gainfully employed and I barely have any expenses at the moment. I have no idea how much money organic farmers make. Not that it matters, but I feel a pang of guilt that Nick felt the need to take me out to such a nice meal. That guilt quickly washes away, however, as Nick pulls me out of the restaurant and into his arms when we step out onto the sidewalk.

"I want you so bad, baby," he whispers, bending so his lips press against my ear. The brush of his heated breath travels right through me. I gasp softly. And I guess he's not too worried about being seen with me in public because he moves his lips to mine, sliding his tongue along the seam of my mouth. I'm about to open my lips to return the heat of his kiss when he pulls back, pressing his mouth to my hair. "God, I want to be inside you. I'm so hard right now. I wish I could... I want you right here."

I laugh. "What has gotten into you?"

He shakes his head and wraps his arms tight around me. He wasn't joking about being hard. His erection pressed against my stomach as every inch of our bodies presses together. "I don't know. Being out with you—knowing we're together. I wanted to touch you all night."

A group of people, clearly very drunk based on the volume of their laughter, pours out of the dive bar a few doors down. Nick tenses up immediately and we both glance over at them, but it's fully dark now and impossible to see anyone's face. I start to pull away but Nick keeps his thick, solid arms around me.

Then it happens. One of the men, a young stocky guy in a Mets jersey, glances over at us and says something. Then another one, taller and somehow vaguely familiar even in the dark, looks over. "I told you guys this town was going to shit. That's fucking wrong." His voice is harsh and the other guys all laugh and a few make disgusted sounds. Damn it. While I certainly don't love being heckled for showing the kind of affection straight people don't think twice about, I have learned how to deal with it. I pretend it isn't happening. I keep doing what I was doing and go deaf for a few minutes. But I don't want Nick to deal with this. I'm sure he heard that kind of talk enough at home as a kid, and I can't imagine how much that must have hurt.

"Ignore it," I say softly but Nick has dropped his arms. I'm not even upset at the loss of contact, I just want to get in the car and go back to his place. "Nick, seriously. Those guys are being assholes."

Shit. Nick is turning toward them now, drawn up to his full height. He looks mad. And intimidating. He takes a few steps in their direction and my heart starts racing. Do I go with him? Is he going to get in a fight? They're still laughing but one of them seems to have noticed what Nick is doing.

"Stop it," I hiss at him in a panic.

"What did you say?" Nick's voice is low but very clear as he approaches the group. I don't know if I've ever heard him sound so angry.

"Dude, is that fucking Patras?" the taller guy says, incredulous. Nick freezes.

The shorter guy leans forward. It's dark outside the bar, but the restaurant's façade is well lit. Someone recognizes him.

"Holy shit. You're right. Hey, Patras, I didn't know you liked cock." The men are guffawing now.

Nick turns back to me, his face totally impassive. I have no idea what to do. I want to touch him, but I don't want to give those guys any more fodder and I don't want to embarrass Nick at all. So I follow his strides, long and heavy, back to where my dad's Prius is parked a block away. When I pull my door shut Nick is radiating anger. He's folded into the passenger seat and even though it's dark I can see that he's upset. But I can't tell what flavor of upset. It's shocking to see him like this. His normally generous mouth is a firm line and his gigantic frame that never ceases to remind me of ancient Roman sculpture now seems scary. Every muscle pulls tight and his hands ball into tense fists. One of those fists collides with his knee, hard.

"Fuck," he shouts, his voice so raw it almost sounds bloody. I jolt at the sound of his rage.

My voice is hoarse when I speak. So many thoughts and feelings are whirring around in my head I don't even know where to begin. "Did you, um, know those guys?" This is not how I wanted to start. This is neither comforting nor is it helpful.

"Yup." Nick sighs heavily. "Dan Rubinsky and Johnnie Brandon. They were both on the football team. Dan…Dan is friends with Jason."

My stomach drops. That is so not good. "It's not like they saw us kissing," I say quickly, still unsure of how to comfort Nick. "You were hugging me. Guys hug sometimes, it's no big deal." I don't have many straight male friends, so I don't exactly know how they interact. But I can hazard a guess that they don't hold each other close outside restaurants or whisper into each other's hair.

He turns to me and all the anger has leached out of his face. He looks so much like little kid Nick, the tall gangly boy who was so open with his emotions it sometimes made me laugh uncomfortably.

"I don't care what they saw," he says and his voice is soft, almost resigned. "It isn't fair that I can't hug my boyfriend after a date. That I have to worry about some idiot saying something that hurts you. I don't care if he tells Jason. I want you so much more than I want to worry about what dirtbags like that think."

I can't help but press my hand over my mouth as he speaks. A smile spreads over my face, slow and sweet like honey. Squealing and kissing him and saying about a hundred things at once all seem like reasonable responses. Boyfriend? I guess the small, hopeful voice inside me that I consistently silence called Nick my boyfriend. But Nick rolled the word out, totally comfortable with it. I grip my knees tightly, running my palms over the fabric of my dark jeans. I'm filled with frantic energy, and I'm not quite sure what to do with it. "Okay. I'll get the stupid thing out of the way first. Am I really your boyfriend?"

Nick's teeth catch the glow from the streetlight as he grins and nods.

"Cool," I say lamely, trying to mask the fact that I want to squeal like a twelve-year-old cheerleader. "But I kind of doubt those assholes will out you. They were, for one, clearly wasted so who knows what they'll even remember tomorrow. And you don't know that they'll say anything to Jason." Nick eyes me incredulously. I sigh, trying to breathe out the worst of the tension in my chest. It doesn't work. "Anyway that's not the first time someone has stuff like that to me. It just makes the person saying it sound ignorant."

"I know," Nick says, almost harshly.

"It doesn't hurt me anymore. So please don't worry about me, okay? I'm pissed you have to deal with this. It's my fault we came out tonight. I was being kind of a diva about the date thing—"

Nick cuts me off, leaning across the console to crush his mouth to mine. "I wanted to be out with you. You deserve a boyfriend who can take you on dates. I'm fine." He breathes against my lips. "And I'll be even better once I have you in my bed."

Chapter Twelve

David

May

The awkwardness I felt at the outset of our date is back when we return to Nick's house. Archie zooms around in tiny circles when he sees Nick, who collapses down onto the floor to wrestle with the dog. I stand awkwardly in the threshold, shoes on, wondering if in the twenty-five minutes it took to drive back to Nick's place he changed his mind. It's not like I would blame him. I imagine having your brother's drunken friends slur hateful words at you and the potential of being outed to your conservative family is a bucket of ice water on the libido.

"I'm gonna take Archie out, okay?" Nick says, standing and brushing off his pants. "I made some lemonade earlier if you want any. Or there's some wine in the fridge." He seems tense again but I can't quite read his mood. This is disconcerting because usually he's such an open book.

"Oh, okay. Sure." I slip my shoes off and cross into the kitchen. I wonder if he made lemonade specifically because he knows it's my favorite. The thought makes me smile. The lemonade is in a vintage-looking pitcher decorated with a stylized citrus motif. Cute. I wonder where Nick gets all this stuff. His house is so pulled together. Everything seems antique, much of it midcentury modern, all in perfect condition, every stick of furniture clean and polished. I take a long gulp of lemonade. It's delicious, with an unexpected hint of mint.

I never would have pictured this life for Nick. Gourmet lemonade in its own special pitcher. The row of potted herbs on the windowsill. The perfect coordination of the kilim rug and the throw pillows on the couch. I didn't even know he liked gardening, much less that he wanted to start a farm. He never mentioned career ambitions growing up, aside from hoping he would get a football scholarship. Then, when he got the scholarship at Syracuse, his dad was violently opposed to him leaving, saying college was a waste of time. He told Nick he owed it to his family to stay. So Nick tossed the whole dream aside with a shrug of his broad shoulders.

When I'd gotten his wedding invitation in the mail out of the blue, I imagined Nick living the life I'd assumed he wanted. Doing things like tailgating at football games and having a "man cave" filled with signed sports memorabilia. But he doesn't even talk about football or basketball anymore. I wonder how much of the Nick I knew was a façade designed to please his father.

The click of the door closing startles me. Archie trots over to the couch and nestles into a plaid flannel blanket that must serve as his bed.

"Sorry that took so long." Nick comes into the kitchen and fills a glass with water from the sink. "Archie must've smelled deer or something because he was going nuts."

I nod and then the only sounds are the hum of the refrigerator and the steady rustling of the curtains as a breeze blows through the open window. When the sun went down the temperature dropped with it. Nick must notice me rubbing my arms because he strides over to the woodstove and makes quick work of lighting a fire. The smell relaxes me and I lean against the counter, watching him.

"Do you want me to head out?" I ask quietly. I feel a tiny bit pathetic and angry at myself for being disappointed at the thought of leaving.

Nick's brows knit together and he gives me a searching look before shaking his head. "Not unless you want to." He starts unbuttoning his shirt, which is distracting. He shakes it off like he'd been wearing a straightjacket rather than a neatly ironed oxford. The white T-shirt he wears underneath is tight and thin. His biceps and the muscles in his forearms all flex with his movements. My mouth goes dry.

"No," I croak. "I didn't know if you were upset."

Nick closes the space between us, warm, powerful arms wrapping around me. He pushes his nose into my hair like he did outside the restaurant. A groan rumbles through his body. "You smell so good," he says softly and I shiver at the warmth of his breath on me.

"Um, you too," I reply, my mind clouded over with the need to slide my hands under his shirt and all over him.

He bends down to look into my eyes and his are dark, the lids heavy. The brush of his lips over mine draws a needy whine from me. Longing rushes through my veins, leaving me reeling. Without thinking about it I grasp at his arms, as if holding on to his solid frame will steady me. Nick's muscles tense then his mouth is on mine again. This is not a gentle kiss. His lips crush against mine and his mouth is hot as he breathes into me. The slide of his tongue against mine has me uncomfortably hard incredibly fast, a cord of desire running from my mouth to my groin.

I need to touch every inch of his skin as I push his shirt up to trace my fingers over the powerful ridges of his chest and stomach. His skin is warm and taut. I want to retrace every line with my tongue. As I bend to kiss Nick's nipple, he growls and his hands fist into my hair, pulling me even closer to him. He's salty against my tongue. When I gently bite down on the hard flesh he arches back, thrusting toward me.

"Okay?" I ask as I reach down to palm him through his pants. He shifts away, breath coming hard and fast and I ease off.

We're still standing in his kitchen, fully clothed. The telltale stabs of pleasure are already making my thighs tense up and my balls tighten.

"Let's go upstairs," he says quickly, as if pausing for even a moment is too much. I follow him up to his room and before I can even think he's pushing me back onto the bed and pulling his T-shirt over his head in a smooth motion. The weight of his body on mine is almost oppressive but I love being crushed down like this. I shift so our erections line up and roll my hips up into him. "Oh god," he moans and slides his hands under me, gripping my ass hard. "David. Baby I..." He kisses me again, desperately. "I can't believe I get to do this."

Warmth floods my chest and I run my fingers gently through his dark hair.

"Mmmm." He smiles against my lips. Then he rolls off me, so we're lying side by side.

I'm still, unfortunately, completely dressed in my blazer, jeans, and shirt. That won't do. Quickly and somewhat awkwardly I strip down to my briefs. Nick's eyes follow me the whole time. He reaches to adjust himself as I lie back down next to him. The need to touch him is overwhelming so I press my lips to his chest, running the flat of my tongue over his nipple again.

"Fuck, David, that feels so good." Nick's voice is gruff and I can see the outline of his impressive erection through his pants.

Thinking of that thick, heavy cock inside me makes me shiver with delight. And a touch of anxiety. "Do you have lube?" I ask. The nervousness is clear in my voice.

Nick sits up and pulls open the drawer of his bedside table. He places a small bottle on the nightstand then lies back down heavily next to me. "Yup."

He kisses me again and what starts as a quick, tame kiss becomes heated as I run the tip of my tongue over his full bottom lip and bite it gently. I can't help myself.

Nick's callused palms cup my shoulders, and he eases us apart, smirking at me. "Hold on, baby. I want to check a few things, okay?"

Check a few things? What? Am I a piece of farming equipment he's running a diagnostic on? But then I remember he doesn't have a whole lot of positive experience and I relax back into the pillows, ready to listen.

Nick draws in a slow, shaky breath and keeps his gaze on me. "Um, so I've been kind of assuming I'll be the one to, uh, fuck you. Top, I mean. But I want to make sure that's what you want. Because I can do it the other way too..." Nick rubs his face. Based on what he's said I get the impression he doesn't like bottoming. Which is lucky for me, because, although I have topped, I really love being fucked.

Wanting to relax him I press a soft kiss to the spot under his ear that I know makes him melt. His eyes fly open and he gasps. I wink at him. "Nope. I want all of this," I trace my fingers over his erection, "in me." Rolling over I straddle him. His eyes go all sleepy. "Start slow, okay? I'll tell you if it hurts. Start with your fingers. And use plenty of that." I gesture toward the lube.

Nick nods and starts running his rough hands up and down the sides of my torso. "Don't worry." I bend down to kiss him again but he blocks me so I end up kissing his long fingers. Not that I mind that either. I like kissing every part of him.

"I have one other question. So, um, last time we did this, you know, since we didn't have lube or whatever I, uh, licked you…" He's all flustered. It's adorable.

"Rimming," I say softly. I had been taken aback by that. The guys I'd slept with in college before Nick hadn't been so immediately willing to go there. "You don't have to do that this time. Not if you don't want to." My cheeks are hot.

Nick's face falls. "Oh. Do you not like it?"

Now my cheeks and the tips of my ears are burning red hot. I should be honest, I suppose. "No, I really, really like it. But don't feel obligated. I know it's not everyone's cup of tea."

Nick sits up and kisses me so hard I worry my lips might actually bruise. It's like he's pouring years of pent-up longing and sadness and regret into the meeting of our mouths. Like this kiss is neutralizing all that anguish and only warmth and desire are left in its wake. Even with my eyes squeezed shut I can see his face. I want this man more than I have ever wanted anything in my life.

"Can I, then?" he asks, his voice a low rumble.

Scorching lust burns in my throat so I just nod enthusiastically. As if I weigh almost nothing he lifts me off him and makes quick work of removing his pants, boxers, and socks, which I notice are mismatched. For a moment he stands at the edge of the bed looking at me, his eyes traveling slowly up and down my body, his thick cock straining toward his muscular stomach.

I start to feel a bit self-conscious. Whereas Nick's body looks like something out of a fitness magazine, I am plain old skinny. I try to jog or follow a workout video on YouTube when I can, and for a while when I lived in Chicago I was doing yoga religiously and managed to get some good muscle tone. But since living here that has disappeared. I silently vow to find a yoga studio and start taking classes again. Nick must notice the moment I tense up because he runs his fingers over the flat plane of my stomach.

"I love your body. I love everything about the way you look," he says gently as he pushes my briefs down. "Everything is so," he traces a hand over the bones of my hips to my erection, causing pleasure to lance through me, "beautiful."

Then he closes his lips around the head of my cock and I'm momentarily lost in a sea of longing. He starts to take me deeper, to slide his mouth down my shaft, and I'm writhing against him. His mouth is all slick suction, and he keeps moaning around my length, each vibration sending waves of pleasure to my balls and ass.

He gags when he tries to take me into his throat and I hate myself for how much it turns me on. That momentary tightness and flood of saliva. He sits back, breathing heavily, cheeks pink. "Sorry," he sighs, dragging his fingers through his hair.

"You don't have to deep throat." I chuckle and lean forward to kiss the tip of his nose.

"Oh, okay," he says, nodding seriously. "I thought that was how you do it."

"You watch too much porn." I laugh but there is no trace of amusement on his face.

"Not from porn." He's staring intently at the books on his nightstand. "That was what Shawn told me."

A mixture of anger and sympathy well up in me. Poor Nick. Of course his first time giving head ended up being with some aggressive masc-for-masc dickwad. I cup his cheek, hot under my palm, and lift his eyes to meet mine.

"Well, that's not what I want. I loved what you were doing but I like licking and teasing and rimming too. You don't need to shove me down your throat, okay?" I wrap my arms around his neck and pull him down so he's lying on top of me, our bare cocks pressing together, skin against heated skin. "Let's leave that for another time. I can't wait for you to fuck me."

Nick seems to relax. "Okay," he murmurs.

Then he's sliding his big hands under my body, gripping and kneading my ass as he moves his hips over mine in a simulation of sex. My whole body clenches and I'm almost paralyzed by the intensity of my desire. My thighs tense and quiver as my stomach flips at the sensation of his hardness answering mine. It's like I can barely remember to take in oxygen, much less string together coherent thoughts.

"God, I want to be inside you," Nick growls. He's holding me just shy of too tight against him.

Running on pure need I kiss his throat, nipping and biting gently on the skin, already rough with stubble. His facial hair grows fast. My hands glide all over his body, trying to memorize every powerful, perfectly sculpted muscle. And I have this sudden uncanny thought, that Nick is an actual work of art. He isn't the son of a cruel bigot father and a kind but downtrodden mother. No. Nick emerged from a block of marble like one of Michelangelo's prisoner statues, every proportion perfect but bound by the stone around him. Every line gracefully rendered as he pushes to break free. Thankfully, Nick's voice, very real and very warm, startles me from my strange thoughts.

"Can you get up on your hands and knees for me baby?"

Everything in me heats at the delicious question and I comply without thinking. I'm rewarded with a swirl of sensations: the heavy throb of his erection pressing against the crease of my ass, the warmth of Nick's body over mine, the tickle of his breath on my neck, the roughness of his stubble as he kisses and nibbles down my spine, then finally the pressure of his hands parting me gently. Every inch of my skin is sensitive, and when his hot, slick tongue glides over my hole I writhe back against him, releasing a small whine that would be embarrassing if I weren't so turned on. He groans against the sensitized skin, the vibration making my cock twitch and leak as he starts to slide the tip of his tongue inside me.

"Nick. Oh my god. Nick. Please." I'm babbling incoherently.

He keeps licking me and moaning and squeezing my ass and bright pleasure starts to roil within me. When he slides a thick finger inside me my whole body jerks, and for a moment I worry that I might actually come from the satiating thrill. I need to control myself.

"Is that okay?" Nick keeps his finger inside, perfectly still, but pulls his mouth away.

"Yes. It's amazing. Please don't stop." My voice is breathy and strained.

Nick bites my ass cheek lightly. "I love this," he says and slides a second slicked finger into me.

A cool trickle of lube is a jarring but welcome distraction to take me off the edge I was teetering over. He must be pouring some directly onto my ass. Unfortunately I'm right back on the brink almost immediately when Nick slides a third finger into me, rubbing the lube inside and stretching me gently. The thickness of his fingers massaging my prostate, the delicious fullness, the sound of his arousal, all guttural groans and hitched breath, coalesce into a vivid pinpoint of pleasure. I'm clenching hard around his fingers, trying desperately not to come.

"Wow." I hear Nick say behind me, low and soft. He shifts his fingers inside me and I buck back into him as he rubs again over my gland.

"Stop." The word spills out of my mouth before I can even think about it and Nick freezes behind me, gently easing his fingers out. I want to weep at the loss. His arms wrap around me and he presses his lips to the heated skin of my neck.

"Baby, I'm so sorry. Did I hurt you?" The concern in his voice pierces through me.

"No," I laugh. "I was about to come. That felt amazing but I..." I trail off, still out of breath and hoping he can piece together that I want him to fuck me now.

He swallows audibly and then he's stroking up and down my back again. I love how rough and big his hands are. And I love it even more when they navigate back to my ass, palming me open.

"Can I?"

The hot velvet head of his hardness isn't pressing, resting against my opening. My mouth is so dry that swallowing does nothing so I nod and try to croak out a yes. I hear the click of the lube bottle again as he slicks himself up behind me. Then pleasure unfurls in every cell of my body at the burn and stretch of him filling me up as he slowly slips into my ass. His breath comes fast and heavy.

I'm desperate to see his face. When I crane my head around to look at him, he's transformed: the olive skin of his chest and neck flushed a deep bronze, his long lashes brushing the thin skin under his eyes as they press shut, his head thrown back, baring his corded neck. I can tell he's trying to slide in slowly, to be as gentle as possible, but that's not what I want. I press back against him, urging him inside. I'm desperate for that intoxicating fusion of pain and pleasure. I'm so full I can barely breathe. I fucking love it.

"You okay?" he groans.

"Uh huh," I manage to say. My fingers grip the quilt hard and my body has gone tense with the concentrated satisfaction of Nick's warm hardness inside me. Tightening around his length, I rock back against him again, urging him on. It's like I've lost my ability to speak and can only communicate with my body. But he gets the message and begins to move at a steady, controlled pace, like it's taking a great deal of effort and concentration not to slam into me. I'm not sure if I'm grateful or disappointed. His hands are on my hips again, grasping me hard as he starts to pick up on my frantic signals and fuck me faster.

Small shocks of effervescent pleasure thrum under my skin. The buzzing heat becomes unbearable when he shifts the angle, bumping my prostate. I cry out and he does it again, with that focused determination he brings to almost everything he does. Collapsing onto the bed, I'm unable to do anything but feel and breathe. Nick's arm slides under me, holding me up. I'm babbling incoherently, clamping down around the thick hardness boring into me. The slap of skin on skin, his heavy breathing and low groans of pleasure, my panting and whining all swirl around me, ratcheting up my need to come.

"Fuck. You're so beautiful. So tight." The sound of his voice behind me, raw with desire, pushes me over the edge.

I reach down to wrap my fingers around my cock and all it takes is a few strokes before pleasure detonates within me, starting in my ass and rippling out to every inch of my skin. My mouth locks open and my thighs are shaking hard. I think I cry Nick's name as I come, but I'm only aware of my slick hand on my erection and the faltering rhythm of Nick pumping into me. He seems to thicken and somehow get even harder with one last forceful thrust. And then I'm filled with and surrounded by warmth as he releases into me and wraps his arms around me.

"Oh...fuck. David. Feels so good." Hot streams of liquid release pour into my ass and the sensation pushes a final aftershock of orgasm through my limbs.

Nick's body is heavy on top of me and I let myself collapse onto the bed, pulling him down with me. And now he's really heavy, but in a good way, like a big down blanket on a cold night. I want to fall asleep, to drift off with him still everywhere.

"Jesus," Nick pants. "That was—You were... Thank you." He starts peppering my neck and hair with swift, soft kisses. "I can't believe sex can feel that good." There's a smile in his voice and I find myself grinning too.

"That was pretty great," I say. This is a huge understatement. I can't even remember the last time I came so hard or felt this satisfied after sex. Every muscle in my body is languid. But my heart races and I can't deny the sharp twist of rising fear. It was all too good. I feel too satisfied. This can't be real. He's going to freak out and shove me away and I don't know if I can recover again. Nick is still inside me, still pressing his lips into my neck, and I automatically constrict around him as he starts to shift and pull out. "Not yet." I breathe the words, worrying I'm delaying the inevitable disintegration of our new relationship.

Once I do finally let him pull out, I start to panic. The worry that Nick isn't going to want me collides with an almost overwhelming tenderness toward him. The knot of emotions swells in my chest and makes tears prick at the corners of my eyes. I need to get it together.

Without thinking, I hop out of bed and scamper to the bathroom, cleaning up and splashing cold water on my face on autopilot. Once my breathing returns to normal and I don't feel like I'm going to collapse into a puddle of mixed-up emotional tears, I glance around the bathroom. Like the rest of the house it is impeccably neat and vintage in its décor. I must have been out of it when I scrambled in here too, because I failed to notice that the bathtub is absolutely amazing. And I love a good bathtub. It's enormous and made of hammered copper. One of those European-style freestanding showerheads dangles above the faucet and a simple white and gray shower curtain falls over one side. The floors and walls are tiled in mottled slate and a white ceramic sink rests on a cool mosaic vanity. Does Nick make mosaics too? It figures.

Glancing at myself in the comically tiny mirror mounted above the sink is a mistake. My eyes are shiny, the pupils still dilated. My cheeks are ruddy like I just woke up from a very satisfying nap. Or got fucked. Nick's heavy footfalls move toward the bathroom and then he appears in the mirror behind me. His mouth turns down and that cute little wrinkle creases the skin between his eyebrows.

"Are you okay?" he asks and when he sees me, his eyebrows draw even tighter together, his wide nostrils flaring.

Oh yeah, I did basically jump out of bed the minute he pulled out of me. And I'm almost positive Nick wanted to cuddle. He wasn't going to push me away. I was the one freaking out, not him. I turn to him, stretching to kiss the corner of his mouth. The muscles in his face relax.

"Yeah. I wanted to get cleaned up. Sorry."

"I wanted to cuddle," Nick grumbles adorably but doesn't meet my eye.

Yup. I was right about that one. As if he can't resist touching me, he rubs his hands up and down my arms. My skin prickles with goose bumps and shiver runs down my spine.

"Was that...not good?" he asks sheepishly.

I feel awful. Of course Nick would interpret my flip response and flight to the bathroom in a negative light. I wrap my arms around his thick neck and press a kiss to his Adam's apple. "Nick, you were amazing. I mean, shit, I came in here because I thought I was going to start crying because it was so good." Heat rushes to my face. I did not mean to admit that. "Anyway. Your bathtub is awesome. Like, I didn't even know tubs like that existed outside of design magazines. I thought copper was super expensive though. Was it expensive? Did you make that mosaic vanity?" Great, now I'm babbling and asking random, possibly intrusive questions.

Thank god Nick lets the subject of my post-sex breakdown drop and starts enthusiastically telling me about how the tub is original to the house. I learn that Jenna made the mosaic vanity but Nick did all the other tile work. As he talks he draws a bath, tipping some bath salts and herby-smelling oil into the water.

"Arnica oil," he informs me. "It's good for your muscles. I use it after I work out. I figure you might be kinda sore?"

The rising steam smells like Nick, all earthy and fresh, and he gestures for me to get in. When I sink into the water, which is painfully hot just the way I like it, every fiber of my being relaxes. My ass is aching a bit but I'll survive. Nick stands next to the tub, looking from my low angle like I imagine the Colossus of Rhodes might have.

"Want to join me?" I ask, patting the surface of the water like it's a couch cushion.

"I know the tub's big but it's not that big." He chuckles. "And I want you to relax."

I scrunch myself up into a little ball and scoot to the back of the tub. "Here, there's plenty of room. Come in, the water's fine. Actually, it's incredibly hot. But I like it."

"I remember." Nick sinks into the water, wincing. The bath is now full to the brim, water sloshing over the side as he shifts his bulk so one foot is on either side of me. I stretch my legs out a little, my feet tantalizingly close to his bobbing cock.

"Um, I don't remember ever taking a bath together," I tease.

Nick splashes water onto his face then runs his hands through his hair. "No. But one time you said you hated the dorm showers because they never got hot enough. That you loved being able to take baths so hot your skin turned red. I, um, got kinda turned on picturing it and I was worried Jason might see. You and I were Skyping and he wouldn't leave me alone the whole damn time." He shrugs. "Anyway, can I ask you something?" Nick reaches for a bar of soap, one of those handmade-looking ones you see at health food stores. As he washes himself the very familiar scent of pine and sage fills the air.

"Sure," I reply, trying to simultaneously process Nick's amazing recall of a conversation we had a decade ago and anticipate what he's going to ask me. That, and quell the renewed flood of arousal from the smell of his soap.

He strokes my throat with his fingertips, his gaze serious. Oh god, what is he going to ask me? Is he upset about those guys seeing us earlier? Do we have to have that conversation in the bathtub?

"How's your skin so soft?"

My laughter, high and only slightly manic, echoes off the tiled walls. "Is that actually what you wanted to know?" I say, rolling my eyes at him. "Moisturizer. Ever heard of it?"

"Whatever. You just have really soft skin. Jeez." He grins and scoots closer to me. I glance down and see that he's getting hard again. His hand slides up to my face, thumb brushing over my mouth. Then he grips my shoulders, drawing me roughly onto him and sloshing more water out of the tub. "Can you spend the night?" he asks against my lips.

We both know I can't, but the invitation fills me with a warmth that has nothing to do with the bath.

A few blissful hours later I slide into my car, wrung out and boneless from round two of sex in the bathroom. My ass is delightfully sore and a few small love bites bloom purplish-red on my neck. I'm exhausted and emotionally overwhelmed. I don't want to leave. I want to fall asleep wrapped in Nick's arms and wake up in the middle of the night to nuzzle his neck and kiss down his chest. I want to hear the long, slow breath Nick always makes the moment he rouses from sleep. Instead, I'm going home to my father's house to wake Jimmy and Daisy up off the couch and apologize profusely for being out so late.

The scent of pine and sage lingers on my skin as I look over my shoulder to back up. I can't subdue my grin, knowing I'm taking a bit of Nick with me as I navigate back home.

Chapter Thirteen

Nick

June

The brown, alien-like form crawls over the tomato leaf, finally settling far too comfortably on the silvery stem. I stare at the insect for a long moment, trying to think of some benefits stink bugs may offer the ecosystem. The gross, rotten cilantro scent it emits prevents it from being a popular food source for birds. In the looks department it's no great shakes, mottled brown and vaguely creepy. And they *are* an invasive species. So it's nothing but a pest. An awful pest that, along with its friends, is invading my fragile, newly transplanted tomato seedlings. I pluck the bug from the stem and stomp on it, maybe too aggressively, with the toe of my boot. I'll have to ask Hector what he thinks about applying some Kaolin clay to this bed. And the adjacent squash and herb beds too. Damn bugs.

Out in the orchard Jenna and Hector chat away, their voices distorted by the distance and breeze. Jenna has been in an uncommonly chipper mood over the past few weeks since she and Anna started hanging out. Jenna doesn't let on much, only says Anna is cool, and funny, and other positive generic traits. But every time I see her she's smiling and kind of spacing out, which seems like a good sign. When I mentioned the potential double date, she was pretty excited about the idea of going kayaking. But with late spring comes the height of planting and the start of weeding and the influx of pests, meaning Hector, Jenna, and I finish each day so exhausted we can barely haul ourselves up onto the porch for a beer or glass of lemonade. We really should hire someone else.

The nights David has come over I've been so exhausted I've made lousy company, spacing out during dinner and dozing off right after sex. I'm pissed at myself for being such a terrible boyfriend. After the night Dan and Johnnie saw us outside the restaurant in Kingston we sort of defaulted to spending time at my place again. I know I should bring it up, talk the whole thing over with David. Honestly I should come out, once and for all, so I don't have to worry. But anytime I think about sitting down with my parents and telling them the truth, I want to scrunch up from the tight discomfort blooming in my gut.

I have to remind myself that I did do at least one good boyfriend thing over the last month. David mentioned his dad was griping about feeling trapped around the house, so I'd invited them over for dinner. I even made a vegetarian, low-salt meal that managed to satisfy all Dr. Webster's new and old dietary restrictions. David told me his dad was doing much better, that he was becoming more self-sufficient for daily tasks, and that his strength and outlook had improved a lot from being able to take short walks outside.

But Dr. Webster was so different from the man I'd known that I could barely believe it was him. The Dr. Webster I knew was, well, kind of kooky. He was taller than David, but they had the same willowy frame and animated way of talking. They made the same wild gestures when they were excited about a topic and the same stony face when they seemed irritated. The Dr. Webster I knew would go on long tangents about politics, pulling facts and statistics seemingly out of thin air to support his claims. He would tug on his salt and pepper hair as he talked, making it stand on end.

I never told David this, but I always thought the hairstyles he spent so much time on, all tousled and pushed back, looked a lot like his dad's hair after a particularly heated tirade. Dr. Webster was undeniably sharp. I knew without a doubt, for example, that the man was totally aware of what had been going on between his son and me throughout high school and David's time at college. He didn't like to pry and didn't care what David did in his personal life. A far cry from my own parents.

But now Dr. Webster is frail with brittle-looking hair. He spoke with effort and spent most of the meal chewing intently and listening to David and I make small talk. But then he'd surprised me at the end of dinner when he'd looked between the two of us, nodding with a trace of one of his old knowing smiles on his lips. David immediately seemed to panic on my behalf, shooting his father a death glare then an apologetic look my way.

David's willingness to keep our relationship a secret caused a weird mix of emotions to well up inside me. On one hand, I was thankful that he was so patient with my need to come out slowly, but on the other hand I was getting frustrated with myself. David, a man who'd been comfortably out since he was thirteen, did not need to be sneaking around as a fully fledged adult.

So, I'd blurted it out, telling Dr. Webster in a convoluted jumble that I was gay and that David and I were trying out a relationship. David's face went an adorable shade of pink, but he'd grinned at me and pressed his leg against mine under the table. And Dr. Webster nodded again, blinked a few times, and said he hoped I made his son happy. So there it was. I was out to another person.

My phone buzzes in my pocket, pulling me from my thoughts and bringing a smile to my face. David and I usually text throughout the day, sending stupid jokes back and forth and sometimes exchanging the kinds of messages that make me grateful I can steal away to have some privacy. When he sent me an unprompted but very welcome naked selfie last week, I'd been so immediately turned on that I'd escaped to the abandoned hayloft in the barn to call David, both of us jerking off and whispering what we wanted to do to each other into the phone. It's been a strange, delightful comfort having David in my life again.

When we were kids I could never seem to get enough of David. Any time I spent at football practice or hanging out with other friends was time I wanted to be with David, talking or watching him do his homework. He's still the first thing on my mind when I wake up, on the edges of all my thoughts throughout the day. I even dream about him.

But when I pull my phone out of my pocket, Jason's name on the screen has my heart beating too fast for an entirely different reason. Jason and I don't exactly have a friendly relationship, especially since I moved out to the farm. Any messages we exchange are about family stuff, or the occasional nonsense drunken text Jason fires off when he's out partying. When I saw Jason at my parents' for Sunday dinner, the past three weeks he acted like his normal obnoxious self, getting too tipsy on beer before we ate and following in my father's footsteps with muttered comments that Lexi could stand to lose a few pounds. For a few days after my date with David, I'd been freaking out that Dan and Johnnie would tell my brother about what they'd seen. But nothing changed so I finally let myself relax into the assumption that the guys had been too drunk to relay what they saw.

Reading Jason's text, though, my worst fear comes true. His message is a screenshot of a conversation with Dan, stupidly nicknamed Dan "Tha Man" Rubinsky in Jason's contacts. I double-tap the image to bring it up large so I can read it. The conversation dates from a few weeks ago.

> Dan: *So your bro dumps Christi and now he's gay, huh?*
>
> Jason: *Dude, wtf ru talking about?*
>
> Dan: *Lol yeah. I saw him w a guy uptown Kingston last weekend.*
>
> Jason: *No way. Stop fucking around man. U were prob trashed.*
>
> Dan: *Lol yup. I was pretty faded. But it was DEF Nick and that weirdo he was friends with in hs. Your bro tried to confront me and shit.*
>
> Jason: *Shut the fuck up.*

I read the conversation over and over. I'm shockingly calm as I try to think of a reasonable reply. Before I can say anything, though, the little gray bubble pops up showing that Jason is typing something else. So I wait, gripping my phone almost hard enough to break it.

Jason: *Something u wanna tell me bro?*

My mind reels for a minute, frantically hoping Jason just wants to know the truth, that he might be supportive. I think about texting him back, even calling him and telling him that David and I are together and that I'm happy for the first time in years. Then my phone buzzes one more time.

Jason: *U shouldn't hang around with guys like that. Pops was right that ppl will get the wrong idea. Or maybe yr into that shit?*

The only emotion I allow in is anger. But even that is short-lived, burning through me hot and fast, extinguishing as quickly as it began. Heaving a sigh I type out a quick response, telling Jason we can talk about it on Sunday. Then I turn my phone off.

I UNBUCKLE THE passenger seat belt protecting the foil-wrapped strawberry rhubarb pound cake. I made it in the middle of the night once I'd resigned myself to the fact that I was not going to be getting any sleep. Thankfully the cake survived the bumpy car ride intact, not that anyone other than Cassie and Lexi will eat any. My mother acts like I'm insulting her cooking anytime I bring over food and Yiayia constantly claims to be on a diet. Dad and Jason can't be bothered to leave the wood-paneled den most of the time.

I glance across the street at David's house, wishing I could forget this whole afternoon and go sit in the backyard with my boyfriend. I grin like a little kid at the word. But the thought of David pushes me out of the car and toward my parents' house. I have to do this. I have to tell the truth. I have no idea if Jason said anything to my dad but at this point I don't even care. After spending the last two days trying to calm down my breathing and putting away a few too many beers before bed in an effort to knock myself out, I'm done. No part of me has any misconceptions that today is going to go well. Weirdly, though, I still feel light and excited as I push open the faux stained glass front door.

"Nico, is that you?" My mother's voice mingles with the sound of sizzling food, the roar of the vent fan over the stove, and the too-loud baseball game playing in the den.

"Hey, Mom," I call back, bending to take off my boots. The house smells the same as always, the scents of garlic, nutmeg and baked cheese mixing with the overpowering scent of "clean linen" air fresheners my mother seems to cram into every other outlet. The walls are crowded with gold-leafed reproductions of dour Greek Orthodox saints, unsmiling photos of our relatives in Corfu, and ornate needlepoint projects completed by my mom.

My sister-in-law Lexi pops her head around the kitchen archway and waves down the hall to me with a bright smile. She always seems so cheerful, easily deflecting my mom's guilt trips and somehow laughing at every stupid joke Jason makes. I wonder how she can handle living in this crowded house with her in-laws, not to mention how she puts up with my idiot brother. Since I last saw her, she's cut and dyed her hair. Jason has a weird obsession with women keeping their hair long and he loves blondes, so I wonder how much grief he's been giving her about her choice to dye her now shoulder-length hair back to its original deep brown.

"Your hair looks beautiful, Lex," I compliment her honestly as I walk into the kitchen. My mother is at the stove, stirring ground lamb and onions in an industrial-sized pan. I bend to kiss her head, then I turn to Yiayia who's sitting at the kitchen table drinking coffee and working on an elaborate jigsaw puzzle of wolves. She plants a light, violet-scented kiss on my cheek before refocusing on finding the middle piece she needs.

"Thank you!" Lexi chirps. "You're the only one who seems to like it. Jason freaked out when I came back from the salon. And Cole started crying when he saw me." I roll my eyes at her in sympathy.

Cassie bustles into the kitchen from the basement, lugging a huge metal container of olive oil. "Nick!" She beams at me and wraps me in a tight hug. I lift her off the ground a few inches, taking comfort in her familiar cigarette and Clinique perfume smell.

"I brought a cake." My sister takes it from my hands with a wink in the direction of our mom.

As expected, my mother wheels around from the stove and glares at the cake, like I brought a live grenade into her kitchen. She shakes her head at the baked good as Cassie unwraps the foil and slides it onto a blue and white china plate.

"Nico, I made koulourakia. You didn't need to bring anything." My mother sighs and returns her attention to the stove.

I've always wondered if my interest in baking and cooking bothers my mother more because she sees it as feminine or if it's because she worries my food might be better than hers. Cassie makes an exasperated gesture behind our mother's back like a teenager.

Thinking of teenagers, I wonder where my younger sister is. "Where's Doria?" I ask, popping one of the braided cookies neatly arranged on a clear plastic platter into my mouth. It's a little dry but still delicious. Absentmindedly I consider tinkering with the recipe I found online for these.

"She's out with that weird friend of hers," Yiayia pipes up, not looking up from her puzzle.

My mother interjects. "That Esther girl. I don't like all that makeup and purple hair. She looks like a witch."

"Ma, she's just goth." Cassie laughs. "And Doria texted me. She'll be back for supper."

I drift down the hall, following the smell of beer and drone of sports commentary. Jason and Theo, Cassie's husband, slump on the dingy tan microfiber sectional. One glance at their glassy eyes and zoned-out expressions tells me they're both stoned. Well, at least if Jason's mellowed out he might not get confrontational about me basically blowing off his gay text panic. Jason flicks his eyes over to me as I walk down the two steps into the sunken den but Theo keeps staring at the gigantic TV.

My father, practically lying down in his recliner, grunts at me as I put my hand on his shoulder in greeting. When I stand in front of him for a beat too long all he says is, "Move it, Nick. You're blocking the game."

Immediately I wish I could go back in the kitchen, or better yet escape with Cassie to the backyard to get her advice on this whole coming out thing. Instead though, I sink down onto the rocking chair in the corner that my mother sometimes sits in when she watches her soaps. The worn basket next to the chair overflows with her celebrity gossip magazines and needlepoint supplies. I wonder if this is the last time I'll be forced to sit in this dingy room, pretending to care about baseball, the only sport I can almost guarantee will make me drowsy, and not talking to the men in my family. After I tell them the truth, will my parents still expect me to come over every Sunday for supper? Will I even be welcome in this house anymore?

"Daddy!" My nephew Cole barrels into the room, clutching a Nerf football in one hand and a pair of ratty Velcro shoes in the other. "Mom says you'll play football with me. Can you?" Cole glances over at me and grins. "Oh hey, Uncle Nick!"

"Hey, bud." I return his enthusiastic smile, even though his presence immediately makes me falter in my whole living-your-truth coming out plan. If Jason and my dad decide I'm some kind of monster for being gay, I probably won't be able to see Cole anymore. No more picking him up from school a few times a month to go hiking or play basketball. No more taking him to the movies with Lexi and Cassie or bringing Archie over here so Cole can play fetch with him in the backyard for hours on end.

Jason's eyes stay glued to his phone screen and for a long moment he doesn't even seem to register his son's question. "Nah, kid. I'm watchin' the game. Go see if that Vinnie kid next door wants to play."

Cole's face falls for a fraction of a second, but I can tell he doesn't want Jason to see his disappointment. He shrugs, jams his feet into his shoes, and dashes out through the back door. The prospect of sitting in this room with my miserable dad, and Jason and Theo too stoned and absorbed in screens to even register anything is so intensely depressing I push up out of my chair and follow Cole into the yard.

"Here," I say, splaying my hands and grinning at my nephew. He throws the football to me and it wobbles through the air, sort of in my direction, landing with a soft thud on the patchy lawn between us. He kicks at the ground, muttering, but I grab the ball and call him over. For the next half hour I work with him on correct grip and form for throwing a spiral. We start with snapping the ball back and forth short distances, gradually increasing as he gains confidence and improves his form.

It's nice to see Cole so proud of himself. Jason spends so much time ignoring him, and although Lexi is a great mom, she tends to baby him and praises him for every little thing without allowing him to work through problems. Not that I'm in any place to judge her as a parent. I know she's doing her best and she's raising an awesome kid. When Cole gets in a few good, clean throws he starts celebrating like an NFL player, prompting the neighbor kid Vinnie to come out and ask to play. The two of them scamper off to Vinnie's yard, leaving me alone to sink down into one of the lawn chairs clustered around the tempered glass patio table.

I laugh to myself as I remember trying to teach David how to throw a football when we were in second grade. Every time I'd thrown the ball in his direction he'd deftly scooted away from it, shooting me a dirty look like I was torturing him. After a few failed attempts he rolled his eyes and admitted he found the whole thing boring and pointless. It was nice, though, having someone I could simply exist with. With all my other friends it was all sports and rough play and teasing and trying to one-up each other to do increasingly stupid shit. David and I could sit on the stoop and talk or lay in the grass to watch the clouds. David would make up silly stories sometimes and I loved getting lost in his imagination. I'd craved his simultaneously calm and lighthearted presence.

Shaking myself out of my memories, I glance over at the small raised bed garden I put in when I was living at home. I'd installed the beds right after high school, not long after I'd started working as a line cook at the diner. I wanted to grow a few fresh herbs, but soon my passion for gardening ignited and I was saving seeds and driving all over the state to check out specialty nurseries. It was nice to see that Lexi and Yiayia were keeping up the garden, even if my herb bed had been replaced with my grandmother's tangle of grocery store cucumber starts, and Lexi had swapped out the asparagus for Big Boy tomatoes.

"Thanks for playing with Cole." Lexi's voice sounds over the creak of the back door. She and Cassie drop into chairs next to me, both of them bearing glasses of the sweet white wine they love. Cassie glances around guiltily before lighting a cigarette.

"Don't tell Theo." Cassie rolls her eyes. "He wants me to get pregnant, so he thinks I should quit."

"You *should* quit," I say in a nagging tone, not meaning it but enjoying teasing her. She's been sneaking around about smoking since she was a teenager, always saying she's on the verge of quitting for good.

"Oh sure, says the guy who used to smoke weed every day." Cassie snorts.

"You try being the oldest son in this family. And being in the closet." Damn. I did not mean to let that slip in front of my sister-in-law. I guess my sexuality taking up so much mental space today loosened my lips too much.

Cassie shoots me a *what the fuck* look. Lexi looks baffled, her heavily filled-in eyebrows pulling together in confusion. She claps a hand over her mouth.

"I fuckin' knew it!" Lexi laughs, doubling over. Neither Cassie or I react at all. "You always notice my hair and clothes and stuff!"

Cassie glances at our sister-in-law out of the corner of her eye. "Um, look at Nick's sorry-ass outfit. He does not have that whole 'queer eye' thing going. No offense, Nick. I'm pretty sure he's just one of the only nice, observant people in our whole family."

Shrugging, I glance down at my T-shirt and shorts. They're not that bad. It's plain on Lexi's face that she wants to start interrogating me. Her lips quirk up in a smile. Thankfully, she doesn't seem bothered by my accidental confession. She's clearly hungry for information but I don't know what to say. I turn to Cassie, hoping she'll be ready with some of her self-help book advice. Since the conversation began she's pulled her wavy brown hair into a loose bun, and her big, caramel eyes are locked on my face.

"I'm telling them today." My effort not to let any of my emotion into my voice fails completely. Even I can hear the stress in my words. "I'm dating someone. Jason found out. But that's not why, I guess. I need to tell them." Saying the words out loud solidifies my conviction. Honestly I don't get why I spent so much time hiding the truth. My family will accept me or they won't. There isn't a whole lot I can do about it.

Cassie nods slowly, taking a long drag on her cigarette before stubbing it out in the overfull ashtray. "Who are you seeing?" she asks softly.

"Who do you think?" I laugh. Cassie knows about my past with David—the result of her grilling me incessantly and trying to solve all my problems once she found out I was gay.

She claps her hands together. "Yay! I knew you guys were, like, soul mates!"

"Wait...who? I'm so confused." Lexi looks back and forth between me and my sister.

"His friend David. The guy who lives across the street you were, like, positive was a model? That dude. He and Nick have been besties since they were in kindergarten. David's always been, I don't know, just super gay. Like, he told everyone in middle school, had the whole artsy drama kid thing going. It pissed our dad off big time. But he and Nick stayed friends and they started messing around toward the end of high school."

"Thank you. That will be all," I cut in, shooting my blabbermouth sister a sharp glare.

Cassie is unfazed. "So why do you think Jason knows? I haven't heard anything. And you *know* if he'd mentioned anything, Mom would not let me hear the end of it."

I pull out my phone and show Cassie the text exchange. Lexi cranes to look at the screen, and when she reads over the texts, she shakes her head. "I'm sorry. My husband is a moron."

As much as I want to commiserate I simply shrug like the whole thing hadn't left me on the razor's edge of a panic attack for the past forty-eight hours. The soft brush of Cassie's hand over mine brings my focus back to the present conversation.

"You know they're not gonna be happy though, right?" My sister's expression is pained, and she tightens her grip around my fingers. "Mom might be okay about it. But since the election, Dad has been..." She cuts her eyes to Lexi as if searching for a way to explain the situation.

"He listens to that stupid radio show all the time. And that psycho host is not exactly positive about the whole gay thing. I hate when he talks that way in front of Cole. There're kids in his class with gay parents." Lexi downs the rest of her wine like a shot.

My father basically eats, breathes, and dreams conservative media. He's never hidden his open disgust with homosexuality. But over the past few years, since the passage of marriage equality and with the increased presence of a gay community in town, his hatred has deepened and become more vocal.

My whole body flinches as Yiayia raps on the glass panel of the crookedly hung porch door. She gestures for us to come inside for dinner. I plant my feet on the ground and breathe. The air feels thin. Hot dread lodges in my throat as I follow Lexi and Cassie into the house.

Supper is the same as always. My mother and Yiayia barely sit, clomping up and down the stairs to the basement "beer fridge" to get refills for Theo, Jason, and my dad. Doria slinks in at the last minute, her choppy bob all mussed, giant flannel hanging down to her knees, reeking of mouthwash and perfume to mask the smell of weed. Once everyone settles in with heaping plates of salad, pasticcio and the weird mix of steam-in-the-bag veggies my mother insists on serving, Yiayia says grace. Cole starts eating his food before she finishes the endless stream of Greek prayer. My leg won't stop bouncing under the table. Even though my mom's pasticcio is one of my favorites, with savory layers of noodles, ground lamb, and spiced béchamel, I have to force each bite down with a gulp of water.

When I hazard a glance at Cassie, she's pushing her food around on her plate. She's clearly as nervous as I am. My dad and Theo heatedly discuss goings-on at the diner, which grabs my attention. Theo recently started putting in kitchen shifts and it kind of seems like he's blowing it. I gather something fell through with the contractor he worked for, but I can't follow their conversation.

Doria's so preoccupied with her phone I haven't even had the chance to say hi. I push down another twinge of regret. Now that my little sister is a junior in high school she has understandably zero interest in spending time with me. If I stop coming by for dinner, I probably won't see her much. When she was still in middle school, when Christi and I first got married, Doria loved spending the night at our apartment. She and Christi would always make me watch horror movies, a genre I hated, but still it was nice. I would make us popcorn and hot chocolate and Christi and Doria would tease me for trying to leave the room anytime something gross or terrifying happened on screen. One of the few highlights from my disastrous sham of a marriage.

Cassie's knee bumping mine under the table jars me from my thoughts and I realize she's glancing between me and our mother. My mom's eyebrows arch to where her fingers knot into her black curls.

"Sorry, Mom, I was spacing out. What?"

She heaves an exasperated sigh. I don't blame her. Half the time she talks, my dad and Jason ignore her completely. "I *said* Katie told me this morning at church that you never called her. I thought you'd want to ask her out on a date."

And there it is. My opening for the big gay reveal, offered up on a silver platter. Drawing in a deep breath I go over all the things I'd planned to say. I'd hoped to drop the topic in casually, although I hadn't been able to figure out the particulars for that part. I would calmly, clearly tell them I'm gay. I would explain that it had been a struggle for me to come to grips with it but I was happy now that I was in a relationship. I would ask, but not plead for their support.

I glance at Jason. He's eyeing me with a mix of disgust and confusion. Cassie has become fascinated with the lace embroidery of Greek keys on the tablecloth.

"Oh yeah, Mom, I don't think so. Katie's nice but I'm kinda seeing someone."

Jason scoffs, his face now radiating full disgust as he mutters something under his breath. My mother looks so utterly thrilled that my old wish that I could just be straight slams into me with shocking intensity. It's a ferocious desire to be the person she wants, to be a son she can be proud of, to be a whole different person. The same desire that led me to marry Christi and push David away.

"Who is she, Nico?" My mom and Yiayia have both perked up considerably. Theo and my dad remain, thankfully, oblivious to our conversation. Maybe I can slip this whole confession in super quickly and wait for my dad to figure it out later.

My breathing thing is back in full force. Even though I know it'll make it worse, I compel myself to draw in deep, even breaths. They come in as tiny sips of air.

"Goddamn it, Nick. Tell her the damn truth. Tell our mother who you're fuckin' with." Jason almost seems to be enjoying this. Like he's been waiting for years for me to mess up and he's savoring the moment.

Lexi and my mother both rush to chastise him for his language. Lexi glances at Cole and my mother eyes my Yiayia. I am motionless. Sometimes in books I'd read descriptions of characters being stunned into silence and I always thought it seemed like an exaggeration. But clearly it's real, because I am. Rationally, I know my heart is beating, that I'm drawing in oxygen, that blood is moving through my veins. But it's like every cell in my body has powered down. I do notice that Jason's agitation has pulled our father out of his conversation with Theo.

"You should tell them, Nick." Cassie's voice is soft.

But I can't get it out. My dad's eyes narrow. Even Doria has looked up from her phone. Is everyone at the table staring at me?

"He's messing around with that fucker across the street. David." Jason spits his name out like bile at the end of throwing up.

"Watch your mouth," Lexi snaps. The command seems to infuriate my father and Lexi withers under his glare.

"Is this true, Nickolas?" My father looks incredulous, desperate for this whole thing to be one of Jason's stupid jokes.

I clear my throat. "Yes." Saying the word, there is nothing. No burst of relief. No swell of fear. Nothing. I look at my father and watch as his features rearrange into a stormy expression.

"I knew him hanging out with that guy was going to fuck him up," Jason mutters to Theo, who nods but looks weirdly bored by the conversation.

"Um, that's so not how it works," Doria drawls.

Finally I manage to string words together, but they're not the ones I'd planned. "I've always been gay. I tried not to be. That's why I got with Christi, but we all know that didn't work." I don't know why I think bringing up my divorce is going to help the situation.

Tears well in my mother's eyes, smearing her mascara and streaking down her tan cheeks. "*Nickolakis mou.* Are you sure? Maybe Christi wasn't the right girl.

You need a family, a good wife. Someone to care for you." Her voice breaks but she looks hopeful, like the thought never occurred to me.

"Mom, I was miserable married to Christi, but it wasn't her fault. She did care for me. And it was wrong for me to lie to her. I was losing it, drinking and trying to escape everything."

I glance at Cole. He looks confused and stressed out by the sudden tension in the room.

I try to calm things down and mollify my mother, sharing a truth I haven't even thought about broaching with David yet. "I do want a family. I want to get married someday and I want kids. I want all of that, just with a husband."

My father stands up, his chair scraping back then clattering against the peeling linoleum. "Enough." He glares at me.

I guess my husband comment probably put him over the edge. The rage etched into his face is so familiar, I'm almost comforted by it. I know what's coming.

His words are slow, deliberate when he speaks. "Do not come back to this house. I don't want to see you. No son of mine will choose this...lifestyle. Look what you've done to your mother. How could you be so selfish?" He shakes his head. "You should be ashamed of yourself." With that he picks up his chair and sits back down, gesturing to my mother to get him more food.

I turn to my mom, apologizing to her for ruining dinner, wanting to apologize for so much more. She says nothing. Then I press a kiss to the top of Cassie's head and pad quietly to the cramped foyer. The silence in the house is heavy as I pull on my boots and close the door behind me, maybe for the last time.

Chapter Fourteen

Nick

June

I'm scooped out and hollow as I walk the short distance to my Jeep and move it across the street to park in the Websters' brick driveway. I don't even know if David is home, but I do know my dad won't want my car on his property. When Dr. Webster pulls open the front door, he must see something on my face, because he claps a shaking, bony hand to my shoulder, regarding me for a long and uncomfortable moment.

"Your mother will come around. Your dad..." He pulls a face and makes a small shrugging motion.

Is Dr. Webster an actual mind reader? I hadn't even told David about any concrete plans for coming out to my family. I couldn't stomach the thought of disappointing him if I made a big deal of it then acted like a coward at the last minute.

"David's in the kitchen."

I try to smile but my mouth is too tight. The attempt is probably pretty grim. Exhaustion washes over me and all I want to do is lie down in David's bed with him on top of me and drift off to sleep. As I walk through the archway into the kitchen an actual grin appears on my face. David is, in theory, doing the dishes. Or at least that's what I guess since he has a sponge in his hand and the sink is full of suds. But he has headphones jammed into his ears and he's dancing around the small kitchen with so much enthusiasm I can't stifle my laughter.

David has always been graceful, and honestly he's a good dancer. Throughout middle school and high school he designed awesome sets for our underfunded school productions. Sometimes, though, he'd been cast in small roles and he was always great. But right now, as he half dances, half cleans in his dad's kitchen, his moves are corny as hell. He bounces and bops around in front of the sink, singing softly along to the music.

I can't even imagine what David could be listening to that anyone would ever dance to. Everything he puts on is weird, depressing indie music that doesn't exactly inspire the need to move. A rising tide of tenderness for him fills the hollow in my gut. He's so fucking adorable in his obscenely tight black skinny jeans and one of those T-shirts he wears that manages to somehow look fashionable despite being plain cotton. I wrap my arms around his waist and he drops the cup he was washing into the sink. It splashes both of us with soapy water but thankfully nothing breaks.

"You scared the shit out of me!" he squeaks a little too loud before ripping his headphones out of his ears and wheeling around to face me. Squeezing him close, I finally feel like I can take in a steady breath as he runs his wet hands up and down my arms. His gaze on me is intent, and I wonder if he's doing the mind-reading he must have learned from his parents. Hoping to distract him for a moment I lean down and kiss the freckles dusting his nose and high cheekbones.

"Sorry," I sigh against his skin. "What're you listening to? I liked watching you dance."

Heat radiates from his face. "Ugh, you are such a creep. How long were you watching me?" David pulls his phone from his pocket and thumbs around, setting it in a clean bowl before restarting whatever song he'd been listening to. An infectious techno beat pours out of the phone's tinny speaker. "It's Robyn. Good music to cheer you up." He looks at me for another long moment. The song sounds kind of familiar, but I've never heard of the artist.

"Wow, I actually like this. It's nice to know that you listen to stuff other than people, like, chanting and crying while playing old-timey instruments."

I grin and grab his hands, moving us to the music. I'm an absolutely horrible dancer, lacking any sense of rhythm, but David doesn't seem to mind as he laughs and does most of the actual dancing while I hold him and let the tension drain out of my body. As the song ends I pick him up, which makes him scoff and mutter something about me being a caveman. Setting him down gently on the counter, I step between his thighs. I kind of love manhandling him and I know he likes it too.

"I told my parents I'm gay."

David's eyes go huge at my words. His hand fumbles around behind him to turn off the music, but his gaze stays locked on mine. "Holy shit, Nick. Did Jason find out?"

I wonder if he'll be disappointed to know that my brother basically did out me. That I wasn't brave and empowered. That I told my parents the truth only when I'd pretty much been forced to. "Kind of," I hedge, staring past David's worried face and directing all my attention to a framed photo of David and his parents hanging on the wall. The three of them sit clustered around a campfire, his mother's long grayish-blonde hair secured in a frizzy braid, her hands clasped in David's. Dr. Webster looks at her adoringly and David appears wildly happy.

Why couldn't my family be like that? David's mom was the most interesting and opinionated woman I'd ever met. She'd been a professor of psychology at Bard and had practiced as a therapist for years. She always considered the silly kid things David and I said deeply, weighing her words before she spoke. She also seemed to have the strongest of the weird, observant listening-skill superpowers their whole family possessed.

David's parents were supportive when David told them he was gay, but they didn't make a big deal about it. He told me about coming out to them in a bubbling, excited rush one afternoon, as we walked home together after one of my boring middle school basketball games. He'd been so thrilled. His joy at putting into words all the things he'd been feeling was contagious. Somehow, even as a little kid, I'd known David and I were similar in that way. There was no way of knowing if being gay was what drew us together, or if we just got along because we were the same age and lived across the street from each other. But I knew that afternoon, as David described his parents' hugs and kind words, that if I told my parents that same truth, it would be the end of my relationship with them.

"NICK, ARE YOU okay?" David's hands gently cup my face, turning my gaze to him. The gesture is possessive and comforting in a way that makes me want to squeeze him close. "What happened?" He's nervous but trying not to show it.

It's draining, explaining the whole thing from start to finish: Jason's text, my mom bringing up dating, Jason telling my family that I was with David, and my father's less than stellar reaction. When I finally finish talking I realize I'm gripping David's thighs too tight, but if it bothers him he's not showing it. Instead, he's looking at me with a soft expression, his plush lips parted and his eyes warm.

"How are you feeling?" he asks softly.

I shrug, not really sure. Although I'll still see Cassie and get updates from her, I'll miss my mom, and Lexi, and Doria, and Cole. I'll even miss my Yiayia's antics. My throat tightens. At the same time, though, the thought of being legitimately out, kissing David in public without worrying that something will get back to my family, is soothing. "Confused," I say finally.

David nods sympathetically. "Can you say more about that?"

I narrow my eyes at him. He's always been good at these feelings conversations. Dragging out a sigh I try to explain myself. "I feel more like myself now. But also like I fucking wasted my whole life trying to be the person my dad wanted me to be. It's so...right being with you." I drag a hand over my face. I'm probably making almost zero sense. "But yeah, being gay is part of who I am. I know that. It had gotten to the point where there wasn't a good reason to keep it a secret anymore. But I—" I pause.

I intentionally left out my mom's comments about kids and a family. The last thing I want is to pressure David, so early into our relationship, with my desire to get married and have a family someday. I have no idea how he feels about marriage, much less having kids. That conversation doesn't need to happen today.

"Family's important to me. And I'll miss spending time with my nephew. I took care of Doria when she was little but I barely know her now. So I guess I kind of feel like I lost them." It's like saying the words out loud makes them real and face falls. I don't have a family anymore.

"Nick." David's voice is feather soft as he twines his arms around my neck. "What do you need right now?"

The answer is out of my mouth before I even have time to process it. "You." I manage to hold back the second word. *Forever.*

Leaning forward slightly, David presses an almost chaste kiss to my lips. Just a brush of his mouth over mine. The cool touch of his soft skin, sinewy thighs on either side of me, and his soothing fresh smell all push the day's stress and loss from my mind.

"How do you want me?" he asks in a lilting tone.

My cock wakes up and my stomach fills with fire. Fantasies flashing through my mind's eye shift from David and I waking up twined together in my bed every morning to me fucking David against the counter right now. Jerking those tight black pants down and sliding the tip of my tongue up and down his thighs until he's begging me to blow him. Dragging him up to his bedroom and letting him ride my dick.

"Can we do that here?" My voice is shaky and I'm not sure if it's from the spear of lust sliding through me or from worry that Dr. Webster could walk in and catch me on the verge of railing his son.

"Well not *right* here." David smirks.

I chuck him under the chin. "No, I mean in your dad's house. It seems sort of rude."

David slides down off the counter so his body presses tight against mine. "We could go up to my room. I remember making out in there once or twice." His grin is devilish.

Now my dick is fully hard and I'm desperate to do more than make out. Although I love that too. I bend down to whisper in his ear. "Will you ride my cock?" I'm kind of embarrassed voicing something I've been fantasizing about for months, if not years.

In reply he pulls me into a searing kiss, slipping his tongue against mine, gripping my hair tight. I'm pretty sure this whole sudden veer in the direction of sex is David trying to pull me out of sulking, but I'm grateful because I don't want to think or talk about anything. It's like my mind won't let me feel anything other than hot, agonizing desire. The only sensations I want are him in my arms and his channel clenching around me as I slide into him.

We scramble up to his room in silence, and the moment he locks the door behind him we're on each other again frantically taking off our clothes. I think I tear his T-shirt as I tug it roughly over his head but if he's upset about it he doesn't say so. David's bed is a double, kind of tiny, the same one he's had since grade school. I yank him down onto it, pulling him so he's sitting in my lap, his bare back pressed to the heated skin of my chest. My heart races. I want to groan at the slide of his ass against my cock but I stifle the sound. Easing myself back, I lean against his headboard and the neat stack of pillows propped against it.

"I've fantasized about this for years," David murmurs as he reaches into his nightstand, pulling a small bottle of lube from the drawer. I wonder if he means having sex in this room or him sitting on my dick. Either way I'm desperate for anything he wants to give. I press soft kisses to his neck. My lips brush his pulse point; his heart beats hummingbird fast. I start to slide slicked fingers inside him, to stretch him and work him up to a fever pitch of pleasure. But he shakes his head no and grinds on my cock.

"Please fuck me. I want you so much," he begs.

So I comply, pushing into his ass in a single well-lubricated thrust. And fuck he's tight. I don't think I'll ever get enough of him hot and clenching around me.

With a sharp intake of breath he starts to move in my lap. I reach around to wrap my fingers around his erection, pumping him in time with his slippery gyrations on top of me. He snakes one arm around my neck and nuzzles my face, breath coming hot and fast against my skin. I can't keep my eyes off him.

"Oh my god, Nick," David whines, gripping my thigh with his free hand hard enough to bruise. I can tell he's trying to be quiet, putting all his energy into his steady movements and holding me tight instead of crying out.

The sensation of him on top of me, controlling the pace and the angle, is liberating and beautiful to watch. He's taking charge of his own pleasure, fucking himself on my cock. It's all too good. I could come at any minute so I breathe in deeply, focusing on running my hand up and down his leaking hardness. Something in me needs to see him come first, needs to know I'm doing this right, needs to know that I'm showing him with my body how much I want him.

"Yes. Just like that. Please," he breathes, starting to move on me faster, gripping my thigh somehow even harder. His channel flexes and clenches around my hardness as he digs his nails into my flesh. The pain blends with the pleasure perfectly and my balls tighten and my cock surges. "You feel so good."

"Mmm. Oh fuck, baby," I groan against his neck, biting down gently on the soft, creamy flesh to stifle the moan building in my chest. "So do you. You're amazing." My gaze rakes over his smooth, corded body writhing on mine, at his parted lips, his long auburn lashes brushing the smattering of freckles across his cheekbones.

His eyes squeeze adorably tight as he comes, his body going still and rigid, head tipping back, ass clenching hard around my dick. He cries out my name, too loud, but I can't seem to care about being discreet anymore. He's trembling and I feel his orgasm racking his body all around me as he spills into my fist and onto his stomach. My chest tightens. But it isn't shortness of breath. I pull him close to me and then I'm pouring my release into his ass, holding back the words on the tip of my tongue. *I love you. I love you. I love you.*

We settle side by side in the tiny bed and I wrap my arms around David, drawing him to me. He's still breathing fast as he cuddles into my chest. I glance around his room, trying to take stock of my emotions. Too much has happened in the past couple of hours so I force my thoughts in a safe direction. I run my eyes over the almost comically tall pile of books on the nightstand: a medical book about stroke recovery, a few art books, one that looks suspiciously like a Scottish-themed romance novel, and a bunch of fiction titles by authors I've never heard of.

The band posters of our youth have been replaced with a few framed pieces of art. I assume these were done by friends or purchased at a gallery, because the styles are different from the delicate, soft realism I associate with David's work. The walls, still painted sage green, reflect the diffuse early evening sunlight filtering in through bamboo blinds. But focusing on the décor of David's room doesn't help and my mind snaps back to the emotions I'm trying to tamp down.

The fact that I love David isn't a surprise. Part of me has always known that I loved him. I was drawn to him from the first moment I saw him working in the garden with his mom when they moved into the house across the street. Then, of course, my feelings for him weren't romantic. I knew he was beautiful and seemed interesting and funny in a way I could never hope to be. When he finally spoke to me on the first day of kindergarten I was dazzled.

"You're Nick, right? From across the street?" He'd perched on the edge of my desk. David was pretty, delicate and light, with a tenderness in his eyes I'd never seen in anyone before. And when he said my name it came out smooth and warm, like a soft pebble on the beach you might slip into your pocket to keep. So different from the harsh barks and nagging sighs I was used to. He'd been immediately friendly, leaning close to me as he asked about my favorite color and chattered on about a book he'd read with his dad the night before. He invited me into a bright, slightly chaotic world so unlike my own life of staying out of my dad's way and trying to cheer up my mom. I never wanted to leave.

Loving David is a strong current carrying me to a still, clear lake. He's my inevitable destination.

"YOU'RE SERIOUSLY CHARGING five dollars for these?" The woman's face pulls into a tight scowl. The object of her anger, I discover, is a pint of plum tomatoes. Hector, who was handling the transaction, freezes. He glances from her to the tomatoes to me.

"Um, yes?" he says, shrugging. Her glare intensifies.

"Why would I pay that?" she snaps, tucking a crisp twenty back into the pocket of her distressed jeans. Oddly I would have pegged her as another Brooklyn graphic designer renting an Airbnb in town and snapping nonstop photos of every mundane thing. But those types don't usually argue about prices. Most Hudson Valley farmers upcharge at urban markets and people from the city usually comment on how cheap everything is "upstate."

"Well... we're the only farm to have the bigger tomatoes this early. They're an interesting varietal—" Hector starts to explain in a warm, even tone.

"Look, lady, if you don't like them, don't buy them." A bored female voice from behind the woman cuts Hector off. The flat intonation and almost audible eye roll reminds me of Doria.

And when Brooklyn Lady stalks off in a swirl of spicy perfume, muttered insults, and shiny blonde hair, I realize it was, in fact, my teenage sister who spoke.

"Wow." I bark out a laugh as Doria drifts up to our market table. Since I last saw her, she's dyed her hair cherry red and has transformed her style yet again. This time she's moved from 90s grunge to 60s beatnik. She wears a thin, sleeveless black turtleneck, cropped black pants, canvas shoes like David wears sometimes, and a huge pair of dark sunglasses. She looks nice. "Thanks for scaring away my customer." I shake my head at her to downplay how touched I am by her snarky defense. She hates when I get all mushy.

Doria shrugs. "So I can assume you still won't be coming over for dinner tomorrow? Our wonderful father hasn't had a change of heart?"

"No," I say quietly, busying my hands with organizing the change in the cash box. "How's everything at the house?"

"Shitty as usual," Doria drawls. "Cassie hasn't really been coming over anymore either. And Lexi has been even more annoying. She was asking me all these weird questions about college the other day." My sister shudders. Even though I can't see her eyes through the dark lenses, I can feel Doria's eye roll. "Mom's all weepy and weird. Dad's still an asshole. So yeeaaah."

I don't even know what to say. Cassie told me on the phone last week that she wasn't talking to our father and also mentioned how depressed our mom had seemed since I came out. Of course Jason and my father stopped visiting the market altogether.

"Sorry if I made things awkward," I say, trying and failing to meet my sister's eye. "It wasn't how I wanted it to go down. Not that I had high hopes or anything. Just, I know I didn't handle it very well."

Doria falls quiet for a long moment and I can tell she's thinking. She's done this since she was a little kid. Her overall lack of concern with things like being polite or adhering to people's expectations means she's perfectly comfortable with pausing a conversation for uncomfortable lengths of time so she can consider her words.

"I never thought you'd tell them." She pauses again for another long moment.

While I try to process the fact that my younger sister knew the whole time I was gay, a chef buys up the full stock of tomatoes that had so offended my previous almost-customer.

"I'm glad you finally did something *real* for once. Plus David's cool as fuck. I like his art. Anyway, it's pretty sweet having confirmation that I'm not the only queer in the family." At this she grins, turns on her heel, and stalks away into the crowd.

I want to call after her. I want to give her the support I never had growing up under our father's roof. I want to ask her if our parents know, although I can guess the answer to that question. I even want to grill her about how she'd figured me out. Instead, though, I can only chuckle and shake my head.

Chapter Fifteen

David

June

Hell is kayaking on the Hudson River in eighty-degree humid heat. I cast a glance at Anna, knowing her flushed face will mirror my misery. Because her incredibly fair skin burns as easily as a newborn baby's, she's all bundled up in a long-sleeve denim shirt, an enormous sunhat, and flowy linen pants. Every article of clothing drenched with river water, she glares at me. Jenna and Nick are both oblivious to our suffering as they do the majority of the paddling in the front of our respective double kayaks. They're carrying on a conversation about solar energy that I would try to care about if I weren't grotesquely sweaty, exhausted, and worried about falling into the damn river. I probably should have mentioned to Nick that I'm terrified of deep water.

"Why?" Anna mouths at me and I can only hang my head in response. For the thousandth time I wonder why we couldn't go out to brunch for a double date like normal people. Or if Nick and Jenna were going to insist on something outdoorsy, at least go on an easy hike or check out the swimming hole Nick had been raving about. But no. We are kayaking.

"Okay back there?" Nick turns around, flashing me his most excited, open grin. All my grumpiness toward him melts away immediately. He's clearly having a great time, so I should at least try to enjoy this activity. Plus he's shirtless. His muscular back, tanned and sweaty and rippling with his movements, pushes the last scrap of resentment from my mind.

"Great!" I reply, trying to force as much cheerfulness into my voice as possible.

Nick chuckles. "Baby, you're a horrible liar. But I was thinking we could stop for lunch on the bank about a half mile ahead. There's a nice place to picnic. We can relax and eat our sandwiches."

An almost orgasmic wave of relief washes over me at the thought of getting out of this yellow plastic deathtrap. Then I the sliding prickle of something disgusting crawls on my neck and I almost overturn the tiny boat in my desperation to claw it off me. Jenna starts shaking with silent laughter at my antics. I can tell Nick is trying hard to take me seriously as he simultaneously steadies the kayak and helps me remove whatever bug is tormenting me. Okay, so it was a butterfly. But it still felt creepy crawling all over me like that.

When we finally drag the boats onto the rocky bank, a process requiring getting absolutely soaked in questionably clean river water, I am very much done with this whole outdoors thing. I have to admit the spot is nice though. Nick rummages around in the cooler as Jenna pulls a mercifully dry picnic blanket out of a storage compartment in the kayak she shared with Anna. While Jenna and Nick make efficient work of setting up our picnic, both looking toned and sun-kissed, Anna and I quickly dart into the shade of a tree to commiserate.

"There was a spider riding next to me the whole damn time." Anna shivers as she strips off her life vest. Apparently Jenna and Nick are such strong swimmers, with all their triathlon training and whatever the fuck else, that they chose to forgo the life jackets. So Anna and I look like little kids along for the ride. But at least we won't drown.

"That fucking butterfly almost killed me." I fan myself dramatically. "And I don't get why everyone thinks they're so beautiful. Have you ever looked at one up close? They're creepy as hell. Only the wings are nice and even those are all chalky and weird."

Anna shrugs. Although she shares my general fear of insects, her animal-rights vegan principles force her to trap wayward spiders and flies in cups and release them back into the wild, cringing all the way. I smash them under heavy magazines and then gag as I chuck the whole thing in the trash can.

"Okay!" Nick gestures for Anna and me to return to the sun-dappled spot where he and Jenna set up lunch. "I packed two kinds of sandwiches. There's roasted red pepper with hummus and arugula. And then there's marinated cherry tomatoes with avocado." He beams at Anna then settles down onto the blanket. My heart, once again, melts. How is Nick so damn thoughtful? He made the two kinds of sandwiches I mentioned in passing weeks ago as being Anna's favorites. The idea that he would go out of his way to impress my best friend makes me want to crawl into Nick's lap.

Anna raises her eyebrows in approval as she settles next to Jenna and grabs one of each type of sandwich. The four of us eat quietly for a peaceful few moments and I start to enjoy myself. This part is nice. The water, from a safe distance, is deep blue, sparkling under the summer sun. Birds call to each other in the trees around us and a gentle, grassy-smelling breeze has picked up. I'm often taken aback by how nice the air smells here. No exhaust fumes or hot garbage or the weird burning plastic smell that used to linger outside my apartment. There's just the mineral tang of water, the rich sweetness of wet soil, and the green scent of plant life. I stare across the wide expanse of the river at the opposite bank and watch as lush foliage sways in the wind.

"So did you guys decide if you're going next weekend?" Jenna asks through a mouthful of sandwich.

Nick shoots her a reproachful look before glancing over at me. Okay, so clearly they've been discussing the argument Nick and I had about going to Pride. After Nick came out to his family, I thought it might be nice to spend a weekend in the city and check out a few Pride events. I loved participating in Chicago Pride with the youth group. Not only was it a ton of fun, but the atmosphere was supportive and inclusive. Nick needs, in my estimation, more of that in his life. I'd argued that it would benefit him to see queer people celebrating their identity and to explore the diversity of the LGBTQ community.

Nick shrugged off the idea, saying he hated crowds and didn't need some big party in the city to be comfortable with himself. He figured it was just something he had to work through on his own. This, of course, spiraled into a fight as Nick started accusing me of being bored with living in a small town and I suggested he was still embarrassed to be with me because I don't try to present as straight.

"Oh you mean the Pride thing?" Anna pipes up. "Because, David, I think you're being a little ridiculous pushing this. Nick doesn't want to go. So what? Why are you being so weird about it?"

"Thank you!" Nick laughs, shoving my shoulder playfully and grinning at Anna. "He acted like I wanted to break up because I don't want to go sweat my ass off in the city and hang around and get drunk with a bunch of people."

The anger from our argument returns in a flash and I shift away from him. "Um, you don't even know what it's like, Nick. It's so much more than that, and if you gave it a chance, you would see how awesome Pride can be. Especially since you just came out."

"Gotta say, dude, I'm on David's side with this one. I went to San Francisco Pride right after I moved to California and it was a blast. There was such an awesome vibe. It was the first time I ever met another queer woman of color. So who knows, Nick, maybe you'd meet other hunky, gay organic farmers." Jenna winks at me. I try not to let myself feel jealous at the mere thought.

Nick shakes his head. "But I don't need to meet other guys. I have David. I don't care about anyone else."

I narrow my eyes at him, unsure if he's being sweet or trying to charm me into ending the argument. So I decide to push back. Just in case. "That's not even what it's about. You grew up in an environment where being gay was coded as wrong. Wouldn't it be nice to celebrate yourself, celebrate us, publicly a little?"

A slight flush creeps into Nick's cheeks and he starts digging around in the cooler, avoiding my gaze. *Shit. Too far, David.* Nick beats himself up about any inclination toward keeping our relationship a secret. Before I can backtrack, though, Jenna's nodding and coming to my defense.

"Exactly! Your stupid dad and other assholes like him can fuck right off. Don't adhere to their bullshit ideals. Go to the city, show off your fine-ass body, make out with your cute boyfriend, and have some fun for once!"

Anna's face blooms bright red. And great…Jenna and I have managed to piss off our respective partners. "Look," Anna snaps, "just because we don't like crowds and aren't into going to events all the time doesn't mean Nick and I aren't proud of our sexual identity. But you two," her gaze flicks from me to Jenna, "you both grew up in supportive families. Plus you both fucking love attention." At this Anna grins fondly.

Glancing at Jenna, I realize she's in the same headspace as me. She probably wants to argue, but she also looks kind of guilty about this whole thing. She grabs Anna's hand and presses a kiss to her knuckles before shrugging at Nick. He still looks a little miffed but when I move back toward him he pulls me close and kisses the top of my head. I want to sigh with relief. Even small arguments with him still make my stomach hurt and send my mind racing in the direction of total relationship destruction. Part of me still refuses to believe this is real.

"Anyway," Nick grumbles, "it's a pointless discussion because I can't take any time off. As it is, we're swamped." This comment sets Nick and Jenna off on a lengthy discussion about hiring additional staff for the summer. I catch Anna's eye, trying to telepathically apologize to her. She turns her nose up at me dramatically for a moment before laughing and shaking her head.

The rest of the picnic is argument-free and we lounge around on the riverbank for a blissful hour, drinking iced tea (that of course Nick made himself and packed in recycled glass jars,) and dozing off in the sun like housecats. Anna takes a million pictures of everything and Jenna teases the two of us for being so into Instagram. Jenna doesn't use social media at all and basically thinks all technology is evil. She still uses a flip phone and everything. Nick has to go and ruin the afternoon, though, by looking at the time and declaring we need to kayak back to the rental place.

"Leave me here," I groan, throwing my arm over my eyes to block out the sun and the reality of getting back in the boat. "This is my home now." Then Nick's warm, thick arms come around me, pulling me up into his lap. I have a momentary flashback of him fucking me in my bedroom after he came out. Now the cold river water doesn't seem like such a bad prospect after all. He covers my mouth with his for a long, perfect moment before yanking me to my feet.

"Oh this is a cute one!" Anna chirps, showing me her phone screen. She snapped a picture of Nick and me kissing. It really is cute. My face tips up toward his and both of our eyes have fluttered closed. Nick's lips turn up in a smile so adorable I want to drag him into the woods and let him have his way with me. We look happy. We look like two people in love. The thought has my heart beating fast. Nick beams at Anna.

"Can you send that to me?" he asks.

"Me too!" I request as an idea starts to take shape in my head. I'm so preoccupied with thoughts of painting as we paddle back, I don't even mind (that much) when a fly lands on my hand and I capsize the kayak.

Chapter Sixteen

David

June

I show Nick my phone screen in disbelief, my heart still hammering in my chest. Holy fucking shit. Six hundred and fifty-two likes. Almost two thousand new followers. I'd posted the painting of Nick and I kissing on the bank of the Hudson early this morning after spending a few days transforming Anna's photo into a dreamy Technicolor portrait. I'd worked in a larger scale than usual and, honestly, I loved how the piece turned out. It was fun rendering Nick in his shirtless glory and backward baseball cap, his arms around me, my face pressed up to his and eyes squeezed shut in delight.

Deciding to post the painting to my page on the first official day of NYC Pride, I labored for far too long over the caption. Writing the stupid captions to go along with my paintings is, without a doubt, the hardest part of sharing my work via social media. I suck at it. But posts with clever captions tend to get more likes. And this, I suppose, is my life now. Trying to be clever so more random people will validate me via the internet. After typing and deleting drafts that escalated in stupidity, I settled for a sincere and hopefully only slightly cheesy end result:

Hi all! This is me and my wonderful boyfriend, Nick. Because Nick is a curmudgeon and a busy organic farmer, we couldn't make it to #NYCPride this year. But I want to take a minute to share our story here in honor of Pride! Nick and I have been best friends since we were kids and recently reconnected when I moved back to my hometown. The two of us becoming a couple helped give Nick the courage to come out to his family. Tbh, it did not go great. This is an unfortunate reality that so many queer people still have to live with. But we can rely on the support of our chosen families, friends, and community. Pride matters. Anyway - thank you all for being a supportive social media fam and caring about my art! Lots of love- David #gaysofinstagram #LGBTQ #Pride #queerart #terribleathashtags

When I pulled my phone out of my pocket after dinner, the screen was so crowded with notifications that hot panic prickled my skin. My first thought was that something was wrong with my dad. But all the notifications were from Instagram. It seemed that shortly after I posted the painting it was regrammed by Kenny Thomas, a queer advice columnist and activist I'd admired since I was a teenager. He posted my painting with the caption: *Really loving the work by @davidwebsterart. Also is it weird that I think this painting is super hot?*

Almost immediately, my page flooded with followers and the post got more than triple the likes I usually got for my work.

Settled onto Nick's couch, I scroll through comments as Nick and Archie both breathe down my neck. My whole body is weird and hollow and numb. This is incredibly surreal. The majority of the comments are supportive, making me grin frantically as I read them. I even have a handful of direct messages inquiring about custom work and commissions. A few of the comments are weird as hell. And naturally there are a few I need to delete. Whenever I come across a hateful comment Nick gives my shoulder a squeeze or kisses whatever part of my face is closest to him. Honestly I think the hateful bullshit bothers him more than it bothers me.

"Wait look, there's a comment from your sister." I chuckle, mentally reading the words in Doria's deadpan voice. I didn't even know Doria remembered my name, much less looked at my Instagram.

Nick squints at the tiny writing on the illuminated screen.

Doriadoriadoria: *hey look that's my brother.*

He barks out a laugh and nods. "Yeah, she mentioned that she likes your work."

It made me happy to discover Nick's coming out to his family had been a comfort to his younger sister. Although he doesn't talk about it much, I know he misses the Sunday dinners and spending time with his sisters and nephew in particular. Since Doria told him she was queer, she and Nick have texted and she even visited him at the farm. As I consider all this, I'm still mindlessly scrolling through the comments. Then I see it and I fumble my phone in excitement.

"What!?" My voice is so shrill and so loud Archie hops off the couch. The dog shoots me a baleful look before trotting up the stairs.

Nick, immediately concerned, steadies my grip on my phone so he can look at it. He's in protective mode, muscles tense and mouth pulled into a hard line.

"No, no," I pant, "it's a good thing. I can't believe..." I trail off and look at the comment again, my eyes going dry and blurry.

> ZakSalkOfficial: *Good stuff. Love your overall take on the male gaze. Keep pushing in this direction!*

Zak Salk commented on my fucking painting. He understands what I'm going for! He called my work good! I try to slow my breathing and roll my shoulders back to relax myself. But nothing works. I'm freaking out.

"Wait, I'm confused." Nick's eyebrows knit together. "Who's Zak Salk?"

"He's an art critic. *The* art critic, I guess. For *The New York Times*. He's gay too. And he's big into social media and holy shit. This is crazy." I jump up and start pacing around the room, my brain whirring and skin overheating.

Nick says something but I don't hear him. I have to make a website. I have to put my e-mail address in my profile so people can contact me by a more legit means than Instagram direct message. How the fuck do I not have a website? I didn't exactly take my own painting seriously. I thought of the whole project as a lark, something to fill my time and expend energy while figuring out what would come next. But this is all very strangely real.

Another tidal wave of questions slams into the shore of my consciousness. Should I make a designated e-mail account for my art? Should I reach out to Kenny Thomas and Zak Salk, thanking them for increasing the visibility of my work and for their kind words? Or would that be overkill? Am I an artist now for real? Can I be an actual artist if I didn't go to art school and I make the majority of my paintings on my dad's back patio?

The weight of a large, warm hand on my shoulder pulls my attention back to Nick. He grins at me and gives me an excited squeeze. "This is awesome! I'm so proud of you!" The brush of his lips over mine barely registers.

I know I should respond and, like, be excited together with Nick but I'm so overwhelmed that I want to go home and stare at my phone for hours and google how to make a website.

"Thanks," I say. I sound distracted and distant even to myself. "I should go. I have so much to do." I'm already walking toward the door and trying to figure out where in the name of all things holy I put my car keys.

"Sure," Nick says quietly, following me to the door, hands in the pockets of his jeans. "Call me tomorrow?"

I nod, slide my feet into my sneakers and finally locate my keys. Okay, when I get home I can probably make one of those easy drag-and-drop-style websites. The ads I hear on every podcast I listen to say the sites are super simple to create. Should I start selling prints? The idea of making money from my art sends my mind reeling in a whole new direction. I'm already halfway back to my dad's place when I realize I basically sprinted out of Nick's house without saying two words to him. I blew off my boyfriend for what? So I could waste the evening struggling to make a website when I could easily do that in the morning? So I can reread comments on a post about the man I ditched?

As I pull the car into the garage, I bang my head against the steering wheel. I am, without a doubt, the worst boyfriend in history. I pull out my phone to text Nick, forcing myself not to get distracted by a barrage of new notifications. But even seeing them makes my stomach flip. Okay, I'll take a quick look at Instagram and then I'll apologize for my crap behavior. But I don't text Nick because I freak out all over again when I see that a queer art blogger direct messaged me about setting up an interview. I'm sitting in the car tapping out a reply when a knock on the car window makes me jump.

Jimmy looks down at me, an amused expression on his weathered face. "Everything okay, kiddo?"

My uncle has always called me kiddo. While I was in grad school in particular, it used to drive me nuts. He would call me to check in and chat and I would pace around in front of the library grinding my teeth harder and harder each time he used the nickname. But hearing it now surrounds me with comfort, like a sip of hot tea on a cold night. I look up at him again, his bushy beard, gleaming bald head, and dark eyebrows. He looks like a hippie Santa Claus and the thought makes me laugh. Too hard. I cover my face with my hands and I realize I'm hysterical but I can't make myself stop laugh-crying.

"Whoa. David." Jimmy opens the car door and grips my shoulders.

When I glance up, I register Daisy standing in the doorway to the garage, her long ash-blonde hair tangled around her striking face. Our gazes connect for a fraction of a second, then she turns and drifts back into the house.

"Sorry," I groan. "I'm fine. Great, actually." Quickly I fill Jimmy in on the events of the last few hours. His face transforms from concerned to thrilled and I'm reminded of how excited Nick looked on my behalf. "But I also suck because I got so overwhelmed and, like, elated that I basically blew Nick off."

Jimmy chuckles then gently pulls me out of the car. "I've known Nick almost as long as I've known you, Dave." Another nickname that used to rankle me. "And I can damn near guarantee that boy is nothing but thrilled for you right now. He doesn't have a selfish bone in his body."

I shrug noncommittally but I know Jimmy's right. I follow him into the living room where my dad sits curled up on the sofa, reading a book on the fall of the Ottoman Empire. Daisy, settled into the French-style armchair by the fireplace, taps intently on the illuminated screen of her phone.

"Big news!" Jimmy booms. My dad looks up, eyebrows shooting toward his wispy white hairline. "Our boy here is officially a famous artist." My father's mouth quirks into a grin, as if he already knows how much his brother is exaggerating.

"No," I laugh. "Remember that Instagram page I told you about, you know, the, uh, website where I'm putting my art?" My dad, who doesn't own a smartphone, was wildly confused when I tried to explain Instagram to him. "Well I guess people are kind of getting into it! I got some commissions and stuff. An art critic from the *Times* even commented on the painting I posted!" Saying the words aloud once again sears the bizarre reality of the situation into my brain.

"Good for you." My dad gives me a long look. "I was worried about you leaving your job at the museum. But this is a good fit. You seem happy."

Something in me relaxes at his words. Secretly, I'd always feared he was disappointed when I didn't follow his footsteps into academia. And when I'd left my job at the museum, the same anxiety clawed at me, the worry that I was letting him down somehow. But one glance at his placid smile and shining eyes tells me he really is proud of me.

I sit down on the couch next to my dad as Jimmy heaves himself into the armchair across from his daughter. A calm quiet settles over the four of us, my dad returning to his book, Jimmy flipping through a magazine, Daisy still playing the game on her phone. Seeing her on the device reminds me of all the things I need to do, and the fact that I still need to call or text Nick. I'm about to excuse myself to my bedroom when Jimmy closes his magazine and casts a nervous look in my direction.

"Dave?" he says, his voice gruff. "Mind if Daisy and I spend the night? She hasn't been sleeping well in the new place. She always conks right out on the couch when we're over here though."

Concern and sadness bloom in my chest. About fifteen years ago, Jimmy discovered my aunt Shelley, a beautiful and vivacious woman, was having a long-term affair with a man she met in an online support group for parents of autistic children. Shelley admitted she was in love with this other man and planned to move to Oregon to live with him. Jimmy was devastated but said he understood. Their life together had become stressful and small and vastly different from what Shelley wanted. He and Daisy continued to live in the little Airstream trailer on a plot of land that Shelley's family owned for generations.

About a year ago, though, Shelley's uncle announced he wanted the land back and basically kicked Jimmy and

Daisy out. Because Jimmy makes do with his modest pension, the two of them ended up moving into a tiny, dingy apartment on the outskirts of town. He hated the place, and I gathered that the change had been extremely challenging for Daisy.

"Of course," I say softly, glancing at my dad. I know before his stroke he'd been trying to convince his brother and Daisy to move in with him. Jimmy has always been like a second parent to me. I'll do anything I can do to make him and Daisy more comfortable. "You guys are welcome anytime." I'm about to roll out the offer for them to stay longer, but my dad's tense expression has me guessing the topic came up recently with the usual result. I don't know if it's pride or a practical consideration we're missing, but I don't understand my uncle's reluctance.

Without another word I shuffle over to the hall closet to pull out extra pillows and blankets to make up the couch for Daisy. My jaw tenses as I drift into the guestroom to check that there are clean sheets on the bed. I hate going in the room that used to be my mom's office. The muted cream walls and the big oil painting of the Hudson River she spent weeks working on transport me back to afternoons spent lying sprawled on the floor watching while my mom graded papers and hummed along to soft classical music. Shaking the memories from my mind I bid everyone good night and climb the stairs, tapping out a message to Nick as I walk.

> David: *Hey. Sorry for being such an asshole and leaving like that. I got a little overwhelmed.*

When Nick doesn't reply immediately like he normally does, worry creeps up my spine. Maybe I upset him. I definitely put my self-absorption on full display. It's not like Nick isn't busy and making time to see me. He's been exhausted lately, sometimes getting up as early as three in the morning so he can work before it gets too hot. And he still makes the time to prepare us delicious meals and then take me up to his bed to drive me insane with pleasure. When my phone buzzes on my nightstand I grin, anticipating Nick's kind, reassuring words. But it isn't Nick. It's Paige, the blogger from earlier, asking if we can Skype tomorrow afternoon. And great, she's inquiring about a link to my website. Sighing, I reach for my laptop.

BY THE TIME the interview is over I still don't have a functional website. I want to write angry letters to the marketing people at the stupid website-building company and let them know that it isn't as easy as they make it sound in their breezy ads. The interview went great though. It was a nice, easygoing conversation. Paige obviously works much faster than I do because within an hour of us talking she has a polished, thoughtful interview up on her beautifully designed website. I almost want to call her back and ask her how she made her site look so nice, but I don't want her to amend the article to inform her readers that David Webster is, in fact, an incompetent idiot. So I post a link to the interview on my Instagram page and go back to swearing at my computer.

A few hours later the site is live. Although for some reason it has a blackish gray background and white text, which I decidedly do not want but cannot figure out how to fix. And the online store page where I thought I could sell prints seems to have disappeared. I remember Nick's farm has a super-nice website, so I call him to ask if he made it himself.

He never texted me back last night and now his phone goes right to voicemail. I tell myself that it's just because he's busy. He usually keeps his phone in the house when he's out doing farm stuff. In order to distract my rapidly overheating brain I start sifting through the custom work inquiries. I respond to all of them with a friendly reply asking the senders to contact me with specifics at my newly minted "business" e-mail address.

Deciding it would be wise to approach this whole being-an-artist thing like a nine-to-five job, I jot down a to-do list. I want to ensure I am consistent with posting new work. The watercolors I've been making are fairly quick to do. So if the people who requested the commissioned work are okay with me posting the images, I'll have at least ten new paintings to put on the page within the next week or so. Plus if these commissions come through I might actually have an income again. The first thing that occurs to me is getting back into yoga, since I've started to miss how good I feel when I work out regularly. I text Jenna to ask her for the name of the yoga studio she teaches at part-time. Her reply is instantaneous and I have to keep myself from asking where the hell her colleague is.

By the time Sunday evening rolls around I realize I haven't seen Nick in over a week and we have barely spoken. Apparently some deer got into one of the vegetable beds and decimated a large chunk of the greens destined for the farm share and market. Nick, Jenna, and Hector were already overworked and now they're frantically trying to replant and construct fences so the deer can't do any more damage. Nick wasn't even upset about me bailing on him the night my Instagram blew up. When I apologized he brushed it off, saying he knew I had a lot on my mind and that he'd been tired anyway.

Something is weird between us. But I've been so busy with commissions, keeping up with my own projects, and figuring out how to sell prints that I don't revert to my usual doomsday prophecy bullshit. For once I allow myself to be reasonable. We're both busy.

Still, I miss Nick with an acute longing. Again and again the same fantasy tugs at me: doing my work at the farm, setting up a little studio space and painting, eating dinner with Nick every night, falling asleep safe in his solid arms. I find myself wondering what he would think of the custom wedding invitations I created for an adorable pair of middle-aged women from Seattle. They'd requested a portrait of the two of them holding hands in the middle of a forest rendered in their wedding colors: sienna, sage, and slate. I couldn't stop picturing Nick the entire time I painted, thinking of how the colors reminded me of him.

All day, every day I wonder what he's doing, what he's thinking, if he's getting enough sleep. I can't stop looking at the painting of the two of us on the bank of the Hudson. How happy he looks. How happy I look. How happy we are together.

After Nick broke my heart all those years ago, I kind of assumed that I would never feel as infatuated with someone as I had for him throughout high school and undergrad. And for a long time my assumption was correct. Julian, my first serious boyfriend during grad school, was so self-possessed, sophisticated, and brilliant I felt like I could never let my guard down around him. He was getting ready to defend his dissertation as I started my second year of doctoral coursework at the University of Chicago.

Even the way we met was too perfect to be true. We literally bumped into each other on the sidewalk outside the library and he was unbelievably classy about asking for my number as he helped me pick up my scattered books and papers. We dated for a year before he moved to Kansas to accept a post doc. I was almost relieved when we broke up, even though the sex was great and he was easily the coolest person I'd ever met. But the week after he moved away I realized I didn't miss him. I'd spent all my time with him trying to listen enough to make sure I didn't sound stupid when I spoke. If he mentioned an author or musician I would nod politely, then conduct obsessive research so I sounded like I knew what I was talking about the next time the topic came up. I was a total, intimidated phony.

Then with Christopher I could be myself, but it was only because the relationship was so passive and neutral that I didn't try at all. I didn't go out of my way to seem especially interesting or sexy because I was distracted with work and Christopher was detached and uncomplicated. Well, at least at the beginning. Even finding out he was cheating, though, didn't exactly upset me. I felt betrayed, but in a disconnected way, like it had happened to a friend and I was mad on their behalf.

But Nick has known me for the majority of my life. He knows what a brat I can be sometimes. He knows how I retreat into myself when faced with stress. And he doesn't care. Instead of making me guess what he wants or how he's feeling, he's honest. It's refreshing. It's also terrifying because he makes me want to be a better person. I want to talk things out calmly and try to be honest about my feelings instead of putting up a front or retreating into my work. Being with him calms me.

Knowing Nick is in my life, I'm invigorated and clear-headed. I want to make Nick happy. Not just content, but genuinely, deeply satisfied. I want to know how to make his days easier and brighter, how to see his open, warm smile as often as possible.

When I successfully make black bean burritos for dinner, the idea occurs to me in a flash. Well, two ideas. The first being that I've been kind of a crappy boyfriend. Nick always makes us amazing dinners despite being exhausted and stressed out by the demands of the farm. He always seems so at ease in the beautiful home he built for himself that I never stopped to appreciate all the effort he puts into the nights I come over for dinner. The realization makes me hate myself. So my second idea is that I will make Nick dinner at his place. I'll buy all the ingredients, find the recipes, and cook him a delicious meal. Well, hopefully it'll be delicious.

I'm not a bad cook, per se, just a simple one. Being raised on nothing but vegetarian health food meant when I started college I went kind of wild ordering delivery and existing on nothing but coffee and baked goods. But it made me feel like shit, so I reverted to the spartan diet of my youth: bland but nourishing meals of steamed vegetables, brown rice, and tofu. But it can't be that hard to make something flavorful, right? Quickly I text Anna, who like Nick is an excellent cook, for some inspiration.

> David: *Help. I want to make Nick dinner but I only know how to make like five things and they're all bland AF.*

> Anna: *Hmm... I made Jenna green curry a few nights ago and she said it was really good. Oh! Or you could do a stir-fry! It seems like Nick eats a*

*lot of protein, so you could load it up with tofu (or chicken *frown emoji*). Just serve it with some rice?*

David: *I like the stir-fry idea. Got a good recipe?*

Anna sends me a link to a cooking blog she reads and I glance over the ingredients and instructions. It all seems pretty straightforward. I got this. I thank her then text Nick to see if he wants to have dinner together. He replies immediately saying he'd love to, but he was up early so it will have to be something simple. I explain that I have it under control, all he has to do is show up at his kitchen table. His response falters a few times before he asks if I'm sure and follows it up with a dubious-looking thinking emoji. I roll my eyes and laugh, weirdly proud of myself as I tell him I'm totally confident I can make him dinner.

Chapter Seventeen

David

July

My confidence has evaporated as I stand in Nick's tidy, well-equipped kitchen, groceries unpacked and frighteningly sharp chef's knife in hand. Nick keeps trying to help but I've poured him a beer, telling him he under no circumstances can intervene. I want him to unwind and enjoy himself after a stressful day. He still looks tired, rolling his neck and rubbing his hands over the stubble that's longer than I've ever seen it. Unable to resist I plant a quick kiss to his rough jaw and he relaxes into me, almost knocking me over.

"Okay," I say primly, stepping back and resuming my spot in front of the cutting board. "So do you have a wok?" I glance down at the recipe I pulled up on my phone. It says I need to heat a wok over high heat to start.

Nick shakes his head. "You can use that big skillet though." He gestures toward a huge stainless steel pan hanging from the pot rack over the island. It seems like Nick built his kitchen with his giant proportions in mind because it's too high up for me to reach, which makes my ears burn with embarrassment. Nick has to get the skillet down for me, chuckling to himself all the while.

I glance back down at the recipe, unsure of where to start. I'm overwhelmed. Anna told me it was important to prepare all the ingredients before I started cooking because the recipe comes together quickly. Fine. Easy. *Mince garlic.* I can do that. I struggle for a moment to remove the papery skin from the garlic cloves only to have one of the peeled pieces skitter off the cutting board and onto the floor.

"David." Nick's voice is tinged with amusement and he's looking at me so fondly I feel myself flush again. "Really, baby, I'm happy to help if you want. You help me make dinner all the time." This is not true. I stand with Nick in the kitchen while he cooks, groping his muscles and chatting mindlessly, but usually my help consists of grating cheese or chopping up some herbs.

"I know you *can* help. But I want to do something nice for you. I still feel bad about being such a shit boyfriend," I mutter, now moving on to slicing up a bell pepper into "matchsticks." Whatever the fuck that means.

I'm too focused on not cutting my fingertips off to look up but when Nick speaks, the concern in his voice is audible. "Sweetheart."

His stool scrapes against the pine floor, then his firm body presses against my back, surrounding me with his woodsy smell. I melt into him, every cell needing more of his touch, vibrating with longing for him. I knew I missed him this week, but the sheer relief consumes me.

"I understand that you're busy. Seriously." Nick's words have the slight ring of him having worked to convince himself too. "And it's been fucking insane here. God, we need to hire someone else. Lexi offered to help out, but she has no experience... Anyway. I'm so proud of you. This is a big deal. So don't feel bad for focusing on your art. Please." He turns me, tipping my face toward his to connect our gazes. His gray eyes are intent on mine.

I heave out a sigh and push him back. If he keeps touching me, we'll end up eating at midnight and he'll be even more exhausted. "Sit down." I point to the stool and he dutifully complies, fond grin back in place. "And say what you want, but you know as well as I do how selfish and myopic I can get when I have a project. You remember when my senior capstone was due. How many times did I call you saying I was going to drop out of college? And don't even get me started on my dissertation. I ignored my dad's calls for like a month." I pause, trying to reign in my thoughts, keep chopping vegetables, and articulate what I actually mean. But then I realize I still have to cut the chicken into cubes and everything goes off the rails.

Something is clearly wrong when I toss the garlic into the pan and the air around the stove immediately fills with acrid smoke. The recipe said to make sure the oil was hot, but I guess it was too hot because the garlic I painstakingly minced into tiny pieces immediately turns black.

"I got it!" I snap, glancing back to Nick, whose face is like stone, revealing nothing. This seems wrong. It definitely smells wrong. But maybe once I add everything else it will be okay? Hurrying because this whole process has taken me significantly longer than I'd hoped, I chuck the rest of the vegetables into the pan. Now it smells better, more like food and less like burning metal. I add the chicken last. The recipe, being one of Anna's, had called for tofu but I used chicken figuring Nick would like that better. I don't cook a lot of meat but how hard can chicken be?

The final result looks good enough. The vegetables are colorful and vibrant and it smells less objectionable now that there are peppers and onions and carrots. As I portion the food onto the stoneware plates Nick laid out, I realize I completely forgot to make rice. *Shit.* But this should be okay on its own, right?

Nick follows me to the table with our drinks, Archie trotting along behind him to take his customary seat at Nick's feet. Nick beams at me before taking a bite. I watch him intently, like I'm one of the zoologists on the nature documentaries Nick likes so much. He chews, much more slowly than usual, then takes a long sip of his beer.

"Is it okay? I know I'm not a great cook but Anna said this recipe's fantastic."

Nick looks down at his plate, then looks at me. The wrinkle between his eyebrows is back. There is no way this food is good. I take a bite. Everything tastes like the burned garlic smell and I realize immediately that I forgot to add the soy sauce. It's simultaneously flavorless and revolting. Plus the chicken has a weird, slimy consistency. I spear a piece on my fork and bite into it before quickly spitting it out onto the plate. It's totally pink inside. Great. So maybe I can add poisoning Nick to my list of romantic accomplishments.

"Don't eat it!" I shriek.

Nick shakes with silent laughter, his big hands covering his face. I'm so angry with myself I almost want to cry. My appetite vanishes like smoke and all I want to do is go upstairs, fill up Nick's giant bathtub, and drown myself in it.

"Thank you." Nick looks at me with a strange expression on his face. At first I wonder if he's mad and being sarcastic. But I don't think I've ever actually heard him use sarcasm.

"For almost giving you salmonella and serving us what might be the most disgusting stir-fry in history?" My voice goes all thin and quivery. Clearing our plates, I tip the food into the garbage. Archie doesn't even beg for scraps like he normally does, so I know it's awful.

Nick follows me into the kitchen. "No. For making me dinner. It was really nice of you." His voice sounds off, kind of stilted and formal, and I start to get mad at him.

"Well, sorry I'm a shitty cook on top of being a shitty boyfriend," I snap, turning away from him so I can start to wash the mess of dishes I created in my failed attempt at cooking. "I mean I know how to cook. Just not like a fucking professional." I grumble this more to myself than to Nick.

He's probably finally realizing he's way too good for me. That I'm nothing but a self-absorbed, bratty failure who can't cook for shit and basically ghosted him for a week because I got too wrapped up in my stupid art on my stupid Instagram. My self-esteem takes a sharp nosedive and the fizzy prickle behind my eyes indicates I'm going to cry. Maybe we didn't see each other this week because he realized he's not that into me anymore. It would make sense. He's fucking gorgeous, and he's a genuinely good person, unlike me.

Intellectually I know I'm spiraling and overreacting to something that isn't a big deal. I messed up dinner. So what? But I'm so angry with myself. And for some reason I'm angry at Nick too. In the thirty seconds since I started cleaning up the kitchen I've managed to convince myself he doesn't want me anymore. And, in a cruel twist of fate, that's when I know for sure. The thought is sharp and bright, like a bell reverberating through my body. I'm in love with him and I am fucking terrified. The fear of losing him again makes me sick. I'm clammy and shaky and hot. Trying to calm down I rake my fingers through my hair, but I only manage to drip soapy water in my eyes. I need to tell him.

"David." Nick's voice is a low growl as his hands press down on my shoulders. I resist hard against his efforts to turn me to face him. If he sees me like this, all flushed and eyes burning from tears and the soap, there's no way he'll want me. But he uses his strength to his advantage and his gaze is hot on my face as he twists me around toward him. I stare at the ground, at his huge bare feet, at anything but his intense gaze. Then his thick fingers are in my hair, forcing my head back, and his mouth crashes to mine. There is desperation in this kiss. Immediately my mind snaps to the way Nick used to kiss me, glancing around furtively before tugging me against him roughly and crushing our mouths together, groaning then sighing with relief.

I'm pinned between the counter and the wall of Nick's body as he wraps his powerful arms around my shoulders, squeezing me and pulling my chest to his torso. His tongue slips against mine and finally my body at least catches up with the wave of sensation. I return the kiss, fisting my hands in his shirt and moaning into the searing heat of his mouth. Lust burns from our joined lips down to my groin.

Before I can do anything or even think, Nick fumbles with my belt buckle and tugs my pants and briefs roughly down to my knees. His movements are jerky and impatient. I'm breathing hard, my head spinning with an intoxicating mix of arousal and emotion. I want this man. Every fiber of my being is crying out for his exhilarating kisses and low, sweet words and for... I hiss at the pressure of his cock against mine as he hauls me up toward him, grinding his hardness against my own.

"Yes. Fuck yes," he says through clenched teeth. His mouth is set tight, his eyes pressed shut, his chest heaving. He bends down to kiss me again, bruising and frantic, panting into my mouth. His stubble scrapes the sensitive skin of my face. Something feels...different. I'm still almost dizzy with lust, desperate for him to be inside me, but something is definitely off.

I open my mouth to ask him what's wrong but Nick grips my shoulders and turns me, bending me over the soapstone countertop. I still have my shirt on and it immediately gets soaked with dishwater as he presses my torso down. When he leans over me his breath is hot against my neck as he ghosts a kiss over my skin. I'm whining and writhing back up on him, making breathless gasping noises as the head of his cock glides against my ass.

"Yeah. Just like that." Nick growls, a low and desperate sound.

I'm still agonizingly hard as Nick spits into his hand and urges a little more firmly against my entrance, but this is too detached, too sudden. I'm reminded of the impersonal hookups I pursued desperately when I first moved back to Chicago for my doctorate. Meeting a guy in a bar and letting him fuck me in the bathroom or hard and fast and quiet while my roommates slept on the other side of a thin wall. Not being sure exactly what I wanted but feeling too swept up in the stream of events to stop.

Maybe I tense up or my breathing changes. Maybe I pull away ever so slightly. I'm not sure. But Nick goes stock-still behind me. Then his warm, callused hands stroke up under my shirt. He leans back over me and buries the tip of his nose into my hair.

"Baby," he breathes into me and I realize he's shaking. I yearn for his heat as he pulls away and I can hear the rustle of him zipping his jeans behind me.

I turn to face him, clumsily tugging up my own pants. Nick's gaze darts down to my soaked shirt.

"Shit. David, I'm sorry." His voice is gentle, but he looks panicked, eyes flashing like a caged animal's.

I pull the wet fabric away from my torso and laugh. "No big deal. It'll dry."

"No. That's not—" Nick pauses. "Fuck, I don't know." He trails off, raking a hand through his dark hair. I watch his sculpted chest rise and fall, breaths coming ragged.

I press my palm to his cheek. His skin is fevered. "Was dinner *that* bad? You don't even want to fuck me now?" I grin, going for levity and even though it comes out hollow I'm rewarded with Nick's smile as he shakes his head and huffs out a laugh.

The moment he gets himself under control is evident on his face. When our eyes meet, his gaze is fond, gray eyes soft. "Thank you for making me dinner. Stir-fries can be tricky to make." He bends to kiss me gently. "And you are *not* a crappy boyfriend." He raises his eyebrows at me like he's waiting for me to agree with him. Finally I shrug and he looks satisfied enough.

"So what was that all about?" I make a vague gesture between the two of us. "I mean something was weird, right?"

Nick nods earnestly, looking for a moment like a nervous little kid. "It's my fault. I'm so sorry if I was too rough. And sorry I got your shirt all wet. I just..." He groans and rubs his hand over his face, clearly frustrated. Finally he sets his shoulders and gives me a long, searching look. "Okay. I'm going to tell you the truth but I don't want you to feel like you have to respond or anything. I have to get this off my chest."

My mouth is a desert. This has been a weird night after a weird week. And sex has never been like that between us. Is there a chance he's trying to break up with me—squeeze in one last pity fuck and then bail? A hot swell of anxiety crashes over me. I say nothing and stare down at the knots in the pine floor.

"All right," Nick starts uncertainly. "So, I want to say I'm proud of you about your art. You're so talented. So when you found out your page was taking off I wanted to give you space to work. I mean, I know I can be intense and the last thing I want you to feel is smothered." He starts wringing his hands and my heart sinks.

The words spill out of my mouth before I can stop them, before I even take a moment to consider what Nick is saying. "If you're breaking up with me, can you get on with it? Put me out of my misery." My breath catches in my throat.

Confusion registers on Nick's face for a moment before he's tipping me forward into his embrace. I'm grateful for the warm rumbling sound of his chuckle. Then he's kissing me again so sweetly, there's no way this is goodbye. Okay, now I'm confused.

"I'm not breaking up with you, you goof. I'm trying to tell you I'm in love with you. I was stressing all week because I was worried you would want to, I don't know, leave or something? I know you said you want to stay here, but I started thinking you changed your mind. That you might go back to Chicago or move to the city. I get that I'm being stupid. But I don't want to burden or limit you or, I don't know—"

I fit my mouth to his to shut him up, pouring all my relief into him, grinning against his lips. His words wash over me like cool water on a burn. Nick is in love with me. *In love.*

Julian and I said we loved each other. But I only said it because he did. I had no idea what I meant when I said the words. Christopher and I tossed the phrase around ad nauseam, but usually it meant *I'd love to stop talking to you* more than *I adore you and want you in my life.*

But when Nick says he loves me I know he means it. The words are as sure and solid as he is.

"I love you," I say without hesitation after I break the kiss. And that clear bell echoes through my body again. Of this I am sure. Naturally, I start laughing hysterically at the sheer absurdity of the situation.

"What's funny?" Nick asks with trepidation.

"I thought you were breaking up with me. I'm over here fucking losing it because I thought you finally figured out you're way too good for me. That you'd lost interest."

Nick shakes his head and puts up a hand. "One, there's no such thing as 'too good for.' You and I are good for each other. Perfect. And I mean it. I love you, David." He blushes and I want to kiss every inch of his perfect face, it's so adorable. "And two, I think you and I need to get better at communicating. It kinda seems like we both spent this week worrying about things that didn't exist."

I wrap my arms around his waist and smile against his chest. He is, of course, right. But it's somehow nice to know that he's capable of the same kind of unreasonable, pointless stressing that I specialize in. That he's not always perfect and honest and direct.

"I know." My voice is muffled by the fabric of his T-shirt. "I want to try to be better, to be less distant and self-absorbed. And please don't worry about me leaving." I tip my head back to look at his handsome face. "To be honest, I do miss living in a city sometimes. But I wouldn't trade being with you for anything. You make me so happy. Happier than my favorite coffee shops or my apartment or the museum." My cheeks heat as I realize how true this statement is. Nick looks touched by my words and I reach to gently guide his lips back down to mine.

Chapter Eighteen

David

July

"Can we go upstairs?" Nick asks, his eyes hooded with obvious desire. I nod enthusiastically, hurrying to follow him up to his bedroom. Archie looks unhappy with us when Nick shoos the dog off the bed and closes the door behind him.

Pleasure unfurls in my belly as Nick undoes the buttons on my sodden shirt, following the motion downward with soft kisses to my chest and stomach.

"I love you. So much." The words are whole and right as they flow from my mouth. I think of how often I had to hold myself back from saying those very words to him before. How I tried to keep my emotions in check so I didn't scare him off. But now Nick beams up at me and pushes me back onto the quilt, tugging my pants down and nipping at the sensitive skin of my inner thighs. As happens often when we end up in his bed, Nick seems desperate to get me undressed, and quickly I'm stripped bare, while he's still fully clothed. His heated gaze raking over my body has the same effect it always does. My cock hardens at the sight of desire so plain and potent on his face but I'm also l tense with the slight self-consciousness and discomfort of all his attention so intensely focused on me.

He straddles me, the fabric of his jeans rough against the thin, sensitive skin of my hips. I can tell he's being careful not to put the whole of his weight on me, but some part of me loves the feeling of his big body crushing me to the bed. Need builds in me, thrumming under my skin and clouding my thoughts. I need to see him, need to run my eyes, my fingers and tongue over every inch of his tanned skin, need to worship the sculpted planes of his muscles.

I try and fail to yank his T-shirt over his head and he grins at me before pulling it off in a smooth, oddly sexy motion. My mouth goes dry at the sight, every inch of him so firm and sculpted. It seems almost unfair that someone so perfect even exists. I grin to myself greedily. He's mine. This beautiful, sweet, wonderful man loves me.

"What are you smiling about?" Nick asks, rolling off me to remove his jeans and boxers. I try not to get too distracted by the sight of his thick, heavy cock as he settles next to me on the bed.

"Um." I attempt to get back on my train of thought. "I was honestly thinking about how hot you are." I laugh but Nick must see some reservation in my face. His fingers graze gently over my collarbones, up my throat, then trace my jaw before tangling into my hair.

"David, you're gorgeous." He kisses me breathless, and it takes a great deal of concentration for me to follow his words. "You get self-conscious sometimes, huh? All tense." Nick runs the pads of his fingers over my eyebrows, relaxing them into a softer expression. "I wish I could show you how gorgeous you are. Like the way you paint me—I see myself through your eyes. It makes me feel good."

"No, I know I'm being ridiculous." I sigh, wishing for a moment Nick couldn't always read me so well. "It's just like your body is so fucking perfect. And your face..." I realize on an intellectual level that Nick's gorgeous, intimidating body is the result of intense workouts, constant grueling farm work, and to some extent genetics. He could have, had his family not squashed the opportunity, been on track to be drafted into professional football. I know that our bodies are simply different, and that my feelings of inadequacy are partially informed by unreasonable cultural notions of masculinity. Besides, one glance toward Nick's rigid cock straining between us tells me he likes what he sees when he looks at me.

Nick stares at me again for a long moment. Then he's wrapping his arms around me, pulling me under him, skimming his hardened palms down my spine to grasp my ass. Desire sluices through me, wave after warm wave of pleasure.

"Nick," I whine under him, his name a benediction. All I want in that moment is to make him feel as good as possible. To feel him bucking and vibrating with need as I take him into my mouth. "Lie down on your back," I command.

Nick rolls off me but seems wholly reluctant to let our bodies part fully. He cuddles close into me, turning to bite lightly on my earlobe and lace his fingers with mine. A moan bubbles from my lips before I sit back and trace my hand down his considerable length. At the first hint of contact Nick arches off the bed, rutting up into my hand.

"Fuck. David. Why is that so good? You need to teach me." Nick's voice is rough but tinged with amusement.

I bite back a laugh. Nick is incredibly responsive, making me feel like some kind of sex god over straightforward things like hand jobs. "You do just fine." I lick my lips and grin at him before closing my mouth around the dusky tip of his cock. The musky sweet taste of his precome explodes on my tongue, making me involuntarily hum with satisfaction around his length. Sliding my mouth lower I allow my eyes to lose focus and I watch Nick's dark pubic hair zoom in and out of my field of vision. He moans brokenly as I take him deeper into my throat, reaching down to cup his heavy balls and massage the spot behind them that drives him wild. He urges me on, groaning steadily and letting his hand rest on my head as I lick and suck him.

"Baby…" he bites out. "I need to be inside you. If you keep doing that"—I press down on the spot, knowing exactly what he means and his hips buck off the bed—"I'm gonna lose it."

"Fine." I swipe a swift kiss to the tip of his erection before draping myself on top of him. As much as I love the masculine scent of him and slipping him deep into my mouth, every inch of my skin is thrumming at the thought of him gliding into my ass.

"I want to see you. I want to see your face when you take my cock," he murmurs, rolling us over and easing me down onto the cool sheets that smell so much like him, all clean air and pine. His eyes lock on mine as he straddles me again, thick thighs flexing on either side of me with the movement of him reaching for the lube on the bedside table. He eases my legs back, opening me. Slick fingers slip into my ass, heavy and adept, pulling thin, needy sounds from me as I spasm around him.

"Oh my god, Nick," I cry out as he begins to massage my prostate, knowing exactly how to render me desperate. I'm so hard every touch, every slippery motion has pleasure burning through me like I could come at any moment, but I do not want this to end. "Please. Your cock. Please." I know I'm begging but my need weighs down on me, viscous and all-encompassing.

"I love you. So fucking much," he says low and almost possessive as he replaces his fingers with his dick.

As always I welcome the momentary burning stretch as he breaches my hole. I whimper and arch into him as he slowly fills me with his hot length in one fluid stroke. Once he's in to the hilt, I open my eyes to see him gazing down at me, gray eyes shining. He leans down to brush his lips over mine. The kiss heats, tongues and spit and the rough scrape of his stubble as he stays still inside, throbbing. Then as if he can't help it anymore he starts to move and I hook my ankles around his waist. I need him close.

After a few months of being together, Nick seems to know my body as well as I do. He knows how to angle his hips to hit the spot inside me that makes me cry out. He knows exactly when to change the pace of his thrusts and wrap his fingers around my cock to tip me over the edge. Sometimes when he's fucking me it's as though I'm on the continuous edge of an orgasm, riding such intense pleasure I can't do anything but breathe and beg and hold on. Now as he slides in and out of me, peppering my face with kisses and breathing sweet words, it's almost too much. The thick swell of need breaks and I'm writhing beneath his broad frame, every one of my muscles going tense.

"Yes. Oh my god yes. Nick." I'm babbling. He starts pushing in harder as he crushes his lips to mine, twisting his fingers into my hair and tugging my head back into the pillows. Watching his big, perfect body flex, knowing he's mine, knowing he loves me, has me moaning his name in a delirious, slick daze. When he reaches between us to stroke my throbbing hardness in time with his steady thrusts, I'm finished. I go rigid, spilling into his fist, arching toward Nick and trying to pull him in deeper as my throat seems to close around his name.

Slowly I come down, relaxing, delighting in the languid sensation of my limbs and dancing blue-white dots against the black field of my vision. Nick groans on top of me, moaning brokenly that he loves me. He thrusts once, hard and deep, then he's filling me with liquid heat and snaking his arms beneath me as he comes.

I'm not sure how much time passes before Nick tries to pull out but I tighten my legs around him, keeping him inside. He presses his nose against mine and I tip my chin to bite the tip of it, smiling. Finally I unwrap my legs and allow him to ease out of me. He immediately hauls me against him, curling around my back and nuzzling his face into my neck.

"I'm so lucky," Nick sighs after a long moment in which I teeter on the edge of blissed-out sleep and satisfied, conscious desire for pillow talk. We're both a mess of come and sweat but I can't dredge up the desire to get out of bed.

I turn to face him, running my fingertips up and down his tight stomach. He bows into my touch like a cat. "Hey," I whisper, sure this is the time to tell him. "I have to say something." In the spirit of confessing our love for each other, I should probably admit the whole truth.

"Okay," Nick says simply. One of his hands navigates to my hair and I relax as he lightly scratches my scalp. I never used to think of myself as a very tactile person, always sliding out of bed after sex to freshen up and tug my clothes back on. But Nick is constantly touching me, pulling me into his warmth, and running those big hands all over me like he can't help himself.

"Warning you—I'm about to be sappy as fuck," I begin, already embarrassed. But Nick looks pleased. "So I was in love with you before. Like, for a long time. I guess it, um, started November of our sophomore year of high school. You won that first home game as quarterback, remember?" I pause and drag a hand over my face. Of fucking course he remembers winning the damn game.

Nick nods slowly, a smirk pulling his lips up.

"Anyway, I was fucking terrified watching you play. You were, like, untouchable on the field. I didn't, and still don't, get the rules of football. But even I could tell you were good. Anna was super pissed at me for dragging her to yet another game. And she was pissed when I made her hang around after. I made her come to so many games and usually you left right after with your other friends so it was pointless."

I realize I'm starting to nervously ramble. "Anyway, that night you waved me down to the field and you, like, hugged me in front of everyone." My heart races at the memory of Nick, surrounded by his rowdy team, grinning under the silvery wash of the stadium lights, lifting me off my feet in a lingering hug. The guy who I spent far too much time daydreaming about, who I knew would never return my feelings, who barely acknowledged my existence at school—held me in front of everyone. My connection to Nick, warm companionship and nervous adoration, shifted then from a crush to something simultaneously thrilling and terrifying.

"I remember," Nick says roughly. "You were the only person I wanted. I mean, I was confused but I knew." He drags in a shaky breath. "You made my life so much better. I needed you. I still do." He places a lingering kiss to my forehead, and the sensation leaves me lightheaded.

The desire to tell him everything pulls the words from my mouth before I have time to consider what I want to say. "When you kissed me that first time. God, I could barely believe it was real. I'm pretty sure I spent the next day trying to wake myself up out of some weird dream."

I take stock of Nick's face, his wide, straight nose, long, dark eyelashes, square jaw, and those slate-colored eyes locked on mine.

"So yeah, I guess I kind of feel that way again. Like I almost can't believe any of this is real. I'm terrified I'm going to wake up alone back in my apartment in Chicago or, I don't know…you'll realize you don't want me after all." The thought dies on my lips. I need to believe that Nick loves me. His actions since we've gotten together consistently show me the truth of his words.

"David." Nick's tone is almost rebuking. "This is real. I know I was terrible to you before and I get that you might find it hard to trust me now. But I love you so much. I want us to be together."

"You're right," I sigh. Part of me wants to roll away from him, to press my back into his chest again so I don't have to look at his intent face. Instead I direct my full attention to the colorful pattern of the quilt. Idly I wonder if he made it, like the curtains downstairs. "I'm not used to feeling this good in a relationship. Honestly, after Christopher and I fell apart, I kind of figured I might take a good long break from serious dating."

"Did you love him?" Nick's voice has gone all low and growly.

"I don't know." I have to suppress a smile because jealous Nick is weirdly cute. "We were together for a longish time, I guess. I liked him for sure. He's smart and engaging and, I don't know, has great taste?" My brows knit together as I try to catalog what drew me to Christopher. "But we were a bad fit. We said we loved each other but I don't think either of us ever felt it. Julian, the guy I dated while I was doing my doctorate, was probably the closest I ever got to being in love with anyone else. But with him I wasn't quite sure. Too much of my mental energy went into being perfect for him. He's a great guy though," I admit, feeling ashamed that I'd been so self-absorbed and closed off with the two other men I seriously dated.

"Do you still keep in touch?"

I shrug. "Not with Christopher. It wasn't a messy breakup or anything but he moved in with his ex pretty much right away and I couldn't be bothered. But yeah Julian and I keep in touch via Instagram and we'll text occasionally. He got a great job teaching at Pratt, so he lives in Brooklyn." I wonder if Julian knows I'm in New York. I guess I should probably text him and let him know. See how he's doing and all. His partner Kevin is a principal dancer in the New York City Ballet and if the glowing selfies Julian posts on Instagram are any indication, they seem to be wildly happy.

I nuzzle into Nick as I let my mind wander, thinking back to lying in bed with Christopher after sex. Usually he fell asleep immediately, snoring softly and leaving me to wonder why I wasn't more satisfied with him. That life seems worlds apart from being in this bed with this man, his loving touches and the perfect way our bodies fit together. I wonder with a weird stab of jealousy if Nick has ever been in love with someone else. So I ask, unable to meet his eye as I do.

Nick shakes his head immediately. "No. I had a huge crush on Matt, that guy I met on the farming forum. But I mean, we couldn't exactly get to know each other that well. We never met in person. I did like him a whole lot though. Both of us kept trying to, like jokingly convince the other to move across the country but that was obviously bullshit. Neither of us could leave." He chuckles fondly and now it's my turn to get all weird and jealous, picturing Matt as a perfect blond version of Nick. I almost want to start wheedling for more information but Nick continues. "And yeah, I mean, I wanted so bad to love Christi when she and I got married. I cared about her. But it was pretty much the same kind of love I feel for my sisters so, yeah. No."

Nick squeezes me tight against him, twining our legs together, and I tuck my face into the crook of his shoulder. With my ear pressed flush against his skin I can hear his heart beating faster than usual in his chest.

"Do you want to get married?" Nick asks, looking sheepish.

I startle, shock launching me upward so quickly I give myself a head rush. "What? We've only been dating for like four months."

"Shit. No, sorry. I'm not trying to propose to you. Believe me, I would try to come up with something more romantic than this. I meant in general, or whatever." Nick shakes his head, laughing before cupping my cheek to lock his eyes with mine.

My thoughts, unsurprisingly, start churning. Thinking of Nick asking me to marry him for real makes me so hot and dizzy I feel like I could pass out. Would he get down on one knee like I'd seen guys do in crappy romantic comedies and a few times at nice restaurants? Would he come up with one of his carefully rehearsed speeches?

"So, maybe not?" Nick guesses, and I realize I never answered his question.

"Oh. Um." Honestly the concept of marriage never seemed like a reality to me. When I'd been in grad school I always felt kind of bad for my married colleagues. They left parties early, looking cranky as they checked their phones, always needing to take another person into account when making professional decisions. My parents had a happy marriage for the entirety of my childhood: anticipating each other's needs, sitting on the porch together on weekends to read the paper and drink coffee, always open with sweet affection. In the end though, my mother's choice not to pursue any treatment for her cancer made me doubt her love for my dad. And for me.

Wow, okay, I need to reel it in. *Focus. Marriage. Nick's question.*

"I'm open to the idea. I guess I want a long-term monogamous partnership. I definitely couldn't handle the stress of dating multiple people or anything like that. Plus I totally appreciate the power and meaning of marriage for queer folks. Having access to that is huge." I hear myself, the distant, clinical tone of my answer. This is not what I want to say. I remind myself of my decision to be honest and direct with Nick. He deserves that. I take a deep breath. "Yes. I would like to get married someday. I don't think I would have wanted that before, but now...I do."

Nick looks at me with a soft smile on his face, like I gave him an incredibly thoughtful gift. Like my words are exactly what he wanted to hear. Then his stomach gives a loud grumble and his hand shoots down, as if pressing on the tight muscles will stop the sound.

"Shit!" I yelp, burying my face in my hands. "We never ate. And you did actual manual labor all day."

Nick waves his hand in the air dismissively. But I know how much he normally eats. He's probably ready to keel over from hunger.

"God, I'm so sorry about dinner." I groan but Nick leans forward, claiming my mouth with his.

"Baby, don't give it another thought. How about we get dressed and I can make us something simple? You can help." If I didn't love him so much the last statement would make me bristle. Patronizing bastard.

"I *can* cook, you know," I snipe. "I probably should have made something more familiar."

Nick smirks at me as he slides out of bed, padding over to the bathroom. His ass is amazing, the taut, muscular globes flexing with his every movement. For a moment my mind shifts away from any thoughts of food or deep talk of our future together. He leans against the doorway to the bathroom for a moment. My mouth goes dry. Truly, he looks like the classical Greco-Roman ideal of male beauty. I take a quick mental snapshot, already rendering the image in indigo ink and watered-down charcoal to match his eyes.

After we hastily wash up and I cast a few longing glances at the bathtub, I follow Nick downstairs. We find Archie waiting patiently at the front door.

"Crap," Nick says. "Would you mind taking him out real quick while I get food together?"

"Sure." I grin, reaching down to rub Archie's wiry head. The dog waggles his whole body in response.

"You want to take a flashlight?"

I would very much like to take a flashlight but I also don't want to seem like a nervous baby, so I step into my espadrilles and follow Archie out into the muggy night air. Immediately the dog darts toward the tree line and immediately I panic. It's so isolated out here, surrounded by dark forest and pretty much nothing else. Nick mentioned seeing bears, and a few weeks ago I swear I saw a wolf although Nick insists it was a coyote. I'm grateful that the moment I whistle for him, Archie comes bounding back carrying a truly gigantic stick in his mouth.

"Are you allowed to bring that in?" I ask in a mock reproachful tone. Archie cocks his head before trotting up onto the porch with the stick—well, log, really. I poke my head in the door to find Nick in the kitchen, moving around with the grace I lacked earlier. Tomatoes and a big bunch of basil are laid out on the counter in front of him. "Hey," I call and his head snaps up, a bit of concern clouding his handsome face "Can Archie bring sticks inside?"

"No." Nick chuckles and relaxes immediately. "He knows better. Tell him to drop."

I give the command and Archie immediately drops the huge stick, tail wagging in circles as he follows me inside. "I meant to ask you why you named him Archie?" I toe off my shoes and scratch the dog's head as he waits next to me patiently.

Nick looks abashed. "It's Archimedes. You know, like the Greek mathematician or whatever. He's a smart dog, so I wanted to give him a smart name."

"I like it." I glance at Archie, who looks between Nick and me expectantly, as if the discussion of his intelligence will merit a treat. "I always wanted a dog. This painter I was obsessed with, Lucian Freud, did these amazing etchings of his whippet, Pluto. It made me really want one. A whippet, I mean. They're super sweet. But I never had time for a dog."

"Lucian Freud," Nick repeats quietly, as if to himself. I hope I'm not making him feel how I used to with Julian.

"What're you making?" I change the subject and drift into the kitchen.

"Some bruschetta. We have more tomatoes than we know what to do with right now." He gestures toward a rustic-looking loaf of bread that I recognize as Jenna's handiwork. She makes sourdough bread that Anna constantly raves about.

"Can you cut that into about half-inch slices?" He's laid the bread out with a serrated knife and cutting board, as if he knew I would come inside, guns blazing, looking to redeem my cooking failure. I make quick work of slicing the bread and I don't fuck anything up. By the time I've finished this task, Nick has chopped up all the tomatoes, sliced the basil into wispy strips, and started arranging chunks of cheese on a colorful ceramic plate.

After a few moments of focused slicing and chopping, Nick and I have prepared a platter of tomato basil bruschetta, a cheese plate, and a fruit salad. Nick pours us each a glass of wine before arranging everything on a wide wooden tray.

"I thought we could eat on the porch." A bit of pink creeps up his neck. It's adorable how embarrassed he gets over these little romantic gestures. I can almost see into his mind's eye, him planning out the candlelit meal on the porch but trying to act like it's no big deal.

"Sounds great!" I reach to brush my lips over his cheek before hurrying to hold open the back door. I have to bite back a laugh when we enter the screened-in porch off the kitchen. Nick did indeed find a moment to light a candle on the small teak patio table. Soft bossa nova emanates from a laptop tucked in the corner. "Well this is romantic," I tease and Nick hurries past me to arrange the meal just so on the table. Archie slips out behind him, settling next to one of the chairs.

Nick plates our food in silence. He must have been starving because he immediately wolfs down three slices of bruschetta and a few wedges of cheese before I even finish a single slice of bread. After he eats a bit he seems to relax, yawning and sinking back into his chair.

"Sorry," he mutters, wiping his mouth neatly on one of the navy linen napkins he set the table with. "I guess I was hungry."

We sit for a while, listening to the soft music and the thrum of night insects. An occasional warm breeze flows through the room, fluttering the leaves of the dozens of flowering plants in terracotta pots. The food is delicious, the tomatoes perfectly ripe and seasoned with crunchy salt and a squeeze of lemon. Nick looks so at ease here on his back porch, his face golden in the flickering candlelight. I'm tempted to let us settle into this soft quiet, but the bigger, more annoying part of me wants to continue our conversation from his bedroom.

"So do you?" I ask, pushing the remains of my meal to Nick to finish. "Want to get married someday, I mean."

Nick bobs his head immediately and enthusiastically, his mouth quirking up into his adorable sheepish grin. "I do. It, uh, was actually kind of a sticking point for my mom when I came out. You know the whole Greek marriage and family thing. I know she always wanted me to have a big family." His eyes meet mine, a little nervous.

"Is that something *you* want?" I ask softly, hoping to set Nick at ease.

"Yeah." The word almost seems to pain him to say. "It's fine if that's not something you're open to. I mean it's not like a deal breaker or anything. I just, I don't know, I sort of helped raise Doria, and I always loved helping Jason and Lexi out with Cole. Like when he was a baby and toddler, seeing him take his first steps, helping him learn to write his name." Nick gets a wistful look on his face.

Again I push myself to be honest. "I have pretty much zero experience with babies or toddlers or anything. But I loved working with middle schoolers and teens at the youth center in Chicago. I definitely like kids. I guess I never thought I'd be in a serious enough relationship for it to come up." Christopher actively seemed to dislike children. Anytime I would gesture toward a cute family when we were out walking or remark over the whimsical displays at one of the toy stores on Clark Street he would scoff and complain about the neighborhood being overtaken by baby-crazy yuppie families.

"Come here," Nick requests, scooting his chair away from the table and gesturing to his lap. His arms wrap around me the moment I settle onto him. "I love you," he sighs into my hair. "Feels good to say that." There's a smile in his voice.

"It does." I agree, but of course I can't let a good moment go unanalyzed so I lean away from him slightly to look at his face. "What do you mean when you say it?" I hope I don't sound as pathetic as I feel asking the question. "I'm not looking for you to do a 'How do I love thee, let me count the ways' sonnet or anything. This isn't like a compliment grab."

"Sonnet?" Nick quirks an eyebrow before he scoffs and shakes his head. "You paid a lot more attention in English class than I did." He turns serious and I can almost feel him thinking, trying to put his ideas in order. Finally he shoots me a pained expression. "Baby, I don't know. I just love you. It's an emotion. I don't know how to describe it or whatever."

I laugh. "Sorry, I wasn't trying to be all weird about it. I mean that, like, when I say I love you I mean I actively want you. I want to wake up with you. And throughout the day I'm always thinking about how you might feel about things. I keep this little, like, tally of stuff I want to tell you about, and..." That soft expression from earlier is back and my stomach does a nervous flip as I try to finish my thought. "Usually the first thing I think about when I wake up is coffee and all the things I need to worry about. But now the first thing I think of is you. When I consider the future, it doesn't seem so scary anymore because I can always picture you in it and that feels like a comfort." The words flow from my mouth easily and I know they're right.

Nick claims my mouth with his, a slight sweetness lingering on his lips from the fruit salad. The tip of his tongue traces the seam of my mouth, coaxing it open and eliciting a gasp from me. He pulls back and for a moment I see myself reflected in his eyes.

"I guess you make me feel like myself. I can be the real me and I can *like* that person. It's always been that way with you. Loving you makes me love myself." The words tumble out of Nick in a hurry as he stares down at the weathered wood of the porch. Heat radiates off his face. Then he shrugs, chucks me under the chin, and taps a kiss to my nose. "I'm gonna clean this stuff up then unfortunately I have to head to bed. Early day again tomorrow." He slides me off him easily then busies himself stacking our plates onto the tray.

"Oh!" I chirp. I'd forgotten to share the only good part of Operation Be a Decent Boyfriend with Nick. "Jimmy and Daisy are spending the night at my dad's. So I can stay over." As soon as the words leave my lips, I realize I basically invited myself to spend the night. Nick has to get up in fewer than six hours. He probably wants to sleep in peace. "Only if you want. No big deal at all if you want me to head home." I work hard to keep my voice bright and casual. Heat steals up my throat and into my cheeks and I'm grateful the porch is so dim.

"David." Nick is looking at me with a mix of exasperation and fondness. "Of course I want you to spend the night. Do you have any idea how hard it is for me not to beg you to stay most nights you come over? I want you all the time."

My face burns and my legs have gone all shaky. As if he didn't say exactly what I needed to hear, Nick pushes through the screen door balancing the tray effortlessly, Archie trotting behind him. Quickly I scoop up our empty wine glasses, wincing when they clatter together. Thankfully they don't break.

Nick is already busy cleaning up the kitchen. His home is immaculate, never a crumb on the counter or a pair of shoes in the middle of the floor inviting me to trip over them. Together we make quick, silent work of cleaning up and I try not to get distracted by the flex of Nick's forearms and biceps as he reaches to hang up pans or wipe down the counter. I must completely zone out because when Nick speaks his mouth quirks up in amusement.

"Where do you go?" he asks without malice in his voice.

I shake my head, trying to come back to reality. "Sorry," I murmur. "Did you say something?"

"I asked if you need a toothbrush or pajamas or anything. I'm not sure if I have anything that'll fit."

"Nope!" I grin at him and stride over to the canvas bag I hung on a hook by the door. "I brought a toothbrush and toiletries and everything. I usually sleep in my underwear." Even though Nick was fucking me an hour ago the idea of sharing a bed with him, of waking in the dark comforted by the steady rise and fall of his solid chest against my face, leaves me achy with desire.

"Oh," Nick croaks and reaches down to not so subtly adjust himself. "Well, okay then. I'm gonna take Archie out again. I'll be right up."

I bound up the stairs, filled with a giddy energy that has me worrying I won't be able to sleep. This won't be the first time I've shared a bed with Nick. Throughout grade school we used to have sleepovers all the time, falling asleep on the floor with our faces inches apart. Even in high school Nick would occasionally sneak into my room, drunk after hanging out with his buddies, and pass out in my bed after begging me to read to him until he fell asleep. I would sit up and watch him, trying and failing to pull apart the threads in my tangled-up emotions.

And once, Nick stayed in my dorm while I was doing my masters at Columbia. We'd spent the weekend together, him driving down to the city, once again filling me with false hope that he wanted me for real. Both nights we'd shared my comically tiny bed, I started awake in the middle of the night, heart hammering so hard in my chest I was sure I'd wake him. I wanted to wrap my arms around him and beg him not to go. But he left in a hurry that Sunday morning, unwilling to meet my eye after a guy on my floor walked in on me taking care of Nick's morning hard-on in the shower.

When Nick bends to kiss my neck and pulls me against him, he startles me enough that I drop my toothbrush into the sink. I have been standing in the bathroom, spacing out, and staring at my own reflection like the neurotic idiot that I am.

"You okay?" Nick asks. He rinses my toothbrush off before squeezing on some all-natural toothpaste and handing it to me. I nod, grateful to have the distraction of oral hygiene so I don't keep diving into dark thought wells.

Watching Nick get ready for bed is also a welcome distraction. He stripped down to navy boxer briefs, which hug his thick thighs and ride up deliciously with his movements. Methodical about everything he does, he brushes his teeth thoroughly, then flosses and gargles with mouthwash. He washes his face carefully with the same delicious herbal soap he uses on his body before smearing a bit of amber-colored oil on his face. I must wrinkle my eyebrows at it because he informs me that it's jojoba oil and that it's great for your skin. And a tiny part of me hates him in that moment because apparently he doesn't have to spend obscene quantities of money to achieve the kind of glow I strive for.

I'm a little embarrassed by the elaborate nature of my own pre-bedtime routine but I find genuine pleasure in taking care of my skin, so whatever. Nick fails to hide a smirk when I push my hair back with a terrycloth headband and pull out a floral toiletry bag full of my products. I don't even look at him as I cleanse my face, mist it with rosewater, apply a serum, and massage moisturizer into my skin. I like the intimacy of getting ready for bed together, the quiet, coordinated movements in a small shared space. I can imagine us doing this a thousand more times side by side. But Nick needs to get a bigger bathroom mirror.

"So that's why your skin's so soft." He chuckles and drags the pad of his index finger over my cheek.

I roll my eyes in response and follow Nick back to his bedroom. Archie is curled up on a blue blanket folded at the foot of the bed. I have a sneaking suspicion that the dog usually sleeps in bed with Nick. "Archie can sleep in the bed if that's where he normally sleeps. I don't want to be the one kicking him out."

"Oh he's a horrible bed hog. And he snores. I don't want to put you through that." Nick pulls open the windows, letting in a sweet-smelling breeze that ruffles the sheer curtains.

Suddenly, profoundly shy I undress and slide under the cool white sheets. Nick flicks off his bedside lamp, collapses onto the bed, and groans as he pulls me to him. I lay my cheek against his chest. Improbably my heart rate slows, all my anxieties melting away as his words echo against my ear.

"Good night, David."

And as I return the words, pressing a kiss to his skin, I find myself drifting into the dark, rolling sea of sleep.

Chapter Nineteen

David

July

When I was eleven, my parents took a two-week summer trip to Paris without me. My mom was giving a talk at Descartes University and she and my father decided to make a vacation of it. I don't remember missing them much. I stayed with Jimmy, Shelley and Daisy in the Airstream and spent most nights sleeping in a tent under the vibrant canopy of stars. Days were devoted to riding horses with Shelley, walking quietly through the woods with Daisy, or going foraging with Jimmy. The latter activity usually amounted to me listening to one of his long political rants that I barely understood. Guilt weighed heavy on me over the course of those two weeks because I'd missed Nick more than I missed my own parents. Jimmy and Shelley's place was in Big Indian, about an hour's drive away, so I only saw Nick once, when I'd finally whined at my uncle enough to get him to pick Nick up so my friend could spend the night camping with me.

My mom sent me two postcards, one depicting the Arc de Triomphe illuminated at night, and the other a beautiful painting of water lilies. I'd been excited to read the details of my parents' trip: the food they tried, my dad's bad attempts at speaking French, the museums they visited. But there was something about the water lilies postcard that echoed through me. I sat on one of the lawn chairs outside my uncle's trailer for hours, staring at the image, trying to memorize the colors and figure out how the painter—Monet, it said on the back of the card—made everything look like a good dream.

When my parents returned, I threw myself into my mother's arms and demanded that she tell me everything about the painting. Her hair flew all around her face on the windy car ride back home as she breathlessly told me about visiting a museum called the Marmottan that had a whole room devoted to these works. One glance at her bright eyes and flushed cheeks told me that she shared my enthusiasm for the water lilies painting.

A week after they returned my mom started working on what she called her Monet garden in the backyard. Off teaching for the summer, she would rise early, throw on her mismatched gardening clothes, and drive with me to the big nursery outside town. Sometimes we even lugged along the Impressionism art book she brought back from France. She would ask me which flowers I thought looked the most like the ones in the pictures. By the time the school year started our yard was transformed into a pastel wonderland of blooms. The goal, she said, was for us to paint the garden out in the open just like Monet himself had done.

After my mom died, I developed a strong aversion to Impressionist art. It didn't take Freud to understand why. Unfortunately, the museum I ended up working at had a huge collection of Monet's paintings and my colleagues always found it odd that I tended to shift my gaze to the polished wooden floor when I crossed through those galleries. Marc had even asked me about my weird Impressionism-hate, but I gave a vague theoretical answer and he left it alone, sensing, I think, that it was a scab I'd rather not pick. When my dad would call me, filling me in on the details of his day-to-day, I hated when he brought up working in my mom's garden. I would go monosyllabic until the conversation shifted back to local politics or him asking about how my research was going.

Now as I pull the massive tangle of weeds that has overtaken the beds since I moved back, the billowy heads of dandelions and clumps of waxy grass seeming endless, I realize my cheeks are wet with tears. I want to rip every single plant from the earth and rake the dirt until it is black and bare. I want to stomp into the kitchen and find the big box of salt we never use and upend its contents onto this stupid garden. Instead I'm careful and deliberate as I tidy up the plots of land my mother and I so loved. I have no desire to stop and consider my grief. I've managed not to think about my mom much, even since moving back, and I do not want to start mourning her now. If I do, I worry I might cry scary hard, shaking and gagging and gasping for breaths that won't come.

My phone starts going nuts in my pocket, ringing even though I'd sworn I'd put it on do not disturb. I dash at the wetness on my face with the back of my hand so I can make out the number on the screen. A Manhattan area code, I think, but I don't recognize the caller. I let it ring one more time, the obnoxious calypso ringtone grating on my nerves before I decide to pick up.

"This is David," I croak, hoping I sound professional and calm instead of like a grown-ass man who was on the verge of dissolving into sobs.

"Hi, David! How are you doing?" The female voice lilts with a posh British accent and the sound is so comforting and familiar I find the corners of my mouth lifting.

"Selima?" I squeak, delighted to hear from my friend.

Selima and I were in the same cohort of our PhD program at Chicago. Although we'd been incredibly close, we fell out of touch after she moved to Manhattan to take a job as an assistant gallerist. After bonding initially over our mutual hatred of getting-to-know-you games at orientation, I'd moved into the crappy walkup in Pilsen she shared with a perpetually flustered anthropology student. Selima would talk me down off the ledge when I started pacing around wildly from writer's block or breaking out in cold sweats over deadlines. She also made amazing Persian food at random hours, sometimes waking me up in the middle of the night to indulge in a feast of herbal sabzi polo and eggplant stew. In turn, I soothed her through her rages at students when they pushed back on grades or dozed off in classes she prepared so meticulously for. She and I were both forever wringing our hands that our students refused to take us seriously.

Selima and I made a great team, commiserating as we slowly became disenchanted with the rat race of academia. As we approached our defenses, we both decided we wanted to look for jobs in museums or galleries rather than slog away as adjuncts at random universities like so many of our classmates.

It was also nice to have a colleague with whom I was intellectually well-aligned. Both of our dissertations had focused on art as a means of community building. Selima's work highlighted Iranian female artists and the intersections of traditional Persian and modern Western artistic sensibilities. My work was, honestly, significantly less exciting, focused on queer public art, Andy Warhol and Keith Haring in particular.

"Yes! I'm so glad to talk to you. It's been a while, hasn't it?"

I nod as she pulls me out of my walk down memory lane. Realizing she can't see me, I respond with actual words. "It's great to hear from you! Sorry I'm so bad at keeping in touch. Are you still at 404 Gallery?"

"I'm not. I accepted a new position last year. That's actually why I'm calling." Something in her voice shifts, going from warm and friendly to crisp and practiced.

Because I'm confused, I stay silent and wait for Selima to elaborate.

She clears her throat softly before continuing. "My boss recently discovered your Instagram page. Which by the way is fantastic. I'm loving your work. Very smart to use social media to promote your stuff like that. But anyway, Mr. Sakamoto is interested in a specific piece— that male nude you posted recently. The one done in blue and gray of the man leaning in the doorway?"

I'd posted the nude of Nick to my page a few days earlier. He was thrilled when I asked him about it, admitting that the idea of me sharing the image publicly, even though no one could see his face, turned him on. Honestly, no one with a body that nice would want to keep it hidden. Then my brain catches up to what Selima just said. "Wait are you talking about *Larry* Sakamoto?" I splutter.

Selima laughs, a bright, tinkling sound. "Yes. I work at Le Eclat gallery now. Directly under Larry. It's been great. I'm learning a lot."

Pride for Selima's success wars with the sheer shock that Larry Sakamoto, owner of one of the most influential contemporary art galleries in the world, has even seen my work. My skin feels about ten sizes too tight and my throat goes so dry I have to work hard to swallow.

"So Mr. Sakamoto is interested in purchasing the nude for his private collection. What are the dimensions of the piece?"

I have no earthly idea what the dimensions of the giant piece of watercolor paper might be. Since I started working in a larger format, I just buy the biggest paper they happen to have at the art supply store.

"Uhhh…" I rocket toward the house, tucking the phone between my ear and shoulder as I scramble to open the porch door. "It's pretty big, I guess?" After an eternity of searching I locate a tape measure in the wildly cluttered kitchen junk drawer and bound up to my room to measure the piece. Thankfully Selima waits patiently, filling the conversation with details about shipping and payment. She still has yet to mention what Mr. Sakamoto is planning to offer for the painting, but honestly I would give it to him for free if it means my work will be displayed in his collection. "Twenty-six by forty. Um, inches. Obviously." Finally I manage to answer her question.

"Wonderful," Selima says and I can hear her speaking to someone in the background. "Mr. Sakamoto will offer seven hundred and fifty for it. As I said, I will e-mail you a shipping label once we're off the phone."

My jaw actually clicks as it drops open. Someone is willing to pay *that* much for something I made? Not just someone. An unbelievably famous gallerist whose Upper East Side mansion frequently features in architecture and design magazines. A man who is literally discussed at length in the art history textbooks on my bookshelf. I wrote about him in my dissertation, for fuck's sake! It's clichéd, but I pinch the skin on my wrist to make sure I'm awake. There is no way this isn't a fever dream.

Selima must interpret my stunned silence as resistance to the price because there's muffled talking in the background, then she offers to go up to eight hundred dollars.

"Great! Um, sold." God, I sound like a fucking moron. "Um, wow. Did you tell Mr. Sakamoto about my work or something?"

"No. He likes to keep an eye on the queer art scene. And he's completely addicted to Instagram." She laughs. "Speaking of, my friend Tia is organizing a group show at Gesture in Bushwick at the end of September. You'd be perfect for it, David. It's all going to be devoted to the promotion of queer arts on social media. Would you like me to put you two in touch? I'd be more than happy to."

"Are you my fairy godmother?" I ask. Apparently I'm wholly incapable of acting professional or filtering the stupid crap flowing from my mouth.

Selima chuckles again. "I'll send you a follow-up e-mail connecting you with Tia. Her stuff is phenomenal. Really great video installations."

"Wow. Thank you so much, Selima. Seriously. Wow." I desperately wish I could string together a coherent thought.

"David, no need to thank me. Your work speaks for itself. I'm so pleased you've chosen to work as an artist. Anyway, I have to run, but I'll be in touch this afternoon."

I end the call in a daze, staring down at the darkened screen of my phone. As amazing as it was to get the attention and barrage of followers after the Kenny

Thomas thing, this is next level. Like actual participation in the actual art world. Of course, I can't let myself be excited about the money, the validation, or the potential to participate in a legitimate-sounding show at a fancy gallery. No, I start freaking out that everyone is going to discover what a complete fraud I am. What if Larry Sakamoto gets the painting in the mail and hates the way it looks in real life? What if this Tia person realizes I have zero formal artistic training and wants nothing to do with me?

I need to talk to Anna. She's amazing at pulling me out of these impostor-syndrome death spirals. But my call goes right to voicemail. Right. Today is a weekday and Anna is at the library doing her actual job.

Okay, Nick. He'll be all calm and sweet and proud of me. Plus hearing his voice always ensures things will be okay. But no luck. He also has real work to do.

I'll try Marc. His phone is never more than a millimeter away from his fingertips. The need to talk to someone, anyone, is burning me up. I'm almost tempted to wake my dad up from his nap. But I need to return Marc's call from the other day anyway. And Marc will actually know who Larry Sakamoto is and can join in on my swirling anxiety and excitement.

Bless him, he answers on the first ring. "Thanks for waiting two whole days to call me back, you fuck." His wry smile is almost audible.

"Sorry. Sorry." I'm about to word vomit at him but he cuts me off.

"No worries. I was calling you to despair over my total lack of career success."

"What happened?" I ask, now worried that this will be a terrible time to bring up the whole famous gallerist buying my art thing.

"I applied for your old job." Marc's statement is followed by the sound of a door slamming shut. "They interviewed me but it was pretty clear they weren't going to choose a dumbass with nothing but a shitty for-profit college graphic design degree."

"Marc." I say his name gently. He would have been perfect for my old job. In his role as my assistant he'd been intimately familiar with the duties and had been better at a good portion of them than I was. "That's awful. You would have been amazing. Why didn't you tell me you were applying? I would have called Lane and recommended you."

"I was embarrassed. It was such a long shot anyway. They ended up promoting Nisa. She'll be better." He sounds like he's trying to convince himself.

There's a long pause in which I page through a variety of comforting phrases in my head but they all feel like platitudes. I know Marc has always been self-conscious about what he views as his unimpressive credentials in the competitive, pretentious museum world. Finally I just settle on a question. "Are you staying on?"

He makes a noncommittal noise. "Ehh. For now, so I don't have a gap in my resume or whatever. And so I don't land myself in debtor's prison. But I'll probably start applying around." He clears his throat and when he speaks again his voice is bright and teasing. "So, is that your fucking boyfriend in the painting you posted a few days ago? Because if so I legitimately hate you. That ass is stupid nice."

I bark out a laugh. "Yeah, it's Nick."

"Ugh, whatever. You have this fucking dream life in dumb upstate New York with your hot as fuck boyfriend and I'm stuck in Chicago going on crappy online dates.

The last guy I got drinks with had snakes. Multiple snakes in a tank in his creepy apartment. And I still let him fuck me." Marc sighs dramatically and loudly.

"Do you want me to add salt to the wound?" I tease, but I'm wary of bringing up the windfall today brought.

"Oh god. What? Did the farmer propose or something? Am I going to have to come to some perfect-ass Pinterest wedding?"

"I miss you," I say, meaning it. "But no. I sold that piece though. The one of Nick."

"Nice!" Marc says, sounding genuinely pleased. "Are you working with that gallery in Woodstock you mentioned?"

"Um, no. Larry Sakamoto bought it." Heat flashes across my face.

There is no sound on the other end and I wonder for a moment if Marc is angry enough to have hung up. Maybe I'm being an asshole mentioning this.

"Holy fucking shit, David. Are you fucking kidding me?" Marc practically screams into the phone.

"No?" I venture. "My friend Selima, my roommate from grad school, works for him. She called me like ten minutes ago about him buying it for his private collection. Like, I guess for his house or something? Crazy, right?"

"Um, yeah! That's amazing. How much did he offer you?"

Marc is never shy about asking personal, slightly invasive questions but it's something I've always liked about him. He's not asking out of some weird competitiveness, he's curious so he asks.

"Eight hundred dollars!" I say, still reeling over the figure. The idea of making that much money in the span of a short conversation leaves me breathless. "And

Selima's putting me in touch with some woman organizing a show about queer art or something. I seriously can't believe this. I am so *not* a real artist." I can't help letting my doubts creep in.

"Bullshit," Marc snaps. "You make art so you're a real artist. You are what you do. Although that means I am a coffee buyer and printer fixer, so..."

"Not true. The materials you put together for the outreach program were amazing. Plus you basically designed my entire website after I made it look like some kind of Geocities monstrosity. You're talented and you know it."

"Yeah your site sucked... But wow! Are you going to do the show?"

I admit that I'm waiting on Selima's e-mail and I doubt anyone will want my stuff for the exhibition anyway. But it would be cool. I can't even imagine showing in a gallery. It was never something I'd considered as a viable option.

"David, Jesus Christ. Well, when you get accepted for the show I'll come up and visit, okay?"

We end the call a minute later and I can't seem to stop smiling. Glancing down at the riot of colorful blooms in my mom's garden and the pile of weeds and dirt strewn all over the patio, I push up my sleeves and return to the task of reinvigorating the Impressionist garden. My mom would be proud.

Chapter Twenty

Nick

September

Lexi's words echo in my head as I flip my phone side to side in my hand. *Your mom misses you, Nick.*

Outside, Jenna and Hector walk my cheery sister-in-law through basic weed identification and gratefully welcome her aboard as a new member of the Laurel Creek Farm family. Their enthusiastic voices carrying through the humid air do little to lighten my dark mood. We decided to take Lexi up on her offer to help out for the summer and fall after Jenna finally put her foot down, saying if we didn't get some additional help, we were all going to collapse from exhaustion. Jenna, as usual, had been right. Since making the joint decision that we wanted to increase production and expand to a few markets in Manhattan, we'd been killing ourselves under the burning heat of the sun. Even two-a-days throughout high school when I'd been desperate to prove myself to my mean-ass coach hadn't left me this exhausted.

As soon as Lexi slid out of her scratched Fiesta this morning, she'd launched herself into my arms, saying she missed me coming over and that Cole had been asking about me. She left out the fact that Jason had probably forbidden his son from seeing me again, but the implication hung heavy between us.

Since coming out not much has changed in my day-to-day existence. I still wake up alone most mornings, work out, toss a tennis ball around with Archie, then make coffee and breakfast before Hector and Jenna arrive for the day. It's definitely been nice not randomly feeling like I can't take a deep breath. And it's been nothing short of amazing waking up some days with David twined around me like a morning glory vine. Seeing his auburn hair all sleep-mussed and falling into sheets that smell like him are more than worth the occasional twinges of sadness.

I hadn't quite been prepared for how much the implosion of my relationship with my family would hurt. Even though the farm work wrings me out, sometimes sleep evades me and I pace the kitchen into the wee hours of the morning. Most nights I channel my frustration into baking the Greek pastries my mom used to send home with me carefully wrapped in takeout containers from the diner. If a flavor is slightly off, it stings knowing I can't pick up the phone and ask her about it. David, Jenna, and Hector eat my handiwork with gusto but they all seem to recognize that I'm pouring my sorrow into the food.

So when Lexi admitted that my mom missed me, something inside me crumbled. Could it be possible for me to rekindle my relationship with her? My dad and Jason are lost causes. They think I'm disgusting. A pervert, as Jason had texted me a few weeks after the ill-fated family dinner. If the misspellings and timestamp on the message were any indication, he was clearly wasted. Unlike my brother, though, my mom hadn't seemed angry or disgusted by me coming out. She'd just seemed sad.

I could talk to her and explain that the hateful things my father says about queer people are untrue. She could come over and have a cup of coffee with David, see how happy he makes me. See how engaging, and intelligent, and caring my boyfriend is. See that we're slowly stacking the bricks to build a life together. The thought has me unlocking my phone and navigating to her cell number, still at the top of my favorites list. Glancing at the little icon next to her name, a picture of the two of us in the kitchen at the diner, shoves a lump into my throat. I tap her number with a shaking finger.

"Nico?" she answers on the third ring. My heartbeat seems to falter at the sound of her hushed, tight voice.

"Hey, Ma." I rake my fingers through my hair. It's damp with sweat.

My mother sighs into the phone but says nothing for a long moment.

Shit. Maybe I should say something. Apologize? Or try to explain myself? Usually in a situation like this I plan out my words so this doesn't happen. So my mouth doesn't clamp into a hard line, leaving me silent.

"I made karidopita. Something was off though. Do you use orange juice or only the zest?" I figure asking her about her walnut cake, a dessert she and I both love, will set her at ease. Nope.

"Nico." She sounds as weary as I feel. "I don't think it's a good idea for you to call me." She pauses. "I use the zest." The line goes dead.

I toss my phone down onto the countertop with too much force. Thankfully it's in a durable case so nothing breaks. Well that was a disaster. I should have understood that my parents want nothing to do with me. I have to make a new family now.

I let my mind drift back to David and the last time he'd spent the night, a few days after he found out his work was accepted at some fancy gallery in Brooklyn. He talked a mile a minute and insisted on taking me out for dinner with money he'd gotten from selling a naked painting of me. It was weird but definitely cool that some famous art guy was going to have a picture of my ass in his house. After David devoured my cock, the minute I pulled my Jeep up the driveway after dinner, he stayed over.

Realistically, I knew that it would start to feel normal, seeking out his lithe body in the night, the shiver that ran down my spine every time our lips brushed, waking before him to listen to his soft breathing and watch his face move as he dreamed. Sure, it was kind of weird but I loved watching him sleep, his beautiful face relaxed and plush lips parted. The next morning when I put a thermos of coffee with milk and honey on the bedside table I'd started thinking of as his, David acted like I had figured out how to transform dirt into diamonds. When he drifted sleepily out to the orchard to find me, wearing only one of my flannel shirts and a pair of black briefs, I was so tongue-tied that Jenna dissolved into laughter and Hector tactfully excused himself to the barn.

The need to hear David's voice is overwhelming, but it's only when his phone goes directly to voicemail that I remember where he is. He's spending the weekend in the city, getting dinner with the friend who told him about the art show and helped him sell his painting. And going to meetings with people from the gallery, I think? He told me the details so fast it was hard to keep track of the information. It was even harder to extinguish the spark of worry that ignited when he told me about spending the weekend in Brooklyn.

Logically, I know he's going to be busy with his art and his friend. Besides, David has reassured me over and over that he's happy in the Hudson Valley. Still, the Neanderthal part of my brain has me wondering who he's staying with. I keep picturing him reconnecting with his sophisticated professor ex-boyfriend and realizing he would prefer life in a city full of art and culture and intellectual stimulation. They'd probably go to some intimate cash-only bar and drink craft cocktails and this Julian guy would put his hand over David's on the table... *Fuck*. I need to get back to work and stop angsting over made-up crap.

Bounding down the porch steps I pause for a moment to look at the farm Jenna, Hector, and I built. New, sturdy fences surround the neat vegetable and herb plots, keeping the deer in the woods where they belong. As beautiful as they are, those assholes can totally destroy a month's worth of work in a matter of moments. Sunlight filters through the leaves of trellised pole beans. The crops are thriving thanks to the drip irrigation system Jenna installed. As my gaze scans over the newly built mobile chicken coop and travels to the freshly cleared orchard, my shoulders drop. I'm proud of this place. Proud of myself. Proud of my new family.

"Nick!" Jenna's voice startles me out of staring at the dry grass under my boots. She and Lexi jog over from the barn.

"Sorry, what's up?"

"Are you planning to work at all today or just hang out around the house?" Her tone is teasing, amber eyes bright. "Because we can replace you with Lexi. This chick is fantastic. She had a great idea too." Jenna makes a *go ahead* gesture to Lexi.

"No. It's dumb. I was babbling." Her tanned cheeks flush and she nervously runs her fingers through her shiny dark hair.

"No!" Jenna shakes her head emphatically. "Lexi noticed the space next to the orchard. You know where your uncle had tossed all that shitty lumber?"

I nod, grinning at Lexi to encourage her. Living with my dad and brother tends to make everyone feel like each idea is stupider than the last. "What'd you think, Lex?"

"Well," she hedges, "I thought it might be a good place to do flowers? You know, like, for sale. No one at our market sells them and I always wanted to buy sunflowers and stuff. Plus a lot of the people doing weddings at the new hotel seem to want local flowers for their bouquets. Anyway, sorry. I know it's super rude to barge in and make suggestions on the first day." She's breathless as she stops talking.

The idea is a good one. And it wouldn't be too expensive to make it a reality. Stupidly my mind also supplies the idea that David would probably love having ready access to fresh flowers. He'd gone through a phase in high school when he was obsessed with painting them. He and his mom would sit in the backyard for hours working in companionable silence as they painted canvas after canvas.

I fix my attention back on Lexi's eager face. "That's a great idea!" I shove her shoulder playfully. "We could start that next season. Plus doing flowers might make us more appealing to the city markets as we expand."

Jenna nods thoughtfully, turning as Hector strides over.

"I loved the flower idea too," Hector pipes up, grin stretching wide across his face. "In fact, I remember suggesting something similar and neither of you were into the idea."

He's teasing but Lexi looks worried, eyes flicking from me to Jenna. Her gaze softens when it lands on Jenna. The two of them seemed to hit it off today. It makes sense. Jenna can set pretty much anyone at ease, and Lexi, after being berated by my brother all the time, could probably use some comfort and friendship.

When Hector and Jenna start discussing pricing for the green Thai eggplants, Lexi's gaze flicks over Jenna's body, pausing on the exposed band of bronze skin between Jenna's shredded jeans and her cut-off Talking Heads T-shirt. So that's how it is. Before I have time to process the fact that my sister-in-law was hardcore checking out my friend, Lexi notices my quizzical expression. She stands up straight like a soldier and shoots me a glare.

"So how's your boyfriend doing?" she asks. *Nice subject change, Lex.*

I laugh. "He's great. In the city this weekend getting ready for an art show. It's pretty awesome. His career is taking off."

"So..." Lexi tips her head in a mock flirty gesture. "Are you guys, like, getting serious, or what?"

I hate that her teasing makes me blush like a kid. I rub the back of my neck. "Um. Yeah, pretty serious. His dad's doing a lot better too, so I'm kind of starting to think about asking David to move in with me. I want to talk to his dad though. See how he feels and stuff. Don't want to push."

Jenna spins away from Hector like a powerful golden top. "Wait. Dude. Shut the fuck up. Are you serious? You're thinking of having David move in here and you didn't tell me?" She scoffs. "Some friend you are."

"Be real, Jenna. I know the minute I even hinted you'd tell Anna. David would know before I could even come up with a romantic way to ask him." I grin at her.

"I wouldn't tell Anna." Her voice is flat.

"Anyway…" I draw out the word, trying to get rid of the awkwardness that unexpectedly infused the conversation. "Do you guys want to come to David's show next week? It's Saturday night at some gallery in Brooklyn. He and Anna are driving down the day before to set stuff up. So I was gonna head down after the market. I invited my cousin Ben too since he's still in New York for a few more months. It might be a good time."

Embarrassment at admitting my plan makes my eyes burn.

"If it's, um, okay with you guys I was going to take Sunday off? See if David wanted to spend the rest of the weekend in the city. Maybe go to some museums or whatever." That, and ask David the questions that have me so nervous I shove my hands deep in the pockets of my jeans so I don't wring them to death.

"Sounds fun." Hector grins. "I'll probably skip the show though, if that's cool. I can get everything finished up in the coop. I'm happy to keep an eye on Archie for you too. And don't worry about taking Sunday off. Heck, take Monday too. The three of us can handle things around here."

"Yeah, especially since you're useless most of the time." Jenna winks at me, snarky merriment firmly back in place. "I'd love to come. I love your man's art."

Lexi kicks at the grass. Of course she can't come. My brother, who loves calling people from any town larger than ours "citiots," thinks going south of Poughkeepsie is a total waste of time. If he knew his wife came with me to an actual gay art show in Brooklyn, he might explode into a fiery ball of protein powder, cheap vodka, and hate speech. Lexi would have to lie about where she was. And I know she's not crazy about leaving Cole with Jason because he just ignores the kid. I wonder if Jason even knows about Lexi working at his gay brother's farm.

"Sorry, Nick," Lexi mumbles. "I don't think..." She shoots me an apologetic look.

I'm wholly convinced my asshole brother does, in fact, have a sixth sense for reaching out exactly when people are most dreading hearing from him because Lexi's phone buzzes loudly in the pocket of her shorts and her face falls.

"Ugh," she groans, rolling her eyes extravagantly. "Jason can't pick Cole up from school. Is it okay if I head out early?"

"Of course!" Jenna and I say in unison and Hector barks out a laugh.

I follow Lexi to her car, telling her about my misguided attempt to reconnect with my mom as we walk along the gravel driveway. Her fingers, the nails painted sparkly pink, dig into my shoulder as she gives me a sympathetic squeeze.

"I didn't tell Jason I'm working here," she admits. "I told him I got a part-time job at a gift shop in Woodstock." She fiddles with her tangle of keys and the key chains Cole always buys for her. "He's been awful. It's like since he found out you're, you know, gay or whatever he has to act like even more of a macho idiot. He's been a nightmare to Cole." She pauses again, catching her lower lip between her teeth. Whatever she's deliberating about saying can't be good. "Jason, um, he told Cole to stay away from you."

My hands clench into fists and every muscle in my body goes rigid. I don't say anything but my hurt and anger must be visible on my face because Lexi reaches up to pat my cheek.

"I told Cole later not to listen to that crap. I said you're his uncle and you love him and that you're a wonderful man. Usually I don't like to disagree too much with Jason because I don't want Cole getting caught in the middle of our shit, but that was..." Lexi shakes her head, looking as sad as I feel. "Anyway, I'm sorry. I know that must hurt you to hear. But I didn't want you to wonder why you never see Cole anymore. You're always so good with him and that kid loves you to death. I'll try to bring him out to the farm soon though. He misses you a lot."

I can't manage to speak so I nod once. Lexi, thankfully, is perceptive enough to climb into her car without another word, casting me a watery smile as she pulls away. As soon as her car rounds the curve of the driveway, disappearing behind a tangle of evergreen trees and underbrush, dozens of possible responses come to mind. Lexi should leave Jason. She should get away from those toxic asshole men and come live here with me. I could even build a cozy little cottage for her and Cole to live in. Then the anger starts bubbling up.

Throughout my childhood my dad did his fair share of political raving. As a kid this talk did nothing but confuse and shame me. It made my stomach hurt and my head buzz. Apparently, however, Jason took our ignorant father at his word and now views me as an actual danger to his son.

I exhale hard through my nose and turn back toward the barn. Everything seems strangely quiet as I begin relentlessly hauling heavy bags of compost to a new garden bed. My mind is a perfect blank as I work. Sweat drips into my eyes and my muscles burn more and more with each trip between the barn and the freshly turned plot of land. A wheelbarrow would make the job easier but I need the pain. Need to exhaust myself.

By the time I've prepared the bed for planting, the sky is streaked with hazy orange and gold and the cicadas sing in the trees. The windows of the house glow yellow. Probably Jenna is grabbing us beers and fishing out a deck of cards so we can unwind on the porch. Instead of joining her though, I head in the direction of the barn to grab the auger and start drilling for fence posts. I'm striding across the driveway when the wind carries the sound of my name to my ears.

Jenna, planted on the top porch stair, is waving a beer at me and making a *wrap it up* gesture with her finger. *Stop working.* Warmth blooms in my chest and I jog toward my house. Our house.

Chapter Twenty-One

Nick

September

When my obnoxious bell alarm goes off the next morning at three thirty, my throat feels like I swallowed sand. Beers on the porch turned into hour-long confessionals. Jenna admitted that she and Anna had some kind of huge falling out but was unwilling to divulge further. I shared my tentative plans with David. And Hector shocked both of us by revealing he'd been seeing Naomi, the beautiful, stone-faced bartender at the dive he frequented, for six whole months but didn't think it bore mentioning. We'd put away a six-pack of Keegan Ale before Jenna decided we needed whiskey and unearthed a very large, very full metal flask from the glove box of her car. And we drank every last burning drop.

Archie, hogging up a majority of my large bed as usual, shoots me a sidelong glare as I try to untangle myself from my sweaty sheets.

"Don't judge me," I chastise the dog and slide out of bed. Unsteady on my feet, I shuffle to the bathroom. No way I'm turning on the light, so I use the flashlight on my phone to guide the way. And no way I'm looking at my dumbass reflection in the mirror. What the hell was I thinking? It's been a while since I got wasted like that. I cringe, remembering the way I'd drunkenly babbled on about how much I love Jenna and Hector. And I actually groan into my hands when I recall my sloppy rehearsal of the question I want to ask David. I'm a fucking idiot. A splash of ice-cold water to the face wakes me up a little. But I need to sweat. I need to run until I can't think.

After pulling on a pair of loose running shorts, an old triathlon T-shirt, and a ball cap with a wide reflective stripe, I tiptoe down the stairs. Jenna and Hector, dead to the world on the couch, don't stir as I feed Archie and quickly jot down a note telling them I'll be back in a few hours. I'm out of the house not long after four. The morning air is a cool relief. The dark quiet of the country road, just the whisper of the wind through the trees and the chattering of birds, soothes me. When I'm out running this early I hardly ever come across cars until I pass through Woodstock. After a mile or two I stop feeling so woozy and disgusting and get into a good, steady rhythm. My breaths come easy as the sweat pours down my neck and back.

It's only when the landscape shifts from tangled roadside wildflowers and swaying trees to the maze of ugly, repetitive strip malls that I realize where my feet are taking me. David's house. The thought that I'm being swept along in his current overwhelms me. That visceral need to see his twinkling green eyes, to hold his lean body close, to hear his voice, and watch him throw his head back as he laughs.

David texted me late last night after his Amtrak train was delayed arriving into Rhinecliff station by over two hours. I'd already been tipsy enough that I responded with a bunch of random heart emojis and a poorly spelled message about missing him. He'd sent an eye roll in response and told me to call him in the morning.

When I round the corner into my old neighborhood, buttery sunlight filters through the rustling leaves in the established oaks lining the street. It's quiet. A few people are leaving for work, trudging to their cars with travel mugs of coffee. Mostly the houses are dark and still. It must not even be seven yet. What the hell am I doing? David hates getting up early, and he didn't get home until after ten last night. No way he's awake. And I'm sure as hell not going to bother Dr. Webster this early.

But as I slow to a jog in front of the Webster family's small stone house, deliberately avoiding looking across the street at the stained vinyl siding of my parents' place, I see lights on in the front window. Of course I neglected to bring my phone with me, so I'll have to do this the old-fashioned way. That means I'll be ringing the bell looking like the hungover ball of sweat that I am. After a long moment spent trying to even out my breathing and willing myself to stop sweating, Dr. Webster pulls open the red front door. Dressed neatly in a pair of pressed khaki pants and a polo shirt, he looks so much healthier than the last time I saw him I almost do a double-take. His eyes are bright, skin no longer gray, and most importantly he's back to flashing his typical wry grin.

"Morning, Nick." He shuffles back and gestures for me to come inside. Guilt prickles my cheeks. I'm fully intruding on Dr. Webster's morning.

"Hey. Um, I'm sorry to bother you so early. I was out running and kind of ended up over here. I know David's probably in bed." My heart starts racing again like I'm still running at a punishing pace. This is the perfect time to have the conversation with Dr. Webster that I've been rehearsing in my head. Well, okay, maybe not the *perfect* time. I would prefer not to be wearing a soaked T-shirt and running shorts, which upon second inspection, are probably a little too short. But it'll have to do. Before the man can even respond, I'm breathlessly delivering the whole monologue I'd discussed at length with Jenna and Hector last night.

There is absolutely no way I can hide the huge smile stretched across my face when I step out onto the back porch. Dr. Webster informed me David got up at five to start painting and had been hard at work, pounding coffee and blasting music since. I take a moment to watch David work, smiling to myself at the sound of him humming along with the music spilling from his headphones. His slim frame hunches at an awkward angle over a giant piece of paper. Precarious piles of what look like pencil sketches and various art supplies cover the table. His hair is even messier than usual and he's dressed in a striped navy and white shirt that reminds me of something a French sailor might wear.

The last thing I want to do is startle him while he's working and cause him to mess up. So I clear my throat. Nothing. I say his name softly. Nope. Finally I walk around to the other side of the table and crouch down so I'm in his line of sight. And I totally scare the shit out of him.

"Nick!" David tears his headphones out of his ears. He's looking at me with such surprise and skepticism that I'm worried he's angry I interrupted his work. "Did you run here?" David's voice is high with disbelief.

I chuckle and nod.

"It's like twelve miles, babe." He shakes his head at me like I told him I'd teleported.

His eyes heat as they travel over my body, lingering for a moment on my sweaty thighs. I imagine his tongue following the path of his gaze.

No. I can't allow myself to get so distracted by David's parted lips and hitched breaths. Not with his dad on the other side of the wall. Not while David is working.

I glance down at the painting fixed to the table with masking tape. Thankfully I didn't startle him into spilling paint or anything, because the piece, even half finished, is gorgeous. Two male figures fill the page. One, a handsome man with shoulder-length dreads wearing a shirt and tie, watches as the other, lithe and dressed in only a pair of compression shorts, folds his muscular body over in a graceful stretch. The lines are fluid and everything looks hazy and dreamlike.

"That's beautiful," I murmur, still taking in the tones of gray and gold.

David's body radiates tension as he appraises his work. "You think? I'm going crazy trying to get these done in time for the show. But yeah, I just got the idea so I'm worried I won't finish the series."

"You'll finish. Don't worry, baby." I'm going for soothing but the moment the words leave my lips I know I said the wrong thing.

David's eyebrows crash together. "You don't know that," he snaps.

"You're right. Sorry." I press a soothing hand to his shoulder and it slumps.

"No. No. I'm sorry. I'm on edge. I got like two hours of sleep and I'm kind of freaking out about the show. I only have four days to finish."

I don't want to sound like an idiot with my useless words of comfort so I trace my fingers along the bridge of his nose and bend to kiss him. David's lips fall open immediately as his cool hands skim down my chest to my hips.

"God, I missed you," I breathe against his mouth.

"Me too. You always know how to make me feel better." He leans back to flash me a cheeky grin.

"Glad I can be of service," I tease, rocking my hips against his.

"Um, yeah. Those shorts...damn. I can definitely forget my troubles for a minute or two." David drags his fingers over my thighs, pulling a low groan from me. But his mention of troubles sends all my stress back in a wave—my brother's decision to label me unfit to interact with his son, my mom's refusal to talk to me, the weird tension between our two best friends.

"I had a pretty weird weekend too," I say. So I can focus on talking instead of getting caught up in my desire to pull him into a searing kiss, I step back to put a few inches of space between us.

"Oh yeah?" Concern blooms on David's face and he immediately starts running his fingers up and down my forearm.

I hastily recap my phone call with my mom and the discovery that Jason actively thinks I'm some kind of pervert because I'm gay. David's green eyes blaze with anger but he shakes his head. Squinting back down at the painting, he bites his thumbnail and turns his head from side to side like a confused puppy. Damn, he's cute.

"Want me to beat Jason up for you?" David's mouth twitches.

"Yeah let's take him down." I grin and pull him against me.

"Ugh. You're all sweaty," David grumbles. I can tell his heart isn't in it. His corded arms wrap around my waist.

"You love my sweat." I nuzzle the top of his head.

He laughs and shoves me away but he can't hide his grin or the slight flush coloring his pale cheeks. I realize how painfully thirsty I am, for water in addition to David, and I gesture toward the condensation-damp, untouched glass on the table. The sun has barely been up for a full hour but the air is already oppressive. David nods and I gulp down the water gratefully. His eyes are locked on my throat, Adam's apple bobbing as I swallow.

"So how was New York?" I wipe my mouth with the back of my hand.

"It was pretty awesome." He's almost bouncing with excitement. "Tia, the show organizer, is so great. As much as I'm panicking about getting everything done, it's amazing to work with her. She's so laid back and supportive. I met the other two participating artists, Meti and John. John's stuff is kind of knock-off Robert Mapplethorpe to be honest, but he seems like a good guy. Plus he has like Kardashian levels of followers on Instagram. Honestly I don't even know why he's doing the show. But whatever. Meti is legitimately the most talented artist I've ever met." David unearths his phone from under a pile of crumpled-up papers to show me pictures of breathtaking, hyperrealistic portraits of a beautiful woman with long, dark braids.

"That's great." I ruffle his hair, proud of him.

"Yeah and it was wonderful seeing Julian and finally meeting Kevin in person."

David keeps talking, telling a detailed story about a dance performance and the inspiration for his latest series. But my mind froze on the name of his ex-boyfriend. All my jealous worry rains down on me like rubble from a collapsing building.

"I thought you were seeing your other friend. Selima?"

"Yeah, I was supposed to stay at her place. The plan was for me to take her out to dinner. God knows I owe her. But she had to fly to LA last minute. Julian reached out on Instagram. I posted this dumb selfie on the train into the city." David grins sheepishly, clearly more concerned about me teasing him about his selfies than me losing it because he hung out with his ex.

"So, what, you guys got a drink or something?"

David rolls his eyes, laughing. "Do you listen? I literally just told you. He invited me to see a show his boyfriend Kevin choreographed. It was super cool, this super modern minimalist production. The three of us got dinner after and I got trashed. You know how much of a lightweight I am. I did not realize a Negroni is basically a straight-up glass of booze. I passed out in the cab ride back to their place. So classy." He puts his head in his hands.

Something inside me goes cold. The desperation to keep my voice calm has me curling my hands into white-knuckled fists. "You shouldn't get drunk in the city by yourself. It's not safe."

David doesn't seem to notice my words. He's back to looking at the painting. My neck goes hot. Is that Julian? Is he actually that attractive or did David just paint him that way? Everything seems to be moving at a delay but my mind races.

I am radiating stress, and although I know it's unreasonable, I realize I'm furious. He could have gotten hurt. He could have ended up shaking and alone in an unfamiliar place not knowing how to pick himself up and get home. The last thing David needs is to wake up some nights drenched in a cold sweat, so angry and scared he doesn't know where he is. My hand lands on David's shoulder and I jerk him around to face me a little too roughly.

His eyebrows raise and his head cocks to the side in confusion. "Nick, what the hell?"

"I said it's not safe to get drunk like that by yourself. Do you have any idea what could have happened to you?"

"Um, I wasn't by myself. I was with Julian and Kevin." He's looking at me out of the corner of his eye like I'm a total idiot. And the rational part of me knows I'm being a jealous, overprotective jerk. But the part of me that takes control is running on pure, white-hot adrenaline.

"So basically you were out getting wasted with your fucking professor ex-boyfriend and spending the night with him?" My voice is getting loud, taking on the rough edge I associate with Jason and my dad.

"Wow. It's not like I slept in bed with them. Kevin's dad is like some kind of real-estate mogul and bought them a three-bedroom brownstone in Fort Greene. Crazy. So, yeah I spent both nights at their place. In a beautifully appointed guest room. Alone. I barely saw them on Saturday night because Kevin had another show and Julian had some work cocktail thing." A defensive edge creeps into David's voice and for some reason it sets me off even more.

"Were you even going to tell me?" I want to stop talking but I can't. "I knew it. I knew you were gonna see him. You probably can't wait to move to some apartment in Williamsburg or some shit so you can hang out with Tia, and Julian, and whoever the hell else all the time."

David's eyes blaze with anger now. "Nick, do you even hear yourself? I went to the city for my *job*. I just happened to get together with Julian and his partner. Honestly, it didn't even occur to me that it would bother you. When staying with Selima fell through, I was glad I wouldn't have to spend money on a hotel room last minute. Nothing happened. And honestly I don't have time for this chauvinistic shit right now. You either trust me or you don't."

My anger recedes as quickly as it came and I shrug like this whole conversation doesn't matter. He's right. But my stomach keeps churning. I'm a total dick. I lost my temper like my asshole father and upset David when the last thing he needs is extra stress. Trying to calm the situation down, desperate to feel a connection between us, I give David's shoulder a gentle squeeze. But he squirms out of my grip and stalks to the other side of the patio.

"Sorry," I croak. "I didn't mean to lose my shit like that. I trust you that nothing happened. I was worried."

When David turns back to me, his face is transformed by anger. "About what? That I'm such a fucking moron that I can't handle myself for two days? That I can't spend a second away from my big, strong boyfriend without crawling back to some other guy?" His breaths come out fast and his voice seems to rise with every word.

"Of course not. Shit. David. I'm so sorry."

"I got along just fine for ten years without you, Nick. So you can save it. Or is it that you refuse to believe that I'm actually going to stay here? You still think I'm some pretentious douchebag who wants nothing more than to like, get shitfaced and kiss ass at parties. I was happy with you Nick. I loved you."

David's use of the past tense impales me with cold dread. "I love you too. Baby, please. Calm down." My voice is raw and low.

"Calm down? I'm so sorry that you have to deal with my emotions. I'm sorry I can't be so fucking in control all the time like you. You know, you can't be all fake nice and tell me you love me and expect everything to work out. That's not how it goes." David's words drip with scorn. "Clearly you care more about getting all fucking jealous than you do about my career. I was excited about this series. I couldn't wait to show these to you. Plus, I'm going crazy trying to finish in time for Saturday. But all you care about is whether or not I'm so much of a fucking slut that I couldn't keep my dick in my pants. Fuck you, Nick."

A long thread of tension thrums between us for a moment. I open my mouth to speak but David holds up his hand and turns away.

"I have to get back to work. And since it's wholly apparent that you can't take my work seriously, how about you skip the gallery opening, okay?"

My heart is beating harder than it did as I'd flown over miles of pavement to get here. For a minute I worry I might pass out. Searching for the words to make this right, to make David turn and look at me and soften, I have no idea what to say. So after a few silent moments I press a kiss into his hair and turn to jog home.

Chapter Twenty-Two

Nick

September

The rest of the week passes in a blur of fanatical work around the farm, aggressive exercise in my basement gym, and desperate, unanswered calls and texts to David. Every restless night since Monday has been a blur of trying to drown my sorrows in binge-watching episodes of *Gilmore Girls* or stress-baking batches of cookies that only Lexi seems to want to eat. No combination of deadlifts, cinnamon sugar, and Stars Hollow can pull me out of my sullen brooding. Only gliding along the track of habit seems to keep me somewhat sane.

By Thursday afternoon even Archie is wary of my presence, shooting me his trademark dog side-eye every time he catches me grumpily mumbling to myself. Every word Jenna or Hector says to me is met with a terse, flat response. Every thought of my argument with David leaves me sore from clenching my jaw and tensing my shoulders. And every time my phone makes a sound I'm frantically unlocking it, hoping David has responded to my increasingly pathetic texts. But it's inevitably a customer or market organizer asking questions I don't have the energy to answer.

The worst part of this whole thing is that I have no idea where David and I stand. Was that his version of a breakup? Does he want space until after the show? I'm unwilling to believe that David would want to throw everything we had away over one stupid, jealous argument. David talks about his tendency to lose his temper, but I'd never been on the receiving end of his anger before. Growing up he was more likely to laugh off my messed up, selfish behavior. At the very worst he gave me the silent treatment for about an hour before caving and flashing that adorable wide smile. Even the night we'd first had sex and I'd been so horrible to him, after I freaked out and pushed him away, he'd tried to talk to me. My stomach curdles at the notion that David is using the excuse of the fight to be done with me for good. That I pressed him too hard, too fast into the kind of relationship I craved with him. Maybe we were never on the same page. But I can't let him go without knowing for sure.

My eyes lose focus as I stare down at the tidy pile of invoices on the kitchen table. Hector normally handles all the paperwork, but I'm so desperate to fill my time I told him I would take care of it. I have gotten zero work done since sitting down. Instead my brain has been beating me up. Repeatedly, I torture myself by picturing the whole life I'd imagined for David and me. David would move into the farmhouse. The two of us would share meals on the screen porch in the summer and cuddle up in bed as the fire crackled and snow drifted down in the winter. Maybe he and I would get married in a small, simple ceremony by the creek. Maybe we'd even be filling out adoption papers.

I glance over at the manila folder holding the plans for my future with David. Heat prickles my nose. It feels like I'm going to sneeze but then I register the wetness blurring my vision and quickly brush the tears away. I wish he would answer my calls. Let me apologize again. Let me tell him how much I love him. Convince him that I care about his career as much as I care about him.

I'm wrenched from my moping by the sound of my phone buzzing where I'd left it to charge on the other side of the kitchen. I leap up to answer. I don't think I hustled so fast even when college scouts showed up at the state playoffs. But the number on the screen isn't David's. Just another random 845 area code. Probably the well-meaning but very inquisitive CSA member who I'd mistakenly given my personal cell number to. She called at random hours to ask highly specific questions about the exact growing conditions of vegetables after consulting with her spiritual healer. I don't want to deal with her but I answer because, honestly, staring blankly at the pile of paperwork is a pretty inefficient method of paying invoices. Plus I need to stop agonizing over David.

"This is Nick."

"Hi." I hadn't been expecting Anna's soothing voice.

"Oh hey, Anna. How are you?" Immediately all I want to do is grill her about David, but I have no idea why she's calling so I try to play it cool.

"I'm okay." She hesitates. "You know what, whatever—I'm gonna drop the bullshit. I'm kind of freaking out. I haven't been able to get in touch with David since he got back from New York last weekend. And when I called his dad's place Richard said David was busy getting ready for the show. But I swear to god I heard My Chemical Romance playing in the background. And you know Richard isn't listening to that emo shit. Bad sign. Have you heard from him? Is he okay? I'm supposed to pick him up tomorrow morning to take him down to the city."

I groan. This is bad. It's one thing for David to shut me out. But he never pushes Anna away. Their best friend bond is sacred. "No." I scrub my hand over my face a few times before continuing. "We got into a fight on Monday morning. He's ignoring my calls and stuff too."

"What happened?" Anna's voice is pitched low with concern.

I explain our fight, not bothering to downplay my overprotective crap, but I try to minimize how angry David had gotten. After all, he was exhausted, and I had treated him like a child.

"He lost his shit, didn't he?" Anna asks. Wow, she sure knows David.

"Um, yeah. Kind of. He told me not to bother coming to his show. I'm confused. Did he ever say anything to you about wanting to break up with me?" I try not to feel pathetic, blatantly angling for information like this.

"No. David's so in love with you it makes me want to puke. He is in it deep with you. Basically you and painting are the only things that dude ever talks about." She heaves an exaggerated sigh that sounds so much like David's I chuckle. "He does this sometimes. I guess you guys were like, on the outs while he was doing his doctorate so you might not know, but David gets crazy over deadlines. Like Papa Richard and I were ready to contact the police levels of dropping off the face of the earth. And usually he's too, like, obsessed with you to lash out but David can be kind of a bitch sometimes. I'm sure that's all it is. I was hoping he was at least talking to you. You calm down his crazy."

I sag with relief at her words while also feeling weirdly defensive. "So I should still go tomorrow, you think? I don't want to be disrespectful. This is important to him and I don't need to ruin it."

Anna snorts so loudly into the phone I have to hold it away from my ear. "Nick. Be real. He is going to sulk so hard if you don't show up. I'm picking him up at nine tomorrow, ignored calls or not. Hopefully he'll at least be rested and won't snipe at me for the whole three-hour drive."

We end the call after I nervously ask Anna for a favor and she promises to update me if David says anything indicating he does not, in fact, want me at his art show. But her words give me hope. By the time I have my weekend bag packed up with the manila folder tucked safely inside, my cheeks are sore from smiling to myself.

THE GALLERY LOOKS nothing like I'd expected. When I imagined a New York City art gallery, I pictured an almost sterile white space with light wood floors, filled with lots of gray-haired people wearing stylish glasses. But Gesture isn't even called a gallery. It bills itself as an "exhibition space" and is housed in a sprawling, graffiti-covered brick building surrounded by auto body shops and building supply companies. As Jenna and I push our way into the crowded, industrial main room, I also realize I'm dressed totally wrong. While Jenna fits right in with her skintight black jeans, cherry red lace crop top, and gold hoops, I look completely out of place in my trusty blue button-down. And I am for sure the only dude in the entire place wearing fucking khakis.

There's a DJ set up in the back corner next to a tiny makeshift bar crowded with beer cans, random bottles of wine, and red Solo cups. People laugh and jostle each other good-naturedly. One guy in a Hawaiian shirt is even dancing alone to the 90s hip-hop booming from the speakers. This whole thing reminds me less of an art show and more of a house party that happens to have great art on the walls. Glancing around, trying not to look too desperate to find David, I'm drawn to a large cluster of black and white photographs of a nude, heavily tattooed man. The photos are dramatic and somehow profoundly intimate. I like them. But not as much as I love David's art.

Gaze pinging wildly, I start to get overwhelmed by the crush of bodies, echoing voices, and thumping music. I can't even see David's paintings, much less his lean frame or auburn hair. I try to swallow, to calm myself down and breathe, but my throat is hot and tight. I need to see David, feel his hand in mine, tell him I'm sorry. Mentally I chastise myself. Today is about David. This is not the time or place for me to deliver the apology speech I'd been looping in my head as Jenna hurtled down I-87.

"How 'bout I grab us a drink?" Jenna squeezes my arm and shoots me an encouraging grin. "Beer?"

I nod distractedly, still scanning the crowd and allowing myself to zone out. I wonder if Ben decided to come after all. He'd texted me yesterday, letting me know he was busy wrapping up his fellowship project but, he hoped he'd be able to make it. Honestly, I could use a dose of his calm self-assuredness at the moment.

"Nick?" A soft, unfamiliar voice pulls me from my thoughts. I turn around to see a young guy, in his early twenties maybe, dressed entirely in black and glancing up at me through his lashes. He's Asian, a head shorter than David, with messy dark hair and gorgeous cheekbones.

I realize I'm staring at him and quickly nod. "Um, yeah. That's me." I rub the back of my neck nervously. This has to be Marc, David's friend from Chicago. David mentioned how beautiful the guy was, and he was definitely right.

"I recognize you from the paintings. Nice ass, by the way. I'm Marc. I used to be David's assistant. And friend." He offers his hand and a mischievous smile. His wrist is wrapped in a tangle of colorful beaded bracelets.

"Nice to meet you." I try to smile politely and make a good impression but at this I might crumble if I don't find David soon. "Um, have you seen David yet?"

Marc rolls his eyes. "Yes, for like two seconds. He was holding it down back there with a bunch of legit-looking art people so I decided to hit up the bar." He rattles the ice in his cup.

I'm thankful when Jenna slides back over, bearing a huge glass of red wine for herself and a Schlitz tallboy for me. She greets Marc warmly, seeming at ease and launching into a conversation about the photos around us while I return to my surveillance of the room. The crowd is diverse in every way possible. A middle-aged woman in a fuzzy North Face jacket chats enthusiastically with an impossibly dapper woman in Levi's and a purple bandeau top. There's a tall person in a gorgeous silver suit who looks so much like David Bowie I do a double-take, even though I know Doria's beloved idol is no longer with us. A shimmering femme guy with long braids takes notes in a leather journal. A guy who looks like a pro-wrestler jokes around with a couple of skinny bearded guys in baggy, ripped T-shirts. I watch with a hunger I didn't know was in me. A part of me mourns the fact that fear held me back from going near any kind of queer-friendly community until I was in my thirties. I should probably check out that queer support group David and Jenna kept bugging me about. After all, the initial visits with Dr. Yan, the soft-voiced therapist David helped me find, hadn't been so bad.

"Shall we?" Marc asks, gesturing toward a yawning archway. "David's stuff is back there."

Bobbing my head so hard I probably should have slipped a disc in my neck, I follow Marc and Jenna through the crowd. The room housing David's work is even bigger than the main room with the photos and bar. My eyes lock immediately on David's paintings. I'm confronted first with a large-scale portrait of David, leaning back into a tangle of pastel blooms. Something about the way he's painted the flowers makes me want to reach out and touch them, like they might be as soft as David's skin. Next, I see a half dozen images I recognize from his Instagram: the two of us kissing on the bank of the Hudson, the abstracted close-up of me jerking us off, a guy I now recognize as Marc leaning toward a handsome stranger across a bar. Then there are the Julian pictures. Julian watching with hunger in his eyes as his boyfriend contorts his body in midair. Julian and his boyfriend in a sun-drenched kitchen, sipping coffee. And the painting David had been working on the day we fought. I try not to feel grateful I haven't seen Julian here in the flesh. But I am.

I feel David before I see him. Something electric travels through my body, waking me up and calming me down simultaneously. David, of course, looks out-of-this-world gorgeous in a thin blue corduroy blazer, a gray T-shirt, and his trademark skinny jeans. I want him so much it hurts but I hang back. He's talking to Anna and a tall, broad man whose back is turned to me. The man looks sophisticated, all graceful gestures and expensive, well-tailored clothes. I assume he's some kind of art collector or something. Trying to play it cool I break away from Marc and Jenna and wander the gallery space, unable to stop smiling because, damn, my man is talented.

When I approach the back wall I freeze. There is a huge painting of me. Unlike the other works, which are all done on paper and framed in light wood, this one is a huge, unframed canvas. Although I know almost nothing about art, I can tell David used a different kind of paint than he typically does. Oil maybe? Or acrylic? It takes a second for me to place the image, but when I do, I can't help but grin.

Chapter Twenty-Three

Nick

September

It's me, beaming across the table like a lovesick kid on our first real date, at the Thai place in Albany. While all David's other paintings play with color and render the images in a slightly surreal mist, this one is hyperrealistic and clear.

"Do you like it?" David's voice is small behind me.

My knees buckle at the sound. I can't even respond. All I can do is turn and pull him close, almost sobbing at the relief of holding him in my arms again. Burying my face in his hair, I breathe in his scent, clean mint and lavender. His brow is a little sweaty when I press a kiss to it.

"It's the moment I realized how much I love you. I finished it last night." David grabs at my shirt and presses his forehead hard into my shoulder.

"It's amazing. You're amazing." My voice is ragged. I squeeze my eyes shut.

"Nick." David leans back and brushes his fingers over my jaw. "I'm so sorry. I always do this. I spiral when I get stressed and take it out on people. Or I pull away. It was fucked up for me to say I didn't want you here. And it was even worse for me to ignore you. I can be such a selfish asshole—"

I cut David off, kissing him hard and lifting him up against me. A tiny squeak escapes his lips and we both laugh as I set him back down on the polished concrete floor. "Don't worry about that now. We can talk later. If you want, I booked us a room at that hotel you said looked cool. The one in Greenpoint? I thought we could stay in the city until Monday." I stroke up and down his back as I talk, hoping I'm not embarrassing him with my blatant affection in front of all of these people.

"God, I don't deserve you. That sounds perfect."

"How're you feeling?" I ask, knowing David needs to get back to talking to the collector guy and the dozens of other people craning their necks, eager to speak to him.

"A hell of a lot better now that you're here." David rolls his shoulders and burrows his face back into my chest like I'm a comfort blanket. The thought that I can reassure him has me feeling all warm and tingly. "But even though I basically spent this whole week losing my shit and acting like a total jerk, I'm excited about the show. Until now I didn't think what I was doing was real. It felt like I was flailing. Wasting my time. But Meti isn't formally trained either. We both got recognition through social media, and it's cool to feel like that's legitimate. Like, I get that I'm a privileged white dude but it's good to have something to offer the world, I guess. I finally fit into an artistic community and—" He breaks off and rolls his eyes. "Sorry, I've probably had one too many glasses of wine. I'm gonna go ahead and cool it with the rambling now."

He grazes another kiss over my lips before turning back to the people he'd been speaking to. I realize the tall guy I'd figured was an art collector is none other than Ben, looking elegant in gray slacks and a white linen button-down. At least one other person in this building is wearing a shirt with buttons. I clap my cousin on his muscular shoulder in greeting and he nods, flashing an almost imperceptible smirk.

Marc and Jenna stumble over, both of them dissolving into laughter, clearly fast and tipsy friends. As Jenna approaches, Anna's lips press into a tight line and she breaks away from the group without a word. But before I can shoot David a *what the hell is going on* look, Marc is yanking him away from me and squeezing my boyfriend's narrow shoulders with what looks like surprising strength.

"David, I officially hate you, by the way. Look at this man." He gestures broadly in my direction, leering. "Just—holy fucking shit. He's all jacked and sweet and I bet he's amazing in bed. Am I right, gorgeous?" Marc jabs a finger at me and heat floods my cheeks. I can only laugh nervously in response. "I don't know what you guys are into, but I would be so down with some ménage action." Marc's warm brown eyes sweep over my body.

Now I know I'm blushing hotly and uncomfortable as hell. Ben shakes his head, looking surprisingly tense. Jenna nods enthusiastically and gives me a thumbs-up. And David looks like he wants to wring Marc's neck.

"Um, hard pass. Thanks though." David cuts his eyes at me and I put up my hands. Nothing wrong with group sex, but I don't think it's my cup of tea. I do have to admit, though, the idea is slightly intriguing.

Marc shrugs lightly and turns to Ben. "And who is this?"

Ben extends his hand and introduces himself in a low, calm voice. "Ben Miller. I'm Nick's cousin. Nice to meet you."

"Marc," he murmurs, sounding much shyer than the man who just loudly suggested a threesome in the middle of a crowded art gallery. His whole demeanor softens as he accepts Ben's hand.

"Well David, I don't want to keep you. Nick mentioned the two of you will be around for a few days, right? I'd love to take the both of you to dinner. Congratulations again on the show." Ben grins fondly at David and I'm weirdly thrilled that my cousin seems to like my boyfriend. I'm also wondering why he's in such a hurry to leave. "I'll call you tomorrow, Nick."

The second Ben is out of earshot and David is tugged away by an owlish woman in a colorful kaftan, Marc pushes up on his tiptoes to speak in my ear. At first I'm nervous he's going to keep teasing me about the threesome, but instead he whispers, "Please, please tell me your cousin is queer."

I bark out a laugh and Marc looks genuinely disappointed, his face falling for a moment before he recovers his cynical smirk. I cannot imagine someone less suited to Ben if I tried. Ben has always been quiet, logical, and withdrawn. And Marc seems anything but withdrawn. I know almost nothing about my cousin's personal life, but I'm sort of convinced it's because he doesn't have one. Every ounce of his energy appears to be channeled into professional success: graduating with a physics degree from MIT then getting another from Berkeley, doing incomprehensible but impressive-sounding research at Harvard, teaching at Columbia. While I know Ben is gay, I have never once heard him or anyone in the family mention a boyfriend. Not that people in my immediate family would be celebrating a queer relationship anyway.

"He is gay actually," I inform Marc in an even tone. His eyes go wide. "But I have no idea if he's single or if he even dates. He's finishing up a fellowship at Columbia this year and moving back to Boston in December."

"Give me his number," Marc demands. He hands me his phone, encased in black leather.

"What? No," I laugh, handing him his phone back. "You barely met him. Plus I'm not going to give out Ben's number to some random dude."

Marc puts his hands over his heart, all mock wounded. "I'm not some random dude. I'm your boyfriend's bestie. Well other than that moody redhead." He exhales loudly and thumbs around on his phone. "Whatever, I'll have to hope and pray I find hot Ben on Grindr."

I don't have the heart to tell Marc I'm pretty sure Ben avoids hookup and dating apps like the plague. Draining the rest of my beer, I chuck Marc under the chin and shake my head in fond exasperation.

The next few hours are filled with half-understood conversations about the art scene, answering random and occasionally bizarre questions about running a farm, and people excitedly recognizing me from David's paintings. One woman even takes it upon herself to ask extremely detailed questions about our sex life that leave me feeling on display, and not in a way I'm into. Occasionally I catch David's eye to send him small signals of encouragement or take a free moment to bring him a glass of the seltzer water he switched to drinking. By the time the gallery starts to empty and the big, barred windows frame an indigo sky, David's shoulders slump and I catch him stifling the occasional yawn.

I scan the thinning crowd for Jenna to see if she and Anna want to grab a bite to eat with us. Finally I spot my friend's golden curls among a group of women chatting in the corner. Catching her eye, I gesture to the door so I can grab my bags from the trunk of her car. As we walk back into the gallery, she shakes her head as I try to pry about what the hell is going on between her and Anna, who seems to have left. Marc has also disappeared. I'd last seen him deep in conversation with John, the tattooed headlining artist who'd surprised me by being incredibly soft-spoken and shy in contrast to his brash artwork.

I'm watching a video of a woman who I assume is Tia, the show's organizer, doing some kind of cool futuristic dance in a white latex suit, when David wraps his corded arms around my waist.

"I sold five paintings." He's grinning sleepily. Poor guy ran himself ragged. I want to scoop him up in my arms and carry him to the hotel.

"Of course you did. You're the best artist in the world." I know he's going to roll his eyes and I chuckle when he does.

"Wanna head out? I'm pretty tired."

I nod and pull up the hotel's address on my phone as David makes the rounds to say goodbye. His cheeks are flushed and his eyes sparkle. His face has been stretched into a grin for the last few hours. I find my heart swelling in my chest with renewed pride.

The moment we slide into the rideshare, however, David conks out. I make small talk with the driver who recommends a favorite pizza place a few blocks away from our hotel. The buildings around us slowly shift from industrial warehouses to crowded brownstones. As we pull up to the large brick building housing the hotel, which I'm hoping is nice, I brush my lips over David's to wake him. His eyes blink open and he grumbles adorably.

"Come on, baby." I shoulder my bag and debate gathering him up and carrying him inside. But he follows me through the door with heavy, shuffling steps. The hotel lobby is eclectic and beautifully decorated, with colorful art adorning the walls, a curved metallic front desk, and lamp-style light fixtures that, while not exactly my taste, work well in the space. It's a far cry from the budget chain motels my father favored on the few fraught family road trips we'd taken when I was a kid. But I want this weekend to be special for David. It's definitely worth it to splurge on a nice place to stay, especially since I barely spend money on anything else.

"Fuck. I'm exhausted." David flops down on the bed as I close the door to our room behind us.

"I'm guessing you didn't sleep much this week?"

"No. I sleep like crap when I'm not in your bed." He shakes his head but then shoots to a sitting position, eyeing my leather duffel bag. "Shit. I don't have any clean clothes. Yet another reason I should have answered your calls." He buries his face in his hands. "Ugh, I am seriously the worst."

I'm unreasonably proud of myself as I pull out the small canvas tote bag Anna packed for me on the sly yesterday morning while David was in a panic corralling all of his work for the show. I toss it to him and he catches it adeptly. He rummages around inside, inspecting the items. When he looks up at me he blinks rapidly, green eyes shining.

"Thank you," he murmurs.

"I wanted this to be a surprise." I sink onto the bed next to him and he leans into me like I'm magnetic. A small sigh escapes his lips. "Even if I hadn't been an overprotective idiot and made you feel terrible, I wanted this weekend to be special for you." David tries to interrupt but I hold up my hand. It's high time to roll out the apology speech. I'm glad when I speak there's no trace of nervousness in my voice. "Baby, I get that you feel bad about icing me out. And yeah, it sucked not knowing if you wanted to, I don't know, dump me or something. But it was wrong of me to get jealous of Julian and act like you couldn't handle yourself. I'm sorry for being such a jerk. I'm so proud of everything you've accomplished. I mean, you go for it, you know? You moved to a new city all by yourself at eighteen. I could never be that brave. I was too fucking scared to even leave my family for college when my dad shut down the Syracuse thing. I accepted it. But look at you. You left a career you'd worked at for years and started over from scratch to help your dad. And you were amazing today. People were falling all over themselves to talk to you and buy your work. I shouldn't have let you spend this week so unsupported—"

David presses his lips to mine and now I want nothing more than to devour him. But he bumps his forehead against my cheek and sighs. "Fuck, Nick. I'm sorry too. I couldn't even answer my damn phone this week. I just, I don't know, I suck at controlling my emotions. I spiral and shut down." His voice is shaky. "When I thought about it later it seemed like you were— maybe kind of...displacing some of your fears about what happened to you onto me? Like you were worried if I was off getting drunk, something bad would happen?"

Immediately I go tense. I want to argue even though David, perceptive as ever, is right.

He presses a soft finger to my lips. "And that's okay, baby. I understand why you were upset. But I had no excuse to lash out at you the way I did. When I get stressed, I lose it. Like, all week I wanted to talk to you but any moment I spent doing anything other than painting felt like wasted time. Like I wasn't going to finish and everyone would realize I'm trash. My dad had to fucking remind me to eat. And I'm supposed to be the one taking care of him. I'm awful." A tear slips down David's cheek.

"David." I run my fingers through the silky strands of his hair. His words are both a balm and a bruise. Unexpected anger detonates inside my gut and hot shame sears my skin. I've failed David. I can't make him see how undeniably special to me he is. And for what feels like the millionth time in my life I curse myself for being unable to put my emotions into words. "That's not true. Your dad's doing okay. You know that." I consider asking him my question now but press it down. Not the right time.

"Nick, I acted like I don't even care about you. But I do. I want us to be together for as long as you'll put up with my bullshit. I love you. And I know saying it doesn't fix everything but...I do."

"I know," I murmur, locking my eyes with his. I want to show him with my body exactly how much I love him. How much I trust him and need him. David's supple lips fall open and his breath hitches.

We fall back together onto the starched white comforter, rustling fabric and ragged panting as David ravages my mouth and writhes on top of me. Everything is frantic liquid heat, mouths and bodies straining against each other. Each slick brush of his tongue against mine sends a searing pulse of hot arousal to my cock. I groan into his mouth as David reaches between us. He dips his cool fingers into my pants and beneath the elastic of my briefs to brush the head of my throbbing hardness. Tangling my fingers into his hair—god, I can never get enough of his hair—I lock him against me. David eases back, turning to try to hide a yawn.

"Sorry," he murmurs and then his mouth stretches into a gigantic second yawn. Something seems to drain from his body, like he's extinguished his final reserve of energy.

David's hand is still down my pants, leaving me on the razor's edge of desperation. But we breathe together, drinking each other in. Holding him on top of me, feeling the ebb and flow of his breath, has me almost whimpering. I listen as his breathing shifts from rapid to steady, heavy to feather soft. David's eyes flutter closed and his lips are slightly turned up at the corners, like he's already fallen into a good dream. Without glancing in a mirror I can see the fond expression on my own face, my goofy, soft smile. Lifting him off me as gently as possible and adjusting the still pulsing hardness bound by my damn khakis, I slide off his shoes, try and fail to remove his jacket, and finally pull the blanket over him. He stirs as I brush a soft kiss over his forehead.

Once I've undressed, checked the lock on the door, and flipped off the lights I settle down onto the plush mattress. For a long moment, I glance around the dim, stylishly appointed room. I'm filled with buzzing energy, almost certain I won't be able to sleep. For one, I'm starving, having forgone the highly recommended pizza in favor of making out with David and ensuring the intact status of our relationship. And two, a quick glance at my phone on the nightstand reveals it's only a few minutes past nine. But the moment I let my eyes drift closed I sink down into the thick warmth of sleep, calmed by the weight of David's body next to mine.

Chapter Twenty-Four

David

September

I wake alone in a pool of sunlight. My brain can't quite place where I am, but my body doesn't care. Warm, crisp sheets slide over my naked skin and for the first time in days I feel rested and whole. My limbs are liquid and the world is cast in the floaty, soft-edged haze of good sleep. Glancing to the side I search for the clothes I'd torn off in the middle of the night when I shook Nick awake and begged him to fuck me. Everything is neatly folded on the nightstand and a small square of hotel stationery rests atop the pile.

Good Morning,

Got up early so I decided to go for a quick run. I have my cell. Oh, and I love you :)

-Nick

P.S. You look so beautiful right now I don't want to leave.

P.P.S. (I'm not sure if that's how you do it?) I just spent five whole minutes watching you sleep. Sorry for being such a creep. And...that wasn't supposed to rhyme. Yikes.

A laugh that sounds uncomfortably close to a giggle bubbles from my lips as I read over the note a few more times than is strictly necessary. After taking a couple minutes to stretch luxuriously in the big bed I pad toward the bathroom. The hotel room is a monument to Nick's profound thoughtfulness: my phone plugged in to charge on the desk, clothes unpacked and meticulously hung in the tiny closet, my toiletries arranged in a neat row next to the bathroom sink. Allowing myself a quick swoon I hang the lightweight gray sweater I'm grateful Nick packed for me next to the shower so the wrinkles can steam out. I'm embarrassingly eager to get ready for whatever romantic stuff Nick has likely planned for the day.

Even though I lived in Manhattan for two years while I did my master's, I never did anything touristy. When I was at Columbia, the vast majority of my time was spent in the library, hunched over my laptop reading badly scanned PDFs or frantically scrawling notes for my thesis. As often as possible I'd carved out time to go to MOMA or the Guggenheim, but I'd done my best to avoid Times Square and I never even saw the Statue of Liberty from any vantage other than through the window of an airplane.

Because I like my showers only slightly shy of painfully scalding, the bathroom quickly fills with steam and I let the water sting the back of my neck and shoulders. My skin pinks and as I run my hands over my face. I can taste the salt of sweat from last night mingling with the sweet taste of the fresh water. Heat that has nothing to do with the shower snakes through me as I remember the delirious longing of the night before. My lips trailing down the ridges of Nick's chest and stomach.

Slicking him up with my spit before he plunged into my ass. His possessive groan as he held me close and flooded me with his release. My cock stands at attention, desperate for any touch. But as I wrap my fingers around my length all I want is Nick. His big arms around me. The bristle of his scruff chafing every inch of my skin.

"Mmm, perfect timing." Nick's low voice snaps me from my reverie. He steps into the shower, flushed and gorgeous, all musk and clean sweat. A tiny whimper escapes my lips at the sight of his big, tight body. The half-smile on his lips disappears as his mouth falls open and his gaze sweeps down to my straining erection. "Is that for me?"

I grin at him, nodding. I'm embarrassed at being literally caught with my dick in my hand but also too turned on to care. He kisses the corner of my mouth and as I'm about to deepen the kiss he backs off, stepping under the stream of water and sighing as he scrubs his skin. I watch the rivulets of soapy water trace down his golden flesh, over planes of hard muscle, and my mouth goes dry. My cock throbs at the sight of him alone.

"Come here." He opens his arms and I comply immediately, moaning as his heavy erection presses against my slick skin. Nick claims my mouth with his roughly, releasing a ragged moan as our tongues slide together. I reach to cup his balls, dizzy with lust as his dick strains between us.

Nick kisses me deeply, holding me close against him. His need, his love, his relief that I'm here in his arms are all so palpable that I find myself whining into his mouth. "Please," I gasp, begging him for anything he's willing to give.

"Fuck, David." Nick kisses all over my face before once again crushing his lips to mine.

I glide the point of my tongue down his throat, nipping at the sensitive flesh and sucking on his Adam's apple. His sharp intake of breath is the only encouragement I need to continue. I lick all over him, loving the lingering taste of his sweat, the rough drag of the stubble on his jaw under my tongue, the way he shivers when I nip at his shoulder. Nick seems desperate, hands grasping at me and mouth gaping open as I bite down gently on his erect, copper-colored nipple. He hisses when I do it again, harder this time. Despite his size, his sculpted muscles and broad frame, Nick appears vulnerable, completely at my mercy.

"Oh god. Baby. Please," he begs and I drag my mouth lower, down the rippling muscles of his stomach and bypassing his heavy, pulsing erection to nip at the thin skin of his inner thighs. I nuzzle into his pubic hair, need ripping through me as I inhale his scent. When my hands connect with the firm flesh of his ass, he groans and a trickle of precome slides down his shaft.

"Good?" I ask breathlessly, still kneading the flesh. I glance up at him through strands of damp hair.

"Fuck yes," he scrapes out. Nick's head is thrown back, eyes squeezed shut.

A hot wave of desire engulfs me and my breath quickens. I'm desperate to be inside Nick, to feel him clenching around me, to fuck him. But interwoven with the heavy blanket of lust is a tiny thread of self-doubt. I have no idea if Nick has any desire to bottom with me. I don't know if he has any desire to get fucked at all. He mentioned not liking it much when he tried it with that idiot Shawn. And the absolute last thing I want is to bring up any bad memories.

Nick is usually pretty open-minded about sex though, comfortable taking what he needs and giving me everything I want. So experimentally I slip a finger into my mouth, slicking it up with saliva, and run it gently around Nick's rim. His cock surges, leaking another stream of his arousal. A strangled sound escapes his throat. I press more firmly and Nick thrusts back against my finger.

"Is this okay?" I check in with him. Arousal courses through my veins.

Nick's gaze is molten as he stares down at me. "Yeah. How did you know?" His voice is raw.

"Hm?" I tip my head to the side but I keep teasing his hole. I'm delighted to watch the effects of my touch play out over his body: his skin prickling with shivers, his muscles flexing, his breath coming in low moans.

Nick hauls me up against him and turns the shower off. He's staring at the water swirling down the drain. "I was gonna ask you if you would fuck me. Is that something you want?"

"I definitely want to." I kiss him, pouring my desire into the meeting of our lips.

Most guys I'd hooked up with automatically labeled me as a bottom, which for the most part was fine. I love getting fucked. And Christopher had baffled me with his construction of a totally false, totally rigid gender-performance dichotomy in our relationship. In his mind he'd been more traditionally masculine, with gym-sculpted muscles and a well-groomed beard he thought would prove it. He never wanted to even let me anywhere near his ass. A "born bottom" he'd called me, usually with a knowing smirk. Only with Julian had I been able to fully explore the joys of the give and take. And, I grin, I guess with Nick.

Before I can fall deeper into my thoughts Nick is pulling me out of the shower and rubbing a towel over my skin. Something about the care with which he dries me off, brushing my hair back from my face, stroking the plush cloth over my arms, pressing an almost shy kiss to my neck, leaves me pliant and needy. I pull his mouth down to mine and the kiss quickly goes breathless, Nick's hands roaming all over my damp skin. He palms my ass and I moan into his mouth. Then he's lifting me up, cradling me in those huge arms, and depositing me gently onto the tousled sheets.

I straddle his thighs, trembling as his muscles flex beneath me and coarse hair tickles my skin. My fingertips ghost up and down his shaft, a light, teasing touch. He groans and reaches for the back of my neck, pulling me down to him. He begins to kiss me, soft, brushing kisses on my cheeks, the sides of my mouth, my nose, then hungry kisses.

"What do you want?" I ask, tightening my grip around his erection. He ruts up into my hand, grasping at the sheets with white-knuckled fists.

"You," he finally manages. "I want your tongue. Then I want your cock."

His words send a pulsing throb of need to my dick and I slide off him, so eager to taste him my mouth is almost watering. "Lie down on your stomach," I order softly and Nick obeys immediately. I dart to Nick's duffel where I'm glad I make quick work of locating the lube. When I slide back into bed, gently easing him open, his body tenses up the tiniest bit.

"Baby," I say, kissing the pert skin of one of his perfect ass cheeks, "try to relax, okay? If there's something—anything—you don't like, tell me. I'll stop. I promise." I rock back to sit on my heels and run my fingertips up and down the notches of Nick's spine. The muscles in his back uncoil and his shoulders relax. More than anything I need him to feel safe. I want this to be good for him. I want him to see what he does to me, know how amazing it can be to let me take care of him.

"Yeah," he says roughly, his face pressed into the bedding, like the one syllable is all he can manage.

I start at his neck, breathing into his ear that I love him. By the time I've traced my lips and tongue down to Nick's ass, spreading his cheeks apart and sliding my tongue into his crease, he's moaning rhythmically and rubbing his dick against the bed. And when I press the point of my tongue against the sensitive skin of his hole his entire body jerks.

"Oh fuck yes," Nick chokes out. "Oh my god."

I swirl my tongue around his rim and he spasms in response. I do it again and again, letting the radiating waves of his heat soak into me, driving me wild with the need to be inside him. When I slip my tongue into him something like a sob escapes his lips.

"David." Nick's voice is scratchy. "Please." He swallows audibly. "Please fuck me."

I moan into his ass in response and fumble blindly for the lube bottle, not wanting to separate our bodies. When my hand finally closes around it I hurry to coat my fingers before plunging one into his clenching channel. I keep still, listening to his soft moans. No tension. No sharp intake of breath. Just soft whimpers as I slide my finger in and out, fucking him gently.

"Good?" I ask and he tightens around me. His hair rasps against the sheets as he nods. Slowly, I slide in another finger, then a third and, fuck he's tight. I hook my fingers, seeking out his prostate. When I find the sensitive spot inside, Nick's hips surge into the bed and a low growl rumbles in his throat.

"T—that feels amazing." His voice is strangled.

I massage the spot until I know neither of us can take it anymore. Seeing him, all power and brawn, laid out like this for me has my cock dripping.

"I want you," Nick gasps.

I ease my fingers out and roll Nick onto his back. I need to see him, let him see me as I slide into him. My cock throbs at the sight of his handsome face so open and wanting. His eyes widen and his lips fall open as I push his knees apart. Coating my hardness with a copious amount of lube and slicking some more around his rim, I tease his hole with the tip of my cock. His jaw tightens and his erection leaks a trickle of hot need. When I slide inside him, so slowly, he groans and lifts toward me. The electricity between us is so potent I'm surprised there aren't sparks when I lace our fingers together.

"More," he bites out.

I grin and flex my hips, pushing in to seat myself fully in his gripping, slick warmth. As he clenches and squeezes in response to my thrusts, it's like he's massaging my cock and it's all I can do to focus on maintaining a smooth, steady rhythm for him.

"You feel so good," I say, riding the rising effervescent swell of my pleasure. The control Nick usually exhibits during sex is gone. He's holding his legs open, angling his hips so I can slip deeper in. When I do he growls and clamps his eyes shut. If I keep watching his face as I fuck him I know I'll come so I lean forward to connect our mouths.

"I need to come," Nick breathes against my face. The smell of his mouth, of his skin, warm spice and sunshine, pulls a needy whine from me.

"Nick," I moan his name again and again as I move inside him. My orgasm tightens my thighs, makes my ass clench, pushes me as deep as possible into his tight ass. I reach between us to grip Nick's slick, throbbing cock. He clamps down hard around my erection as I start to jerk him. Everything in my body is taut, like a cord stretched so tight the slightest touch will cause it to snap. Then Nick is coming, spilling jets of hot pleasure between us, groaning his release and coating my fist as I loosen my tight grip on his dick.

His orgasm is my permission to come, my body rigid as I thrust one final time deep into Nick's slick heat. The pleasure rolls through me as I stare down into his eyes. The burning trust, the love in his gaze undoes me. The cord breaks and everything goes slack as I collapse down onto him.

We pant together for a long moment, me still half hard inside him. I relish the liquid heat of my body, every muscle wrung out and relaxed.

"Wow," Nick finally says, his voice growly. "That was...damn."

"Good?" I ask, brushing my lips over the hinge of his jaw before easing out of him.

He winces slightly but before I can even run my fingers over his hole and check if he is okay, he's laughing and wrapping me up in his arms. Our sweaty bodies press together and Nick taps his forehead against mine.

I turn on the sass immediately and smack his shoulder. I'm weirdly energetic despite being so thoroughly drained. "Hey, I haven't topped in a while. You don't have to laugh at me."

Nick shakes his head, the deep chuckle still rumbling in his chest. "I was so fucking nervous. And it was so fucking good." The smile slides off his face and his gaze turns fond. "You were amazing." He cups my cheek and kisses me.

What begins as a soft touch of lips heats until I'm moaning into his mouth, wanting him again despite my satisfied exhaustion. But as usual, Nick's body has other ideas, specifically a need to replenish expended calories, and his stomach gives a loud grumble.

"Ugh, sorry." He rolls his eyes at himself. "I'm starving. Do you mind if I eat?" He gestures toward a paper bag I hadn't noticed on the dresser.

Guilt flutters in my stomach. Naturally I forced the poor guy to skip not one, but two meals. "Oh my god." I shake my head. "Of course not, baby. I'm so sorry. I passed the hell out last night and made you skip dinner. You didn't make plans, did you?" My cheeks are warm.

"Nah." He grins and slips out of bed.

After a quick trip to the bathroom to wash up, he hands me a cardboard coffee cup and some kind of buttery-smelling pastry wrapped in parchment paper. By the time I've unwrapped it and taken one bite of the perfectly made almond croissant inside, Nick is already halfway done with a gigantic bagel breakfast sandwich.

"Ben called me this morning. He asked if we wanted to meet for dinner around eight? He said he'd make a reservation. You can invite Marc if you want too. Did he stay in the city?"

"That sounds great." I take a sip of my tepid coffee. "Anna offered to put Marc up for a few days, so he's probably back upstate? He's gonna visit for a week or so since he just quit at the museum."

I should probably check my phone but my desire to get out of bed is basically nil. Instead, I return my attention to the croissant. It's delicious, the ideal balance of rich, flaky dough and crunchy candied almonds. Glancing over at Nick, I expect him to look as perfectly content as I do, but he's staring down at his coffee cup, eyebrows knit together.

I set my food aside and scoot over to him, shuffling to sit between his legs and face him. "Everything okay?" I ask, trying not to immediately worry. Maybe I hurt him. Maybe he wasn't ready for that.

He nods and glances at his duffel bag. His expression does nothing to soothe my concern, however. "Yeah." He rolls his shoulders and gives me a shy smile before lifting me away from him so he can slide out of bed. "Can I ask you something?" Nick's back is to me as he rummages in his bag.

My heart starts hammering. But it's not out of worry now. I know this will be a good question. "Mmmhmm," I hum and recline back against the pillows.

When Nick turns back to me, still gloriously naked, he's clutching a manila folder in his hands like it's a life raft. He opens his mouth to speak but seems to think better of it and thrusts the folder at me. I grin as I flip it open. My eyebrows shoot to my hairline. Inside are four pieces of paper printed with what look like plans for a tiny cottage. When I glance up at Nick, he's rubbing the back of his neck, eyes locked on the papers.

"I thought I could build you an art studio." His voice is pitched low. "I was thinking over by the greenhouse because you said it gets good light. You know, so you have a place to work."

Butterflies race around in my stomach and I look down at my fingertips to find them trembling. I'm almost dizzy because there is no way everything can be this right. "Nick…" I reach for him, needing him close.

He settles across from me and gestures to the plans. "It would be pretty small. I thought around two hundred square feet, maybe? This south-facing wall could be mostly windows." He runs the pad of his finger over the lines on the page.

My eyes burn and all I can do is stare down at the rapidly blurring image.

"Can you say something, David? If you don't like it, I can change it. I can build it however you want."

Finally my body catches up with my churning brain and I launch myself at him with a huge smile pulled across my face. "You're so fucking perfect."

Nick grips my shoulders, inspecting my expression. "You like it?"

"I love it. And you." I'm giddy and can't seem to stop smiling.

Nick snaps into earnest speech mode, eyes shining with sincerity, shoulders square as he sits up straighter. "I was hoping maybe you would move in with me at the farm. I know it's a little isolated up there, but I figured I could build you the studio so you could focus on your painting. Have a space of your own."

I feel my smile falter as the weight of my responsibility crashes down on me. "Nick. That sounds incredible. Really. But my dad can't be alone. Yeah, he's doing way better but his doctor still says he needs consistent care. He's not fully independent yet."

Anticipating Nick's disappointment and trying to hide my own, I stare out the window at the network of fire escapes on the façade of the building across the street. Nick's hand is warm as he guides my face back to his. He looks so pleased with himself I find myself cocking an eyebrow at him.

"I, um, talked to your dad. I wasn't trying to go behind your back or anything," Nick says in a rush. "But I wanted to hear from him how he was doing when I started thinking about this. He told me Jimmy and Daisy are going to move in with him. I guess your dad sort of figured you might want to move in with me. So he mentioned the idea to Jimmy. I know Daisy does well there and your dad told me Jimmy agreed that they would move in if you decided to move out. They could all take care of each other."

Something clicks inside me, like a key turning in a lock. Home. The place where Nick and I spent so much time—forming ourselves, exploring each other, and testing our desires—will be my home. The place I'd feared would break the bond with the man I loved will be the locus of a whole unfolding future. That image of the two of us sharing a life, the image I'd been too afraid to even dream of, coalesces into something real, like a single brushstroke transforming an entire composition from mundane to sublime.

"I want us to take care of each other too." Nick smooths my hair back from my face and strokes down my jaw. "What do you think?"

I'm nodding frantically because I can't seem to open my mouth to speak. Nick's familiar face fills my field of vision. I trace every classical masculine line with my eyes, my fingers, my lips so I can carve this moment into my memory. Willingly I tangle myself in this complicated web of feeling. I hope never to be set free.

Nick takes me into his arms. I'm home.

Epilogue

David

A Year and a Half Later

The farm is awash in undulating shades of gray, blue, and white. Plumes of powdery snow drift across the fields, rendering everything in soft focus. The air carries the crack of frost and caress of wood smoke. It's quiet. Well it was quiet until Archie and Pluto started going crazy, barking and whining at the door of my studio. I peer out through the wall of windows overlooking the iced-in forest, thinking maybe I'll see a deer. But there's nothing. A glance at my phone reveals it's only two fifteen. Nick isn't due back from the winter market in Albany for at least three more hours.

Archie settles back in his spot next to the tiny woodstove but Pluto is still pacing by the door, glancing out through the steamy glass pane. He's a nervous dog, an ex-racing whippet, and I love him to pieces. I call him over and he comes immediately, nuzzling his thin snout into my hand and then hoisting as much of his small, wiry body as possible into my lap. Nick tells me I spoil him, which I think is pretty rich coming from a guy who started making his own homemade dog food when he found out the stuff we were feeding the dogs got recalled.

Nick surprised me with Pluto last June. I'd gotten back from an exhausting day in the city, meeting with the artistic director for the fashion line that had commissioned me to do illustrations for their upcoming look book. The opportunity had been thrilling, but the reality was less rosy. The creative director constantly changed her mind and routinely demanded my presence at truly pointless meetings in the company's Soho office. Once I arrived, the willowy receptionist would usually inform me that the director was busy and request that I "wait for one sec." One sec usually turned into hours spent twiddling my thumbs in the minimalist conference room.

When the director finally graced me with her green-juice-chugging presence on this particular day it was to completely change the nature of the project. No more androgynous models for the illustrations, despite the fact that this was a gender-neutral fashion line. She wanted me to paint the clothes floating in space, disembodied from the human form. When I mentioned to her that the choice smacked of gender nonbinary erasure, she'd given me a blank look and told me to "try it out." I'd gritted my teeth and nodded, mentally tossing all my completed work into the compost pile back home.

When I'd stepped into the Rhinecliff train station parking lot that night, cranky and in desperate need of a long bath, Nick was there, flanked by not one, but two dogs. Archie was his usual calm self, tail wagging as he sat and waited for me to pet him. But the other dog, a skinny white whippet, was all over me: pawing at my legs, licking my face, tail flying in wild circles.

"Who's this?" I'd asked as I struggled to pet both dogs and crane to kiss Nick at the same time.

Nick looked sheepish. "This is, um, Pluto. Well his name at the shelter was Rascal, but I didn't think that suited him. But you can name him whatever you want. I've been calling him Pluto."

Not for the first time since I'd moved in with Nick, I wanted to swoon like one of the Victorian maidens in the romance novels my mom used to read. Nick had an amazing recall for the tiny, random desires I expressed. And he seemed to be making it his life's mission to fulfill every last one of them. How he remembered me mentioning over a year ago that I'd wanted a whippet was a total mystery. Half the time I couldn't remember what I'd eaten for breakfast.

Pluto whines again, his eyes still fixed on the swirling landscape of early spring snow. I scratch behind his ears and he seems to settle a bit.

"Focus," I say to myself and turn back to the piece of watercolor paper on my desk. The large stainless steel surface is a mess of crumpled-up papers, uncapped pens, and pencil shavings. Nick would be appalled.

Since I'm not really working anyway I start tidying up a bit, tapping the papers I deem worth saving into a neat pile, sliding the pens and pencils into the ceramic mug that in theory is meant to hold them, then quickly sweeping all the remaining crap into the garbage can. There. I look down at the desk for a moment. The antique drafting table Anna and I found at a flea market is one of my favorite things about my studio, not that the whole place isn't wonderful. Nick and Jenna surprised even themselves with how quickly and beautifully they built the tiny cottage from reclaimed wood and recycled construction materials. As hard as I try to keep the beautiful knotty pine walls clutter-free, they are almost always plastered with sketches, inspiration photos, and half-finished pieces.

I smile softly as I glance at the painting mounted above my desk. My mother's oil painting of the Hudson River. My dad surprised me with it the day I moved out, carefully wrapped in brown paper with a short note scrawled on the back. *I know you always loved this one. We were lucky to have her and I'm lucky to have you. We're proud of you.* How he intuited my level of attachment to the piece, my need for those exact words of validation, I have no idea. But I'm grateful every time my eyes flick over the soft brushwork and swirling waves of cool blues and browns.

The dogs explode in a wild fit of barking again and a spark of worry flashes down my spine. All three of us hurry to peer out the door, only to find a dark sedan pulling up to the house. The car looks vaguely familiar, and for a moment I worry it might be Jason. When he found out Lexi had been working at the farm, he'd shown up drunk and shaking with rage, hurling insults and accusations at Nick. But Jason drives a souped-up muscle car, which this decidedly is not. I squint at the car again.

When Mrs. Patras climbs out of the driver's side I tense up, desperately hoping she's alone. While I haven't had any contact with Nick's parents since he came out, I have a strong suspicion his father wouldn't have an abundance of kind words to offer me. Nick's mom hugs her puffy gray coat around her and begins shuffling toward the house. No one else gets out of the car. I open the studio door a crack to call to her, but of course both dogs wriggle through the opening and tear down the path in her direction. *Fuck.* Pluto is going to jump all over the poor woman.

Scrambling to yank on my boots and not even bothering with a jacket, I take off after them. Archie, well-behaved as always, is sitting calmly, waiting for her to greet him. But Pluto is a mess, yipping and trying to climb her legs in a desperate effort to lick her face.

"Sorry!" I call, jogging over. "Pluto! Get down!" I need to get better about training him.

Nick's mom strokes Pluto's back, and the dog leans into her touch. She looks uncomfortable and I rack my brain for the right words to set her at ease.

"Um, Nick isn't home," I say, dropping my gaze to the frozen ground. I shiver when a gust of wind slams into me. "Do you want to come inside?" I gesture toward the house.

"Sure." Her voice is soft. "That would be nice."

The dogs follow us up the porch steps and into the small entryway. I hurry to wipe their paws with the rag Nick hung up by the door. He hates when they track in mud, which they always seem to be doing. A decidedly awkward silence descends on the house as I take Mrs. Patras's coat and flip on a few lights. Her eyes sweep all over the living room, darting from the giant potted cactus to the paintings on the wall to the crowded bookcases, and I realize this must be her first time in Nick's house. Our house.

"Um, do you want a tour?" My voice is strained and I will myself to stop fidgeting like a nervous kid. Plus that was a dumb question. The house isn't big enough to merit some kind of grand tour.

"That's okay." She shakes her head and lapses back into silence.

Wow, I guess she doesn't want to make this easy on me. "Can I get you something to drink, then? I was going to make myself some tea."

Nodding vaguely, she traces her fingers over the fabric of one of Nick's hoodies hanging by the door. I shuffle into the kitchen, busying myself with the kettle, measuring out tea leaves, and tipping a splash of milk into a small pitcher. My heart might actually give out. And of course I left my cell phone back in the studio, so I can't even text Nick and tell him his mom just showed up out of the blue.

When I place two steaming mugs of Earl Grey on the kitchen table and gesture for Nick's mom to sit, she seems to have relaxed a bit. I haven't seen Mrs. Patras since college, but she looks almost exactly the same. Curly black hair, now shot through with a few threads of silver, half clipped back. Aquiline nose and brown deep-set eyes, all unlike Nick's. But when she sets her shoulders and turns to me, clearly ready to deliver some kind of proclamation, she looks so much like her son I can't help but smile.

"I wanted to say I'm sorry." Her voice is brittle, and she takes a large sip of tea. "Oh wow, that's hot." She laughs lightly and I relax.

"Did you want to say that to Nick? Apologize, I mean?" I don't want to push, but I'm not the one she needs to say those words to. "He won't be back for a few hours, I'm afraid."

I startle when she places her hand, warm and soft, over mine on the table. "I want to tell you I'm sorry too, David. I know you make my Nico happy. You always have." Her eyes are shining and she looks away.

"He makes me happy too," I offer lamely. She's staring at the kitchen, taking in the gleaming pots and pans hanging above the island, the tidy rows of preserves and vegetables Nick put up for the winter, the big bouquet of dried lavender hanging above the sink. "Do you miss him?" I ask, my voice gentle. Sadness radiates from her every pore. And I know Nick misses her, even if he doesn't like to talk about it much.

She nods slowly, not taking her eyes off the beautiful kitchen her son built.

"We're getting married," I admit.

I can't hide my grin as I remember the night in October, Nick's birthday, when I'd asked him the question I knew both of us were dying to speak aloud. Anna had helped me make dinner earlier in the day. We'd settled on butternut squash soup since I could keep it warm on the stove and not worry about messing anything up. When Nick walked in the door, all windblown and smelling like the apples he'd been harvesting in the orchard, I'd leaped on him, winding my legs around his waist, kissing all over his face and nuzzling into his neck.

I loved the kisses we shared in greeting. Nick bending down to brush his lips over the back of my hair as I worked. Me clambering all over him when I'd missed him so much I couldn't stand it. Gleeful pecks when we had exciting news to share. Hungry kisses when we'd spent the day apart but were desperate for each other. Perfunctory kisses when one of us was distracted or irritable. I cherished all of them.

I'd wanted to make the night special. Serve the dinner that I was relatively certain was not disgusting and the expensive bottle of champagne I'd bought in town. Maybe light a fire and ask him the moment he slid inside me. But no. Instead I'd blurted the question the moment he set me down and bent to untie his boots. His hands had stilled on the laces and he glanced up at me, lips twitching.

"Did you just ask me to marry you?" he asked, his smirk shifting into a full-blown grin.

"Yup!" I chirped, not even angry with myself for ruining my whole elaborate plan.

"That's funny," Nick mused. "Because I was going to ask you at Christmas. I guess you beat me to it." He stood, brushed my hair away from my face, and kissed me.

I try to shake myself out of the memory because I don't want to start picturing what happened next in front of Nick's mother. When I glance at her the expression on her face is unreadable. I wonder what I should say.

Nick and I talked about the kind of wedding we wanted. And the look on Nick's face when the words "courthouse ceremony" escaped my lips had told me everything I needed to know about his feelings on that idea. We ultimately decided to get married here, at the farm. A big party with lots of delicious food, good music, and our friends and chosen family. When I'd laced my fingers together with Nick's and asked, as delicately as possible, if he wanted to invite his parents, his response had come in the form of a single shake of his head.

"When is the wedding?" Mrs. Patras looks as wary as I feel, like we both know we might be wading into dangerous waters.

I rub my hands, which are now very clammy, on the knees of my corduroy pants. "Um, in July. The fifteenth. We're getting married here. Over by the creek." I gesture vaguely in the direction of the woods, before realizing this information is likely meaningless to her. My whole body is getting sore from tensing. *Fuck it, I'm inviting her.* She clearly cares about her son, and if I piss Nick off, I'll deal with it. "You can come," I blurt.

Her eyes go wide. Then a timid smile plays at her lips. She looks younger and for a moment I see the woman who used to send me home with bulging containers of baklava and knitted me a heavy wool scarf because she worried I was so skinny I'd freeze during a particularly cold winter.

"Thank you," she whispers as she rises to wash out her mug at the sink. I want to tell her not to bother, but then think better of it because she's already finished by the time I open my mouth. She wheels on me wearing an expression, half fond, half nagging, that reminds me so much of the times she used to snap at Nick to stop watching TV and do his homework that I have to tamp down my laugh. "Are you having kids?" she asks.

A loud laugh erupts from my chest. "Science hasn't gotten us there yet, I'm afraid," I deadpan.

She rolls her eyes in exasperation. "Stop clowning. You know what I'm asking you. You're going to adopt, right?"

I shrug because this is for sure not a conversation I'm about to have with her right now. The same timid smile transforms her face, and she brushes a kiss over my cheek. Her smell, white linen perfume and bleach, tugs me so hard back to my youth that I barely register her leaving.

"DAVID? ARE YOU okay?" Nick's tense voice startles me awake. I fell asleep at the kitchen table, head in my crossed arms. Sitting, staring into space, and trying to figure out how to tell Nick that I invited his mom to our wedding without his permission must have somehow worn me down into sleep. The house still smells like Earl Grey and Mrs. Patras's perfume.

"Sorry." My voice is sluggish as I lean forward and stretch. I wonder how long I slept. The ache in my back and groggy daze suggest at least an hour.

Nick tosses a bundle of mail on the table before wrapping his arms around me. His face is cold. I shiver at the touch of his skin against mine but nuzzle into him anyway.

"Your mom was here today, and I invited her to our wedding." The words explode from my mouth.

Nick sinks down in the chair next to me, the same one his mother had occupied. He even wears her same unreadable expression. "Why?" he finally asks. He sounds exhausted.

"Do you mean why was she here or why did I invite her?" I'm not trying to be difficult.

Nick looks at me sidelong and shakes his head. "I guess both," he laughs.

"She was here because she wanted to apologize. Then she said we seem happy, so I mentioned the wedding. And then it seemed like she wanted to come? I don't know. I'm sorry if I did the wrong thing." My face turns hot and I stare down at the grayish wood of the table.

Nick presses his cold fingertips against my cheeks, trying to soothe my blush like it's a burn. "No, baby." He lifts my chin with one thick finger. "Thank you." His expression is so tender I almost want to look away, still feeling sometimes like there is no way I deserve someone so good.

"Oh!" I pipe up, hoping to lighten the mood. "Your mom totally nagged me about having kids. Like she legit asked about adoption."

Nick shakes his head and groans. "Oh my god she's so fucking *Greek* about everything. She hasn't talked to you in a decade but of course she's totally cool with pressuring you about grandkids." But then he grins at me, raising his eyebrows. "But I mean...we are, right?"

"Can we please get married first, you weirdo?" I slide off my chair and into his lap.

"Absolutely." He kisses the tip of my nose, then my lips.

As I relax into Nick's embrace, breathing in his woodsy smell, I realize I do deserve all of this. This life: the man I've wanted for so long, coming together in the dark, waking up to coffee and sleepy smiles, my studio, the wedding. None of it is a composition I can simply paint over. It's all tangible, real, alive. And we built it together.

Acknowledgements

This book is deeply personal to me and I'm so thankful that I found the words to tell this story.

Tara thank you so much for plopping down on a bench in Boston and reading this through and getting it.

Rebecca, Sionna, SM, and Emily, thank you so much for your thoughtful and supportive beta feedback.

Endless gratitude to Julia Ganis for polishing this book and giving me the exact edits I needed to help my first novel shine.

Thank you to my family for listening to me alternately stress and gush about writing for the past few years.

And the deepest love to my wonderful group of Portland queers. You are the people I need and I'm so grateful to know you.

Finally, to all survivors. Thank you for being here.

About the Author

KD Fisher is a queer New England-based writer of authentic, heartfelt LGBTQ+ narratives. KD grew up all over the United States, bouncing from North Carolina to Hawai'i to Illinois, and finally settling in Maine where she spends far too much time at the beach.

When KD isn't writing, she can usually be found hiking with her overly enthusiastic dog, obsessing over plants, or cooking elaborate meals. She loves classic country, perfectly ripe tomatoes, and falling asleep in the sun.

Website: www.kdfisherromance.com

Facebook: www.facebook.com/kdfisherauthor

Twitter: @kdfisher_author

Instagram: www.instagram.com/kdfisherauthor

Pinterest: www.pinterest.com/kdfisherauthor

Also Available from NineStar Press

Connect with NineStar Press

www.ninestarpress.com

www.facebook.com/ninestarpress

www.facebook.com/groups/NineStarNiche

www.twitter.com/ninestarpress

www.tumblr.com/blog/ninestarpress